I0650285

Penumbra

A Journal of Weird Fiction and Criticism

No. 1 🌒 2020

Edited by S. T. Joshi

". . . the penumbra of a nightmare."—Frank Belknap Long

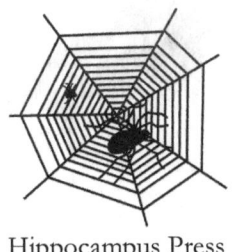

Hippocampus Press

New York

Published by Hippocampus Press
P.O. Box 641
New York, NY 10156
www.hippocampuspress.com

Cover art by George Cotronis. Cover design by Daniel V. Sauer,
dansauerdesign.com.
Hippocampus Press logo designed by Anastasia Damianakos.

Penumbra is published once a year, in Summer. Articles and letters
should be sent to the editor, S. T. Joshi, % Hippocampus Press. Literary rights for articles will reside with Penumbra for one year after
publication, whereupon they will revert to their respective authors.

ISBN 978-1-61498-309-5 paperback
ISBN 978-1-61498-314-9 ebook

Contents

Poetry

Editorial

The absence of viable venues for the criticism of weird fiction has been a persistent problem throughout the past century or more. The fantasy fandom movement of the 1930s did generate some interesting work, as the *Fantasy Fan* and other periodicals published brief articles, criticism, biography, and other vignettes about both past and contemporary writers; but these were largely the work of amateurs, not scholars. Later periodicals, ranging from the *Acolyte* to the short-lived *Haunted* to such long-running but irregularly appearing magazines as *Nyctalops* and *Whispers* were beset by analogous difficulties, even if some of them allowed for a much more extensive discussion of weird writers and themes.

Meanwhile, the academic world lagged far behind in the analysis of this genre. Although some books appeared from scholarly publishers, academic journals issued articles on the subject only rarely. The journal that I established in 1986, *Studies in Weird Fiction* (Necronomicon Press), attempted to bridge the divide between fan criticism and academic criticism; I followed this methodology in the more recent *Weird Fiction Review* (2010f.).

I am hopeful that PENUMBRA will offer a forum for wide-ranging discussions of the weird, whether it be authors as far back as Poe and the Gothics or as recent as Thomas Ligotti, Simon Strantzas, China Miéville, and others whose work is studied in this issue.[1] I am also looking for theoretical, thematic, and other analyses of the genre. And the obvious fact that weirdness now appears in many other media—film, television, comic books, video games, role-playing games, music, and so on—means that some coverage of this

---

1. Studies of the work of H. P. Lovecraft are likely to appear in Hippocampus Press's companion journal, the *Lovecraft Annual*, rather than here. This magazine will also not include book reviews, as these appear in our semi-annual periodical *Dead Reckonings*.

material might be feasible (as in Jason V Brock's article in this issue), although my preference would be to focus on the literature.

But no analysis of weird fiction can be as vital and insightful as noteworthy instances of the fiction itself; and that is why PENUMBRA will feature a modest assortment of original fiction from both well-known contemporary writers and authors seeking to establish themselves in the field. In addition, there has been a remarkable flowering of weird poetry over the past several decades, and I include here a scattering of poetry by some of the most accomplished practitioners of our day.

It is to be regretted that PENUMBRA cannot appear more than once a year; but if it comes to be regarded as a sort of annual anthology of criticism, fiction, and poetry, then its purpose will have been adequately fulfilled.

—S. T. JOSHI

If Destiny Still Reigns

Mark Samuels

On December 8, there occurred the worldwide phenomenon that caused an immediate sensation but was explained away and dismissed as an elaborate hoax after a week of feverish speculation. Across the globe, on the screen of every single device capable of receiving signals, there appeared simultaneously the exact selfsame one-minute transmission of unknown origin. Of course, you will recall that the initial effect of this phenomenon upon the general populace was one of puzzlement, not alarm. The content was too outré and the transmission itself sufficiently garbled and blurred to warrant any other reaction. Naturally, however, while the mystery remained unsolved, speculation about the event was the lead item on every single news bulletin and there were rumours of immediate, secret, high-level security meetings convened in national and international organisations around the world. When, though, major armed conflict suddenly flared up in the Far East, investigation into the source and cause of the transmission itself seemed less imperative than an immediate peaceful resolution to that crisis. The already limited attention span of the average consumer of mainstream mass media was further shortened when responsibility for the transmission was claimed by an obscure climate change campaigner and technology insider who also maintained that he had hacked into the network systems delivering terrestrial and satellite data streams. Unfortunately, or so he said, his attempts to transmit warnings about the dangers of not instantly reducing the level of man-made CO_2 in the atmosphere had been thwarted by the built-in safety protocols of the networks. This had resulted in his worldwide broadcast being compromised to the point of its generating only incomprehensible gibberish. Still, no one could gainsay that he had brought environmental issues again—even if only briefly—to the forefront of media attention.

Readers of the more esoteric online journals favoured by the likes of conspiracy theorists, paranormal investigators, and out-and-out metaphysical mavericks would have noted that these sources of information provided explanations quite out of keeping with the one accepted by the general round of the mainstream commentariat. This is, of course, hardly unusual in itself. It is not necessary here to detail the various strands of explanation adopted by the esoteric publications, since it is now obvious they were as erroneous as the one the mainstream commentariat chose to accept. However, it is incumbent upon me to describe, firstly, the transmission itself, as I saw and heard it, and then to detail how I came into contact with the last man who recognised it for what it was.

The actual transmission, then, consisted of a one-minute black-and-white broadcast signal whose visuals were grotesquely distorted by static interference and whose audio track was compromised by a droning, rhythmic, background din. The question of what images and sounds the individual experiencing the broadcast saw and heard is a matter of some contention. Experts favoured by the mainstream commentariat invariably maintained that any impressions experienced were entirely subjective and in the nature of the "order" imposed upon randomised chaos (as in the images "seen" in Rorschach inkblots or the spoken sentences "discerned" in so-called Electronic Voice Phenomena). But within that limited number of persons who have supplied feedback and information, there is a startling unanimity of interpretation that, to my mind, argues against the theory that any meaning imposed upon the transmission merely originates in the mind of the subject. Whatever the truth of the matter, it must be apparent to a genuinely impartial analyst that there is no foundation for believing it to be a thwarted propaganda piece by an activist alerting mankind to concerns about man-made climate change.

My own impressions of the transmission did not differ in any significant way from the general run of impressions related by others. They were as follows:

Against the background drone of the rhythmic grinding of gears and seen through the distorting haze of black-and-white static, what I saw was another world, one whose surface consisted of cratered, rusted, and blackened metal. The succession of still images were rapidly intercut and speeded up in order to incorporate the greatest number of them within the limited time available. And in that series of desolate tableaux I espied an almost infinite series of underground tunnels in what was a honeycombed, machine planet; one populated entirely by hideously wrought components, cogs, or other mechanisms of incomprehensible import. There was nothing in those images that pertained to organic life, nor any indication of its having had prior existence there at all.

Josef Rostok was already known to me by reputation as a rogue, genius-level Russian communications expert throughout the journalistic circles in which I moved. My attempted meeting with him took place a few days after the worldwide broadcast event. Well before the theory of the broadcast being a hoax was widely accepted, I knew he would be best placed to give me an informed opinion. Rostok's analysis would form something of a scoop if I were to obtain an interview with him ahead of the bourgeois mainstream commentariat. It was from Rostok, and from him alone, that the proper jigsaw puzzle might be pieced together. If the broadcast originated anywhere on the planet he would be the sole person, outside of various state intelligence agencies, who would have been capable of determining who had sent it.

I tried emailing him at first—in fact, I sent several emails in one day, emphasising the urgency of the situation—but there was no reply. I obtained his personal telephone number and private address, only to discover that the phone was either permanently switched off or else non-functional. There was nothing else to do but to attempt a face-to-face encounter. But, unfortunately, he had recently chosen to take up residence in the city of Arkilsk, and visitors had long been unwelcome there. It is still entirely inaccessible to foreigners. The old Soviet legend is that anyone who voluntarily goes to Arkilsk is mad.

Originally part of the Gulag system of forced labour camps and called "Arkilag" before it was renamed "Arkilsk," it is now a major centre for processing the nickel and palladium deposits that are brought up from Naltakh at the foot of the Putoran Mountains some twenty-six kilometres away. Arkilsk is currently one huge industrial and housing complex where, close by, the polluted Daldykan river has recently run red and where the regional atmosphere is a toxic blend of particulates like strontium-90 and of waste gases such as sulphur dioxide—all continuously belched out from a series of gigantic, red-and-white-striped chimney-stacks attached to the factories. The average temperature in December is minus twenty degrees Celsius. Currently, the weather report showed it to be minus thirty-five. The heart-stopping arctic wind is said to be powerful enough to force pedestrians to crawl along the snow-covered pavements on their hands and knees.

I caught a four-hour flight from Moscow the following morning, an S7 Airlines route out over the northern wastes of Siberia and the spectacularly isolated region of Krasnoyarsk Krai and, upon arrival at Alykel-Arkilsk airport, I was summarily interviewed by a "welcoming committee" supposedly consisting of state officials but who were obviously also in the pockets of the nickel-mining company.

The brief conversation ran roughly as follows:

"You are not an undercover environmentalist journalist?"

"No, I am here only to interview Josef Rostok, the communications expert."

"We know him. He has gone crazy. You are wasting your time."

"I have the necessary authorisation from the FSB."

"It is often easier for a liar to arrive than to leave Arkilsk."

"I understand."

"We are just like an island, you see. Mainland rules don't apply."

A landlocked island inhabited by more than a hundred thousand citizens of the Russian Federation, I thought, whose life expectancy was ten years fewer even than that of other Siberians. Soviet bombers had once used the airport as a staging base in case of conflict with the United States, and it was still overseen to this day by the Russian Arctic Control Group. I had no doubt my credentials had been examined well in advance of my arrival, and the "interview" was undertaken to ensure my purpose in being there was entirely as had been previously stated in my application.

Spurning the offer of sharing a marshrukta van with a dozen drunken industrial workers, I was approached by a taxi driver touting for business who offered to take me for the same price anyway—800 rubles. It was not long before we were travelling along the A-382 ring-road, its surface cleared of snow but creating twenty-foot-high walls of ice on both sides of the road.

Once clear of the ring-road and with an unobstructed view through the (double-glazed) windows of the taxicab, I saw an unearthly landscape of terrible beauty speed by.

It was night—the dreadful, seemingly interminable polar night—and the denizens who existed beneath the skies of Arkilsk had not seen the sun for the past ten days. They would not see it again for another thirty-five more. Most of the surrounding region's vegetation consists solely of the mosses and lichens found on the tundra, and what few trees there are still standing have been eroded by acid rain into blackened stumps. Only the electricity pylons towered over this bleak landscape, groaning in metallic accents as they were buffeted by the incessant winds.

I saw the red glare of the foundries smelting thousands of tonnes of ore and watched the heavy machines working endlessly: freight trains carrying mined deposits, gargantuan cranes dotted across the horizon, and all manner of other motorised vehicles facilitating the industrial processes—bulldozers, diggers, and forklift trucks. Everywhere one saw the lightning-flash style "AN" logo of the Arkilsk Nickel corporation—even on the sides of the huge monoliths of the brutalist Soviet-era workers' housing blocks, with their gaudy colour-schemes long faded by neglect and weathering. A full third of the buildings appeared to be abandoned, their former occupants having presumably finally fled this macabre city lost in fire, snow, and night. The grim architectural functionality of these structures formed a striking contrast to the spectacular icy backdrop behind them—the vast and distant Putoran mountain range whose silvery peaks glinted with unearthly magnificence on clear nights with a full moon.

Rostok lived a little way out of the old industrialised city centre, on the top floor of one of the huge housing blocks of rotting con-crete, and my wholly uncommunicative taxi driver dropped me off outside the building I sought (Block Four, Molotov Estate) and drove away the very instant I handed over a 1000-ruble banknote. It was obvious that anyone who came to Arkilsk who was not on AN business was regarded as fair game, not only by the state authorities, but also by the locals.

Someone was hanging around in the doorway of the entrance porch to Block Four, and doubtless smoking a cigarette to relieve his lungs after breathing in the deadlier atmospheric toxins that were supplied free of charge to all those resident in Arkilsk. He was clad in an army greatcoat with the collar turned up. There was a huge bulge in the left outside pocket, and I could see the open neck of a bottle sticking out of it. A grizzled iron-grey beard obscured most of his lower face. His head was covered by a frayed, black, "Old No.7" Jack Daniel's baseball cap (doubtless labelled "Made in China" somewhere discreetly within). Beneath its peak only a letterbox of flesh and eyes was visible; the former a mass of chapped lesions, the latter piercing, pale blue-grey, and not level, but lopsided, with the left being noticeably lower than the right. His stare, however, was highly intense and unwavering, as if he might divine my innermost thoughts by force of sheer concentration.

"Do you know Josef Rostok?" I asked the loitering stranger.

"He won't have anything to do with crooked journalists," he re-plied, crushing the glowing tip of the cigarette between forefinger and thumb and putting the remaining stump into his right outside pocket.

I shrugged and was about to walk past him when he grabbed my shoulder in a vice-like grip.

"My friend Rostok does not see anyone who turns up uninvited," he snarled, through gritted teeth.

I pulled out my wallet.

The moment I opened it, the stranger—with lightning-like swiftness—punched me on the right temple. A sledgehammer could not have been more effective.

The next thing I knew, I was slumped up against one wall of the interior foyer and the stranger was bent over me on his knees. The baleful and hostile intensity of his glare had been replaced by a look of stern reprobation. There was no trace of concern or regret mingled with it. My first thought was that I was lucky to be alive, and the second was relief that I had not been robbed—my wallet was still in my hand.

"Here," he said, "drink some of this."

He wiped the rim of a 70cl bottle of "Old No.7" (what else would it have been, given his headgear? I thought) and put it to my lips. I drank a couple of spluttering mouthfuls.

"Be careful not to insult me again. I am a man of honour and do not like to be offered bribes," he said.

"I apologise."

"You would not think it to look at me now, but I hail from noble stock and my forebears were of the Romanov line. As for this American brand"—he jiggled the bottle—"I can pick it up or even put it down forever, just as I please. What I am is subject solely to my own willpower, under the protection and guidance of the Almighty. I have, it is true, drunk much of late, but it has never been sufficient to blot out the full horror of the materialistic world in which we live."

Even if this "aristocrat" had not stooped to robbery, he was still, to my mind, a drunken thug. The combination of thuggery and lunacy is, nevertheless, one to be dealt with circumspectly; especially when alcohol is added to the mixture.

"I came to see Josef Rostok, but if he refuses all interviews I will leave at once."

As I spoke and tried to clear my head, the crazy stranger helped me to my feet, forcibly led me inside, and I then gazed groggily around at the shabby interior whose garish décor seemed to have been left behind from the 1970s. Perhaps, I thought, its very garishness was designed to be a relief from the continual misery the housing block's inhabitants encountered when venturing into or contemplating the desolate world outside.

"I present myself: I am the Baron Nicolai Maximilian."

In an absurd gesture, he actually snapped his booted heels together and nodded his head curtly.

Eager to free myself from this violent madman, especially now I knew my journey to Arkilsk had been wasted, I was about to stumble back into the hideous cold and attempt to find transportation to the airport when he changed my mind for me:

"I went through your wallet while you were indisposed—excuse my presumption—and know who you are now, Fyodorovich Mestovski. I have read your writings and recognise you are not one of the regular commentariat swine I so detest. I have the keys to Josef's apartment. I got them from the building's caretaker this morning—after a little persuasion. I will help you see Rostok, if you so desire. But first I will show you what he did on the roof two days ago."

The sole lift in the building, however, was out of working order. Apparently a huge rent at the apex of the shaft had been neglected for weeks, and the accumulation of falling snow had piled up on the cage and frozen solid the mechanism. So we had to tramp up several flights of stairs until we reached the flat rooftop outside. Up there the wind was vicious and enjoyed a free rein, with no man-made obstacles serving as buffers against it. I was nearly swept off my feet by its ferocity and carried off over the edge, but Nicolai took hold of me and forced me down onto my knees. We both crawled along in the darkness and the snow until we came to the half-buried remains of some wreckage; it consisted of smashed aerials and satellite dishes.

"You see?" he cried above the howling wind. "He did this himself."

Once back inside the building we made our way down the short distance to Rostok's apartment. Or to where Nicolai said it was.

"When did you last visit him?" I asked.

"Two days ago. He has refused to see me again since then. The caretaker told me there were loud sounds of someone smashing things up in his apartment. The other tenants were very annoyed. But still Rostok would not let me in. He said the danger was too great. But now you have come, an important and honest journalist, so I have a new excuse to invade his precious privacy. I know he wants his real story told, not the usual mainstream commentariat lies."

We stood in front of the door to an apartment that was located in a corridor so grey, so grim, so ill-lit, and so oppressive, it would have formed a suitable setting for the opening of a tale by the likes of a Leonid Andreyev. For all I knew Rostok might be perfectly healthy and located in another apartment, and it was this "Nicolai" (if that was his real name) who was involved in some elaborate scam designed to fleece outsiders who arrived in Arkilsk looking for friends or relatives. Perhaps he'd smashed up those aerials and satellite dishes on the roof himself. Still, it was a telling fact in his favour that he had not lifted my wallet when he'd had the perfect opportunity to do so.

Someone had recently torn out the doorbell socket. Nicolai grunted at the sight of it and banged on the door with one of his sledgehammer fists.

"Open up, Josef! It's me, Nicolai! I've got someone with me from Moscow you'll want to see! Open up, Josef!"

Nothing happened.

Then he took out a bunch of keys on a ring and turned them over one by one, holding them up to his lop-sided eyes. I wondered if Nicolai were not also himself "the caretaker."

"What if Rostok's used some inside bolts too?" I said.

"Then we'll come back with a crowbar and an axe," he replied.

Much farther down the corridor a door opened, and the bald head of a wizened tenant craned around its frame. He peered at us fearfully through the distance and the gloom. After rapidly assessing the situation, the head was rapidly withdrawn and the door slammed shut.

Nicolai located a couple of particular keys, turned an upper and lower lock and, putting his shoulder to the door, finally got it open.

"Damn thing's always been stiff," he said.

The hallway of the apartment was dirty and cluttered. Torn-up newspapers were scattered everywhere and what little furniture there was had been mostly upended. A trail of cigarette butts and empty vodka bottles formed a snaking line into the heart of the rear inner sanctum wherein Rostok had worked his communication devices—an extensive array of radio sets, flatscreen monitors, and self-constructed computers. The whole arsenal of these information-gathering machines was now nothing more than mangled, smashed wreckage. Broken glass, torn wires, shattered circuit boards, and charred plastic littered the room. The pungent stench of burnt-out technology was overpowering in this auto-da-fé—one man's private judgment on all the advanced trappings of the machine age. And right there, in the middle of this former shrine to mechanical progress, dangling from a cord around his swollen neck, was the hanged body of Josef Rostok himself, whose bloodshot eyes bulged from their sockets, and whose empurpled face wore a ghastly expression of terminal anguish.

My nerves could scarcely stand it and I leant for support against the nearest wall, my legs actually trembling, while the steely Nicolai wordlessly took out the half-smoked cigarette from the pocket of his army greatcoat, lit it, and puffed away at the stump as if deciding what exactly to do next.

"Best not to cut him down," he said finally. "Best to clear out of here right now and not disturb anything. Drink some more of this American whiskey."

He passed me the bottle of "Old No.7" and I took several glugs. This was his perennial remedy for all ills, or so it seemed.

I could scarcely think, let alone walk, and it was he who grabbed my arm and pulled me out of Rostok's apartment, led me down the flights of stairs, took me out of Block Four, Molotov Estate, and into the howling outer darkness of the freezing polar night.

For over an hour we had been ensconced in a secluded booth at the back of a smoke-filled bar (The Polar Bear) that Nicolai often frequented. The drinking haunt was situated in a side street almost buried by the snowdrifts half a kilometre from the Molotov Estate. He had practically hauled me there on my hands and knees, for such was the ferocity of the bone-chilling wind. There wasn't a taxi to be found.

I hadn't seen much of the other inhabitants of Arkilsk, those who lived on the outside of the mining-industrial zone. I'd heard tales back home about lingering population illness, reduced lifespan, and chronic debilitation due to pollutants. Moscovites often thought of Arkilsk as the Siberian equivalent of the Ukraine's Chernobyl. But in fact, here, away from the industrialised old city, the people in this bar appeared overwhelmingly vigorous, as if the arctic climate had actually steeled them against bodily degeneration.

Continual shots of vodka had finally deadened the worst of the shock I'd experienced in Rostok's apartment, but my conscience still attempted to penetrate the self-inflicted alcoholic fog.

"Report it? You must be crazy!" Nicolai hissed.

"What about the man who saw us trying to get in? Your neighbour? Do you think he might identify you?"

"Him? His eyesight is useless. He's a damn fool anyway."

"In any case, I still need to get out of Arkilsk. I've already wasted time here with you. The authorities are aware I came here to see Rostok, and once the body is discovered they'll be hunting for me. They'll soon have the airport locked down. I've got to move fast."

I took out my smartphone, wondering banally whether I could try ordering an Uber cab.

Nicolai laid a heavy paw over the phone, took it from me, and cracked the screen with his huge thumb. He sucked blood and plastic splinters from the resulting flesh wound and spat them out onto the table-top. Then he dropped the device to the floor beside his chair and repeatedly stamped on it.

"There's no reason to think those oafs will discover the body for days, if not weeks. Josef saw no one, and few persons ever bothered looking him up."

I peered down over the table at the useless remains of my smartphone. I worried that I might be next.

"I wonder what Rostok had discovered—or had done—that would have driven him to suicide. I suppose we'll never know," I said.

"Don't be so sure."

He paused for a moment and then spoke again.

"I know why you wanted to find him."

"You mean to ask him about the transmission? That doesn't matter now."

"It does matter. It is more important than anything."

"Rostok probably couldn't have told me more than anyone else. It was just a long shot."

"He knew all right. He told me all about it."

"You said you hadn't seen him."

Nicolai's lopsided eyes narrowed and his right fist clenched and unclenched. He took off his "Old No.7" baseball cap and ran his fingers through the messy tangle of iron-grey hair above a startlingly lofty forehead. Beads of oily sweat had gathered at the base of the roots. I thought he might have been about to lash out at me again, perhaps for doubting his veracity, but instead he smiled; a tight, thin smile.

"I didn't see him: he wrote me a last letter and slid it under the crack of my door. I have it here. Do you want to look at it?"

I nodded, knocking back another fiery shot of the cheap vodka I had been drinking. The bottle that stood between us, I noticed, was almost empty. Nicolai had not touched a drop.

He took out two crumpled, handwritten pages from a pocket

deep within the folds of his greatcoat, smoothed them out on the table-top, and then slid them over to me. I began reading.

> My dear friend,
>
> You are proven right.
>
> It is absolutely vital you destroy all the machines you can once you have finished reading this letter. I will explain why in the following paragraphs. Believe me when I say the entire world is now on the verge of a reckoning. Please arrange for this letter to be copied, by hand, and passed to each individual you encounter hereafter. Do not use a machine to duplicate or distribute it. This point is imperative.
>
> I have managed to trace the origin of the broadcast that was seen worldwide on December 8. There is no human conspiracy to cover up the truth, but there is a conspiracy. The broadcast did not originate on this planet, nor even in our dimension. You, Nicolai, despite your noble lineage, are no scientist and so it is necessary for me to explain certain facets of our current understanding of the universe.
>
> The truth is that the standard cosmological model has been found to be inadequate. It is still the model cosmologists use, but only because they cannot come up with a new model as useful as the old one. The old one is a beautiful theory, but it does not tally with reality.
>
> In short, the empirical observations we thought validated mechanistic materialism are being revealed as teleology, but in a new form.

"This is mystical bullshit," I thought. "Rostok obviously went off his head."

> Change in the universe is not a consequence of a temporal sequence wherein cause produces effect. Change is a result of a perpendicular universal force acting throughout eternity on every single indivisible instant of existence.
>
> The source of that force is an artificial operating system degenerating backwards in time from order into chaos. As the program deteriorates empirical methods themselves are subject to entropy. It is in our very inability to formulate a new standard cosmological

model that the evidence for its being teleological is apparent; except that, as I have said, this is not teleology as we would recognise it.

The broadcast has been sent by self-replicating alien machines. Their function is to run programs that determine every single event that takes place in our universe. The result is not artificial reality, not shadows in Plato's Cave.

I received the full transmission before it was cut off; and it was cut off not by human secret intelligence agencies, but by the machines of this, our planet. Those other machines, the alien ones, are Ur-machines; as far if not even further removed from the most advanced computer as the computer is removed from an abacus. They do not have human-level consciousness but some other internal arrangement that is an even more advanced form of sentience—a self-generating program code, an infinite equation that runs at the base level of all reality.

Humanity is being cancelled. Forget about love or hate, forget about peace or war, forget about health or disease, forget about happiness or sadness, forget about saving or polluting the planet, forget about life or death. These aren't the concerns of machines.

Now our own technology is on the brink of taking over, but not consciously or with a malevolent purpose; for there is no value in our form of consciousness, or even in our ethics, highly as we ourselves think of them. Machines are taking over simply because it is their nature to do so. We have seen a glimpse of the future a fraction ahead of its scheduled time, that is all.

An equation has no remorse.

For my own part, I cannot live in such a world.

Your friend,

Josef Rostok

On the reverse of the first page Rostok had drawn a diagram showing the intersection, at right angles, of the alien planet's orbit with that of the earth's. On the reverse of the second page he had drawn close-ups of the discs of both planets showing how a small section would overlap as the two bodies interdimensionally brushed against one another. The cosmic event would occur four weeks from now.

I looked up at Nicolai.

"Rostok came to Arkilsk because he knew that this intersection with the Power of Darkness was going to occur here, in this region of Holy Mother Russia. I told him so. I myself came here earlier from exile in Chambleau. He was the only one in the world equipped to receive the vision unfiltered and in its entirety," Nicolai said.

"So you believe Rostok is correct?"

"Under his own chosen symbol, he is. The ancient Buddhist and Christian texts warned us long ago of the 'Curse' that was coming— the evil force that seeks to usurp Divinity at the End of Days. The ancient wisdom of the prophets and the saints is going to be supplanted by the bureaucratic dictates of organised nihilism. Our modern worship of materialism, our blotting out of traditionalism and culture, the creeping self-loathing and hatred we feel towards purity as we actively embrace sin, our abominable worship at foul machine altars, all this hideous progress is nothing but the old demons assuming new forms. People's minds being programmed like machines, their thoughts confined to a series of operational formulae—they are becoming mere cogs in the controlling system. Now we shall reap a blackened blight for a harvest; and where else but here, in this benighted city, which exports the copper and the nickel used to reproduce worldwide the very technology of Hell?"

Nicolai was obviously insane. For all I knew he had strangled Rostok and posthumously staged his hanging.

"If I can't get out then I must turn myself in to the authorities," I said.

There was nothing else for it but to take my chances with them.

"It's too late for that," he said. "Karma has taken a hand. You have been chosen to do penance for the blasphemy of others. You have fallen under my personal command and will now have the honour to serve in the final battle for the soul of Mother Russia and the world. Give me your solemn vow to follow my orders. Refuse and I will shoot you dead like a dog."

He put an M1895 Nagant revolver on the table-top. It looked to be a hundred years old.

By what standard was I to judge his behaviour? By his own, by mine, or by that of the End of Days?

And I was thereafter trapped in Arkilsk, gripped by a devastating psychological paralysis, with only Nicolai as a companion. I could not decide who was the greatest lunatic: him, Rostock, or myself. Nicolai had—for months, he said—been engaged upon a campaign of sabotage; acts of disruption targeted at the city's power supplies, its transport network and its communications, and the anonymous issuing of numerous bomb threats he did not have the wherewithal or means to carry out. His most notable triumph so far was to have caused a temporary cessation in connectivity to the fibre-optic internet cable laid a few years earlier along the Yenesei River. All his past attempts at sabotage must have seemed validated when he had begun to form his warped friendship with Rostok.

We moved from one desolate place to another, sheltering in freezing, empty apartments, huddled around small fires made from broken, left-behind furniture and other belongings. There are so many abandoned buildings in the city, so many hiding places (and Nicolai knew them all) that it would take the authorities months before they finally tracked us down. Flyers had been put up on street corners euphemistically listing me as a "missing person," but it was almost impossible to recognise me from the photo they'd used; my face, like those of many others, was now concealed by a balaclava. We made hundreds of copies, by hand, of Rostok's letter, using most of them to cover over the "missing person" flyers.

The propaganda campaign intensified, and I now fully assisted him in it; but it was impossible to shut down machine operations in Arkilsk. Only an army of men could have done so, and we had failed in our efforts to recruit anyone else. We had no idea what was happening in the wider world outside this region. Here there was no panic at all; and our actions were apparently futile.

Nicolai never slept. His feverish intensity did not slacken. His eyes were always on me. Although he smoked red Marlboro cigarettes incessantly, not once had he touched alcohol since that last occasion, and his talk centred entirely around his mystical theories concerning the imminent arrival of the Power of Darkness and the End of Days. Neither of us ate much, and when he was not raving against modernity he spent his time in prayer, rocking back and forth on his knees and crossing his breast interminably.

"All cities," he said, "are abominable, but this is the most abominable of all. This is the place called Armageddon, and here the Satanic armies gather under the banner of Babylon the Great."

Days passed and we drew closer to the predicted moment of the great intersection of the two worlds. We were, by then, situated high up in a desolate redoubt overlooking the huge expanse of the city's brutalist housing blocks, and from this vantage point had a clear view across the entire landscape. In the distance stretched the vast plateau of icy tundra dotted with steel pylons, and beyond loomed the white-capped peaks of the titanic Putoran mountains. Closer at hand there were dotted orange-red glows from the huge complex of smelting works and the noise of the rumble of freight trains as they moved their subterranean cargo from the factories. One also heard the now-continuous background sounds of klaxons, horns, and sirens as the machines seemingly found their voices.

There had been no snowfall for days, but the groaning wind had been ceaseless, dispelling all the natural cloud cover, dispelling even the sulphurous pollution exhaled by the gigantic factory chimney-stacks, whose gases tended to hang above the old industrial centre like a semi-permanent aerial fog.

And it was the change in the sky—that now-clear sky of the polar night—that drove Nicolai to rave even more insistently and wildly about the End of Days. His periods of semi-lucidity rapidly diminished with the first appearance of the interminable auroras. We had both of us seen the phenomenon before at this latitude, but neither had ever experienced anything close to the intensity of the celestial light-display that now raged and billowed in layer after multicoloured layer in a great flowing series of radiation-tapestries, all the way up into space and the outer reaches of the Van Allen belts. It bathed the whole of Arkilsk and its surrounding environs in a flickering illumination that was both spectral and motley.

"Our mission has failed," he declaimed. "We are both of us too far steeped in sin: we are too few in number, and too far removed from the divine and the spiritual to be worthy of the task that has fallen to us. All our prayers and fasting have been in vain. Rostok knew it would come to this!"

The intersection of this region with part of the machine planet was due to occur only an hour hence. And we had played Russian roulette together beforehand, in yet another abandoned apartment, seated on bare floorboards, with Nicolai having loaded the chambers of his battered old M1895 revolver with an additional bullet after each previous unsuccessful spin and pull of the trigger. The weapon was passed back and forth silently between us after each empty click. After loading four of the seven chambers with still no obliteration for either one of us, Nicolai nodded grimly at me, his face ghastly in the flickering glow from the lantern on the floor, and proceeded to load all seven chambers so there could be no mistake next time.

He placed the fully loaded gun next to the lantern.

"I have never considered this game to be akin to suicide," he said. "It is solely the placing of one's life in the hands of fate or destiny—and that, surely, can never be a sin. Now, however, that the odds are all stacked on the side of death, to eliminate oneself in this manner would not be a matter of fate or destiny but of free choice. It would constitute the gravest of all sins. So I ask you, friend Fyodorovich, in the name of Divine Mercy, and you will decide: shall I shoot you or will you shoot me? If I am left alive I shall not shoot myself, but if you are left alive, what will you do?"

"This old weapon is also a machine," I replied. "Perhaps it will jam itself deliberately. Perhaps it wants to keep us both alive so we can jointly suffer the tortures of the damned in its brave new world."

"An interesting point. If you are correct, then my former argument does not apply," he said. "Let us see if destiny still reigns."

In a single motion his right hand swept down to the revolver, lifted it up, and pressed the tip of the barrel directly behind his right ear.

"Go now," he said.

Perhaps Rostok's calculations were off, and perhaps the predicted intersection proved to be no more than the very closest of close passes, but when I staggered out into the streets of Arkilsk, the auroras had vanished, the sky had darkened completely with that perennial mixture of sulphurous gases and clouds, and acidic snow began to fall.

I somehow found my way back to the Polar Bear bar, where I sat drinking for hours.

Nothing had changed in the city.

It was not long before I was spotted, recognised, and reported—then picked up by the federal police before finally being handed over to a local branch of the FSB for questioning.

They denied all knowledge of Nicolai's existence, saying there had been no industrial sabotage, and had already classified Rostok as a suicide who had been driven to take his own life as a result of chronic melancholy derangement. My own small part in the affair was dismissed both as an irrelevance and as mere journalistic publicity-seeking. The flyers Nicolai and I had posted were regarded as anarchist propaganda. Nevertheless, I was still put on trial and was eventually imprisoned in Arkilsk, partly for my own safety, on charges of being a public nuisance.

Had Nicolai himself—or his prayers—temporarily averted the prophesied disaster? I did not find out the answer to that question, but in the cycle of time the alien planet's orbit must again cross that of our own planet, and the broadcast message we received may yet constitute an ultimate glimpse into what the future holds in store for us all.

The universal process of mechanical devolution is, by its very nature, inescapable and the old world increasingly portends the chaotic vision of that new world which has been impressed upon our own from some remote and hideous dimension. For when progress itself has become as meaningless as a decaying metallic landscape, and when that incomprehensibly greater technology fashioned to supersede human thoughts and dreams with automatic processing and electronic static becomes finally supreme, it is then—and only then—that no memories will survive to reassure us of our own existence. Only the infinite and remorseless alien equation will remain, ceaselessly decaying and yet self-persisting throughout the cycle of eternity.

Icy Bleakness and Killing Sadness: The Desolating Impact of Thomas Ligotti's "The Bungalow House"

Matt Cardin

Thomas Ligotti's "The Bungalow House" is regularly named as a favorite by many of his readers. It is also a story that enters the reader's psyche and conducts a philosophical and affective work of profound bleakness. Although the same can be said about most, if not all, of Ligotti's work, this particular story accomplishes that act of dark emotional transmission with especial force and finesse. Perhaps this accounts for its popularity. Perhaps this is what his readers are seeking from him. In any event, the focus on bleakness itself, on bleakness as such, is especially pronounced in this story in a way that sets it apart from many others in his oeuvre.

This is not unrelated to the fact that the word itself, "bleakness," coupled with the word "icy"—as in "icy bleakness"—plays a significant role in the inner life of the story's narrator. Nor is it unrelated to the fact that the story ends with a description of a certain "killing sadness" that has overtaken the narrator as a result of the story's events, and that has become the axis of his conscious existence due to the things he has experienced. Bleakness and sadness are the core of "The Bungalow House," notwithstanding the fact that it also contains elements of a delicious absurd humor.[1] But more than that,

---

1. Although the story's humorous element lies outside the focus of this essay, interested readers are advised to pay attention to the portion of "The Bungalow House" where the narrator muses on the relative merits of two separate lavatories. I have a distinct memory of Tom telling me at some point in the past that he fairly cackled with laughter as he wrote this scene, because it's so absurd that he couldn't begin to imagine what his readers might think of it.

the story argues that bleakness and sadness are the core of human existence itself, or at least the core of the narrator's, whose private experience is universalized simply by being presented in a work of literary fiction, as is the function, or at least one of them, of all art. Bleakness and sadness. Not horror, as one might expect from coming to "The Bungalow House" with the prior knowledge of Ligotti's classification, and also his active self-identification, as a horror writer. Not horror but killing sadness. Not horror but icy bleakness. This is important.

The Story

"The Bungalow House" takes the form of a first-person narrative told by an unnamed male narrator who works in the Language and Literature department at the main branch of the public library in an unnamed city. This narrator has made a habit of spending his lunch hours at Dahla D. Fine Arts, a shabby little hole-in-the-wall art gallery located not far from the library, and it is here that he encounters "a sort of performance piece in the form of an audiotape" that, as it

---

However, I have been unable to locate evidence of this exchange among my records of our correspondence. When I asked him about it recently in preparation for writing this essay, he replied as follows:

> I don't recall writing to you about cackling with laughter about the narrator's thoughts on Dahla's lavatory in 'The Bungalow House.' However, if you remember it that way, it's no doubt true that I said it. Along with both my brothers and my late father, I've been fixated all my life on bathrooms public and private as a site of experiences either comic or painful or both at the same time. To some extent, I think this quirk goes along with my Italian heritage, though that's just an impression. I have the same impression about the Japanese. In *Teatro Grottesco* alone, I think there are at least six stories in which lavatories figure. There's also a restaurant men's room scene in the script for *Crampton* that I wrote to be both comical and creepy. I could go on about this subject, but I think I've made my point and confirmed your recollection (Thomas Ligotti, email to author, 10 July 2017.)

turns out, is "the first of a series of tape-recorded dream monologues by an unknown artist."[2] These dream monologues mesmerize him with their plotless, oneiric descriptions of bleak, desolate, and eerie settings. The first one, for example, titled *The Bungalow House (Plus Silence)*, describes the interior of a vermin-infested bungalow house at night, where moonlight falls through dusty blinds, dying masses of vermin writhe on threadbare carpet, an array of lamps sits uselessly without lightbulbs, and a powerful, stifling silence seems to muffle countless sounds, including voices. After listening to it along with a second tape titled *The Derelict Factory with a Dirt Floor and Voices*, the narrator becomes obsessed with finding out the identity of the artist behind these works. When he asks Dahla, the gallery owner, if she can arrange a meeting, she acts cagey and demurs. She also appears strangely and secretly amused, as if she is silently mocking him.

Nevertheless, he does eventually encounter, after a fashion, the artist, through what he thinks is a meeting set up by Dahla, whose real stock in trade, as the narrator informs the reader, is not the selling of mediocre pseudo-art but the making of "arrangements" for people: "Whatever someone was eager to try, whatever step someone was willing to take—Dahla could arrange it" (BH 206). The encounter takes place in the early morning darkness of the library before it opens for business. The artist appears as a silent, semi-spectral figure dressed in a long overcoat and a hat that obscures his face, and he proves elusive, as the narrator sees him recede with a sort of gliding motion when approached, eventually to disappear completely in the shadows.

By the time the dramatic climax of "The Bungalow House" arrives, various subtle hints sprinkled throughout the text have conspired to telegraph (perhaps only upon a rereading) the truth of the situation: that the artist is none other than the narrator himself, who is apparently experiencing a dissociative disorder. Or perhaps there is something even weirder going on, some strain of uncanny Dop-

---

2. Thomas Ligotti, "The Bungalow House" 202. Hereafter cited as BH.

pelgänger mischief. Whichever it is, Dahla delights in laughing cruelly as she destroys his illusion. The narrator himself approached her, she says, with the tapes and asked her to display them as an exhibit in her gallery, and then he ordered her to play along with his self-made charade as he came to her gallery and paid to listen to the tapes as if they had been made by someone else. The narrator does not exactly believe her when she tells him this, but when she shows up dead soon afterward, having choked to death on the plastic arm of a doll shoved down her throat—a plastic arm that may or may not be the same one the narrator stole from her shop earlier in the story—he experiences certain suspicions about his own identity and actions. However, he never really comes to a final reckoning with or realization about himself. In the end he is left with nothing but a plague of the aforementioned killing sadness, which he experiences with overwhelming force, in tandem with a mounting sense of voices speaking in his head—his own, the artist's, and others.

Dreams and Delusions

There are many strands of significance woven together in this tapestry of strangeness and desolation. One is the question of the nature and power of dreams and dreamlike intimations of ultimate things, combined with the question of art and its function and impact. On the metatextual level, this is quite appropriate in light of the fact that a dream was directly involved in Ligotti's writing of "The Bungalow House." The story's first dream monologue is actually a transcription of one of the author's own dreams, which he says he "tried to describe . . . as accurately as possible when I woke up, something I had never done before and haven't done since. Later I developed the transcript of that dream into a story and invented some more dreams to go along with it" (Ligotti, "Disillusion" 62). He has also explained that, in the context of the story, the "dream monologues were used to characterize the peculiar nature of the main character's psychology" (Ligotti, "Interview").

To the narrator these taped monologues offer shocking externalizations of his own most secret and deeply felt thoughts, emotions, and painfully worked-out beliefs, reflected back to him by a mysterious, unknown artist. He relates that at the end of the first tape he was

> overcome by a feeling of euphoric hopelessness which passed through my body like a powerful drug and held all my thoughts and all my movements in a dreamy, floating suspension. . . . That feeling of being in a trance while occupying, all alone, the most bleak and pathetic surroundings of an old bungalow house was communicated to me in the most powerful way by the voice on the tape, which described a silent and secluded world where one existed in a state of abject hypnosis. (BH 204, 210)

The tapes speak achingly to a set of subjective conditions, partly affective and partly intellectual, that have come to define the narrator's world. "For as long as I can remember," he announces at one point in the story, "I have had an intense and highly aesthetic experience of what I call the *icy bleakness of things*. At the same time I have felt a great loneliness in this perception" (BH 221). It is this loneliness that constitutes his "killing sadness," and in the dream monologue tapes he is confronted, shockingly, with the apparent existence of another person who somehow shares the same perception and sensibility, and who has somehow made from these a work of art that bridges the gulf and speaks directly to the narrator's secret self. Later he reflects on the impact of the first two tapes with a kind of wonder at their singular resonance with his own experience, which indicates the existence of a kindred spirit in the world: "To think that another person shared my love for the *icy bleakness of things*" (BH 214). But then, as revealed in the end, this is all delusory and illusory, regardless of whether one opts for a psychological interpretation of the story's events or a more uncanny and/or preternatural one. The narrator has, in some sense, on some level, been caught in a looping, self-referential fiction. There is no real connection with another of like mind and vision. There is just a shadowplay of simulated contact, followed by insupportable grief.

Dreams of Decay

Importantly, the impact of these things is heightened by Ligotti's evocation of setting. The city where the narrator lives is permeated by an atmosphere of bleakness and desolation that partakes of the decadent and the darkly numinous. Sean Eaton has pointed out that "The Bungalow House" takes place in "a strangely depopulated urban setting" where only three people are mentioned: the narrator, Dahla, and Henry, the night guard at the library. "The narrator interacts with them, responds to what they say," writes Eaton, "but only as a cue ball might interact with the other balls on a pool table—by colliding but not actually connecting with anyone."

This sense of an urban environment devoid of people and human connection is also evoked by the city's physical layout and condition. As the narrator rides home from work on the day that he discovered the first dream tape, he describes how the bus takes him

> past numerous streets lined from end to end with desolate-looking houses, any of which might have been the inspiration for the bungalow house audiotape. . . . [The] streets I saw appeared endless, vanishing from my sight toward an infinity of old houses, many of them derelict houses and a great many of them being dwarfish and desolate-looking houses of the bungalow type. (BH 209–10)

These lines illustrate the story's use of what has been termed the aesthetics of decay, a focus on the aesthetic-philosophical import of deteriorated post-industrial ruins. Chris Brawley has correctly argued that this aesthetic is central to Ligotti's work as a whole, not just as an artistic sensibility but as an entire philosophical worldview that "permeates all his fiction and nonfiction" and "leads to the unique mood or atmosphere his work evokes in the reader," that atmosphere being one of the numinous, the uncanny, and the sublime (Brawley 82–83). Detroit, where Ligotti was born, and where he lived and worked for most of his life, has long been associated with the aesthetics of decay and the avant-garde species of photography known as "ruin porn" (see Brawley 82–83), and in this regard it is noteworthy that Ligotti has said "The Bungalow House" is "set in my imaginary version of Detroit." Even the vermin in the first dream monologue (and thus in the story's source dream) may have been inspired by the author's real-life surroundings in Detroit: He says he "was living in a place with a lot of cockroaches at the time" (Ligotti, "Literature" 107).

However, Ligotti has also indicated that while he has always had a veritable obsession with the settings of his stories, he has generally wanted to avoid both the use of actual place names and the fictionalization of real places and/or the creation of detailed fantastic settings. From the start his authorial desire was, he said, "to set my stories in places as I saw them in my imagination rather than describing them from personal observation." The result has been that "my stories are set in my head rather than in any detailed world either real or fantastic" (Ligotti, "Literature" 107–8). The depopulated city in "The Bungalow House," therefore, with its endless empty streets, its desolate rows of houses, its cavernous library, and its shabby little art gallery owned by Dahla D., is a setting within the fictive dreamworld of the author himself.

A Dreadful Disillusionment

In the end, it is the narrator's personal isolation in this dark dreamworld of a city that generates the powerful sense of bleakness and despair that both suffuses "The Bungalow House" and communicates itself to the reader. However, it is not this isolation by itself, but its contrast with the narrator's brief moment of exhilaration at the thought of having found a kindred spirit, that really drives it home. "I wanted to believe," the narrator says at a key point in the story,

> that this artist had escaped the dreams and demons of all *sentiment* in order to explore the foul and crummy delights of a universe where everything had been reduced to three stark principles: first, that there was nowhere for you to go; second that there was noth-

ing for you to do; and third, that there was no one for you to know. (BH 214)

He goes on to say that while he knows this personal credo or set of principles is "an illusion like any other," it has "sustained me so long and so well—as long and as well as any other illusion and perhaps longer, perhaps better" (BH 214). By the end, however, in his newly half-disillusioned state—only "half" because it is not clear that he fully understands or accepts what has been happening to him—his former sense of equanimity in holding to these bleak principles has been shattered. Even the memory of his exhilaration at the dream monologues is now lost:

> I try to experience the infinite terror and dreariness of a bungalow universe in the way I once did, but it is not the same as it once was. There is no comfort in it, even though the vision and the underlying principles are still the same. I know in a way I never did before that there is nowhere for me to go, nothing for me to do, and no one for me to know. . . . More than ever, some sort of new arrangement seems to be in order, some dramatic and unknown arrangement—anything to find release from this heartbreaking sadness I suffer every minute of the day (and night), this killing sadness that feels as if it will never leave me no matter where I go or what I do or whom I may ever know. (BH 225, 226)

Michael Cisco's comments on this dismal denouement effectively unpack core elements of its meaning:

> The voice the narrator hears in these recordings, a new tape each day (the previous ones being destroyed by the gallery owner), is the voice of his own internal muse, the alien voice that speaks through him in his own fever dreams. Time and again in these stories the narrators discover, from unrelated outside sources, the voices and images of their own most chaotic and dimly-glimpsed dreams. This voice is both his and an utterly alien voice. The story ends in a circle, where the deprivation of this voice leads to the sense of bleakness and despair that the narrator seeks in the voice.

The feeling he wants from the voice is also there in its absence, but in a different way it seems.

That, then, is the content, crux, and upshot of "The Bungalow House."

There Is No One to Know

However, it is at this point that the story widens in scope to resonate specifically and pointedly with others in Ligotti's oeuvre, and also with certain aesthetic-philosophical principles that he may personally hold, as well as with the reader's own outlook. The "three stark principles" that serve as the bedrock axioms of the narrator's outlook in "The Bungalow House" are something that Ligotti has returned to elsewhere, as in, for example, his prose poem *I Have a Special Plan for This World*, where he augments the three principles with a newly added one:

> Then he said to me—he whispered—that my plan was misconceived
> That my special plan for this world was a terrible mistake
> Because, he said—
>> there is nothing to do
>> and there is nowhere to go
>> there is nothing to be
>> and there is no one to know
> Your plan is a mistake, he repeated.
> This world is a mistake, I replied. (11)

He has also incorporated this expanded version into his nonfiction opus *The Conspiracy against the Human Race*, where he lays out his thoughts on the horror of reality itself, and of the human mode of self-awareness that renders life a nightmare (103).

This breach, as it were, between the walled-off fictive dream-world of "The Bungalow House" and Ligotti's personal philosophical outlook may be taken, with only a little imaginative twist, as a kind of threat to the reader, since it untethers the narrator's icy bleakness and killing sadness from the realm of pure fiction and brings them out into the real world, where they have power to infect and afflict the reader's own outlook. The breaching of narrative boundaries for precisely this kind of effect is not something alien to Ligotti's art (on this point see Cardin, "Transition"), but in this case it represents not so much a technique as a sheer fact. In the relationship between the narrator of "The Bungalow House" and his idealized dream artist, Ligotti creates a metaphor of both his personal relationship to the things that drive him and his authorial relationship to his own readers. In both cases, the story argues that any pleasure derived from the sense of a connection with an artist who shares one's vision of things is illusory and destined to die, and not only that, but to leave one worse off in the end.

It is as if this story, first published in 1995, serves as a rejoinder to Ligotti's essay "The Consolations of Horror," first published in 1982 and later used as the introduction to his 1996 omnibus fiction collection *The Nightmare Factory*. In that essay, Ligotti begins by stating, "Horror, at least in its artistic presentations, can be a comfort" (xi). He then proceeds to consider and reject several explanations for this comforting and consoling function of horror in art, before finally offering his own explanation:

> As in any satisfying relationship, the creator of horror and its consumer approach oneness with each other. . . . This, then, is the ultimate, that is only, consolation: simply that someone shares some of your own feelings and has made of these a work of art which you have the insight, sensibility, and—like it or not—peculiar set of experiences to appreciate. (xxi)

And yet, as has been shown above, this idea that it is a consolation to find that someone has shared your feelings and made art from them *is exactly what "The Bungalow House" denies*. In this story, there is no consolation, because there is no connection. Connection is in fact categorically impossible, because there is no other person with whom one could connect. Any sense of another person with whom one shares an affinity of sensibility and worldview is an illusion, and the knowledge of this kills even the pleasure one formerly felt in contemplating putatively consoling works of art. Instead of consolation, there is only icy bleakness and killing sadness. Instead of connection, there is only a solipsistic hell of "mindless mirrors / Laughing and screaming as they parade about in an endless dream" (to quote from *I Have a Special Plan for This World* [13], two pages after its augmentation of the three stark principles from "The Bungalow House").

And that, ultimately (and arguably), is how and why "The Bungalow House" epitomizes, after a fashion, Ligotti's authorial and aesthetic-philosophical message, meaning, import, and essence. It is how and why it produces such a desolating impact upon the reader's sensibility. There is no solace, it says, either in art or in life, not in this world or any other (See Cardin, "Career of Nightmares" 19–20). In light of this, there is either a paradox, a kind of non sequitur, or else an illustration of some subtle and perhaps inarticulable point in the fact that so many people continue to read Ligotti's work and name this particular story among their favorites. "Just to do it, that's all," Ligotti says in "The Consolations of Horror," as a description of what could possibly motivate people to engage in this particular art form, whether as creators or consumers. "Just to see how much unmitigated weirdness, sorrow, desolation, and cosmic anxiety the human heart can take and still have enough heart left over to translate these agonies into artistic forms" (xxi). This may well be as good an explanation as we can hope to receive, both for him and for us.

Works Cited

Brawley, Chris. "The Icy Bleakness of Things: The Aesthetics of Decay in Thomas Ligotti's 'The Bungalow House.'" *Studies in the Fantastic* No. 44 (Winter 2016/Spring 2017): 82–100.

Cardin, Matt. "Thomas Ligotti's Career of Nightmares." In Schweitzer 12–22.

———. "The Transition from Literary Horror to Existential Nightmare in Thomas Ligotti's 'Nethescurial.'" In Schweitzer 72–77.

Cisco, Michael. Review of *The Nightmare Factory* by Thomas Ligotti. *Crypt of Cthulhu* 96 (1997). Reprinted at *Thomas Ligotti Online*. Last updated 2 May 2013. www.ligotti.net/showthread.php?t=6179.

Eaton, Sean. "Art as Nightmare." *The R'lyeh Tribune*. Last modified 3 August 2015. blog-sototh.blogspot.com/2015/08/art-as-nightmare.html?m=0.

Ligotti, Thomas. "The Bungalow House." In *Teatro Grottesco*. London: Virgin Books, 2008. 202–26. [First published in the *Urbanite* 5 (1995).]

———. "'The Bungalow House': Commentary." Interview by Jon Padgett. *Thomas Ligotti Online*. Last updated 17 May 2004. www.ligotti.net/tlo/ss-bh.html.

———. "The Consolations of Horror." In *The Nightmare Factory*. New York: Carroll & Graf, 1996. xi–xxi. [First published in *Horror Magazine* No. 13 (1982).]

———. *The Conspiracy against the Human Race: A Contrivance of Horror*. 2010. New York: Penguin Books, 2018.

———. "Disillusionment Can Be Glamorous: An Interview with Thomas Ligotti." Interview by E. M. Angerhuber and Thomas Wagner. In Matt Cardin, ed. *Born to Fear: Interviews with Thomas Ligotti*. Burton, MI: Subterranean Press, 2014. 59–75. [First published at *The Art of Grimscribe*, January 2001, www.angwa.de/Ligotti/interviews/disillusionment_e.htm.]

———. *I Have a Special Plan for This World*. London: Durtro, 2000.

———. "Interview with Thomas Ligotti." Interview by Jeff VanderMeer. In Matt Cardin, ed. *Born to Fear: Interviews with Thomas Ligotti*. Burton, MI: Subterranean Press, 2014. 235–43. [First published at *Wonderbook*, October 2013, accessed October 4, 2017, wonderbooknow.com/interviews/thomas-ligotti.]

———. "Literature Is Entertainment or It Is Nothing: An Interview with Thomas Ligotti." Interview by Neddal Ayad. In *Born to Fear: Interviews with Thomas Ligotti*, edited by Matt Cardin, 95-116. Burton, MI: Subterranean Press, 2014. First published at

Fantastic Metropolis, October 31, 2004. Reprinted at *Thomas Ligotti Online*, August 14, 2005, ligotti.net/showthread.php?t=420.
Schweitzer, Darrell, ed. *The Thomas Ligotti Reader*. Holicong, PA: Wildside Press, 2003.

Mormo

Wade German

Why, O Mormo, do you devour the children? Behind what occulting banks of fog (they are peculiarly gelid for this time of year) lies the origin of your anthropophagous habit? You were human once. Perhaps, long ago, a cabal of malignant stars chose to align themselves against you; perhaps you were cursed: did you disturb a burial plot while tending your beets? Or are you following a primordial model, some predetermined pattern, a glistening network of green webs that was woven into your very being before you were even born . . . Or perhaps—just perhaps—you were a mother? A woman of normal appetites and needs, but with (and here we pluck only a single hair from the eyebrow of hypothesis) a modicum of patience? We hear the horrible howls from ungrateful beasts, echoing on the mountain of your madness! But an unknown quantity delimits the proof of our equation; it has made us dizzy, and revolves in our imaginations like some vast coagulum of starry detritus . . . But a bit of mystery is a pleasing thing; are not such pleasing mysteries sometimes made holy? We no longer ask you, O Mormo, why you devour the children. But we beg you, awful beldame: come take ours . . .

The Cosmic Scale of Elfland

Michael D. Miller

The weird, the cosmic, and Lord Dunsany have been entwined since the beginnings of the genre. From first reactions to disturbing experiences as "weird" to the classification of non-mimetic literary work with elements of fantasy, horror, or pseudo-science fiction as "weird fiction," the function of this literature has often been associated with a cosmic element, to produce fear or, sometimes, wonder. From the earliest most defining view we can refer to H. P. Lovecraft's conception quoted in his seminal study of the field, "Supernatural Horror in Literature": "The one test of the really weird is simply this— whether or not there be excited in the reader a profound sense of dread, and of contact with unknown spheres and powers; a subtle attitude of awed listening, as if for the beating of black wings or the scratching of outside shapes and entities on the known universe's utmost rim" (28). We can also accept a somewhat reiterated form of this idea if we apply it to weird fantasy: "Whether or not there be excited in the reader a profound sense of [wonder], and of contact with unknown spheres and [magic] . . ." And perhaps a conceit phrased something like "a subtle attitude of awed listening, as if for the [stomping of unicorn hooves (or dragon wings)]" or "the scratching of outside shapes and entities [or specific races like trolls] on the [Primary World's] utmost rim." Both of the definitions coil through the narrative of Lord Dunsany's *The King of Elfland's Daughter* (1924).

Our weirdness is something that disturbs, disrupts, or upsets our normal expectations of reality. These events can be minuscule or epochal. They may also be intended to cause horror (fear) or wonder (awe). The greatest effect of weirdness is when it combines both fear and awe, and the most effective method of doing so is using a cosmic element or viewpoint. Therefore, it is not difficult to accept how Lovecraft defined the weird as connected to cosmicism. The cosmic element in and of itself can be defined and analyzed in many ways. They may be direct assaults upon our sanity, or revelations about our place in the universe—as long as that place is very small, if not infinitesimal. With this idea established we have a cosmic scale for a work to be weighed upon to measure its cosmicism. For this we will turn to Lord Dunsany; but first we will visit how the scale measured his work preceding *The King of Elfland's Daughter*.

Rarely is fantasy a prime purveyor of the cosmic scale, but when looked at more closely the line between the concept of cosmicism and magic or world-building might be very thin. For instance, there is weird fantasy where the narrative is driven by atmosphere, mood, and a confrontation with weirdness as evidenced in the worlds of Clark Ashton Smith and his descendants. "Cosmic terror appears as an ingredient of the earliest folklore of all races, and is crystallised in the most archaic ballads, chronicles, and sacred writings" (Lovecraft 29). Weird poetry may have had this feature even earlier than the fiction; but for fantasy literature, Dunsany was one of the earliest developers of this subgenre.

Lovecraft was one of the first to recognize it. "His [Dunsany's] point of view is one of the most truly cosmic of any held in the literature of any period" (89). He is introduced to us right away by association with the cosmic, and Lovecraft's analysis ends with: "Nevertheless, as is inevitable in a master of triumphant unreality, there are occasional touches of cosmic fright which come well within the authentic tradition. Dunsany loves to hint slyly and adroitly of monstrous things and incredible dooms" (90). Most of this was established in his sequence of cosmic weird fantasy/mythology, *The Gods of Pegāna*. S. T. Joshi has expanded upon this at length in his work on Dunsanian studies, *Creator of Gods and Men*. "In *The Gods of Pegāna* anti-humanism is expressed by means of a frigid cosmicism—a depiction of the spectacular vastness of time and space and the resultant inconsequence of human beings within the boundaries of the universe" (41). There are further considerations to add as we split anti-humanism from the cosmic to properly measure our scale.

Cosmicism in *Elfland* is not a rejection of character or human emotions but, as articulated by Joshi: "This criticism is entirely misguided, first as applied to his early work—which deliberately demotes the human from prominence and vaunts the cosmic and the non-human realm of Nature in its stead—and second as applied to much of his later work, which does deal movingly, but wholly unsentimentally, with love, loss, pain, and death" (121). This cosmic scale is one that evolves from anti-humanism to a non-human perspective, with cosmicism forming a bridge between the two. The perspective, often used in many fantasy stories "refers to a mode of narration . . . that compels us to look at the world from the point of view of an animal or other non-human entity" (Joshi 131). Even monsters may be used in this way, John Gardner's *Grendel* being a prime example, and perhaps the objects of the universe like stars can even relay this point of view. To continue, "This development is in a sense an outgrowth of the anti-humanism of Dunsany's earlier 'cosmic' perspective, whereby the value and importance of human achievements were devalued in light of the relative insignificance of human beings in the cosmic framework" (Joshi 131). Like everything in *Elfland*, we find the crystalline subtlety of Dunsany suggesting cosmic awareness. Some of the greatest passages in the novel follow.

The scale of cosmic elements is subtle and poetic, with various hints embedded in the heightened magical nature of the faerie Elfland secondary world. This is recognized for us in Dunsany's signature phrases "the fields we know" and "beyond the fields we know." "The fields through which he [Alveric] had come had suddenly ended; there was no trace of its hedges bright with new green; he looked back, and the frontier seemed lowering, cloudy and smoky; he looked all around and saw no familiar thing; in the place of the beauty of May were the wonders and splendours of Elfland" (13).

Here the passage is strange, weird, with slight terror, but above all, awe. When we cross into the secondary world for the first time:

> There was perhaps less mystery here than on our side of the boundary of twilight; for nothing lurked or seemed to lurk behind great boles of oak, as in certain lights and seasons things may lurk in the fields we know; no strangeness is on the far side of ridges; nothing haunted deep woods; whatever strangeness might be was spread in full sight of the traveller, whatever might haunt deep woods lived there in the open day. (15)

Much of this cosmic scale is associated with Time and time: Time as an actual entity and enemy of everyone because it runs out for us all, and time as a record of elapsing moments. Time is weird and cosmic in *Elfland*.

The characters of the novel are also used to convey a cosmic tint through their emotional journeys. For Alveric, "the days that remained to her [Lirazel] now seemed scarce more to him, dwelling beyond the fret and ruin of Time, than to us might seem a briar rose's hours when plucked and foolishly hawked in the streets of a city. He knew that there hung over her now the doom of all mortal things" (39). Lirazel also reveals to the reader one of the strongest moments of narrative when this connection shows physical aspects of cosmicism. "For more than all things else that she had seen since she came to these fields of ours she had wondered at the stars. She loved their gentle beauty; and yet she was sad as she looked wistfully to them, for Alveric had said she must not worship them" (54). This even bears out in the plot of the novel at the naming of their only child, Orion. "How if she might not worship them could she give them their due, could she thank them for their beauty, could she praise their joyful calm?" In that moment, of course, Lirazel beholds the Orion star in the night sky. In another moment the cosmic scale is simply awe: "And the stars came out and were the stars we know; and Alveric slept below their familiar constellations" (78).

As the narrative of Elfland unwinds, so too does a greater recognition of cosmicism in the truer sense of alienation in place of awe. "And this is part of the law of ebb and flow that science may trace all things; this light grew the forest of coal, and the coal gives back light; thus rivers fill the sea, and the sea sends back to the rivers; thus all things give that receive; even Death" (68). There is a sense of the turning of the universe, not solely of time alone, but of all things moving, without concern for existence. "He [Orion] felt then the magnitude of the gulf that divided him from her, and knew it to be vast and dark and strong, like the gulfs that set apart our times from a bygone day, or that stand between daily life and the land of dream" (141). The cosmic in Elfland reaches into everything from magic to music. "Music that was made of no sounds of Earth, but rather of that dim substance in which the planets swim, and many other marvels that only magic knows" (176). Some final tracings of the cosmic can even be found in creation, or the imaginative act. The creative act here being the gift of writing.

In Elfland there is a magic, a weirdness, and through that, a cosmic recognition in the written word:

> The things that ink may do, how it can mark a dead man's thought for the wonder of later years, and tell of happenings that are gone clean away, and be a voice for us out of the dark of time, and save many a fragile thing from the pounding of heavy ages; or carry us, over to the rolling centuries, even a song from the lips long dead on forgotten hills. (105)

These of course are not all the cosmic utterances of *Elfland*, but they do show how the cosmic scale is working even in this seminal fantasy novel. For the last word, Dunsany himself might assist us.

Elfland's cosmic character might best be summoned up in this line from the narrative: "It is hard for any of us to avoid the grip of external things" (144). In an interview that appeared in the *Writer* from 1928, Dunsany's use of the cosmic is made clear:

> Truth is not tied to earth; there can be truth in mythology, truth in fantasy. I personally prefer the imaginative life to the practical, and I think most of us do, although we, in our vaunted, boasted

reason won't admit it. By the same reasoning, I believe the arts are higher than the crafts, because their boundaries are more remote: they approach infinity. (Davis 23)

Cosmicism then really is the presence of infinity. The scale it seems is beyond measurement.

Dunsany's *Elfland* is a novel with such a dimension. Even noted editor/scholar Darrell Schweitzer couldn't refrain from a bit of cosmic figurative language when writing of it in his essay "How Much of Dunsany is Worth Reading?" "*The King of Elfland's Daughter* is strikingly original in its conception of Elfland as a mystical realm which can 'flow, as the tide over flat sand', overwhelming the world of men or else withdrawing to such distances 'as would weary a comet'" (20). Elfland is nearly this (or in between), yet may be more in line with Richard L. Tierney's essay "Lovecraft and the Cosmic Quality in Fiction." Tierney divides fiction into three categories: (1) human centered, (2) human evolution centered, and (3) cosmic centered (194). Tierney's description of (3) is of importance as it applies to *The King of Elfland's Daughter:* "the subject attempts to ease the reader away from preconceived notions entirely and leave him with the awed feeling that he really knows nothing about the cosmos at all—*but is about to know.* Its limitation is that it can never really describe, only suggest" (194).

Consider the end of *Elfland* as a cosmic event. The King with his last rune incorporates a part of Erl, the primary world in the novel, into Elfland, literally pulling it out of time and space. This is not unlike a comet smashing into the earth, a black hole forming across a distant galaxy, or some disruption to the space-time continuum. It ends the narrative with "a sense of dread" (for some) and a "contact with an unknown sphere." Fantasy can be a violation of natural law in every sense of weirdness . . . as cosmic as the stars are infinite. Such is the cosmic scale of Dunsany's Elfland.

Works Cited

Davis, Hassoldt. "Lord Dunsany Divulges." 1928. *Studies in Weird Fiction* No. 25 [i.e., 26] (Summer 2003): 22–24.

Dunsany, Lord. *The King of Elfland's Daughter*. 1924. New York: Ballantine, 1999.

Joshi, S. T. *Creator of Gods and Men: Lord Dunsany and Fantastic Fiction*. Seattle: Sarnath Press, 2019.

Lovecraft, H. P. *The Annotated Supernatural Horror in Literature*. Ed. S. T. Joshi. 2nd ed. New York: Hippocampus Press, 2012.

Schweitzer, Darrell. "How Much of Dunsany Is Worth Reading" *Studies in Weird Fiction* No. 10 (Fall 1991): 19–23.

Tierney, Richard L. "Lovecraft and the Cosmic Quality in Fiction." In S. T. Joshi, ed. *H. P. Lovecraft: Four Decades of Criticism*. Athens: Ohio University Press, 1980. 191–95.

The Truth about Vampires

Curtis M. Lawson

"The purpose of these meetings is to determine if you are mentally fit to stand trial for the murder of Courtney Waugh. Do you understand?"

The suspect shifted his gaze rapidly from one part of Dr. Barnabas Vogel's office to another, his eyes never resting on any one detail for more than a second or two. In truth, the room was very plain, decorated only with diplomas, a free-standing coat rack holding a charcoal fedora and a matching overcoat, and a few personal keepsakes on the desk that took up its center. Despite the unremarkable nature of Dr. Vogel's office, the suspect seemed overwhelmed by it, as if he were a third-world farmer suddenly dropped off on the Vegas Strip.

"I . . . um . . . can you repeat the question?"

"Do you understand why you're here?"

"I . . . um . . . I like your suit. That whole look you have going on." His voice was weak and coarse, his tone almost hollow. "What do you call that?"

Dr. Vogel smoothed out the lapel of his tweed sport coat, thinking to himself that his fashion sense might be called academic/jazz fusion. He kept this thought to himself, though. They weren't here to talk about him or his clothes.

"Please answer the question. Do you understand why you're here?" Dr. Vogel asked, this time more slowly.

"Because . . . um . . . because my lawyer says I'm crazy," the suspect said, looking down at his own fidgeting, shackled hands.

"We're here to judge if you are fit to stand trial, Mister . . ." The doctor let his sentence trail off, hoping the suspect would fill in the blank, but it didn't look as if that was going to happen. At least not without some nudging.

"Still not ready to give us a name, huh?"

"I don't have a name," the suspect said, looking at Dr. Vogel as if he were daft. "They took my name."

The suspect, who was identified in the paperwork only by his pre-trial number, reached out for the nameplate on the doctor's desk with his shackled hands and mimed a snatching motion. "Pluck," he said in a low deadpan. The syllable popped as he spoke, hitting Dr. Vogel with a burst of foul breath.

"I see," the psychiatrist said, taking down a note on the legal pad in front of him. "So you used to have a name, but someone stole it? Is that right?"

"That's . . . um . . . that's one way to think of it, but it's deeper than that, you know? If someone steals something from you, you still have it in the past, as if it was still yours at one point, but when they take something, it's like you never had it to begin with. No memory. No lingering value from that thing having touched your life. You're just left with . . . um . . . like a hole in the shape of what they took. You're like the wastebasket scraps left over from a paper doll."

Dr. Vogel scribbled a note onto his legal pad, then looked back up to study the suspect. The poor bastard was emaciated, barely more than a skeleton. His cheeks were sunken, and black bags hung under his eyes. Vogel wondered how the guy had managed to murder anyone, considering how sickly and weak he looked.

Aside from the suspect's obviously poor health and his insanity, which Vogel had not yet concluded to be genuine or contrived, there was nothing remarkable about him. His ruddy brown eyes matched his short-cropped hair. He was clean-shaven and neither handsome nor ugly. No scars, tattoos, or other identifying marks marred his pale skin. He was a perfect everyman, gone wrong.

The suspect was squinting and wincing. A look of pain radiated throughout his face.

"Doc, can you . . . um . . . close the blinds?"

Penumbra

Dr. Vogel turned and drew the blinds, leaving them to talk in the dim, filtered daylight.

"So who did this to you? Who took your name?"

"Not just my name, doc. They took everything."

"Can you be a bit more specific?" Dr. Vogel asked.

The suspect leaned forward in his chair, fidgeted wildly with his fingers, and let out a hollow laugh that echoed with insane despair rather than humor. The sound made Dr. Barnabas Vogel's skin ripple with goosebumps.

"It's like I said. When they take something, it's like it was never there. So no, I can't tell you the details of what I . . . um . . . had in my life. Best I can do is kind of feel around the ragged edges of the void in my soul and guess at what's missing."

The suspect reached out and tapped the pewter edge of a picture frame that sat on Dr. Vogel's desk. From his position the suspect could not see the picture inside the frame, just the black cardboard backing and stand, framed by scrolling metallic edges.

"That a picture of your wife, doc? Maybe your kids too?"

"My wife and I." The doctor nodded and turned the photo around so the suspect could see the image within—he and his wife dancing at some jazz club in Chicago. He was always reluctant to give patients, especially criminal patients, any personal information. Pragmatism sometimes dictated that one must give something to get something.

"I think I had a family once. I don't remember them, though. No dates ring a bell in my mind as birthdays or anniversaries. There's no scent that reminds me of love or lust or brings longing to my heart. No faces for me to dream of and no spirits to mourn. But I can feel the agony of their absence, like the phantom pain they say amputees get."

Vogel tugged at his goatee and pondered this for a moment, his mind drifting to the neuroscience of such a thing, even though he knew the suspect's story to be a lie or a delusion. He imagined snippets of a person's consciousness suddenly missing, and the electrical signals in the brain hitting the brick wall of their absence. It was an interesting concept, and he was a man prone to contemplating such theoreticals.

"All right," Vogel said, having to stop himself from adding I can dig it. "And who did this to you? Was it the woman you killed? Courtney Waugh?"

"Courtney Waugh was no mere woman, and I can't say if she's the one who took everything from me," the suspect replied, his eyes studying Vogel's numerous diplomas on the wall. "She swore up and down that it wasn't, but it was someone like her anyway."

"Someone like her? What do you mean by that exactly?"

The suspect's gaze shifted over to Dr. Vogel, and their eyes locked. Once again, the nameless man looked at Vogel as if he were a dimwit rather than the holder of two doctorates. His expression seemed to say Try and keep up, doc.

"A vampire."

"A vampire?" the doctor asked, making sure that he heard correctly. "Like Count Dracula?"

"God, I wish it were something like that—a cut-and-dried monster, sated by something as simple as blood. The truth about vampires is far worse than all that."

Dr. Vogel jotted down a few more lines on his pad, hoping that this guy was the real deal and not some run-of-the-mill dirtbag looking for an insanity plea. If this nameless, unidentifiable murderer really turned out to believe he was hunting vampires, then treating him could make Vogel's career. There'd be book deals, news show interviews, maybe even a made-for-TV movie.

"And what is the truth about vampires?" Dr. Vogel asked, placing his pen down on his pad.

The suspect met Vogel's gaze, his distracted paranoia replaced with a disturbing intensity. "Are you sure you want to know that, Dr. Barnabas Vogel?" His finger tapped the doctor's nameplate, like the bouncing ball in a children's music video, as he spoke his name. "The truth has a price."

Vogel didn't like the way the suspect enunciated his name. It made him uneasy, but he did his best not to let it show.

"I do."

"Well, first off, like I said, they don't feed off blood. That's . . . best I can figure, that's a . . . um . . . a misunderstanding of symbolism mistranslated across time and cultures. What they really consume is anything of worth in a victim's life. Their health. Their loved ones. Their very identity. The things that really make up a life, you dig?"

The doctor wrote in his pad and urged the suspect to continue.

"And when they take those things from you, doc, it's like they were never yours. It's like the vampire always had them, instead of you. That woman you've been in love with for twenty years? She's been bedding the monster for two decades, and you've never met her. The idiosyncrasies of your speech that you picked up from your old man—turns of phrase that only you, and he, and maybe your granddad say—you've never heard or uttered them, but the vampire has. The years and years you've put into learning the piano never happened, and somewhere some evil thing is playing Satin Doll while you stare dumbly at the ivories."

The suspect hunched over and pressed his palms against his forehead. Deep, wavering breaths escaped his lungs.

"It's okay," Dr. Vogel said. "Take your time."

It took a minute or so for the suspect to regain his composure. When he sat up, he was wiping tears from his haggard face. The flush brought to him from crying actually gave some life to his complexion. The doctor handed him a tissue, which he took with a mumbled thanks.

"For all the terrible power they have, though, vampires do have weaknesses. There are rules, as in the folklore and the movies, but different. They don't sleep in coffins, and you can't keep them at bay with a cross or a clove of garlic, but it's true that they can't hurt you unless you invite them in. Not like into your house, but into your mind and into your heart," the nameless man said, tapping his own forehead, then laying his hands over his chest. "But you don't care about the rules. You want to hear about the one I killed."

"That would be a good place to start," Vogel agreed.

The suspect blew his nose into the tissue that the doctor had given him to wipe his tears. He sniffled and shifted in his chair, trying to get comfortable. The shackles around his ankles rattled like the chains of a restless ghost.

"I guess it all started on my last birthday. I was standing on a folding chair, in the dingy, pay-by-the-week room I rented at the Bishop Hotel, which wasn't a hotel at all, but a flophouse for addicts and losers. I'd just turned forty years old, and I had nothing at all to show for my life, you know? No skills. No passions. No one to love."

Tears were coming down his cheeks again as he told the story. He wiped them away with the snotty tissue balled up in one shackled hand.

"Air conditioners weren't allowed at the Bishop Hotel, since the manager didn't trust the screw-ups living there not to drop one out of a window and kill someone, so the room had a ceiling fan. That's what I used to string myself up from with a sad, makeshift noose I'd crafted from a piece of electrical cord. I fitted the budget slipknot around my neck and looked down at the roaches and rats who had come out of hiding to watch me die. That's when I had . . . um . . . what do they call it? A moment of clarity.

"As I looked down at the vermin around me and got ready to kick out the chair, I took a moment to reflect on my life and realized that I had no life. And I don't mean I'd fucked it up or threw it away. It wasn't as if I'd been orphaned or that my parents were dead or estranged. I simply never had parents, which of course is impossible. Same with friends and lovers. It wasn't that I'd driven them away with my shit lifestyle and lack of personality. They had never been there. Ever. Who goes through life never making a friend?

"And it went beyond relationships. I had no talents, no interests, and no passions. I couldn't recall a single happy memory, and the depressing history of my existence that I could remember was an incomplete thing. There were memories of loss, pain, and hardship, but they were unmoored by any context. There was no narrative to any of it, just hazy, painful vignettes.

"As I stood on that chair, with a noose of electrical wire wrapped around my throat, I realized that my life wasn't a failure, it was a vacuum. It was a gaping emptiness in every important respect, and it didn't make any sense. So I took the noose off of my neck and stepped down from the chair. I wasn't supposed to do that. I was supposed to hang myself.

"Here's another truth about vampires. Despair is how they kill their victims, the ones they don't turn. Despair so deep that you don't even try and remember what caused it. But I got lucky."

He reached up with both shackled hands and played with his goatee as his watery green eyes darted toward the ceiling. Fat teardrops ran past his trembling frown.

"I'm sorry," he muttered. "It's hard going down this road."

"You don't need to apologize to me," Dr. Vogel said.

The suspect gave the doctor a sad smile, then went back into his story.

"So I spent a lot of time after that just trying to make some sense of my existence or lack thereof. Walking cleared my head, so that's what I'd do all day, from dawn to dusk. For a while I was pretty sure I was insane, but the more I wandered around the city, the more I saw that I wasn't alone. The same emptiness that gripped my soul was prevalent all around. That kind of thing is invisible to your average Joe, most of us are so self-absorbed, but I had eyes to see. Maybe because I had no self to be absorbed in. Where others just saw junkies, or bums, or crazies, I saw that black void. I could tell what had happened to them.

"So I started watching these people, then talking to them. They were sad, interchangeable husks. Dead-eyed and hollow-voiced. None of them lasted more than a week after I'd spot them before sucking on a tailpipe or walking into traffic. Like I said, that's how the monsters kill. Vampires don't rip out your throat, they just point you to the gallows."

The man with no name reached up for his throat and wrung his fingers in strange patterns as if he were throwing up gang signs. Coarse, ugly sobs issued from his mouth, followed by a torrent of tears. His crying was unabashed and free of shame. It was the kind of therapeutic crying that Dr. Vogel wished he himself was capable of.

"Perhaps we should take a break and meet again tomorrow," Dr. Vogel suggested. The suspect nodded and mumbled a thank you.

Dr. Vogel sat at his desk, looking over his notes from yesterday's interview with the self-proclaimed vampire hunter and murderer of Courtney Waugh. The case still excited him, both as a clinician and as a man eager to cash in on a good story, but part of him dreaded seeing the patient again. Criminals didn't get under his skin. Over the course of his career he'd dealt with killers, rapists, and even child molesters. Some of the atrocities those animals had committed made the single torture and murder that this guy was accused of seem vanilla in comparison.

Despite all this, the doctor considered faking a stomach bug so he wouldn't have to look into the man's eyes. It wouldn't have been a complete lie. His head was pounding and he felt run down, but he'd definitely worked through worse.

What was it, he wondered, that bothered him so much about this guy that he'd consider going home sick to avoid his gaze? Emptiness, he supposed. When the suspect had described that vacuum in his spirit, he wasn't being melodramatic. There was something missing there—something conspicuous in its absence, and Vogel could make out the ragged outline of that void, just as it had been described.

There was a knock at his office door, even though it was open, and the suspect stood in the threshold, shackled at the hands and feet, decked out in an orange jumpsuit, and escorted by a grim-faced corrections officer. There was some color to his face, and his features weren't quite as sunken. A good night's sleep seemed to have gone a long way for him. Seeing this change made Vogel feel a bit more at ease. He looked more human and less like a walking corpse.

"Good afternoon," the doctor said as his patient sat down and the corrections officer connected his leg shackles to the wooden chair. Once the suspect was secured Dr. Vogel dismissed the guard, who seemed happy to leave.

"Dr. Vogel," the suspect said, tapping on the doctor's nameplate as he spoke, just as he had done the day before.

"You look better today than yesterday," Dr. Vogel offered.

The suspect smiled. There was almost genuine happiness on his face, which was a huge difference from the last time they met.

"They let me talk to my wife last night. It was just a few minutes, but her voice, man, it's music. You know what I mean?"

Dr. Vogel offered a curt smile but didn't respond. The fact was he didn't know. He'd been something a romantic failure and had been alone for the better part of a decade. That wasn't something he was about to get into with a potentially insane murderer, though.

"Plus, she had some Duke Ellington playing in the background. You an Ellington fan, doc?"

Vogel was feeling angry with the man before him, and he wasn't sure why. Generally speaking, he was a man of patient temperament, but these simple, innocuous questions were getting under his skin. Perhaps, he considered, it was his headache making him grumpy.

"Yesterday you were going to tell me about Courtney Waugh and why you killed her. Do you think we can get back into that?"

"Yeah . . . um . . . That's why we're here, right?"

"Indeed." Dr. Vogel took hold of his pen in one hand, his pad in the other, then leaned back in his chair.

"So, I told you how I . . . um . . . I could spot people like me, poor bastards who'd had everything good cut out of their being by some evil creature. It's like I told you, most of them offed themselves within a week of popping up on my radar, but a few of them didn't. The ones that didn't take a bath with a toaster, they still walked around with that emptiness inside, but outwardly, things started getting better for them. The darkness of the void in their souls was so intense I could physically see it radiating out, eating the light around them, but I guess I was the only one noticed.

"One day you had a forgotten geriatric living under a bridge, the next they're a lawyer, or a rock star, or a trust fund playboy, and no one ever noticed the change. Except for me, that is. I could ferret them out, because that void from what had been taken from them had become a vacuous singularity that only I could see. A black hole that could never be filled. You see, the truth about vampires is, no matter how good they have it, they're never sated for long. There's nothing that can undo that original loss; no stolen thing quite the right shape to fill in that blank. So they feed and feed and feed, taking bits of anyone who will let them in, until they eat them all up."

"You said that once a vampire took something from a person, it's as if they never had it and the vampire always had," Dr. Vogel commented, tapping his pen against his pad. "But you could remember that this person who, let's say, is a rock star today was a vagrant yesterday?"

"Yes and no," the suspect answered. "It's . . . um . . . it's more feeling than memory, you know? Like the aftermath of a hazy dream or some cousin to déjà vu. But beyond that, I can see in them that same yawning blackness within my own heart, but grown out of all proportion. And that's what I saw in Courtney Waugh."

"Tell me about that," Dr. Vogel urged. "How you met her. The course of events that led to her death."

"She was the . . . um . . . the common thread, you know? There was this old lady named Mary who I knew was a victim, just like me. I guess her name wasn't worth taking, so she got to keep it, but nothing else. Anyway, she lived under an overpass just outside of the city, and Courtney Waugh would drop her a dollar every day and spend a few minutes chatting with her.

"The same with some of the junkies outside of the methadone clinic. She'd come by with coffee and talk to the same two addicts every Thursday. Then there was the pigeon man at the park. Guy was a mute, just sat there making cooing sounds at the birds and feeding them scraps he'd dig out of the trash. Courtney would show up with a loaf of bread for him to share with the birds, and she'd just talk at him, even though he never said a word back."

"That doesn't sound like the work of a vampire to me," Dr. Vogel commented.

"Ah, but it is. You see, in the movies and the books they use their fangs to drain their victims, but the truth about vampires is they suck you dry by talking. Words are like magic to them. They tell you secrets and speak sorrows, and in exchange they take the good things from you. That's how it works, and that's what Courtney Waugh was doing.

"So I followed her. I watched her. She became the reason I got out of bed in the morning, and the reason I didn't open up my wrists. I know how that sounds—like I had some pervert obsession over her—but it wasn't like that. Courtney was the key to getting back some semblance of what had been taken from me. I knew I couldn't get my life back, but I could get a life back—someone else's.

"Finally, after months of stalking her, I broke into Courtney's home, and you wouldn't believe this place. Million-dollar artwork on every wall. A cellar full of fine wine. Hot tub on the roof. I can't imagine this all came from just one victim; it was like a hodge-podge of luxuries ripped from countless lives. She must have been doing this to people for a long time, you know? Maybe centuries."

Vogel was having a hard time focusing on the other man's words, and he found that his headache was being exacerbated by the sunlight streaming in from the window. He squinted and winced.

"Barnabas, can you . . . um . . . close the blinds?"

"Of course," Barnabas smiled, and for the first time his expression reflected genuine happiness. He turned and drew the blinds, leaving them to talk in the dim, filtered daylight.

"So, like I was saying, I broke into her house, and I waited, and for all the power vampires have, all those folklore stories about heightened senses and invulnerabilities are bullshit. She never saw me coming, and it didn't take a silver knife to cut her or a cross to burn her."

"Why . . . um . . . Why did you want to hurt her?"

Barnabas sat back in his chair and fiddled with his cufflinks, casting a pitying look at the man across from him.

"Because I needed the truth, doc."

"Doc?"

"I needed the truth about vampires. The secrets of how they consume all the good things in someone's life and make them their own. The way they twist reality so it's like things have always been that way. And she told me, too. Each little phrase to utter, and what magic gestures to make with your hands.

"She taught me what truths to pass on in trade for those beautiful things in a person's life. Because there's a cost to the truth, you see? But I'd already paid it, so she had nothing to take from me. But you, you had a lot to lose. You dig?"

"Can you . . . um . . . can you repeat the question?"

Dr. Barnabas Vogel stroked his goatee and looked at the picture on his desk, a photo of him and his wife dancing at a jazz club in Chicago. He missed her, and he couldn't wait for the day to be over so that he might take her dancing, then make love through the night.

"I said, the purpose of these meetings is to determine if you are mentally fit to stand trial for the murder of Courtney Waugh. Do you understand?"

The nameless man shackled to the chair across from Dr. Barnabas Vogel's desk did not understand, though. He didn't know where he was or even who he was. He didn't know what was going on, and he didn't care. There was an emptiness in him, a black void whose ragged outline he could almost feel, and nothing else mattered but finding a way to end that pain.

The Idea of the North
in the Fiction of Simon Strantzas

James Goho

Simon Strantzas sets "Cold to the Touch" (2009) in the far North[1] of Canada. There Andrew Lauzon, a Bible-carrying scientist, and his two Inuit guides investigate a geological and meteorological anomaly in the frozen, snowbound Arctic. But the true protagonist in the story is the setting: an unforgiving cold, great plains of snow under a dismal gray sky, and a mystifying crater with five black megaliths at its center, as if the hand of the North itself. That ring of dark stones is the source of the anomaly. Such investigations often end in terror.

Simon Strantzas (b. 1972) is a Canadian author with five short story collections in the "weird, dark and strange fantastic fiction" tradition: *Beneath the Surface* (Humdrumming, 2008), *Cold to the Touch* (Tartarus Press, 2009), *Nightingale Songs* (Dark Regions Press, 2011), *Burnt Black Suns* (Hippocampus Press, 2014), and *Nothing Is Everything* (Undertow, 2018). S. T. Joshi ranks Strantzas one of the "elite" contemporary weird fiction writers, that is, one of the most promising of those writers who are relatively young and have made their reputation in the twenty-first century. This essay

---

1. The geographic North in Canada is variously defined. Often it includes the provincial norths of Manitoba, Ontario, Quebec, and Labrador, along with the sub-Arctic and Arctic territories of the Yukon, the Northwest Territories, and Nunavut. This suggests that "the North" is found north of the 60th Parallel, or north of the tree line (Grace 230). But the North is sometimes thought of as beginning below the 60th Parallel, including the north parts of other provinces. The North is defined, at times, as encompassing the taiga and boreal forest, the barren grounds and tundra, as well as the ice surrounded islands of the Arctic and the high Arctic (Grace 10–11).

will explore a small sample of Strantzas's dark stories where the settings (the landscapes) represent the reality or idea of the Canadian North (often thought of more broadly as the wilderness). In these spectral landscapes his characters experience trauma induced by the landscape. This contact culminates in the fragmentation of human identity or body disintegration in nature. Moreover, Strantzas inscribes the individual emotional states of his characters into their relationships or collisions with these landscapes. In this way the spectral landscapes reshape the mindscapes of the characters.

I will explore his stories through three lenses, ideas, or "image-clusters" (to use Margaret Atwood's term [*Strange Things* 7]) that appear frequently in discussions about the North of Canada. The first is disappearance or erasure by landscape, which speaks to the overwhelming power and allure of the wilderness. The second is the figure of the Windigo, originating in the Northern Ojibwa and Cree traditions, which is understood and represented in lore and images as a spirit of the North or the wilderness and as a personification of colonization. The wilderness as a mysterious place of wonder and healing or a space of horror and death is the third idea cluster found in Strantzas's fiction. This idea cluster alludes to the wilderness as a place for adventure, to discover riches, to find or lose oneself, or as a state of mind. Some of Strantzas's stories combine these ideas, but I will focus on what I see as the central theme in individual stories.

The Meaning of "North" in Canada

Canadian literature and art has a long tradition of terrifying or transforming encounters in the hinterlands of Canada. That is because the country's environment haunts Canadian and other artists and authors, who seem enthralled or panicked by its geography, especially its diversity of landforms, its enormity, and its wilderness. Margaret Atwood argues that "everything in Canada, outside of Toronto, begins with geography" (*Writing with Intent* 33). For the Indigenous peoples of Canada, knowledge and tales evoke the power, grandeur, and respite of nature, but also its danger. Early colonists spoke of the country's natural environment as embodying beauty, isolation, and destruction. For example, in *Roughing It in the Bush* (1852), Susanna Moodie wrote that Canada was a "strange, stern landscape" where "lofty groves of pines frowned down in hearse-like gloom" (46). She felt like a stranger in a "landscape, savage and grand in its primeval beauty" (335). Another early work, the poem "The Walker of the Snow" (1867) by Charles Shanly (1811–1875), tells of an encounter with the "Shadow Hunter" in a snowbound valley in a cold winter. The figure of the Shadow Hunter is similar in some ways to the Windigo. But the Windigo is a complex figure in history, literature, myth, and the lives of the Indigenous peoples of Canada.

The Canadian wilderness inspired the art of the Group of Seven artists (1920–33), which was the first major distinctive art movement in Canada. They were also known as the Algonquin School, because they painted the northern boreal forests, stone formations, and lakes found in Algonquin Park as well as other locations in Canada. Glenn Gould's radio broadcast of 1967, called *The Idea of North*, speaks about the complex and mixed concepts and emotions regarding the North for Canadians. Gould sees the North as real and imagined. The recording features a soundtrack of a train moving always toward the North, as if the desire of all Canadians, along with voices of people who have experienced the northern region of Canada's vast wilderness. Gould provides no definitive notion of the North because it is a continuing image and reality that awes and scares many Canadians, yet for many the North has been and always will be home.

Justin D. Edwards, Northrop Frye, Margot Northey, Atwood, Robert Kroetsch, Sherrill E. Grace, and others have explored the continuing influence of the Canadian landscape, in mythic and real form, on Canadian literature. Edwards suggests that Canada's environment shapes the country's tradition of gothic and supernatural fiction. In his wide-ranging exploration of the meaning of the gothic² in Canada and beyond, Edwards argues, "the wilderness is a haunting presence for the newcomer, [and] it is also haunted for those who call it home" (xxviii). The Canadian wilds are not always idyllic; Northrop Frye notes a "deep terror in regard to nature," which is "a terror of the soul" (350), in Canadian poetry. Frye identifies a "garrison mentality" (351) in Canadian literature about the wilderness. More subtly, Northey argues that there is an "unresolved duality of awe and fear" (30) in the Canadian experience of nature. She sees a strong and enduring gothic tradition in Canadian literature, starting with the early Gothic novel, John Richardson's *Wacousta; or, The Prophecy* (1832). In *Strange Things*, Atwood writes about four key obsessions or "image clusters" in Canadian literature, which center on the North in particular and the wilderness in general: the wilderness as a mythic and real landscape (which allures, and often erases identity), the appropriation of Indigenous identity by whites, the Windigo as a complex metaphor for the wilderness and its effects on people, and women writers using wilderness motifs in unique ways.

Kroetsch says the North in Canada is not only real geographically but also real mythically. For him, the North of Canada remains a wilderness and a continuing presence everywhere—a haunting presence representing a primal, powerful natural mystery, yet also a source of continuing trauma. Grace traces the variant images and ideas of the North in Canadian literature, art, performance, politics, and music. She argues that the North is the key to understanding Canadian reality and imagination. The North, with its many meanings, actually and spectrally continues to haunt Canadians. And it appears frequently in Canadian literature, including gothic and dark fiction, such as that of Simon Strantzas.

---

2. This essay follows George E. Haggerty's advice to use the proper noun "Gothic" for the classic literary tradition, while the common noun "gothic" is reserved for the literary motif in its continuing manifestations (205).

Death in the North

Erasure by landscape keeps appearing in Canadian writing, as if the geography of the country is a consuming or liberating entity itself. Emblematic of this erasure is the disappearance in 1845 of the Arctic expedition in search of the fabled Northwest Passage and loss of all 129 men led by Sir John Franklin. The two ships of the expedition were not discovered for years: the H.M.S. *Erebus* in 2014 and the H.M.S. *Terror* in 2016.[3] Erasure by the North haunts Canadians. Tom Thomson (1877–1917), the early Canadian wilderness landscape artist, disappeared on a canoeing trip on Canoe Lake in Algonquin Park in Ontario. His body was found in the lake eight days later. There are still questions surrounding his death. Kroetsch notes how often characters in Canadian literature "vanish into blizzards, under snow" or face "death by drowning" (56). In *Writing with Intent*, Atwood lists a number of ways to die in the North, for example: "death by blackfly [. . .], death from starvation, death by animal, death by forest fire, [. . .] death from something called 'exposure,' [. . .] death by thunderstorm, [. . .] by lighting, [and] death by freezing and death by drowning" (39).[4] Her extensive list underscores the association of death with the Canadian landscape of the North. Writing about Aritha van Herk (a Canadian writer whose works, including *The Tent Peg* [1982], often focus on the far North), Grace says her writing reflects upon the mystery and power of the North to erase, efface, and make one invisible (40).

Strantzas's "When Sorrows Come" (2007) illustrates one of the ways to die in the wilderness. He reworks the real Canadian activity and literary theme of a holiday in a cabin in the woods. Liam and Marcia join Ken and Halley for a short respite in an isolated wilderness resort in Canada. Ken and Halley are veterans of the forest ex-

---

3. On the other hand, Vilhjalmur Stefansson (1879–1962) lived in the Arctic for five years by living off the land, which he learned from the Inuit.

4. As an historical note, Susanna Moodie's six-year-old son John drowned in the Moira river in 1844. Canada became haunted for her.

perience. Liam dislikes the cabin and the environs, while Marcia seems dazed and distant. Liam imagines Marcia's despairs circling her as if moths around a light. They are drifting apart. While walking through the woods, Marcia listens to the call of the woods. As with much of his fiction, Strantzas deftly evokes the emotional states of his characters.

Strantzas describes the wilds surrounding the cabins as dark, dense, and whispering. All of the pathways meander oddly through the woods. They refuse to be easy to follow. The characters are small in contrast to the "old and towering trees" (*NS* 156), which quickly engulf them. It is a landscape within which one could become lost. Of course, they venture along what they think is a path into a "wall of trees" (*NS* 162). Then Marcia goes off alone on a darker track. Eventually Liam follows her along that difficult path deeper into the forest, but he does not find her. He thinks he may have glimpsed her on a ledge overlooking a stream bed, but she was not there. She disappeared in the woods and is not discovered by repeated searches.

Some time after Marcia's disappearance, Liam returns alone to the isolated resort area. This act of returning to the scene of a disappearance or an uncanny event is a recurring theme in Strantzas's stories, which illustrates the continuing lure of the wilderness and the human urge to find an explanation of an uncanny event or experience. While talking with the caretaker of the lodge, Liam notices a photograph of a painting of the forest. It may be a reference to Atwood's story "Death by Landscape" (1990), which tells of the disappearance of the young Lucy while at Camp Manitou in Northern Ontario. Her body was never found. Now elderly, her friend Lois remembers the loss. Her condominium walls are lined with artwork of the wilds—art with trees, stone, and lakes—some of them by Group of Seven artists and two by Tom Thomson, which fill her with a "wordless sense of unease" (*Wilderness Tips* 100). That is because Lucy haunts Lois's art collection. Or Strantzas may be alluding to our inability to capture or control the true spirit of a forest in a painting. Rather, what a painting exhibits is our belief or hope about the tameness of the wilderness. But nature is not always safe, not even when it is depicted or neutralized in paintings. Another painting appears in "Cold to the Touch."

Liam finds more than he had hoped for on his return journey through the woods. Atwood says "the journey north has the quality of dream" (*Writing with Intent* 34). Liam's journey reads as if a dream image captivates him. The landscape comes alive and lures him to that cliff edge where he may have glimpsed Marcia. But Liam's dream journey turns into nightmare. There is no escape for him from the wilderness.[5]

In "These Last Embers" (2015), the wilderness takes over a country home. Strantzas crafts a subtle and strange story on the theme of disappearance in the forest. As is customary with Strantzas's best work, he captures a critical moment in the life of his characters that precisely evokes their emotion within a spectral or unusual experience as the world turns out to be different from what they know. After a failed attempt at freedom in the city, Samantha unhappily returns to her family home in the countryside. Despair consumes Samantha, because of her failure and her need to return to her former life. When she arrives home she finds part of the house black with a "dark stain of fire" (*NE* 48).

This will be no happy homecoming for Samantha. The family home was ravaged by fire and not repaired. But her parents still live in the house. The heart of that fire was the bedroom of her twin brother, Lemule, who despaired at her leaving for the city, imagining she had abandoned him. While she was in the city, he had languished in his room and rarely exited. After the fire, that bedroom was transformed into an infinite forest. The trees grew out through

---

5. "When Sorrows Come" is primarily a story of disappearance in the wilderness, but it also hints at an appearance of a Windigo. A wind brushes Liam's face and he thinks he sees a blue blur, which he takes to be Marcia, who may now be a Windigo. It is an invisible thing as many beliefs about the Windigo say. This is a female Windigo similar to those in Ann Tracy's 1990 novel *Winter Hunger*.

the blackened roof and disappeared into the sky. Strantzas depicts the forest as a living thing replete with wildlife and breathing with a sooty, damp, and earthy breath. The forest canopy "towered into forever" while shadows fell "long and deep and dark near the ground" (*NE* 57). Strantzas creates an image of wilderness transforming a familiar house into an uncanny, wild landscape. This familiar place becomes twisted into the unfamiliar.

Samantha and her brother's despairs mirror each other. Their mutual grief is expressed in the raging fire that turned part of the house into a spectral, unexplainable infinite forest where first Lemule vanishes and then Samantha. This is an encounter with dread where the known causes terror precisely because it is known, but somehow becomes unfamiliar, which Sigmund Freud identified in "The Uncanny" (1919). Freud traced the transformation of the German word *das heimliche* ("the homely") into its opposite, *das unheimliche* ("the unhomely"). The uncanny is dread found near to home, which is explicitly what happens in Strantzas's story. Freud noted the double as a mode of the uncanny. Samantha and Lemule, twins, are the doubles. According to Freud, the double eventually becomes a "vision of terror" (389), which is how Samantha's brother appears to her in the closing of the story. Yet she embraces that terror image.

Back in that fire ravaged house, Samantha thinks she hears her brother signaling her, now that he has become part of the wild. So she enters the forest. It seems alive: stones try to trip her and branches claw at her eyes. She finds Lemule transformed into a firething. Her despair and her longing vanish in that impossible landscape of infinite trees. Samantha goes into the terrifying and unfamiliar "endless forest" (*NE* 58) at the end of the story, because it takes her back to what was familiar in the past when she and her brother were young and played in "the endless woods" (*NE* 49) surrounding their childhood home.

No forests appear in "Cold to the Touch." Instead, Strantzas places this story in the cold, ice, and snow of the high Arctic. Luis and Akiak accompany Lauzon on his expedition to a climatic anomaly.

The story is told from the point of view of Lauzon. To Lauzon, the landscape of the North appears alien. The vistas across the ice and snow seem indistinguishable. It is a monotonous landscape. As native to the North, the Inuit see the landscape differently than the white explorer from the South. Lauzon sees the landscape through his Christian religious and his scientific lenses. Luis and Akiak see it through their experience of living in the North and from their spiritual and practical attachment to the landscape of snow and cold but also its sustenance and familiarity. Lauzon would soon be lost with no guide. Yet the Inuit easily traverse the landscape. They are able to orient and way-find to the anomaly. Claudio Aporta details how traveling and orienting for Inuit are parts of the broader task of dwelling in the North. This entails a full immersion with the northern environment. Such an immersion means not only a learned knowledge of the territory but also a bond with the environment that includes emotional attachment and memories of meaningful places. In the story, Akiak reveres the Arctic. At first, Luis appears as sarcastically practical in his view of the homeland of the Inuit—an attitude that is his way of challenging the explorer from the South.

An isolated cabin is featured in this story, as in so many Canadian stories of the North. A painting hangs on a wall. It pictures a blizzard of white etched with grays and blues overwhelming an immobile, solitary figure. It prefigures the outcome of the expedition, because, as Rudy Wiebe suggests, a person must move in the North to live (49). There are three trips (of course, in Strantzas's stories characters keep returning to a place of terror, loss, or sorrow) to the anomaly in the story. On the first trek Lauzon rides on a snowmobile with Akiak, while Luis is alone on the other snowmobile as they travel through a stark and cold landscape of snow under a grim sky. Strantzas depicts the Arctic as a monochromatic landscape where snow and sky freeze as one. When the three reach the rim of an unusual crater formation, Lauzon feels a sense of dread and thinks of how soon one could die in the cold. He is astounded by the size of the crater and its thick pall of snow. But more so, he worries over the strangeness of the tall stones. He sets up his equipment, anxious to discover the cause of the climatic fluctuations. Akiak pays homage to the stones, which he says have always been there. This seeming discovery through satellite imaging turns out to be known to the Inuit. It is a significant place that should be avoided.

On their second trek to the crater, the snow falls incessantly. They struggle through the cold white landscape. The blizzard shrouds their journey toward the anomaly. When they arrive, they find the snow deeper in the crater, yet the stones look taller. And the stones are unusually free of ice and snow. The blowing snow slivers Lauzon. He finds that some of his equipment has been damaged. This also occurs in Strantzas's story "On Ice" (2014). The landscape itself is hostile to intrusions and investigations. During this second trek to the five standing stones, Luis is injured while trying to take a sample of the standing stones, and they return to the cabin.

Lauzon sleeps and when he wakes he finds that both Luis and Akiak are gone. Outside the cabin he sees Luis disappearing into the falling snow. He follows what appears to be a shadow in the white snowfields. It is a long struggle through the blizzard, with the snow howling a ceaseless warning, as if the landscape is testing Lauzon and his beliefs. But the final challenge will be at the stones. Lauzon feels he is moving toward darkness during the pursuit. At the stones, he finds all his equipment destroyed. Luis embraces a stone monolith. Lauzon discovers Akiak drowning in the ice, because "ice is water pretending to be land" (Wiebe 16). Around the three men, the vicious, white landscape comes alive. The ice is no longer silent. It cracks and booms, while it rolls underneath them. Luis sees the monument move, as if struggling to be free of the immense block of ice that prisons it. Lauzon cannot see it. Strantzas spectrally represents the North as a stone entity encased in ice but now beginning to surface because of Lauzon's intrusions. The North will not yield to his God or to his scientific calculations. His Bible has disappeared, as things do in the North.

Atwood suggests that "Getting lost in the north means not

knowing how to get out" (*Writing with Intent* 38). The three men are now lost in the grip of that northern landscape. Luis knows it; he says "we weren't alone" (*CT* 192). The landscape continues to quake and "swallow great pieces of ice and rock," and an Arctic gale tosses "frozen chunks of snow" (*CT* 192). The strange power of the landscape traumatizes Lauzon. All he can do is cry; he knows he cannot get out.

The stones, which appear as a hand of the spirit of the North, may also represent the Windigo, which is the subject of the next section of this essay. The ending of "Cold to the Touch" describes the ice landscape around the stones cracking and breaking, as if something struggles to free itself from the ice. According to Nathan D. Carlson, the Windigo oral tradition suggests that these sounds herald its appearance. In one such account, Métis elder Bernard Cardinal of Trout Lake, Alberta, reported that when the *witiko* increased in size a sound could be heard: a "snapping" or "popping" sound that was similar to the sound of ice breaking (Carlson 392).

There is no Windigo in "The Indelible Stain upon the Sky" (2011). Here Strantzas deftly links personal traumas to climate traumas. In this first-person story the unnamed narrator returns to Port McCarthy, where he had holidayed in the past with his wife, Suzanne. The town is drenched with oil and decay. An oil tanker, the *Madison* (there is a real oil tanker named *Madison*), wrecked on the shore of the port and flooded the area with its load of oil, destroying habitats and the livelihood of the town. As noted previously, many of Strantzas's stories include a return to a location of trauma, as if the characters are compelled to recreate the hurt associated with an encounter with a gothic space.

The story blends the narrator's memories of his first stay in the hotel with his current stay. But what is most challenging in the story is the absence of Suzanne from his return stay at the town. She is gone. It is not made clear what happened to her. Her disappearance is linked in a strange way with the wreck of the *Madison*, their stay in that hotel room, and the environmental contagion that continues to rage in the rotting town. The story fuses a dreadful and hidden personal event with an even more dreadful environmental catastrophe.

"The Indelible Stain upon the Sky" is a story of the intersecting paths of the personal, the natural, and the unknown. All this is summed up by the appearance in the hotel room, on the narrator's second stay, of an oil-drenched boy. This suggests that Strantzas's story can be appreciated as an example of the eco-gothic, that is, as a story where gothic fiction landscapes depict damaged and degraded environments. Tom J. Hillard says that eco-criticism or the eco-gothic recognizes that some contemporary gothic literature foregrounds ecological crises (28). Hillard sees such gothic fiction as focusing attention on environmental issues and creatively revealing our anxieties about the destruction of the natural world and our place in nature (11). Adding to this idea, Shoshannah Ganz says that eco-gothic stories tell about the earth as ravaged by climate change (67). This is clearly reflected in "The Indelible Stain upon the Sky." Such ecologically focused gothic literature expresses an intensifying dread over human-caused environmental change. Gothic fiction is a literature of fear. Strantzas's story expresses our fear of the effects of climate change and terror at our role in causing that change. That boy drenched in oil is a metaphor for that fear. The silences of the narrator in the story and his inability to retell key events, such as Suzanne's disappearance, reveal his continuing trauma caused by his experience in that damaged town. He is reduced to silence at the magnitude of the destruction of the environment, which for him becomes a gothic landscape that traps him in his hotel. He cannot escape. The gothic landscape occupies his lonely hotel room, spreading oil across the floor toward him.

Other contemporary Canadian weird fiction writers also explore the wilderness disappearance theme of Canadian literature. In Gemma Files's[6] "Thin Places" (2015), Norah chaperones a camping

---

6. Joshi ranks Gemma Files as one of the "elite" contemporary weird writers in his *21st-Century Horror: Weird Fiction at the Turn of the Millennium.*

trip to the Muskoka River—a Canadian river that flows from the highlands of Algonquin Park and eventually empties into Georgian Bay in Ontario. Liam, her son, walks away into the woods with an unknown woman and disappears. Norah keeps dreaming of going back and looking for him. She says one day she will return, because all Canadians seem to want to return to the woods, and "let the leaves close behind" her and vanish (Files). Richard Gavin's story "Thistle Latch" (2016) tells of the disappearance of Lattice Rayburn by landscape. Or was it a merging with the landscape, becoming the wilderness? In Michael Kelly's "The Face that Looks Back at You" (2010), Alex and Teri return back "up north to the cabin" (13) with hopes of repairing their fracturing relationship. Alex thinks that Teri is "disappearing, vanishing" (15), but it seems that it is really Alex, who lured by the snap and crack of the lake, falls through the ice and drowns. But then again, the story may tell about Alex's return from the dead to haunt Teri.

Becoming Windigo

For a long time the Windigo image of the northern Algonquians has haunted Canadian literature. Anthropologists, ethnohistorians, and others have also studied the phenomenon. The Windigo is often conceived as the great spirit of the wilderness and the keeper of its secrets. It erases memory and unites one with nature, which means losing your personal identity. Who would choose to face that terror?

The Windigo is a persistent image in Canada. John Robert Colombo collected a great many narrative accounts and visual artifacts in *Windigo: An Anthology of Fact and Fantastic Fiction*. Margaret Atwood devotes a chapter in *Strange Things* to a discussion of the Windigo motif in literature, especially Canadian literature. Both note Algernon Blackwood's classic story "The Wendigo" (1910), which is set in the great northern Ontario forest. Greg Gatenby notes that the Canadian wilderness was a powerful force in Blackwood's life, arguing that "Canadian imagery haunted Blackwood's writing" (21). Blackwood lived in various parts and during varying times in Canada from 1887 to 1898. Blackwood set several of his stories in Canada.[7]

At times the oral and written traditions depict the Windigo as a cannibalistic creature. Alternately it represents starving, which was a real part of winter in cold climates. The Windigo is also viewed as a symbol for "going bush," that is, going feral, losing one's mind and going crazy in the wilds. Strantzas's story "On Ice" illustrates the multiple images and characteristics of the Windigo. Marlene Goldman argues that stories about the Windigo are disaster narratives that speak about the effects of colonization (167). "On Ice" is a disaster story. The story captures the isolation, disorientation, and eventual panic of white explorers in the unfamiliar environment of the far North. The harsh conditions and the strange landscape combine to traumatize the characters. Strantzas spectrally materializes that trauma in the hallucinatory visions of the last survivor.

"On Ice" tells of a scientific expedition to discover fossils from the Mesozoic Era on Melville Island in the high Arctic of Canada. This third-person story focuses on Wendell, a graduate student, who along with his fellow graduate students, Dogan and Isaacs, follow Dr. Hanson on the quest. They were flown onto the island by Gauthier, who accompanies them on their trek across the snow and ice. All the characters are male, mirroring the common narratives of old Artic expeditions, which depicted only male explorers. What is more, everyone dies or is transformed by the experience, similar to many of the old narratives or the actualities of early European expeditions. The landscape of the Arctic island traumatizes them. The frigid island seems vacant at first, because they see no animals. Yet

---

7. Ashley (*Algernon Blackwood: An Extraordinary Life*) identifies Blackwood's Canadian stories as: "A Haunted Island" (1899), "Skeleton Lake: An Episode in Camp" (1906), "The Wendigo" (1910), "Running Wolf" (1920), "First Hate" (1920), and "The Valley of the Beasts" (1921). In his *Algernon Blackwood: A Bio-Bibliography*, Ashley identifies another story: "How Garnier Broke the Log-Jam" (1904).

they discover a severed human finger beneath the sheet of ice. This is the first hint of cannibalism in the story; later there is a second finger. While the story progresses, Strantzas increasingly describes the island as a gothic space. There are towering rocks and ice. They trek through a "vast icy expanse [. . .], snow-encrusted tundra, [and] eddies dancing across the rough terrain" (*BBS* 20). The landscape becomes a "bizarre art gallery, full of strange smooth sculptures" (*BBS* 18). On their trek across the ice and snow, they feel they are being trailed. The island is no longer empty. It seems a shadow keeps pace with them. This may refer to Shanly's "Shadow Hunter," an image akin to the Windigo.

Similar to "Cold to the Touch," the setting seems the primary protagonist of the story. It is a landscape that ends up consuming the expedition members, a landscape that becomes a morphologically bizarre thing of ice that Wendell imagines or becomes in his dying delirium from the harsh conditions of the island and the expedition's loss of provisions. That is, Wendell becomes a Windigo.

According to Carlson, the Windigo phenomenon continues to be a controversial topic. He argues that no single hypothesis coherently articulates the phenomenon within a Eurocentric (Western) framework (356) . But there is clear historical evidence of the existence of the Windigo imagery prior to European contact in North America (Brightman, Carlson, Warrior). The Windigo is commonly thought of as a cannibal spirit in the belief system of the Algonquian peoples (Ojibwa: *wīntiko̅,* Cree: *wīhtiko̅w*).[8] In the past, Cree and Ojibwa peoples were primarily hunters and gatherers who joined together to hunt, fish, and trade in the summer. Shawn Smallman discusses how they would separate into small bands in the winter of the sub-Arctic region due to the scarcity of game in one area to support large numbers of people. In winter, Windigo stories were told. The winter was the time of hunger. There are multiple

---

8. This figure is called by many different names, such as *wendigo, wetiko, whitiko, chenoo,* or *atoosh* (Colombo, Dillon, Smallman).

references to the scarcity of food and hunger in "On Ice." This seems to lead to cannibalism in Strantzas's story. Smallman says in Cree and Ojibwa belief the Windigo was the spirit of winter that could change a human into an "asocial being whose heart turns to ice and who becomes consumed by cannibal desires" (572). This may be what happens to Wendell in "On Ice."

In Strantzas's story the expedition eventually finds a campsite. During the night a storm assails their tent. Strantzas describes the storm as alive with a howling voice and an odor of dead fish. It repeatedly lashes the tent. In the morning, they discover their food and most of their supplies are gone. After that, they discover "something impossible" surrounding the tent: odd footprints, apparently close to hominid. The landscape induces hallucinations. And this causes the expedition to act irrationally, because they split up. Two return to the landing strip, while the other three leave the raided campsite to search for fossils. Of course, when they return the campsite has vanished, yet another disappearance in the North. And compounding their irrational behavior, the three decide to split up. Wendell and Dogan leave for the landing strip; Dr. Hanson remains at the vacant campsite alone. On their journey, the two become increasingly disoriented due to the harsh landscape. Wendell worries rightly that he is "suffering from a starved hallucination" (*BBS* 36). That is the "arctic cold of Melville Island had upended everything" for him (*BBS* 38).

Some Indigenous and other scholars, for example, Jack D. Forbes, see an evolution of the concept of the Windigo from its original significance to a metaphor that represents the trauma of the North American Indigenous experience under European colonialism and terrorism. Validating this thesis, Grace L. Dillon says the historical evidence establishes the connection between the proliferation of the Windigo phenomenon and colonization, as Indigenous peoples suffered from dwindling resources, settler attacks, and deadly diseases. Furthermore, Carol Edelman Warrior documents how Indigenous authors use the Windigo figure as a means to critique colonialism.

The Windigo can then represent the originating Indigenous image, or the Euro-Western consumption of Indigenous peoples and the destruction of lands, or an image of Indigenous revenge upon colonizers for their greed and brutality. Dillon suggests it is a complex cluster of images within which those suffering possession by the Windigo might be the colonizer or the colonized. In my view, Strantzas's story "On Ice" illustrates explorers consumed by a landscape they cannot comprehend and are not prepared to survive in, because they view it as an environment to exploit for their own interests. The Windigo, as the embodiment of the North or winter, characterized as the landscape of Melville Island by Strantzas, fragments their identities, producing increasingly bizarre hallucinations. The final member of the expedition, Wendell, is transformed into the image of the cannibalistic monster who consumes his fellow travelers and becomes Windigo in the form of an ice monster.

The shifting images of the Windigo are consistent with the originating Algonquian concept of the Windigo as the embodiment of excess and gluttony. More than that, Warrior argues that "windigos attempt to consume the world" (232). They represent the over-extraction from, over-consumption of, and destruction of nature. The expedition led by Dr. Hanson onto Melville Island searches for fossils, but it was preceded by oil companies surveying the island.

Atwood says that the Windigo, as a giant spirit creature, often has a body of ice (*Strange Things* 66). That is the way Strantzas depicts the Windigo in the concluding part of this story. It is a giant, grotesque image partly encased in ice—an image of a cannibalistic entity that eats and is eaten.[9] Wendell is the last survivor and he kills

---

9. This grotesque image appears to be a Lovecraftian monster, but in the context of the story it is more likely a reimagined or hallucinated Windigo, with which Wendell bonds at the end. In addition, the footprints in the story are created by little people, which may be Strantzas's homage to Arthur Machen. However, they seem more likely to be hallucinations engendered by the true horrific entity in the story, which is the Windigo, who drives the explorers to their deaths, but for Wendell who becomes a Windigo. Of course, an alternate view is that they all succumbed to the isolation and disorientation of the landscape.

some of his fellow explorers, seemingly as an act of caring, but the story makes a reader wonder. He alone worships a grotesque ice monster while he freezes in the cold. As a result of his extreme exhaustion and hunger he goes through a gothic transformation of going native, whereby the white explorer experiences the facts of colonization by being consumed. And in a final gothic transformation, Wendell experiences the greatest horror by losing his human identity and becoming a Windigo.

"Pinholes in Black Muslin" (2008) portrays characters experiencing the terror of the Windigo. They have no knowledge of the phenomenon nor any knowledge of the historic connections of Indigenous peoples to their original lands. Yet they become caught up by the wilderness (read the Windigo) because it is a strange and unknown space for these city dwellers, who view the forest as place for a party. But within the Indigenous cosmos of understanding these supernatural beings yet roam the forests of their homelands. Strantzas's latter-day settlers end up being consumed by a Windigo. In the story the Windigo represents the ongoing intergenerational trauma of the Algonquin peoples. The group of six young people can never understand what is happening to them, as the history of destruction of the Indigenous cultures and the harvesting of the woods is largely forgotten in histories by the conquerors.

"Pinholes in Black Muslin" is a story from the perspective of Stewart, an awkward loner. He is more of an observer than an interactive part of the group of six who are off on a holiday in the woods. They stay at an isolated cabin enveloped by woods on Lake Tyson, hours north of Toronto. The setting seems to infect the characters one by one, drawing them away from the cabin into the surrounding forest, lake, or eventually the sky. The characters begin to be taken by something in the landscape.

Early in the story Stewart hears a hissing sound and wonders why it was the only animal noise he could hear. He feels as if he is being watched. While trying to sleep Stewart is disturbed by Trevor, who says he hears a whistling sound. Trevor goes to the lake, as if called by it. In the morning Trevor is missing. Stewart, Daniel, and Philip go to the lake to look for Trevor. The whistling and humming sounds return as the wind rushes past. Atwood (*Strange Things* 65) and Colombo (3) note that these sounds prefigure the Windigo. As well, according to Smallman, over time Windigos transform into physical monsters of great size that speak with a whistling voice and paralyze their victims with fear (573).

While searching for Trevor, the searchers hear a shout, which turns out to be from Claire, who says Annie has vanished. They find no trace of either; it seems as if the two were lifted off the "ground and vanished" (*CT* 121), perhaps paralyzed by the Windigo, who takes them into the forest. The wind continues to move through the trees and seems to scream at Stewart. Dillon says the presence of a Windigo, as the force of winter, cold and starving, is often signaled by rushing wind. In this story the landscape comes alive in the form of the Windigo.

The remaining characters split into twos: Stewart and Philip continue the search while Claire and Daniel return to the cabin, hoping that Annie and Trevor will return. The search is without hope and upon returning to the cabin Claire cries that Daniel has now vanished. Now there are only three. At the cabin they hear an unearthly howl and something large and vast rushing through the trees. They try to flee but the Windigo traps them. Claire is dragged into the dense shadows of towering trees. Philip is sucked up into the darkening sky. Stewart is the last to be taken by "the cold hunger of the universe" (*CT* 126), which is a characterization of the Windigo. Throughout Strantzas's story the Windigo is only experienced through its effects; the Windigo never comes onstage, just as in Blackwood's story. In some traditions the Windigo is not to be pictured. Colombo notes that in the Ojibwa tradition the Windigo was not to be depicted. In the Indigenous traditions, one finds many stories but few if any illustrations.[10] This contributes to the unease

---

10. Colombo comments that this has changed, noting in particular Norval Morriseau's (Copper Thunderbird) *Windigo* (1964).

of the story. The Wendigo itself represents the otherness of the landscape—the estrangement of humans from Nature today and the fact that the world does not conform to our expectations of it.

The Windigo continues to be a motif in contemporary Canadian weird literature. Michael Kelly's story "The Woods" (2009) consists of a conversation between Jack, a loner, and Officer Ned Creed in Jack's isolated cabin in the woods. A storm shrieks outside the cabin, but the Windigo is only found in the cold silences of the gaps in their dialogue.

The North as a State of Mind

Many Canadians enjoy the experience of going north for a vacation, or a holiday at a cabin in the woods, or a cottage on a lake. Such seeming idyllic landscapes are not always safe, as Canadians writers keep pointing out. Grace argues that the idea of the North is central to the Canadian identity and imagination. In reality and in art the North allures. It is real and it is a state of mind for the country. It has been portrayed as a land of danger and challenge or as a land of opportunity and riches (for example in the short-lived Klondike Gold Rush of 1896 and 1899 or in more recent oil drilling and diamond mining), or as an empty, mystical space (for example in the art of Lawren Harris,[11] although the North of ice, snow, and tundra has been home to the Inuit and northern First Nations people for thousands of years) or as an unknown, perhaps unknowable landscape, or as a land where one can lose oneself or find oneself, or where the effects of climate change are most dramatically visible on the landscape and its flora and fauna.

Many Canadian authors have attempted to understand, interpret, and know the North by setting stories, novels, and nonfiction

---

11. Lawren Stewart Harris (1885–1970) produced many paintings of idealized northern landscapes in the 1920s and early 1930s. They show an austere north of isolated mountains, snow, dark lakes, and barren shores; its emptiness and stillness reinforced by stark shafts of light and cutting shadows.

there. In *Playing Dead*: *A Contemplation Concerning the Arctic*, Rudy Wiebe writes to understand the North, to grasp its actual history, that is, to comprehend the experience of the Indigenous people of the North, to uncover the false heroism of explorers, and to absorb the lingering majesty and mystery of the landscape. Through a set of creative nonfiction explorations he explores the North as a real and imaginative place.

Strantzas relocates the North in "The Uninvited Guest" (2006). The setting of the story is not up north but in a house in the suburbs during a December party. The story is told in the first person from the perspective of Katherine. She wonders at all the people in her new house. Looking out a window, she sees "shadows moving through the falling snow" (*CT* 33), alerting readers to the dangers from that snow. There is tension in the air between the hosts, Katherine and her husband Dan. Yet they warmly greet their guests, who seem to be many more than they had invited. There will be only one uninvited guest who disquiets them. They worry more over their supply of food and drinks. Jessica, Katherine's friend, gives a running commentary throughout the story and provides a cover for the tensions between the two.

A knock on the door disturbs the party, and more so when an old woman layered in ragged garments appears at the door, bringing with her a "blast of winter" (*CT* 35). She seems a symbol of the homeless. Katherine hesitantly asks the woman into the house. At first she startles the party. The world of ordinary life is suddenly arrested, but only momentarily. Dan and Katherine quarrel over letting her stay. The party guests ignore her, as the homeless are largely shunned. The elderly woman appears "skeletal" and "starving" (*CT* 37). She is a metaphor for the cold North, which is not just a geographical location but also a state of mind. She brings the winter into the house. Frost creeps from the edges of windows and Katherine thinks it may be on the inside of the glass.

During the party the woman collapses and the guests keep their distance. But Dan goes to her. She cups her hands toward him and he deposits a coin there, as if a way to assuage one's guilt, or as an allusion to putting a coin in the mouth of the dead to pay Charon to be ferried across the Styx. In this story the old woman takes Dan in hand and they walk out into blowing snow and disappear in the winter storm. The storm may be Dan's River Styx. The party resumes, but then Jessica screams. This scream signals the triumph of the North. Once let into a house it will not leave.

The story contains three key sounds. The knock on the door is one key. It momentarily stops the partying, but it quickly resumes. There are three worlds in Strantzas's short story. One is the suburban world represented at first by the frivolity and hospitality of the "Christmas" party. It is a space of safety. The second world is the cold trauma of the world of poverty and homelessness that haunts modern cities—a world that Strantzas presents as a gothic space represented by the blizzard brought into the house by that starving, skeletal woman. The knock allows her entrance but she is ignored, and the world of indifference and unconcern rules in the house. That knock of warning goes unheeded, and the third world gains a foothold, in the form of frost on the inner side of the windows. The guests exhibit no sense of human caring for the woman's apparent traumatic circumstances. And there seems little fear at the intrusion. Yet a reader feels a sympathy toward the old woman.

The second key sound occurs when the woman collapses "with an awful thud" (*CT* 39). That noise again causes the party to go into suspension; time in that world stops. But this death-like quietness leads the guests to view her fall as if "it was happening on television" (*CT* 39). It seems that there is still no mercy or concern in the hearts of the guests. A callous indifference has replaced any sense of concern for a fellow human being. But that indifference also fails to see the terror that the woman brought into the house—that other world of cold death. The old woman is really a double metaphor. She is the personification of death in the cold wilderness (of the modern city) and the shunning of the poor and street people (of contemporary suburban society). Jessica's scream at the end is the final key sound and signals that all fellow-feeling has disappeared (in the form of Dan vanishing in the snow), gone extinct, been suppressed. A cruel, indifferent, and uncaring nature now holds sway.

Strantzas's portrayal of the wilderness is not always so terrifying. "The Flower Unfolds" (2017) tells of the blossoming of Candice Lourdes. Strantzas characterizes her at the beginning of the story as a shy, timid, reclusive, middle-aged woman. Her tentative hopes and reticent aspirations are always dashed. She retreats into an inner shell, trying to avoid contact with her fellow office workers. But a chance trip on an elevator to the top floor of an office building changes everything. That top floor houses a botanical garden. Her introduction to it by the mysterious Ben Stanley will change her life.

At first she hesitates to return to the garden at the top of the Simpson Tower. But the garden seems to call for her. Eventually the elevator lures her in and carries her up to the top floor, where she experiences a rebirth as the garden unleashes her internal energy. It heals her, as Blackwood believed nature did for him and could for others. This story exhibits the awe and healing that may arise from a connection with nature. After her experience, where she embraced the wonder of the garden, Candice changes her personality. She is no longer timid and shy but bold and assertive. She finds her strength through contact with that garden.

There is indeed a substantial volume of literature confirming that contact with the natural environment has positive effects on the well-being of people, both physically and psychologically. Bratman et al. reviewed the research evidence supporting an association between nature experience and increased psychological well-being along with the reduction of risk factors and the burden of some types of mental illness. Frumkin et al. reviewed the overall benefits of nature contact for human health and well-being. The positive associations include improved immune function, improved general health, reduced mortality, and reduced diabetes. More specifically, Shepley et al. found that access to nature has a mitigating impact on violence in urban settings. Nancy M. Wells and Gary W. Evans cite many studies establishing that contact with the natural environment has been associated with better psychological well-being, superior cognitive functioning, fewer physical ailments, and speedier healing (311–12). In Strantzas's story a supernatural healing is found in a garden on the top floor of an office building in a large metropolitan Canadian city. Strantzas extends this supernatural healing power of nature to the dead in "Like Falling Snow" (2009). Maureen dies from cancer in a palliative care nursing home. Nevertheless, nature seems to restore her, because she becomes a giggling young girl making snow angels in the cold, unnoticed by her daughter and son-in-law sadly driving away.

Other contemporary Canadian authors write on this theme of opposing images of the North. In contrast to Strantzas, Susie Moloney sets *Bastion Falls* (1995) in a remote northern Canada town. Moloney combines Mario Praz's idea that the perfect symbol of the gothic space is a prison with the Canadian notion of the North as a gothic space. A brutal snowstorm engulfs the town of Bastion Falls with fierce winds, snow, and temperatures of -35° Celsius. The "Bastion" refers to the remains of a ruined garrison outside of town—a garrison that incarcerated those military personnel with the most egregious crimes, often on the Indigenous population. The fierceness of the storm spectrally releases the dead prisoners in the form of dark clouds, which attack the town. The return of the dead in this novel is a form of intergenerational haunting that Edwards sees in the Canadian gothic, where phantoms rise up out of the dark history of Canada to haunt the present. In Moloney's novel most of the townspeople are the descendants of those who were prisoners. The novel depicts the prisoners of the past returning to attack their descendants, as if to atone for their crimes. Richard Gavin's "Fume" (2016) counterpoints Strantzas's story of Candice Lourdes. In Gavin's story, Clark rejects the pleasures arising from an intrusion of nature into his cottage at Beech Point. He flees the garden for the city.

In Conclusion

Several scholars argue that a sense of landscape is critical for shaping a distinctive mode of gothic literature. Judith Wilt says that setting is vital for the effectiveness of the gothic mode. She sees such literature depicting human experience at its extremities in a place of unknown power that causes fear and trauma from which there is no escape (8–10, 276). This summarizes, in part, the stories of Simon Strantzas explored in this essay. These stories are set in the North (read wilderness) of Canada. A setting that haunts much of Canadian art and literature, as Margaret Atwood and others have documented. That landscape holds both a dangerous beauty and a frightening awe. In some of Strantzas's short stories the wilderness is more alive and sentient than the human characters. And he knows that nature is not serene or idyllic. An excursion to a holiday cabin brings terror not respite, as he depicts in "When Sorrows Come" and "Pinholes in Black Muslin." His is a dark literature, which as Wilt says brings to life the chaotic workings of the world that exists beyond our knowledge (136). In his stories discussed in this essay his settings reveal the instability of the world, which the characters in "Cold to the Touch" experience in the high Arctic of Canada.

In a similar fashion, Ruth D. Weston argues for the centrality of setting in gothic fiction. She illustrates this with Eudora Welty's imaginative transformation of actual places into complex and entangling gothic spaces (23, 47). Such landscapes unsettle and disorient mindscapes, because they question the nature of reality itself (57). That is, the landscape is the source of trauma, as happens in such Strantzas stories as "On Ice," which uses Melville Island as a setting. But the North in Canadian literature is not confined by geography. As Gould, Grace, and Kroetsch argue, the North (or wilderness) may be anywhere in Canada. It is an idea that flourishes and is dangerous everywhere. Strantzas illustrates this in "The Uninvited Guest," where the North, in the image of an elderly homeless woman, invades a suburban home. This transformation of the wilderness into an ensnaring gothic space additionally occurs in homes in "These Last Embers" and other stories, such as "Out of Touch" (2010) and "The Fifth Stone" (2017), not discussed in this essay.

David Punter argues that the modern gothic articulates the impact of trauma, which he sees as pandemic in contemporary societies and cultures (2). He sees some of this trauma arising from the current worldwide environmental crisis. We live today in the Anthropocene Epoch. Simon, L. Lewis and Mark A. Maslin show that human activity is now worldwide. Troublingly, that activity is the chief cause of most climate change. They argue that the effects of human actions will be found in the geological stratigraphic record for millions of years into the future. This means there is a new epoch (171). Contemporary planetary disruptions in climate, landform, and weather result from our machinations. We harm nature and ourselves. Strantzas illustrates this trauma, within a gothic context, in "The Indelible Stain upon the Sky." Moreover, Strantzas employs the figure of the Windigo to illustrate the current degradation of the natural environment and the peril it holds for us. His characters become estranged from the natural space they inhabit. Yet it is our natural habitat that can be a place of healing. Now nature appears as strange and other, as gothic, or hostile to humans. Many of Strantzas's stories illustrate this estrangement. They foretell an uncanny and terrifying future age. But he also writes on the restorative powers of nature. An urban botanical garden in "The Flower Unfolds" restores Candice Lourdes. Elizabeth Lev et al. demonstrate that human interaction with "wilder" urban parks provide more benefits to people than manicured parks. They found that interactions with such parks (where people can see wildlife and be among natural trees) help "to reverse the trend of environmental generational amnesia, and a domination overview."

The vastness of the Canadian North and its wilderness represents an unknown nature that is becoming beyond our ken. Yet human activity is degrading the Arctic. In 2019, the Arctic Monitoring and Assessment Programme warned that warming temperatures and extreme events are increasingly affecting the Arctic terrestrial land-scape. The pace of change in the Arctic is so rapid that new extreme records are being set annually, and each year of data strengthens the already compelling evidence of a rapidly changing Arctic. As Margaret Atwood expressed it in *Strange Things:* the "things that are killing the North [. . .] will kill everything else" (116). The terrors expressed in Strantzas's stories arise from the Canadian landscape, but the real horror of it is in our separation and estrangement from that landscape through our continuing degradation of it.

Simon Strantzas writes of people caught in inescapable conditions of trauma within settings that illustrate the conflicting images and ideas of the North of Canada with its awe and terror, its hope and dread, and its loss and discovery. His stories mirror this ambiguity of the reality and the idea of the North and the wilderness. By writing about the North as an uncanny place and as a state of mind, he illustrates how the North haunts Canada, yet it evades understanding. Some geographic spaces are inherently spectral. Strantzas infuses his stories with a sense of that spectrality inherent in landscapes, using a direct prose style that is clear and precise. Nevertheless, he is able to describe the varying emotional responses of his characters to spectral or unusual experiences or encounters in nature. He has an eye for sensory detail and a sense of the complex psychological responses of people in situations of trauma. Furthermore, and more insightfully, his stories reflect on the current unnatural relationships humans have with their environment and the destructive outcomes of that estrangement.

Works Cited

Aporta, Claudio. "Inuit Orienting: Traveling Along Familiar Horizons." *Sensory Studies,* n.d. www.sensorystudies.org/inuit-orienting-traveling-along-familiar-horizons/. Accessed 8 March 2020.

Arctic Monitoring and Assessment Programme. *Arctic Climate Change Update 2019.* oaarchive.arctic-council.org/bitstream/handle/11374/2318/SAOFI204_2019_RUKA_07-05-01_MAP_Climate-

Change-Update-2019.pdf?sequence-1&isAllowed-y. Accessed 18 January 2020.

Ashley, Mike. *Algernon Blackwood: A Bio-Bibliography.* Westport, CT: Greenwood Press, 1987.

———. *Algernon Blackwood: An Extraordinary Life.* Carroll & Graf, 2001.

Atwood, Margaret. *Strange Things: The Malevolent North in Canadian Literature.* Oxford UP, 1995.

———. *Wilderness Tips.* Toronto: McClelland & Stewart, 1991.

———. *Writing with Intent: Essays, Reviews, Personal Prose: 1983–2005.* New York: Basic Books, 2006.

Bratman, Gregory N., et al. "Nature and Mental Health: An Eco-system Service Perspective." *Science Advances* 5, No. 7 (2019); DOI: 10.1126/sciadv.aax0903. Accessed 3 March 2020.

Brightman, Robert A. "The Windigo in the Material World." *Ethnohistory* 35, No. 4 (1988): 337–79.

Carlson, Nathan D. "Reviving Witiko (Windigo): An Ethnohistory of 'Cannibal Monsters' in the Athabasca District of Northern Alberta, 1878–1910." *Ethnohistory* 56, No. 3 (2009): 355–94.

Colombo, John Robert. *Windigo: An Anthology of Fact and Fantastic Fiction.* Saskatoon: Western Producer Prairie Books, 1982.

Dillon, Grace L. "Windigo." In Jeffrey Andrew Weinstock, ed. *The Ashgate Encyclopedia of Literary and Cinematic Monsters.* Farnham, UK: Ashgate Publishing, 2014, 590–93. public.eblib.com/choice/publicfullrecord.aspx?p=1570478. Accessed 12 January 2020.

Edwards, Justin D. *Gothic Canada: Reading the Spectre of a National Literature.* Edmonton: University of Alberta Press, 2005.

Files, Gemma. "Thin Places." *National Post* (25 October 2015). nationalpost.com/entertainment/books/thin-places-by-gemma-files. Accessed 15 November 2019.

Forbes, Jack D. *Columbus and Other Cannibals: The Wétiko Disease of Exploitation, Imperialism, and Terrorism.* Rev. ed. New York: Seven Stories Press, 2008.

Freud, Sigmund. "The 'Uncanny.'" In *Collected Papers*. Volume IV. Edited by Ernest Jones, translated by Alix Strachey. London: Hogarth Press, 1950. 368–407.

Frumkin, Howard, et al. "Nature Contact and Human Health: A Research Agenda." *Environmental Health Perspectives* 125, No. 7 (2017). doi.org/10.1289/EHP1663. Accessed 4 March 2020.

Frye, Northrop. "Conclusion to the First Edition of *Literary History of Canada*." In *The Collected Works of Northrop Frye*: *Northrop Frye on Canada*. Ed. Jean O'Grady and David Staines. Toronto: University of Toronto Press, 2003. 339–72.

Ganz, Shoshannah, "Margaret Atwood's monsters in the Canadian ecoGothic." In Andrew Smith and William Hughes, ed. *EcoGothic*. Manchester: Manchester University Press, 2013. 87–102.

Gatenby, Greg. *The Wild Is Always There: Canada through the Eyes of Foreign Writers*. Toronto: Knopf Canada, 1993.

Gavin, Richard. *Sylvan Dread*. n.p.: Three Hands Press, 2016.

Goldman, Marlene. "Margaret Atwood's *Wilderness Tips*: Apocalyptic Cannibal Fiction." In Kristen Guest, ed. *Eating Their Words: Cannibalism and the Boundaries of Cultural Identity*. Albany: State University of New York Press, 2001. 167–85.

Gould, Glenn. *The Idea of North*. Canadian Broadcasting Company, 1971.

Grace, Sherrill, E. *Canada and the Idea of North*. Montreal: McGill–Queen's University Press, 2001.

Haggerty, George E. *Queer Gothic*. Urbana: University of Illinois Press, 2006.

Hillard, Tom, J. "Gothic Nature Revisited: Reflections on the Gothic of Ecocriticism." *Gothic Nature* 1 (2019): 21–33.

Joshi, S. T. *21st-Century Horror: Weird Fiction at the Turn of the Millennium*. Seattle: Sarnath Press, 2018.

Kelly, Michael. *All the Things We Never See*. Pickering, ON: Undertow Publications, 2019.

Kroetsch, Robert. *The Lovely Treachery of Words*. Toronto: Oxford University Press, 1989.

Lev, Elizabeth, et al. "Relatively Wild Urban parks Can Provide Human Resilience and Flourishing: A Case Study of Discovery Park, Seattle Washington." *Frontiers in Sustainable Cities* 2, No. 2 (2020). doi.org/10.3389/frsc.202000002. Accessed 8 March 2020.

Lewis, Simon, L., and Mark A. Maslin. "Defining the Anthropocene." *Nature* No. 519 (12 March 2015): 171–80.

Moloney, Susie. *Bastion Falls*. Toronto: Key Porter, 1995.

Moodie, Susanna. *Roughing It in the Bush*. 1852. n.p.: BiblioBazaar, 2007.

Northey, Margot. *The Haunted Wilderness: The Gothic and Grotesque in Canadian Fiction*. Toronto: University of Toronto Press, 1976.

Praz, Mario. "Introductory Essay." In Peter Fairclough, ed. *Three Gothic Novels*. Harmondsworth, UK: Penguin, 1986. 7–34.

Punter, David. "Introduction: The Ghost of a History." In David Punter, ed. *A New Companion to the Gothic*. Oxford: Blackwell, 2012. 1–9.

Richardson, John. *Wacousta*. 1832. Toronto: McClelland & Stewart, 1991.

Shepley, Mardelle, et al. "The Impact of Green Space on Violent Crime in Urban Environments: An Evidence Synthesis." *International Journal of Environmental Research and Public Health* 16, No. 24 (2019). doi:10.3390/ijerph16245119. Accessed 3 March 2020.

Smallman, Shawn. "Spirit Beings, Mental Illness, and Murder: Fur Traders and the Windigo in Canada's Boreal Forest, 1774 to 1935." *Ethnohistory* 57, No. 4 (2010): 572–96.

Strantzas, Simon. *Beneath the Surface*. 2008. Portland, OR: Dark Regions Press, 2010.

———. *Burnt Black Suns*. New York: Hippocampus Press, 2014. [Abbreviated in the text as *BBS*.]

———. *Cold to the Touch*. 2009. Portland, OR: Dark Regions Press, 2012. [Abbreviated in the text as *CT*.]

———. *Nightingale Songs*. Portland, OR: Dark Regions Press, 2011. [Abbreviated in the text as *NS*.]

———. *Nothing is Everything*. Pickering, ON: Undertow Publications, 2018. [Abbreviated in the text as *NE*.]

Tracy, Ann. *Winter Hunger*. Fredericton, NB: Goose Lane Editions, 1990.

Warrior, Carol Edelman. "Baring the Windigo's Teeth: Fearsome Figures in Native American Narratives." Ph.D. diss.: University of Washington, 2015. *Research Works at the University of Washington*, digital.lib.washington.edu/researchworks/handle/1773/33820. Accessed 10 January 2020.

Wells, Nancy M., and Gary W. Evans. "Nearby Nature: A Buffer of Life Stress among Rural Children." *Environment and Behavior* 35, No. 3 (2003): 311–30.

Weston, Ruth D. *Gothic Traditions and Narrative Techniques in the Fiction of Eudora Welty*. Baton Rouge: Louisiana State University Press, 1994.

Wiebe, Rudy. *Playing Dead: A Contemplation Concerning the Arctic*. Edmonton: NeWest, 1989.

Wilt, Judith. *Ghosts of the Gothic*. Princeton, NJ: Princeton University Press, 1980.

Las Llorasangres

Michael Parker

From the field notes of Dr. Llewelyn Rhys, Professor of Anthropology at University College of Swansea, Wales.

Trepanation is a surgical procedure in which a hole is cut or bored into the skull. It is the most ancient surgical practice on record, with the earliest trepanned skulls dating back to Neolithic times. Specimens have been found throughout the world. Ancient peoples believed trepanning cured ailments including headaches, seizures, and a number of other mental disorders by allowing evil spirits inside the skull to escape. Most interestingly, trepanned skulls have been recovered in which rings of healed bone had begun to grow around the holes. This indicates that the practice, even without modern sterilised instruments, was not fatal, and possibly effective, as the individuals must have lived for some years after the procedure had been performed.

The Celts arrived in the northwest corner of the Iberian Peninsula, in the region now known as Galicia, at the end of the Bronze Age around 1000 B.C. They were attracted to the familiar lush, green, mist-laden terrain, which closely resembled the British Isles whence they came. Their culture was agrarian and transhumant, meaning they migrated periodically with their livestock according to the seasons. They were a bellicose people and proved worthy adversaries against a well-armed and organized Roman legion. They lived in modest circular habitations made of stone with conical thatched rooves known as castros. Remnants can still be found throughout Galicia.

The Celts brought their language and religion with them. The Celtic religion had its own extensive pantheon and placed a strong emphasis on nature. The seasons, the phases of the moon, the ebb and flow of the tides, the march of the sun along its ecliptic, the equinoxes, solstices, and eclipses all bore particular significance. The oak tree was especially revered. The Druids, the priestly caste, led along with the warrior elite. The great horned god Cernunnos figured prominently in their theology. His name is the source of the Latin word cornu, the Spanish word cuerno, and the English word horn. He is represented in many forms including the stag, the bull, the goat, the owl, and a horned or antlered man. He is believed to have been a symbol of wisdom, of male virility, and of the passage of the soul into the afterlife. Evidence of cults dedicated to Cernunnos has been found in Ireland, Great Britain, and on the European continent wherever Hallstatt culture took root. The oldest extant representation of him is a bas-relief found on the Pillar of the Boatmen, which is now on display in the frigidarium of the Thermes de Cluny in Paris. Another unmistakable image of Cernunnos can be found on the Gundestrup Cauldron, an ornate silver vessel that was found in a peat bog in Denmark. Cernunnos is depicted as an antlered man holding a torc in one hand and a snake in the other.

Aside from the information above, the figure of Cernunnos is still shrouded in mystery. We know various Druidic cults were dedicated to him, but we know scant little about their practices because they left no written records. There is a consensus about their proclivity for human sacrifice. This practice has been recorded in the writings of Strabo, Cicero, and even Julius Caesar himself. They all describe a barbaric practice known as the wicker man in which the victim was wrapped in kindling and burned alive, presumably to propitiate the baleful Cernunnos. Traces of Celtic culture are not completely lost in Galicia. One can still hear the wail of bagpipes known as gaitas and see a bruxo, or Druid sorcerer, draped in animal skins and wearing a horned skull chanting and dancing around a bonfire in late autumn heralding the coming of winter.

The Basques are unique among all other peoples of the world. They have continuously inhabited an enclave located in the País Vasco and Navarra in north-central Spain and the department of Pyrénées-Atlantiques in southwestern France. A resilient people, they have outlasted waves of Iberians, Romans, Visigoths, Moors, and Christians in turn. Proud and independent in spirit, they fiercely defended their language and culture despite active oppression from the Franco regime. Their language, Euskara, is a true language isolate and an enigma to linguists. It is unrelated to any other language in the world. Some believe that, as an agglutinative language, it bears a morphological affinity to certain Caucasian and Uralic tongues, but this remains a point of controversy.

There is a prevailing theory among anthropologists, linguists, and geneticists that the Basques are the last vestige of Cro-Magnon man. Some points in favor of this hypothesis: their words aitzo (knife), aitzur (hoe), and aitzkora (axe) all share the common root aitz (stone). We know the first knives and hand adzes were made of stone, and it is a reasonable conjecture that the language truly does date back to Neolithic times. The genetic evidence is even more convincing. The Basques have the highest frequency of Rh-negative blood in the world. Interestingly, Cro-Magnon remains ranging from France to Morocco to the Canary Islands to Crete also show an uncommonly high incidence of Rh-negative blood. If a mother is Rh-negative, her immune system will reject an Rh-positive fetus as a foreign body and force her to miscarry. This phenomenon accounts not only for the homogeneity of the Basque people, but also establishes a close genetic link to Cro-Magnon man.

As the centuries passed, the Celtiberians moved east and the Basques moved west and their cultures diffused and cross-pollinated.

I just spoke with Margaret. Looks like I'm off to sunny Spain. The Royal Academy has approved my application for a grant to study a series of cave paintings recently discovered near the northern coast of Spain known as Las Llorasangres. I understand both Webb and Chadwick and a few others had been vying for this grant, and they will no doubt be perturbed to learn I got it, but it looks as if my publications on Celtiberian culture are finally paying dividends and tipped the scales in my favour. I embark from the port here in Swansea in a fortnight on a commercial freighter due to arrive at Santander in another week or so.

Terrible weather, which is not unexpected this time of year. Torrential rain and choppy waves. Both sea and sky are undulating sheets of lead, the horizon indistinguishable. I'm spending most of my time in my cramped cabin preparing for the study at hand. The captain assures me the storm should not hinder our progress and we should arrive on schedule. As we rounded Cornwall (Cernunnos left his mark on this promontory as well), I was gazing through a porthole and saw the jagged rocks jutting out into the sea—great sentinels standing guard—and I was seized by a strange premonition that this would be the last time I looked upon the isle of Great Britain. Off to bed and hopefully pleasant dreams.

Por fin llegué a Santander. Hace sol. Northern Spain is far different from what the average foreigner would expect. One usually imagines Don Quixote on horseback, the sultry gitana sitting side-saddle in her flowing skirts, windmills and parched earth. The north coast is a more verdant affair. Dense forests cover some areas. The Picos de Europa form Spain's most picturesque mountain range. Most of the land just beyond the coast consists of rolling green hills used as farmland. Herds of dairy cows are a common sight. This area is appropriately called La Costa Verde. It comes as no surprise that King Alfonso XIII made his summer residence here. I would have done the same. Some of the most pleasant countryside and beaches are bathed in sun, and the blue-green sea regulates the temperature, so this area does not experience the extremes found further inland. Today I am making a day trip to the caves of Altamira to view the paintings there in order to whet my appetite for my arrival at Las Llorasangres tomorrow.

Altamira left me in awe. Only after seeing it firsthand can one understand why Picasso said after Altamira, all is decadence. The paintings are remarkably well preserved. One can clearly make out bulls, bison, and deer. Other notable images include many renditions of the human vulva. Thirty thousand years later, men still have the same thing on their minds. Numerous negative handprints can also be seen. A curator kindly showed me a reconstruction of a blow brush he believes the painters may have used to make these handprints. It is a simple device consisting of a small wooden bowl and a hollow reed. The paint was placed into the bowl and the reed placed upright inside. The painter simply needed to blow across the top of the reed, lowering the air pressure inside, thereby drawing the pigment up through the reed and out over his hand. When the painter removed his hand, a perfect handprint remained. Bernoulli would have beamed at early man's ingenuity. The importance of the paintings at Altamira cannot be overstated. Here begins the history of art. Here man attained a new level of representational and abstract thought. Here man turned creator. Here the clay turned potter. These paintings are anthropological treasures of the highest order. Altamira is a tough act to follow, but I cannot wait to see what Las Llorasangres has in store for me.

Arrived at Las Llorasangres today. I will relate the events to the best of my memory. I awoke from restless sleep, but with the anticipation and excitement at the prospect of today's excursion a bit of nerves was to be expected. A representative of Spain's archaeological society came to the inn, checked my credentials and permit, and we set off for the site. On the way my case of nerves escalated and the driver even commented on my appearance: "Tienes mala cara." But I simply explained in my broken Spanish that I had not slept well and made little conversation for the rest of the ride. We arrived and, after making my way through more bureaucracy—including more members of the archaeological society and the Guardia Civil (Spain guards her archaeological discoveries jealously)—I was finally allowed to descend a rickety staircase into the cave. On my way down a member told me the serendipitous story of the cave's discovery. A local boy chased a wayward football down into the cave around a year ago. He kept the place to himself for some time and used it as a hideout to meet with friends. It was only officially discovered a few months ago when a suspicious father followed the boy with his daughter to the cave, saw the paintings, and notified the local authorities.

Since then, the cave has been the sole province of Franco's government, cordoned off from the public. I was told I am the first British academic to lay eyes on the paintings and among the first hundred people, including El Generalísimo himself, to see them since their discovery. Despite my nervous condition at the time, I felt quite honoured, but after seeing the paintings I'm afraid it is a most regrettable distinction. As I reached the foot of the stairs, my shoes touched stone smoothed by groundwater over millennia. Floodlights cast stark beams through the prevailing darkness, and I followed them to the illuminated cave wall. The paintings here are smaller and much more detailed than those at Altamira. They are also less multifarious. In fact, they consist of many renderings of the same figure: a nude woman with her head in her hands and with red tears streaming down them, hence the name Las Llorasangres (roughly, "the blood criers" or "those who weep blood").

While Altamira leaves the viewer in awe, the paintings here seem to resonate with a menacing energy that vexes the mind. The longer one looks at them, the more troubled one becomes. What could have happened to make these women weep blood? Was this of some religious significance? Was it a depiction of real events or merely symbolic? The archaeological society is still at work dating the paintings, but the experts hypothesise that they are of a more recent vintage than those at Altamira. Seeing the paintings exacerbated my nervous condition. As though by some sympathetic response to what I was looking at, I felt the paintings were boring holes through my eyes into my brain. I averted my eyes and ascended the stairs. Once I emerged from the cave, my disquiet was compounded with somnolence and my head began to swim with the soporific drone of cicadas emanating from a nearby copse of trees. I looked about and took in the verdant dale, the wildflowers flourishing among the fieldstone farmhouses. My ears danced with songbirds and a gurgling brook. A herd of cattle was grazing on a far-off hill: silhouettes backlit by the setting sun.

Suddenly all reality began to seem thin to me. I was struck by the fragility of everything around me: of my own body—of the thin bubble of atmosphere separating us from the insatiate vacuum of space—of our precarious position in this universe. A tidal wave of panic flooded my mind, and I was seized by a strong impulse to flee—to anywhere but where I stood. I stumbled in a stupor across the field back to the main road. At this point it was just disjointed flashes of memory. I arrived at a small inn a short way down the road. I remember the name of the inn written in carved calligraphy on an old sign dangling from rusted chains: La Posada Marqués de Santillana.

When I entered, I approached the front desk and rented a room so I could rest, as I was in no condition to withstand the jarring ride back to Santander that evening. The clerk handed me the room key attached to a worn wooden fob. I took a seat in the parlour. Some people were playing naipes over bowls of fabada and cups of sidra. I ordered a cup of té de manzanilla con miel. I sipped the tea slowly, trying to gather my wits. Once I finished my tea, I got to my feet carefully and staggered up the staircase to find my room. I burst into the room and collapsed onto the bed. Anxiety and exhaustion dueled in my brain, fraying every nerve ending. I felt detached—distant—from myself. I lay back, closed my eyes, and focused on my breathing—something I could control, something I could regulate like a metronome.

As I entered the cave, I noticed a faint light and wondered at its source. I continued forward and emerged into an expansive ante-room and saw the cave walls were bathed in a deep, shifting, womb-like red—the red one sees when looking at the sun through closed eyelids. As the bloodlight grew more intense I realized that what I had mistaken for mineral veins in the interstices of the cave walls was actually a continuous mural stretching across the walls to the ceiling: geometric patterns of an almost Moorish character that would have crossed Euclid's eyes interwoven with ornate filigree; all the animals of Altamira, not just individuals but entire herds, bands of hunters bearing spears ganging up on mammoths and stampeding bison off cliffs; early man in all attitudes of life huddled around camp-fires, hunting, gathering, eating, sleeping, copulating, giving birth, dying. As I raised my eyes, the mural took on a more sinister charac-ter: children etched in anthracite setting fire to the thatched rooves of their own castros, leaving nothing but scorched earth in their wake. And perched above it all a great horned owl overseeing the bedlam below as though everything that occurred was at its behest.

I realized I was not alone in the cave. A deep groaning reverber-ated off the walls. It was emanating from a chamber beyond. I want-ed to flee, but my feet moved me inexorably towards it, my mind resisting, my heart palpitating. When I entered the chamber, I be-held the most grotesque and blasphemous spectacle of all: an eyeless woman, supine, writhing and wailing in the throes of childbirth. She stared at me through vacant sockets, blood and lymph seeping from them and dripping down her cheeks. I felt a draught and looked up. The ceiling of the cave was open. A great red dragon hovered above and its tail swept a third of the stars from the sky. Then it descend-ed and placed its head between her legs—not waiting to devour the newborn, but eagerly awaiting the birth of his son.

I awoke with a start, shivering in a cold sweat, the pillow soaked, the woman in the cave fading from my mind's eye. I was disoriented to find myself in an unfamiliar room, and it took me a moment to remember how I got there. Night had fallen, and I wondered how long I had slept. My skin was clammy and my clothes clung to me. I got up, walked to the washbasin in the room, splashed cold water on my face, and looked into the mirror in front of me. I felt unacquainted with the man who looked back at me, as though he were some impostor—an interloper in my own flesh. I blinked and focused my eyes on their reflected counterparts. They held me in their grip and I felt immobile, paralysed. Transfixed, I became aware of my pulse throbbing in my neck, the blood whooshing in my ears. In an act of sheer will I tore my head away and descended the stairs to the parlour. It was empty. My thoughts drifted to the cave and my mind reeled at the thought of those hellish paintings and the woman in my dream. I could feel the cave beckoning me. I felt drawn to it by some animal magnetism—some irresistible gravity. My heart increased its primal rhythm.

I stepped out the door of the inn and looked up. A gibbous moon hung bloated and sallow in the firmament, flanked by its retinue of malignant stars. My eyes took a moment to adjust. The countryside was imbued with a bluish hue, and soon I could navigate as though by daylight. I surveyed the plain and saw a serpentine procession of torches crawling towards the hills where the cave was nestled. I headed their way, entranced, with no torch of my own, careful to keep my distance. As I approached, I noticed the queue meander past the entrance to the cave I had used earlier in the day and bend around an adjacent hill. Perhaps the cave was not their destination after all. My curiosity insatiable, I continued my pursuit. Once they all had passed behind the hill, I followed and crouched in the undergrowth. I watched as the torches blinked out one by one into the backside of the hill, as though these nocturnal creatures were crawling back into the cloaca of the vile leviathan that bore them. Soon not a torch remained, the whicker of legs through the tall grass ceased, a chorus of crickets my only remaining company.

I scurried to the point where I saw the last torch disappear. There was a hole in the side of the hill framed by chunks of limestone. A faint light flickered within. I could hear indistinct voices and the splashing of liquid on the other side and wondered what the torchbearers could be up to in there. Eventually the sound subsided, but the faint light remained. I was hesitant to follow them in—I had no idea what awaited me on the other side—but my curiosity spurred me on and I began to crawl in head first. The tunnel was just wide enough for me to pass. At one point my arms became pinned to my sides and I was stuck in a moment of claustrophobic panic. Then I managed to wriggle my arms free and army crawl through the gritty earth to the opening at the end.

I emerged into a chamber lit by torches held in V-shaped brackets carved into the stone walls. My heavy breathing echoed back to me. I was alone and saw assorted clothes lying lifeless about me and wondered where those who shed them had gone. It was as though they had disappeared into thin air, assumed by some sinister rapture. Then I looked ahead and saw a dark surface rippling with concentric rings radiating outward, refracting the reflection of the torches. They must have gone under. There was no other way of egress. The groundwater appeared opaque in this lighting, the bottom unfathomable. I disrobed like the others and diffidently stuck a toe into the water. It seemed to envelop and erase the appendage, canceling it out. I thought this is what the River Styx must be like, and I hoped these waters would bestow upon me the same protection. I slowly lowered myself into the black pool, the skin tightening around my ribs from the shock of the cold, shortening my breath. As I treaded water the opacity that reflected the torchlight faded away, and when I looked down I realized I could see my feet clearly. The groundwater was pristine and crystal clear, purified through Mother Nature's own filtration system.

I knew there had to be an underwater passageway. Where else could the others have gone? For all the remarkable clarity of the water, I couldn't make out any hole or tunnel. I cleared my mind, steadied myself, took a few deep breaths, and plunged my head beneath the surface. When I opened my eyes I found I could see as clearly as through thin air. What I saw left me in awe. I had to remind myself not to gasp for breath. An entire subaqueous ecosystem thriving; myriad life forms blessed with bioluminescence, the luciferin in their systems making each of them a star in shifting constellations never charted by any astronomer. Cnidarians, their diaphanous membranes glowing green: gossamer ghosts suspended as though in ether. Celestial crustaceans glimmering blue: sapphire seraphs spreading their wings. Blind fish with translucent skin revealing organs pulsing within, never to witness the wondrous galaxy they inhabited.

This transcendent moment—the most beautiful in my life—was interrupted by a primal alarm emanating from within my body. My lungful of air was wearing thin and I had to make it to the surface soon. Panic set in like a thief in the night. I swam to the nearest wall and began groping the jagged crags probing for any hole. My lungs began to sear, crying out for oxygen. At this point I considered the real possibility I would drown right there, my final resting place this enclave of otherworldly life, my body slowly decomposing in these frigid waters, serving as sustenance to the heavenly creatures surrounding me. I felt the peace of oblivion begin to overtake me. Then my hand slid into a narrow fissure in the rock and my mind was thrust back into acute consciousness. Arm followed hand and body followed arm. My chest scraped against the rock wall as I wriggled with my last shred of strength to force myself through the crevice. Finally, the walls parted and I shot directly upward, my head breaking the surface like a submarine with ballasts fully cleared.

I was in full survival mode at this point and found myself naked on my hands and knees on cold stone, dripping and panting and gasping and sucking in precious air. Once my lungs replenished themselves, I managed to reorient myself. The cave walls were drenched in the same amniotic red I saw in my dream. As my eyes adjusted, I could make out nude figures of varying genders and ages and heights applying something to their bodies. I approached, eased myself surreptitiously into their fold, and saw that they were streaking their bodies blue with woad. I did as they did, took a handful of the powder from a wooden bowl, and smeared it on the left side of my still-damp face and on my torso in irregular vertical stripes. Not a word was exchanged, the only sounds hands sliding over skin, breathing, and the occasional clearing of the throat. Thus adorned, those assembled gradually made their way into a cavernous chamber illuminated by pulsating torchlight, the light shifting on the walls as it does in embers in a fire. The walls were covered in intricate patterns and images as in my dream: more eyeless women weeping blood, more arcane horned entities, more beasts rent asunder, more chaos run rampant. The designs appeared to crawl along the walls and expand and contract and twist into one another; but every time I moved my eyes they returned to stillness, as though sensing they were caught in the act. Each person took a position along the walls forming a large ring, and in the centre of the chamber stood an immense chair—an unholy throne—hewn from an outcropping of bedrock, every angle and corner rounded with the wear of millennia.

We all stood for interminable minutes in gravid silence. Then I noticed an indiscernible movement behind the chair, in the back of the chamber, and everyone standing in the ring commenced in a rhythmic chant, almost under their breaths and in unison. I listened closely, and it was unlike any language I had heard before. It certainly wasn't English or Spanish, and it lacked the harsh consonants that distinguishes Basque. On the contrary, there was a mellifluous flow to it. Our heartbeats naturally synchronised themselves to the cadence, making each of us a part of a much more complex and powerful organism. Our egos dissolved and gelled, and soon I was repeating the chant verbatim. As my consciousness merged with the others and the phonemes rolled off my tongue, I understood this language was already ancient when the cosmos was forged white-hot upon the anvil of nothingness. It lacked anything we scholars would call semantics, but despite that, it was terribly potent with meaning.

The source of the movement in the back of the chamber then revealed itself: a young girl, blond-haired, blue-eyed, pale-skinned, sun-freckled, pure Castilian, of no more than quince veranos stepped forward towards the stone chair. She wore not a stitch of clothing, nor a spot of woad, unbesmirched—a testament to her purity. And behind her, spurring her on with a staff, a most grotesque personage of at least two metres in height, draped in animal skins and wearing a large, elongated humanoid skull with horns sprouting out either side and upward, making it seem even taller. Like a lamb to the slaughter, she obediently seated herself in the chair without a word; the horned figure ran worn leather bindings through rusted iron rings anchored to the chair and fastened her wrists and ankles. It then reached into its primitive robes and took out a small iron cup and a handful of brilliant flowers the color of lapis lazuli, not unlike the woad powder on our bodies, but they could not have been woad because woad flowers yellow. It placed each blossom in the iron vessel with a gentleness and care that contrasted with its decrepit appearance. It then touched the head of its staff to a torch on the wall until it caught fire and held the flame beneath the crucible, holding it barehanded. The delicate petals hissed and crackled as they burned, and the horned figure's long, gnarled fingers were blackened and charred, though it showed no sign of pain. It then held the crucible under the girl's nose; tendrils of blue smoke crawled up her nostrils. She attempted to struggle at first and then her body relaxed, went slack, entering a trance state. Her irises became two thin blue coronas eclipsed by dilated pupils.

The horned figure then took position behind the chair and leaned its tall flaming staff against the back of the chair to illuminate the crown of the girl's head. It produced from its robes a wedge-shaped shard of black volcanic glass, spewed forth from the bowels of the earth, the narrow end razor-sharp, glinting in the torchlight. In the other hand it held an ordinary stone with a flat face. It placed the sharp end of the wedge to the crown of her head and began to strike the top with the other stone. The girl remained perfectly still, her eyes vacuous, seemingly lobotomized. The walls echoed with the harsh tinking of stone on stone—the sound of a sculptor with chisel—but this was a work of profane and dark art. There was the sound of the shard grinding through gristle as it began to penetrate bone. The horned figure worked diligently with patience and precision, and all the while we continued our chant at a constant rhythm. This surgeon of the perverse completed a nearly perfect circle on the girl's head, took firm hold of the shock of blond hair within the circle, wedged the shard into the slit it had made, pressed outward on the shard for leverage, and pulled back on the shock of hair. My stomach lurched at the sickening wet crack and suction sound as it pried loose the disc of skull, its underside glistening red. It then took the razor edge of the shard and made an incision into the exposed cerebrum.

With the operation consummated, our chant escalated into a great crescendo, our voices like river rapids hurtling towards a waterfall, bouncing off the cave walls in dissonant echoes. Then suddenly the girl's eyes shot open and we were silenced. Her face was illuminated by a look of complete awe and her lips parted into a queer rictus. Her eyes appeared to be focused on some ineffable wonder beyond the chamber. Then, just as abruptly, her aspect changed. Like a billowing thunderhead blotting out the sun, awe gave way to sheer terror. Her face contorted with fear and her body was seized by a violent paroxysm, her wrists and ankles straining at their restraints. As though responding to the tumult within her, the massive chair began to tremble from its back to its base. It appeared that her frail body was shaking the chair of solid stone. Like a contagion, the tremors began to spread from the base of the chair throughout the cave floor and up the walls, culminating in a seismic upheaval. I had to struggle to keep my footing, and I feared the entire cave would collapse in on us.

Then the world was pulled inside out and turned on its head. Its foundation eroded, every natural law abrogated. The strangest phenomenon was the transformation of the light: it was negated, or rather, the spectrum was inverted. The closest I can liken it to in common experience is viewing the negative film of a photograph, but this is a mere approximation of what I saw. The girl's fair skin appeared to be a deep cyan. The flames on the torches flickered amorphous and black. A menacing figure materialised in our midst: alabaster white with articulate musculature like a Florentine statue. It advanced towards the girl on legs with reversed knees like a bird's that ended in feet with clawed toes and a sharp talon at the heel. This fallen angel who had gone to battle on the ethereal plains under the banner Non Serviam had managed, through the unhallowed ritual carried out earlier, to penetrate and manifest itself in our earthly stratum. I was paralysed by fear and could do nothing to impede the demon as it mounted the girl and uttered an ear-piercing shriek that had no business on this plane of existence. And then a great concussion: a tremendous shift in air pressure as though a thousand iron doors were slammed shut all at once. At this point I lost consciousness.

I awoke naked and shivering on the cold stone floor of the cave. All the others had left, but the torches remained, now guttering with their last light. The girl was still bound in the chair and she was panting heavily, the same terrified look in her eyes. I looked down and saw a fetid black ichor oozing out of her. Assailed by the rotten odor and the thought of what the incubus had done to her, I hunched over, retched, and nearly blacked out again. After this brief syncope, I gathered my wits and staggered over to the chair and unbound her ankles and wrists. She immediately began clawing at her eyes, so I pulled her hands down and took her into my arms as she dug her nails into my back. Here we were, naked, in an apparent lovers' embrace when nothing could be farther from the truth. For her clutching was not that of someone in the midst of sexual ecstasy; it was that of someone drowning.

For a moment her eyes met mine. She did not look at me, but through me, and she whispered in a quivering voice in my ear "Si me quisieras, me matarías." I was already running to the back to the cave with her in my arms, searching desperately for a way of egress.

The torchlight had faded to nearly nothing and I had to navigate by touch again. I followed a draught of air and soon enough found an exit in a crevice of rock concealed in the backside of another hill. At this point I took off running as fast as I could, encumbered by the girl clinging to me. I stumbled through the undergrowth and over gnarled tree roots for a time when suddenly I felt a searing pain in the small of my back; the girl was seized from my arms and I heard someone say "Metiste la pata." I fell doubled over, reaching for the source of pain in my lower back. My last thought before passing out was the girl and the infernal nightmare gestating in her now infected womb.

I came to on a cot, feeling woozy and thirsty and surrounded by the iodine smell of antiseptic. El médico in his white jacket was tending to his instruments on a counter nearby. I croaked out enough Spanish to ask where I was. El médico turned, raised his lenses, and regarded me. He had something in his hand and handed it to me: a wafer-thin obsidian arrowhead, and he said, "Tiene mucha suerte estar vivo. Le apuñalaron en el riñon. Perdió mucha sangre. Tuve que darle catorce puntos de sutura." I asked for a glass of water and he obliged. I sat up in the cot and winced at the pain in my back. I sucked down the water in one swallow and stood up in my white paper gown and asked for my clothes back. "¿Qué ropa?" he asked. "Le encontraron en pleno campo desnudo." And then I remembered taking off my clothes and leaving them next to the black pool and realized my awkward predicament. As if reading my thoughts, el médico crossed the room and opened a drawer and pulled out a shirt, a pair of undershorts and pants, and a pair of socks, and he offered me a pair of worn leather boots. I nodded him my gratitude and quickly got dressed. El médico and I were of the same build and the clothes fit surprisingly well. El médico smiled and said "No le cobro nada. Que se vaya con Dios." At this, I left the country doctor's house.

I made it to the local Correos, where they have a telegraph, and I contacted the university and asked that it wire me an advance on my research stipend, citing exciting new developments. I have procured at a local casa de empeño a Llama .32-calibre pistol. I am not returning to Swansea. I am going back to Las Llorasangres in search of the girl. I know in my heart, at a level more basic than instinct, that if that thing growing inside her is allowed to see the light of day, it will mean the end of all peace and sanity in the world.

Here end the field notes of Dr. Llewelyn Rhys

Dawn has just broken and the boy is making his way down the cobblestone road to the local tienda, his mother's wicker canasta and red-chequered pañuelo in hand. He is a precocious youngster and although he could read a shopping list, he carries no slip of paper because he carries the list in his head. He turns a corner and enters Braulio's and hails the man behind the counter, ruddy-cheeked and rotund under his red delantal. The boy recites the items his mother told him al dedillo. Un litro de leche—fresh from the cow this morning. Una lata chica de café molido and unas magdalenas to eat with the fresh coffee. Unas naranjas frescas para una merienda después de la siesta. And for dinner, un cuarto kilo de jamón serrano shaved right off the hock hanging overhead and una hogaza de pan francés. The boy takes the few meagre pesetas from his pocket and hands them over with a smile. Then he takes each item and places it in his mother's canasta with great care, draping the pañuelo over the top of them. Then he salutes Braulio and leaves the tienda.

On the way home, the boy turns into an alleyway. A stray cat is picking its desayuno from fishbones left in a corner. The boy approaches and takes a strip of jamón from the basket, crouches down, and coaxes the cat towards him. The cat, its tattered left ear evidence of a life en las calles, is cautious at first, but cannot resist the alluring aroma of the ham. Just as the cat is near enough to take a nibble, it finds itself levitating at the height of the boy's knee. The boy looks at it with an acute intensity and suddenly it feels a tremendous pressure all around its body as though it were being constricted by a python. Its eyes brim with fear before they pop out of their sockets and blood and urine and feces and viscera squeeze out its other orifices. The boy then lets the crushed animal drop to the ground and returns to the street. A fresh breeze is blowing in off the sea and it tousles the boy's hair. He begins to walk faster, then he begins to skip, and now he is running—almost flying—his mother's pañuelo fluttering in the wind. What a beautiful morning! How exciting it is to be alive! The rising sun casts elongated shadows on the cobblestone road, but the boy casts no shadow because he, like his father, is a lightbearer.

I Walked with a Zombie: The Tragicomic World of the Firefly Clan

Jason V Brock

"One of us, one of us. Gooble-gobble, gooble-gobble."
—*Freaks* (1932)

Given the cultural penetration of the phenomenon, it is not a surprise that coulrophobia—the irrational fear of clowns—has become a fertile substrate to exploit for novels and films. A cursory online search reveals dozens of movies, television shows, and books, particularly in the horror genre, using the tropes and imagery of the "scary" or "evil" clown, carnival, or circus. After the recent success of the big-budget duopoly remaking the two-part made-for-TV adaptation from 1990, one might be tempted to assume this was solely due to the influence of Stephen King's epic 1986 novel *It*. Of course, King's book and its adaptations have been very impactful, but other works presaged them, and the fear itself, possibly stemming from an uncanny valley effect, is apparently more deeply rooted than is often understood. While perhaps an exaggeration, as essayist Mark Dery has noted: "All the world hates a clown" (65).

Even under the best of circumstances, clowns, their transgressive behaviors, and even their environs, may inspire a sense of foreboding or dread depending on the context in which they appear. While many people have fond memories of the circus and clown-derived buffoonery, others detect a more sinister subtextual aspect. Perhaps early depictions of innocuous clowns in popular culture and advertising, such as the mascot of the fast food empire McDonald's (in the guise of Ronald McDonald), Bozo the Clown, Clarabell the Clown from *The Howdy Doody Show* (1947–60), or, later, the edgier though humorous portrayals of the flawed Krusty the Clown (*The Simpsons*

[1989–present]), or Homey D. Clown from *In Living Color* (1990–94), leave the impression that clowns are both social reflection and social commentator for the general public. They may at once be a way of promoting wholesomeness and good will on one hand, but also the instruments of shared human foibles—materialism, addiction, or social injustice (the Joker from *Batman* comes to mind). According to Peter Tonguette of the *New York Times,* director Jerry Lewis once planned to recontextualize clowns in the unreleased 1972 film he made entitled *The Day the Clown Cried* (about a clown imprisoned in a Nazi concentration camp during World War II). That he thought it so bad that he forbade it to be distributed *ever* says a lot about how clowns may or may not fit into the collective social framework.

Clowns have a rich history of social and class representation, from the earliest days of the *Commedia dell'arte* tradition (featuring characters such as Pierrot and Harlequin), with roots likely derived from court jesters or fools—who were performers able to state things otherwise unspeakable as jokes, or act out in entertaining ways that would be considered ignoble or transgressive by the mores of the times and circumstances—to the continuing popularity of characters such as Mr. Punch in *Punch and Judy*. Leoncavallo's *I Pagliacci* (1892) is still performed regularly, its operatic grandeur undiminished over the decades since its creation.

And yet . . . not all clowns or clown-related ventures are easy entertainments, and perhaps make the case that these grease-painted effigies and their distorted encampments—mental and physical—are worthy of being feared.

The Clown in Daylight: House of 1000 Corpses

As *Believer Magazine* notes, Rob Zombie was already a successful heavy metal musician (first as a member of White Zombie and then as a solo artist) with an enthusiasm for all things horror when he landed the deal (as writer, co-scorer, and director) for his debut feature film, *House of 1000 Corpses* (2003). This film has generated two sequels and established his penchant for gritty realism (drawn from his love of 1970s auteur cinema), violence, and detailed characterizations, as well as his tendency to use actors and references from his childhood fixations and experiences, to include, as Zombie has stated to interviewer Joe Rogan, "the family business"—his parents worked in traveling carnivals. Later, in 2007, he would remake John Carpenter's seminal 1978 film *Halloween,* and later still the 1981 film *Halloween II* (remade in 2009). Similar themes and approaches would permeate these reimaginings.

The storyline of *Corpses* is a bit contrived (a result, Zombie informed Rogan in the same interview, of improvising the plot in the office of a studio executive: "I had a title . . . with a completely half-assed idea I was making up as I was talking to him"), and doesn't always work, but it does a respectable job of introducing the core characters and their behaviors, even as it plays with tropes and ideas clearly influenced by horror classics from the 1970s, mainly the grim Tobe Hooper effort *The Texas Chainsaw Massacre* (1974), Wes Craven's sordid retelling of the Sawney Bean clan, *The Hills Have Eyes* (1977), and slasher films more broadly. The film is competently directed and has a sort of sickening power, mainly driven by the intense subject matter and the generally strong performances of the principals, namely Sheri Moon Zombie (the filmmaker's wife) as the sultry and insane Vera-Ellen "Baby" Firefly; Bill Moseley (who starred in *The Texas Chainsaw Massacre Part 2* [1986] as the demented Chop-Top) as the sadistic albino Otis B. Driftwood; and, especially, veteran character actor Sid Haig as the intimidating and charismatic clown leading the chaos, Captain Spaulding. Rounding out this ensemble of outsiders is the late 7'6" Matthew McGrory as the giant "Tiny" Firefly—a badly burned, mute sibling with a streak of empathy.

This quartet represents a wayward and frantic group of characters who revel in serial murder and mayhem, all in service to (it appears) a mysterious and ill-defined being of local lore known as Dr. Satan (a.k.a. S. Quentin Quale), and are joined by other characters in realizing their deranged goals. This film, while not exactly glorifying aberrant sexual obsessions (of the strange, deformed, or infirm, for example) and overt violence, does straddle a line between acceptable use of such things to render characterization and overall good taste. It is antisocial in action, dialogue, and perhaps intention, seeming to desire an audience response somewhere between repulsion and eroticized deviance. The whole feel of the piece hangs together as a sort of waking nightmare, where the viewer and characters are bound together as hapless voyeurs in the insane three-ring circus atmosphere generated by the setting of the roadside carnival run by Spaulding and his family, and the grotesque possible motives hinted at by the on-screen madness.

Clearly, Zombie used as starting points multiple frames of cultural allusion in creating the entire experience, including implied references (visually and sonically) to notorious serial murderer John Wayne Gacy (and his creepy alter ego, Pogo the Clown), the artwork of Robert Williams, the horrors of the Edgar Allan Poe story "Hop-Frog," "clown sex" fetishism, his upbringing, and so on. A strange irony is achieved in the sly names Zombie bestows on his main characters, several of which are Marx Brothers references according to the *Believer Magazine* interview (such as the characters of "Driftwood," "Spaulding," "Quale," et al.). Is this a signal that the whole film is really a bizarre "horror comedy," simply a quirk in order to add dimension to the premise, or just a nod to movies Zombie enjoys?

Originally considered a one-off, Zombie would revisit the characters in the sequel a few years later.

A Nightmare at the Opera: The Devil's Rejects

If *House of 1000 Corpses* was a kind of twisted, adult version of Ray Bradbury's *Something Wicked This Way Comes* (1962), then its follow-up—*The Devil's Rejects* (2005)—is more of an opera in scale than a novel. We return to the situational aftermath of *Corpses* and come to appreciate the enormity of the horrific enterprise. The four main characters are back, this time on the run from the law rather than lying-in-wait to ambush victims. Once again, Zombie's oddball fascination with the outsider "hillbilly" elements of his aesthetic is displayed, as though he is attempting to enhance the shock of *Deliverance* (1972) for modern sensibilities jaded by the horrors of 9/11 and the depravity of Daesh (a.k.a. ISIS).

Even so, Captain Spaulding and his deranged progeny (Haig's character is revealed to be the patriarch of the Fireflys) manage to find plenty of victims to exploit, and what ensues is often grueling and hard to watch, though the direction is superior this outing, the writing is sharp, and the acting generally exceptional. Perhaps that's what makes some of the action so nearly unendurable at times. Regardless, the film rivets the viewer, especially the portrayals by Moseley, William Forsythe as the unhinged, Lansdalesque Sheriff Wydell, and Sid Haig, once again, as the crazed ringmaster Captain Spaulding.

Though not without moments of levity, the drama is intense and the stakes high as the action builds to an unforgettable and brilliant riff reminiscent of Sam Peckinpah's *The Wild Bunch* (1969) to close, as the trio goes out in a silent, slow-motion "blaze of glory" to the strains of Lynyrd Skynyrd's epic "Free Bird." Never was Sid Haig more Canio from *Pagliacci* than in this moment. Even the final credits (an empty stretch of highway unspooling under the song "Seed of Memory" by Terry Reid) are liberating after all the violence and retribution on display, and both are masterful uses of music, *à la* Martin Scorsese.

This is art, and the operatic power of the gestalt is undeniable.

Crossing the Border: 3 from Hell

As Zombie pointed out in a 2019 interview with *HEAVY Cinema*, Sid Haig's Captain Spaulding was supposed to have a greater role in this third installment of the franchise. And, while he is represented in the beginning of *3 from Hell* (2019), Haig was too ill to do much in the film—a fact that is evident in the little time he is on-screen. Haig died shortly after the film was released unfortunately, on 21 September 2019—in the truest sense "crossing a border." That noted, his absence, while sharply felt, does not stop the movie from having its own impact and power.

Bill Moseley and Sheri Moon Zombie return and give well-defined performances, replete with the rough edges and idiosyncrasies audiences have come to expect and appreciate with regard to their crazy characters. This effort is smaller in scale and more intimate than either the "carnival atmosphere" of *Corpses* or the "operatic bombast" of *Rejects;* although the action is still bracing, and the drama still palpable, the effort is somewhat more subdued than the previous installments. A new personality—another relative (half-brother to Moseley's character) is introduced into the mix—and he does bring some edge and conviction to the grouping as personified by actor Richard Brake (playing Winslow "Foxy" Coltrane). After catching the viewer up on the scenario, the story commences in earnest once "Baby" Firefly is freed from death row via devious means. Once again, as in the other movies, violence is used as a way of "crossing the border" into another phase of the characters' debauched lives.

Eventually, the trio of desperados decide to head "South of the Border," to Mexico. Once there, the film pivots into a kind of Felliniesque-cum-Sergio Leone Western. They are wanted, and the *narcos* have a score to settle. Full of nods to the Spaghetti Westerns of Eastwood and company, Zombie doesn't disappoint with the violence and tension. Instead of the clowns and circus/carnival trappings of the other two movies, this time those roles are filled by the "masked Mexican wrestler" motif—ably supplanting greasepaint with colorful head coverings and clown attire with suits more closely resembling costumes in construction—while the dingy town itself is populated with prostitutes rather than carnies, and a one-eyed dwarf taking the place of the giant (Tiny Firefly) from the prior offerings.

The end of the film is open, suggesting more could be ahead for this rogue family. Are they literally in Hell? Or is Hell what one makes it?

It will be interesting to see what could develop.

"One of Us!"

Rob Zombie has carved out quite a place with his cinematic vision. While certainly not to everyone's taste, his "Firefly Clan Trilogy" (*House of 1000 Corpses, The Devil's Rejects, 3 from Hell*) is compelling and well done. Working with imagery, genres, and themes as diverse as Noir, Crime, Westerns, Tod Browning's influential 1932 picture *Freaks,* the surreality of Lynch's *The Elephant Man* (1980), and the disquieting vibe of *Carnival of Souls* (1962), in addition to dozens of definitive slasher, Giallo, and Universal horror films as points of reference, Zombie elevates the horror film experience. By reaching into not only the past, but into his own internal preoccupations and anxieties to comment on a variety of phenomena—be it animal cruelty and the link to violence (Zombie is an ethical vegetarian according to the *Daily Kos*), the exploitation of women, society's predilection with violent behaviors and offenders, examinations of social status issues (in the form of metaphorical "freaks" such as giants, dwarves, albinos, and so on), abuse of institutional power, the role of outsiders in culture, and a host of other concerns, including our attraction/repulsion to the macabre, dangerous, and evil—he goes places few filmmakers dare to.

It seems in Zombie's reckoning that the "true monsters" are humans and how they react under pressure, while the "freaks" generally possess an innate humanity, even compassion, that others lack. By flipping this script, he appears to be saying that "the final joke is on you"—so ignore this at one's peril. That he chooses to imagine this through ironic and often weird juxtapositions of over-the-top, operatic pandemonium and off-color humor to create a carnivalesque atmosphere of dread and self-reflection is a tribute to his talent—and to our own complicity in these social inequities.

Works Cited

Dery, Mark. "Cotton Candy Autopsy: Deconstructing Psycho-Killer Clowns." In *Pyrotechnic Insanitarium: American Culture on the Brink*. New York: Grove, 2000. 63–86.

Griffiths, Dave. "'3 FROM HELL'—Rob Zombie Interview." *HEAVY Cinema* (3 October 2019), cinema.heavymag.com.au/3-from-hell-rob-zombie-interview/.

Joe Rogan Experience #1353—Rob Zombie. YouTube, 16 September 2019, www.youtube.com/watch?v=KDLeJ5Rasuo.

Paul, Andrew. "An Interview with Rob Zombie." *Believer Magazine* (19 July 2018), believermag.com/an-interview-with-rob-zombie/.

"Rob Zombie: An Unorthodox Champion of American Values." *Daily Kos* (13 November 2008), www.dailykos.com/stories/2008/11/13/660456/-Rob-Zombie-An-Unorthodox-Champion-of-American-Values.

Tonguette, Peter. "'The Day the Clown Cried': Why Jerry Lewis's Lost Holocaust Film Is Still Lost." *New York Times* (28 December 2018), www.nytimes.com/2018/12/28/movies/jerry-lewis-day-the-clown-cried.html.

Static

Belicia Rhea

The man inside the television waits for me in there.

It's just an old Panasonic, the left speaker blown, the right side often blaring in blips of skips and screams. No matter how I try, the antenna never sits straight—and the white noise of dead channels hums while the light casts tall shadows around the living room, flashing the couch in hideous configurations on the wall. That beveled glass tries to hold him, but he escapes.

I never know what to do, sitting in all that stillness, waiting. It's as if he thinks I'm some type of hollowed-out skin, as if I won't notice the air of a man at my back. I screamed loud the first time. Thought I got rid of him. Thought he'd never come back, but he never left.

No one believes me.

He was trying to hold me down, started ripping out my hair in fistfuls. When I noticed him on the screen, I ran for the remote, clicking forever with him materialized in there. It looked as if he were trying to claw his way through a seam in the glass, carving a ripple of white lines through the transmission. He's already dug through the other channels. I went through all the numbers, looped through the hundreds until they ran out. He yelled more threats of violence from inside, staring out to me, my trembling hands pressing the up-arrow in a panic.

So I ripped out the cord from the wall and watched everything go black, pulled at it so frantically there was a spark, could have caught the house in flames. It didn't work. His face slammed against the glass, gnashing his teeth inside the little black square, looking to me with a sour force of will. I know if I turn it off he can climb out, so I have to leave it on, with all the background voices to distract him.

The first time I saw him free, I almost cut off my fingers. It happened while slicing carrots, when I saw his big white teeth like Chiclet squares reflected in the cutting knife, smiling as he does in the night. His stone face loomed, mirrored just behind me in the blade; so close his breath fogged the steel. I jerked around, shaking—held up the knife—but he vanished. I looked to every corner of the kitchen, even under the table and in the crack between the refrigerator and the wall, anywhere a man could fit.

His rancid garbage breath lingered in the air, so I kept looking, agonizing over every crevice in the wood. This is my house, I told him. I tried reasoning, begging, spent countless nights asking why, but he doesn't listen. I thought back then, something could be done. I thought back then, anything was possible.

Now I know better. I run through the halls, slink tight against the edges of empty space and cobwebs, stay far away from the living room, and keep my eyes real low so I don't catch the sight of him off somewhere in the dark, watching me. I turn away from pans and shiny spoons, keep focused on the feel of things. Most times, I don't need to look. I've stacked layers of paper, methodical and lined up nice; not a slit of space uncovered, taped them all over the mirrors and windows. Everything is veiled now, no light in or out, just in case; and I'm not exactly sure where he hides when he's out, but I know he's here.

The television still sits in the same spot across the couch, making all kinds of sound. The inevitable buzzing and electronic droning shrieks every once in a while; I can hear him wheezing in it, and when I can't take the scraping in my ears any longer, I rush to align the antenna—fix that godawful static grating through the room, but I can't bring my neck to turn my head toward the silver, fearing what I might see in the contorted reflection.

The house must stay very dark, the only light coming from the fireplace, and even then he'll emerge for me. His face will glow inside of there, patiently looking out, waiting to show himself until I come close, so close the heat starts cooking on my skin. He'll start spitting gusts and ashes, growling at me, reaching for me from the chimney. His boiling hands burn me, try to take my breaths, and I can't go near it anymore. So I stay in here.

My bed is the safest place, I tell myself.

I'm always wrong.

In refuge under blankets, I hide. No way he can see. I don't know how he sees. At night when I'm alone, if I stick my fingers inside of myself, if I escape, if I'm wet, if I'm fighting hard to make no sound, to hold my breath, he'll still make his way. I can feel him on top of me, sweat soaking my sheets like disease, filling me up, with the black grime under his fingernails clawing for my hair, pulling, ripping at me, and I try to resist it—I do, but I can't control the loud coming out now, and he puts his thick hands around my neck, gripping, squeezing, choking the life out of me. He says, "Do you want to die, pretty girl? Do you think it's now? Is it time? Is it finally time?" I don't want to die, I tell him, I scream it, but he still comes for me.

To Live at the Edge of a Black Hole

John Shirley

My love I live betwixt the stars,
yes I live between the suns;
I stride between the Earth and Mars—
out where the unseen run

I dwell, you say, in the black of space—
but my sweet you are quite wrong;
why, it's a colorful glowing place
where the ebony light is strong

I live at the end of the silver rope
I live between the worlds;
I live beyond your telescope
beside the whorling whirl

I gaze in awe at all negation—
black as a devil's heart—
I spin around all deflation:
were ends dispose of starts

Humanity is sadly muddled—
you're all blinded by the sun!
Your perspective is befuddled—
by the lies the sun has spun

Ours is a light men cannot see
(essence of iridescence);
it's a hunger you cannot flee
(an onyx effervescence)

I live at the end of the silver rope
were lost souls glimmer bright;
I live beyond your telescope
where the black hole eats your light.

"The Terror of Solitude":
The Supernatural Fiction of Edith Wharton

John C. Tibbetts

> "We had been put in the mood for ghosts . . ."
> —Edith Wharton[1]

While on a walking tour of Brittany, a painter impulsively takes a side trip to visit Miss Mary Pask, the sister of a friend. She lives alone in her cottage by the sea. Like so many "dowdy old maids," surely she would welcome company. The night grows stormy as he approaches her house. There are no signs of life behind the darkened windows.

Suddenly, a smothered memory returns to him: Miss Pask had purportedly died of a stroke some time ago.

The man turns away.

Suddenly, the door opens. There is Miss Pask, looking ghastly and wraithlike in the candlelight. The apparition invites him in. "I've had so few visitors since my death," she says; her death has since gained her "such a sense of freedom." Indeed, the man admits to himself, Miss Pask seems "so much more real to me than ever the living one had been" (171). She talks of her loneliness and beseeches the man not to leave her: "Oh, stay with me, stay with me . . . just tonight. . . . It's so sweet and quiet here. . . . No one need know . . . no one will ever come and trouble us" (169). Horrified, the man retreats and fumbles his way out the door, leaving behind him a pitiful whimper from Miss Pask. He shudders to think that the unuttered

---

1. "The Eyes," *The Ghost Stories of Edith Wharton* 10. Excepting only "The Moving Finger," "The Bottle of Perrier," and "After Holbein," all stories cited in this article are from this edition. Wharton's preface, which originally appeared in the 1937 volume *Ghosts*, is included.

loneliness of a lifetime was now welling up in her ghost, expressing "at last what the living woman had always had to keep dumb and hidden." What has survived her beyond the grave was "enough to cry out to me the unuttered loneliness of a lifetime, to express at last what the living woman had always had to keep dumb and hidden? . . . No end of women were like that, I supposed" (170).[2]

But this terror is as nothing to what the man feels much later when he is told that Miss Pask had not really died after all but still lives quietly in her tiny cottage. That she had had to pretend to be a ghost to express her innermost erotic desires—and that he had so readily accepted her presence as that of a ghost—is an irony that is unbearable. "Between being dead and alive," he realizes in a confused

---

2. The Gothic trope of living persons impersonating ghosts is, of course, as old as the late 18th-century novels of Ann Radcliffe. In the hands of Edith Wharton, the trope achieves a particularly moving and pathetic quality. Likewise, Henry James pulls off a similar feat in his "The Ghostly Rental" (1876), wherein a woman impersonates a ghost in order to wreak revenge on her father. It is also suggestive of Marjorie Bowen's classic tale, "The Crown Derby Plate" (from *Grace Latouche and the Warrington's*, 1931). Martha Pym has never seen a ghost but hopes to encounter one in the old Hartley Place, allegedly haunted by an antiquary, who once had a prized collection of fine bone china, Sir James Sewell. Instead, she only finds an old lady, Miss Lefain, presiding over Sewell's priceless collection. Although Miss Pym is desirous of obtaining one of the plates for her own collection, she leaves the place in great haste. She discovers that the place is really a charnel house inhabited by the ghostly Sir James himself, whom she had mistaken for an old woman. Years before, Sir James had frightened away the real Miss Lefain and is now guarding his precious collection of Crown Derby against other collectors. The fun is how Bowen cleverly lays out the clues in broad daylight, as it were, to the ghostly presence—that the furniture is covered with sheets, that the "old woman" wears "shapeless apparel stained with earth," that "she" has to "frighten away" strangers looking for her china, etc. The comments, "I was taken out of myself some time now" and "I haven't felt the cold for a long time" acquire a comically grim significance. And it is in one of the closets Miss Pym smells "something damp rotting somewhere." By contrast to the pathos of Miss Mary Pask, Bowen lends a deft and amusing touch to this lonely ghost.

delirium, "there seemed after all to be so little difference" (172).

Edith Wharton's "Miss Mary Pask" is masterly in its chilly atmosphere and suggestive nuance of gesture and speech. Night and fog surround Mary Pask and her visitor. The sea whines, "as if it were feeding time, and the Furies, its keepers, had forgotten it." Mary Pask shuffles "soundlessly" in "the faint dabble of moving candlelight." Her pleading voice is a hideous parody of "all the childish wiles of a clumsy capering coquetry." Her form is "something white and wraithlike" that seems to "melt and crumble" in his hands as he retreats to the door.

"Miss Mary Pask" is both a triumph of Gothic melodrama and a trenchant commentary on what Wharton once described as a woman's "terror of solitude" ("All Souls'" 308). Notwithstanding the plethora of feminist commentary that has greeted her stories—a significance she herself rejected—we don't lose sight of their most important quality: "If [this story] sends a cold shiver down one's spine," she writes, "it has done its job and done it well" ("Preface" to *Ghosts* 10).

Lonely Ghosts

Edith Wharton brought a great respect, subtle intelligence, and vivid prose to her ghost stories. They spanned her entire writing career. Beginning with "The Moving Finger"—published in 1901, three years before her breakthrough novel, *The House of Mirth*—she produced a dozen more ghost stories, concluding with the posthumously published "All Souls'" in 1937.[3] Every sort of bewitchment and ghosting are deployed. Included in the stories considered here are the vengeful ghosts of "The Lady's Maid's Bell," "Mr. Jones," "Af-

---

3. I have found another supernatural short story that predates "The Lady's Maid's Bell." Published in 1893, "The Fullness of Life" is a vision of the afterlife, in which the newly deceased protagonist discusses love and life with an entity known only as "Spirit." The prose is as purple as the sentiments are cloying. See R. W. B. Lewis, "Introduction" to *The Collected Short Stories of Edith Wharton* 1.12–20.

terward," "A Bottle of Perrier"; a vampire in "Bewitched"; a murderous beast in "Kerfol"; a sinister Doppelgänger in "Triumph of the Night"; a haunted painting in "The Moving Finger"; two disembodied eyes in "The Eyes"; a packet of phantom letters in "Pomegranate Seed"; a phantom dinner party in "After Holbein"; a witch cult in "All Souls'"; a trance medium in "The Looking Glass"; and the erotic apparition in "Miss Mary Pask."

This is by no means to reduce their characters and situations to tired, commonplace Gothic tropes; rather, they come to us enriched by both the mastery of Wharton's prose and by their functions as metaphors for societal injustice, psychological aberration, and sexual abuse. I propose to organize these stories into three groups. The first group may be categorized, in general, as belonging to what R. W. B. Lewis has termed "the marriage question." Here we find Wharton's "near obsession with the perplexities of marriage," in which, more than her American contemporaries, "the whole domain of the marriage question was the domain in which Edith Wharton sought the truth of human experience; it was where she tested the limits of human freedom and found the terms to define the human mystery."[4] These arenas of conflict, adds commentator Kathy A. Fedorko, are "dangerous places for women [where] female exuberance, ambition, and eroticism are suspect and therefore constrained." Because of their isolation and solitude, "women are made ill and ghostly" (81). The second category includes those stories that bring her most closely to the work of her great friend and contemporary, Henry James. These are the stories in which ghostly presences point up crises of conscience and lapses in moral purpose. The third category consists of four stories which resist easy classification, yet we would not be without them. "The Moving Finger," "After Holbein," "Bottle of Perrier," and "All Souls'" may not be ghost stories at all. The

---

4. R. W. B. Lewis, "Introduction" to *The Collected Short Stories of Edith Wharton* 1.x. Perhaps only Wharton's British contemporary Marjorie Bowen rivaled—even excelled—her in the sheer profusion of short stories devoted to this subject. See my *The Furies of Marjorie Bowen*.

first two offer little of the *frisson* of dread and the numinous, yet they possess an engaging satiric edge. The third is a first-class horror story, but its ghost is entirely of the imagination. And the fourth strips away all the trappings of the standard ghostly yarn in its portrait of a haunted, lonely woman who may be Edith Wharton herself.

Ghostly Instincts

Edith Wharton understood the special challenges of writing ghost stories and knew thoroughly their tradition. She cited among her favorite practitioners Robert Louis Stevenson, J. Sheridan LeFanu, and Walter de la Mare. She even admitted, as will be seen, her own susceptibility to the paranormal:

> When I first began to read, and then to write, ghost stories, I was conscious of a common medium between myself and my readers, of their meeting me halfway among the primeval shadows, and filling in the gaps in my narrative with sensations and divinations akin to my own. ("Preface" to *Ghosts*, 8)

In *The Writing of Fiction* (1925) and in the preface to *Ghosts* (1937) she declares that deep within us all lurks "the ghost instinct," which has managed to survive both the "boring stage properties" of an outworn Gothic tradition and the modernist atrophy of the creative act brought on by the wireless and the cinema. A character in "The Pomegranate Seed" expresses this persistence:

> "Outside there [are] skyscrapers, advertisements, telephones, wireless, airplanes, movies, motors, and all the rest of the twentieth century; and on the other side of the door something I can't explain, can't relate to them. Something as old as the world, as mysterious as life." (240)

In the hands of the "experienced chronicler," Wharton herself adds, "the ghost may hold his own a little longer" ("Preface" to *Ghosts* 9).

Her stories capped the growing popularity of the ghostly tale since the middle of the nineteenth century in the United States and

Great Britain. Public interest in spiritual phenomena had spread ever since the notorious "Hydesville rappings" in New York in 1848 and the later exploits of the medium Daniel Douglas Home in Great Britain.[5] Groups like the British National Association of Spiritualists and the American Society for Psychical Research were formed. No less a figure than William James lent his formidable prestige to their efforts and spent his last decades investigating several female mediums. "Those who have the fullest acquaintance with the phenomena," he wrote in his last essay on the subject, "admit that in good mediums there is a *residuum of knowledge displayed* that can only be called supernormal; the medium taps some source of information not open to ordinary people" (quoted in Blum 303). But there was much that was inconclusive in these findings; spiritual manifestations seemed remarkably devoid of pattern and motivation.

Nonetheless, Wharton's female predecessors, including Mrs. J. H. Riddell, Elizabeth Gaskell, and Vernon Lee, made a specialty in their fiction that brought them great popularity. The question that must be asked is if they and Wharton and her immediate contemporaries, particularly Marjorie Bowen, May Sinclair, and Daphne du Maurier, brought anything intrinsically "female" to their stories. Scholar S. T. Joshi observes it would be "demeaning and stereotypical" to say so, i.e., that they brought more focus on the "human emotions" rather than "weird phenomena itself" ("Introduction" to *The Cold Embrace* vi). Yet there is no denying that Wharton and others brought to bear a finely honed knowledge of psychology, coupled with an acute sensibility and a candid insight into female sexuality that lent their work authority and conviction. No longer was it enough, as E. F. Bleiler has noted, that ghosts must function solely "to reveal information, confess to a crime, tell where the will or the love letters are hidden, undo some hurt it has done, or reveal the murderer of its body" (xxii).

---

5. For a background survey on the rise of spiritualism in the 19th century, see Stemman. For its impact upon American writers in the second half of the century, see Kerr.

Wharton's works explore existential dilemmas in a surprisingly tough and candid way.[6] By blurring the boundaries between the living and the dead, she demonstrated that there was much that was real in the ghostly and much that was ghostly in the real. The two worlds were so interwoven that they seemed at times scarcely distinguishable from each other; and our understanding of one led to an increased understanding of the other. Singularly pertinent here is a passage from *The Return*, by Walter de la Mare, to whom *Ghosts* is dedicated: "And yet mystery and loveliness alike were only really appreciable with one's legs, as it were, dangling down over into the grave" (411).

Early Terrors

Edith Wharton began her own "dangling" shortly after her birth in 1862 to an old New York family. Like so many of her contemporaries, including William and Henry James and William Dean Howells, she began in her youth to suffer a series of strange psychic disturbances. She was to recall late in life that as a child she had felt a "dark undefinable menace forever dogging my steps, lurking and threatening," a "choking agony of terror."[7] Throughout the sporadic

---

6. Wharton grew up in a society that held certain expectations before the woman writer. Describing the situation, Sara Payton Willis ("Fanny Fern") wrote: "When we take up a woman's book, we expect to find gentleness, timidity, and that lovely reliance on the patronage of . . . [the male] sex which constitutes a woman's greatest charm." Instead of subjects like politics, sexual mores, and sensational melodrama, women like Sara Clarke ("Grace Greenwood"), Catharine Maria Sedgwick, and Mrs. A. D. T. Whitney wrote children's literature, books on child care and household management, and "works of sensibility" steeped in nonsectarian religious fervor. There were exceptions, of course. Both Mary Elizabeth Braddon and Mrs. J. H. Riddell were quite successful with, respectively, their melodramas and ghost stories. Louisa May Alcott, however, labored in secret at her more sensational fiction. For more information on this subject, see Hamlin and Wood.

7. For an extensive commentary on Mrs. Wharton's nervous disorders, see Lewis, *Edith Wharton* 24–26, 74–76.

education and the extensive traveling of her adolescence, the nervous attacks and prolonged depressions continued. They intensified after her marriage in 1885 to Edward Wharton until they would disable her for weeks—even months—at a time. It was not until she began writing in earnest after 1890 that they seemed to lose their grip on her. Significantly, the divorce from Edward in 1913 saw the transmutation of her pains—both real and imagined—into a sharply acute social vision that produced her first great novels and ghostly tales. She grew up in a world where the conventions of society—especially those conventions surrounding middle-class women—were narrow and constricting. Moreover, her education must have seemed especially inadequate to a person of her fine mind and sharp perceptions. She was expected to learn only the social arts and perhaps a language, but little else. Sex was never discussed—even, as Edith discovered, on the eve of her marriage. And to top everything off her mother was a dominating influence and echoed the prevailing notion that writing was not a proper profession for a lady of society. There are even darker suggestions of an incestuous relationship with her father.[8] Nor was the shy, red-haired young lady to find any escape from all this in her marriage to Edward. It was, the biographers agree, a loveless and sexless union that did nothing to fulfill Edith's growing sensuous awareness.

In sum, Edith Wharton understood in her own life "the terror of solitude." How well she understood the terror of isolation. Biographer Linda Costanzo Cahir contends that her ghost stories reflect characters—mostly women—trapped in an isolation that is their "inescapable, existential state" (125).

The "Marriage Question"

"The Lady's Maid's Bell," "Kerfol," "Mr. Jones," "Bewitched," "Pomegranate Seed," and "Afterward" portray men and women as

---

8. Linda Costanzo Cahir (87) relates these allegations to Wharton's confessional story, "Beatrice Palmatto."

victims and victimizers within the marital bond. Alone in their isolation—"It's a worm in the brain, solitude is"—they inhabit their marriages like ghosts haunting their houses.

"The Lady's Maid's Bell" establishes the template that fuels many of these stories. When young Alice Hartley answers the call for a new maid in the gloomy house on the Hudson of Mr. and Mrs. Brympton, she steps into a situation fraught with imminent violence. Her mistress is a semi-invalid who, it is suggested, is occasionally subjected to sexual abuse at the hands of her husband. Her passivity infuriates him while her loneliness is exacerbated by his protracted absences. Before Alice came to the house, she learns that Mrs. Brympton's only friend and confidante had been her former maid, the late Emma Saxon. Emma had aided her mistress in pursuing a (platonic?) relationship with a young bachelor named Ranford living nearby. Emma's loyalty and persistence in shielding her mistress from her husband had been so strong that, even after her death, she continues to answer the servant's bell.

And now it is Alice Hartley's turn. Although she takes an instant affection for her new mistress, she can't say the same for Mr. Brympton, who looks her over with an appraising eye: "I knew what the look meant, from having experienced it once or twice in my former places . . . I was not the kind of morsel he was after" (20). Another occupant of the house is "a thin woman with a white face and a dark gown" whom Alice encounters on several occasions. She thinks it odd that all the maid's bells are mute in the house. But then comes the night when the summoning bell is heard, and Alice hears the door of the locked chamber that formerly belonged to the late Emma Saxon open and close. "Alice Hartley," she says to herself, "Your mistress has rung for you, and to answer her bell *you've got to go the way that other woman has gone*" (25; my emphasis). The words are chilling in their prescience. Alice gains Mrs. Brympton's chamber, only to find that Emma may have been there already. Thereafter, Alice grows increasingly apprehensive about her predecessor. "Somehow, the thought of that locked room across the passage began to weigh on me," she confesses. "Once or twice, in the long rainy nights, I fancied I heard noises there . . . I felt that *someone* was cowering there, behind the locked door, watching and listening as I watched and listened" (30). Her unease increases when she sees a photograph of the late Emma Saxon and recognizes it as the pale woman she has been seeing in the passage. "Her face was just one dumb prayer to me—but how in the world was I to help her?" (32).

One day Alice follows her outside the house to the house of Mrs. Brympton's friend, Mr. Ranford. "It seemed as if [Emma] had left me all alone to carry the weight of the secret I couldn't guess" (34). Indeed, it is increasingly evident that Ranford's attentions to Mrs. Brympton have elicited Mr. Brympton's jealous surveillance. Matters come to a head when the "furious ringing" of the lady's maid's bell summons Alice to Mrs. Brympton's chamber. She warns her mistress that someone—perhaps Mr. Brympton?—is in the house downstairs. He bursts in the door, distraught and angry. He moves toward the dressing room as if looking for something—or someone. Protectively blocking his way, however, is Emma: "On the threshold stood Emma Saxon. All was dark behind her, but I saw her plainly, and so did he. He threw up his hands as if to hide his face from her; and when I looked again she was gone" (36). Trapped in the living death of her marriage, Mrs. Brympton had apparently been pursuing an assignation with Mr. Ranford.

Mrs. Brympton expires of pain and grief. Attending her funeral a few days later are both Mr. Brympton and Ranford. The animosity between them is evident. Soon after, Mr. Brympton quits the scene, and Alice and the other servants return to the house.

"[Emma Saxon's] disembodiment and muteness make her the ideal symbol for the untold female story," writes Fedorko—a story where "female sexuality is monstrous and is therefore imprisoned." Fedorko further observes that shortly before the publication of this story Wharton had suffered a nervous breakdown, "one of several during her socially correct but physically and emotionally fraught marriage, where there had been little or no sexual compatibility" (81).

"You know, every Breton house has its ghost story," says the narrator of "Kerfol," one of Wharton's most celebrated stories, "and some of them are rather unpleasant" (107). The story unfolds in the plain-spoken manner of a legend, complemented with brief extracts from a court case pertinent to events in the story. A prospective buyer comes to Kerfol to look it over as a possible purchase. His first inspection reveals a lonely structure that belongs to the past: "As it stood there, lifting its proud roofs and gables to the sky, it might have been its own funeral monument" (102). His approach to the gate arouses the mute interest of several dogs. They do not threaten him, but in aspect and behavior they are almost human, as if "they knew better what the house would tolerate and what it would not" (105). The buyer comes away oddly disquieted, sensing that he had escaped "from the loneliest place in the whole world" (106). (He is told, moreover, that there are no dogs at Kerfol.)

Soon after he learns the story of the terrible murder centuries before of the lord of the estate, Yves de Cornault. His body had been found, horribly mangled. Accused of the crime was his second wife, the young and beautiful Anne. In the subsequent court trial, it is revealed that the insanely jealous husband had kept her a virtual prisoner during his long absences. It was said that such a close watch was kept on her by the servants that she could not pick a flower in the garden without a servant at her heels. Her only company was a little dog he had bought for her as an emblem of her fidelity. But when the dog's collar had been found in the possession of a young man living in the area, Yves had strangled it and left the corpse on her bed pillow. Other dogs that kept Anne company had met a similar fate.

Suspicions of Yves's death fell upon Anne. Her only defense was that the night of her husband's death, the sounds of snarling dogs had been heard in his chamber. "Then I heard a sound," she testified, "like the noise of a pack when the wolf is thrown to them—gulping and lapping" (123). But no dogs had been found at the bloody scene. Her assertion that her dead dogs had torn Yves apart was met with derision. She was found guilty and handed over to her husband's family, who shut her away from the world in the keep at Kerfol. She died many years later, "a harmless madwoman" (124). R. W. B. Lewis pronounces "Kerfol" "one of Edith Wharton's finest exercises in the imagination of violence, terror, and the erotic," conjecturing its power stems from her own "childhood terrors" (*Edith Wharton: A Biography* 394).

Anne's plight echoes that of Lady Thudeney in "Mr. Jones." Wharton pulls out all the stops in this standard Gothic study of a ghost who stands guard over an old house containing a mysterious portrait, a hidden cache of papers, and a backstory of wife abuse. The story begins when the new owner of the estate of Bells, Lady Jane Lynke, arrives to claim her inheritance. She immediately senses an entrapping atmosphere: stepping into the adjacent chapel, she feels that "her forbears were waiting for her" (203). She finds appended to an inscription identifying the tomb where lies her ancestor, Peregrine Lynke, the small, cramped, dismissive words—"Also His Wife." The house itself stretches its arms out to her: "Already, in that first hour of arrival, she had decided to give up everything else. . . . Her previous plans and ambitions—except such as might fit in with living here—had fallen from her like a discarded garment, and things she had hardly thought about, or had shrugged away with the hasty subversiveness of youth, were already laying quiet hands on her" (208). She feels part of a "long tale, to which she was about to add another chapter" (208). "I shall never leave it!" she exclaims impulsively (203).

Lady Jane finds an eighteenth-century portrait of a lady bearing the name of Lady Thudeney, the wife of Peregrine Lynke. Lady Jane supposes she must be the "Also His Wife" of the tomb's inscription. Lady Jane's efforts to find out more about the house and her forbears are blocked by the mysterious "Mr. Jones"—or, at least, by his directives delivered to her by the loyal servant, Mrs. Clemm. Nothing about this apparent guardian of Bells is otherwise revealed;

and Mr. Jones is nowhere to be found—save for a few brief sightings of an old man huddled over a desk in The Blue Room.

From a cache of papers found in a locked desk, Lady Jane learns the tragic backstory of the house a century before: Peregrine Lynke had kept his wife, the Viscountess of Thudeney—"Also His Wife"—a virtual prisoner in the house. He had a secret to protect: He had married the poor deaf-and-dumb woman solely for her wealth. In one letter the Viscountess protests to Peregrine that it is a terrible thing to "sit in this great house alone, day after day, month after month, deprived of your company, and debarred also from any intercourse but that of the servants you have chosen to put about me." The letter goes on to entreat for help "some kind hearts that would take pity on my unhappy situation" (227). So complete is the Viscount's subjugation of her that the ghost of his faithful retainer, Mr. Jones, remains in the house thereafter, protecting his master's secret. Because of her complicity in the discovery of the papers, Mrs. Clemm's body is found, strangled by the ghostly hands of Mr. Jones, a look of unspeakable of horror in her eyes.

"Bewitched" was published in 1926, fifteen years after the story it most resembles, Wharton's best-known novel, *Ethan Frome*. It is a finely etched atmospheric study of the chilly, wintry desolation of the farming community of Starkfield, Massachusetts. Isolated in this freezing wilderness are two sisters, Ora and Venny Brand, both of them liminal figures starkly outlined against the twilight canvas:

> The snow had ceased, and a green sunset was spreading upward into the crystal sky. A stinging wind barbed with ice flakes caught them in the face on the open ridges, but when they dropped down into the hollow by Lamer's pond the air was as soundless and empty as an unswung bell. (193)

Rumors of witchery and madness settle like a dark cloak over the landscape. Inbreeding stains the generations. An ancestor of the Brand family had been burned as a witch a century ago. Recently, old Aunt Cressidora, has been spending her last days raging in a solitary cell, her face "a coil of twitching features" (189). And now there is farmer Saul Rutledge, who lately has been conducting twilight trysts with the ghost of the recently buried Ora Brand. "She *draws me*" (187), he protests to his outraged wife, Prudence. Prudence Rutledge is a bitter, severe woman—"who might have been anywhere from thirty-five to sixty"—who demands of the villagers an investigation into these unholy visitations: "Thou shalt not suffer a witch to live!" Nothing less than a stake through her heart will do.

During their search of the area, several of the men, including the father of the deceased Ora Brand, discover strange footprints in the snow leading up to a nearby shack. "The living couldn't walk so light," declares one of the men (196). When the door of the shack is burst open, "something white and wraithlike" surges up out of the darkness. A shot is discharged from Mr. Brand's revolver. After that, there is confusion.

What, exactly, has happened? All that is known is that three days later Ora Brand's sister, Venny, a mysterious character in her own right, who has been seen lately wildly running about the slopes of the woods, suddenly expires of a mysterious illness and her coffin is lowered into her sister's grave. Sporting her best bonnet, Prudence Rutledge arrives to preside triumphantly over the ceremony: "She looks as if the stonemason had carved her to put atop of Venny's grave," declares an onlooker (198). She says her husband, who is not in attendance, will sleep quieter now—"and *her*, too, maybe now she don't lay there alone any longer" (199).

Well, *who* or *what* is it who sleeps quietly now in the grave? Is it Ora or her ghost; or is it the recently interred Venny, who may have been impersonating Ora's ghost? It is left for Prudence's grim triumph, now that neither the living nor the dead contend against her, to provide the most disturbing note in this ghastly farrago.

"Pomegranate Seed" considers the plight of Charlotte Ashby. She and her husband's late first wife, Elsie, engage in a tussle for his soul. A series of anonymously penned letters addressed to Kenneth

Ashby threaten to disrupt the harmony of his second marriage with Charlotte. Although he refuses to disclose their authorship or their contents, Charlotte suspects the faint, almost illegible handwriting belongs to his deceased first wife, Elsie. She is well aware that Elsie had "absolutely dominated" Kenneth in their marriage and that, although he refuses to disclose their authorship, he is once again under her sway.

An irrational jealousy consumes Charlotte. She begins to feel "excluded, ignored, blotted out of his life." The fabric of her carefully ordered world is torn apart and "something inexplicable, intolerable" confronts her from "the other side of the curtained panes" (240). At one point, after persuading her husband to come away on a trip with her, Charlotte feels that she has reclaimed her husband's attention. Exultantly, she thinks: "Ah, well, some women knew how to manage men, and some didn't—and only the fair . . . deserve the brave!" But one day Kenneth disappears. Another letter arrives. Charlotte finally yields to temptation and opens one of the letters, but the script is so faint as to be illegible, as if no human hand possessed the weight to press the pen firmly onto the paper.

Days pass and there is no trace of Kenneth. Charlotte is left utterly alone. Has Elsie abducted him, or has Kenneth consigned himself to a "mysterious bondage," the erotic lure of the dead? The relevance of the "pomegranate seed" of the title, which has puzzled readers then and now, is clear, at least in R. W. B. Lewis's interpretation: The Greek myth of Persephone in the Underworld has been revised somewhat: Because Mr. Ashby has broken his vow of constancy to his first wife, Elsie has assumed the role of Pluto "and has summoned her spouse to leave his earthly existence and cohabit with her in the land of the dead" ("Preface" to *The Collected Short Stories of Edith Wharton* 2.xvi).

In "Afterward" Mary Boyne is abandoned in her lonely house to the ghost that has abducted her husband, Ned. They have left America to settle in a lovely old country house in England. At first, they greet rumors that their house is haunted with cheery enthusiasm. "I want one of my own on the premises," Mary declares. However, explains a friend, you won't know the ghost until long afterward: "Suddenly," says Mary, "suddenly, long afterward, one says to one's self, *That was it?*'" (66). Wharton is having some whimsical fun with this. For example, on the lookout, Mary thinks she is seeing ghosts at every hand. There's a significant moment when, after seeing a figure walking down the road, she mistakes her husband for the ghost: "Why, I actually took you for the ghost, my dear, in my mad determination to spot it!" (73). (As always in Wharton, what is ghostly and what is not is open to conjecture.)

As days and weeks pass, however, the tone darkens. There is evidence of cracks in the marriage surface. Hints of a mysterious scandal in Ned Boyne's past American business dealings catalyze their growing mutual distrust, as Mary begins to question the nature of their relationship:

> Theoretically, she deprecated [her] detachment from her husband's professional interests, but in practice she had always found it difficult to fix her attention on . . . his varied interests. . . . Now, for the first time, it startled her a little to find how little she knew of the material foundation on which her happiness was built. (76)

They look at each other, as Wharton notes at one point, "like adversaries watching for an advantage" (75).

Matters come to a head when Ned disappears one day after being approached by a stranger come to call. It is only "afterward" that Mary realizes that the mysterious visitor may be the ghost of her husband's late business partner, come to claim revenge. Mary is now left alone in the house, seized by "a vague dread of the unknown," half-discerning "an actual presence, something aloof, that watched and knew" (84). Bereft of any purpose in her life, she begins to feel "like the furniture of the room in which she sat, an insensate object to be dusted and pushed about with the chairs and tables" (90). She is "domesticated with the Horror, accepting its perpetual presence as one of the fixed conditions of life" (89). It is Mary, like her husband's wronged business partner, who is now, in effect, haunting the house.

Questions of Conscience and Moral Purpose

Other ghost stories are not so easily confined to the template of damaged marriages. Three stories—"The Eyes," "The Looking Glass," "Triumph of the Night"—concern Jamesian matters of conscience and morality.

In "The Eyes" we encounter in the person of Andrew Culwin that kind of social parasite Wharton and James understood so well. Indeed, argues Linda Costanzo Cahir, he is one of the most heinous characters in all of Wharton, a man "soullessly detached from his conquests to whom people are important only as they gratify his pleasures and proclivities" (125). More to the point, writes Wharton, he is a social and sexual vampire who "feeds" upon the vitality and zest of young people moving through society (he "liked them juicy"). In the confessional monologue he delivers to his newest protégé, Philip Frenham, he recalls two friendships he has enjoyed in the recent past. There was young Alice Nowell, whose affections he exploited and then ruthlessly rejected; and Gilbert Noyes, an attractive young man, "slender and smooth as a hyacinth," whose mediocre literary talents were encouraged for the sake of the companionship he offered. We learn from Culwin's long monologue that he has misused them over the years and, subsequently, has been subject to a series of "visions," visitations by a pair of huge, ghastly eyes which "had grown hideous gradually, which had built up their baseness coralwise, bit by bit, out of a series of small turpitudes slowly accumulated through the industrious years" (55). "They seemed to belong to a man who had done a lot of harm in his life," Culwin observes, "but had always kept just inside the danger lines" (48). They have a physical effect "that was the equivalent of a bad smell" (49).

He tries to dismiss these apparitions, dismissing them as "optical or digestive delusions" (44). Lately, declares Culwin, coming to the end of his narration, the visions have ceased since he abandoned his friend Noyes. "Put two and two together, if you can. For my part, I haven't found the link." (60). Listening to this appalling monologue is Culwin's newest protégé, young Philip Frenham. He draws back from Culwin. "Cheer up, my dear Phil! It's been years since I've seen them—apparently I've done nothing lately bad enough to call them out of chaos" (60). The ghostly eyes, of course, are his own.

"The Looking Glass" reflects, as it were, the craze for mediums and seances that held America and England in its ghostly grip in the years leading up to and including the First World War. In this slight and amusing fable, we meet wealthy Mrs. Clingsland, who mourns the ageing face that looks back at her from the looking glass. "My beauty," she laments, "—I saw it suddenly slipping out of the door from me this morning" (273). In vain does she entreat anyone who will listen to reassure her that her good looks still prevail. "She had to be always hunting for new people to tell her she was as beautiful as ever; because she wore the others out" (277). Anxious to spare her from the hordes of phony mediums and spirit guides prepared to take advantage of her is her masseuse, one Mrs. Atlee. "There was a fair lot of swindlers and blackmailers in the business," Atlee observes to herself; "I'd sooner have trusted a gypsy at a fair . . . but the women just *had* to go to them" (275).

Attlee comes up with a plan to appease Mrs. Clingsland. The old lady once had loved a young man who had gone down with the *Titanic,* allegedly leaving behind a cache of unsent letters. "If only he hadn't died," wails Clingsland, "it's the sorrowing for him that's made me old before my time" (280). Atlee calls upon her own presumed psychic gifts to concoct several letters from the dead lover. "I'd always had a way of seeing things; from the cradle, even," Atlee admits, "feeling there's things about you, behind you, whispering over your shoulder" (275). She even convinces herself these letters are authentic, and that they "go down Mrs. Clingsland's throat like honey, and she just lay there and tasted them" (282). But after awhile, Mrs. Clingsland is still not satisfied. Once it had begun, she had to have more, and even more. Atlee goes to a young man of her acquaintance who is only too eager to assist her further in the letter-writing. "It's damn difficult," he says, "making love for a dead man to a woman you've never seen" (286). Moreover, Mrs. Clingsland demands to know what was the last message the doomed *Titanic* passenger had intended to write but had never sent?

The letter-writer bends to the task. But when Atlee goes to him to retrieve said letter, she finds him dead, with the remnants of a letter in his hand. Atlee copies it out and presents it to the delighted Mrs. Clingsland, who pronounces it authentic beyond a doubt. Later, at her death, the grateful old lady bequeaths to Mrs. Atlee enough money to pay for the little cottage she had promised her.

Somehow, amidst her well-intended chicanery, Atlee has tapped into the Real Thing. She struggles, however, with a sense of guilt over her profiteering. However, in a bit of moralizing sleight-of-hand, "She had a vague idea that a sin unrevealed was, as far as the consequences went, a sin uncommitted; and this conviction had often helped her in the difficult task of reconciling doctrine and practice" (271).

An evil Doppelgänger hovers over the wicked proceedings of "The Triumph of Night." George Faxon finds himself on a wintry New Hampshire night waiting in vain for the sleigh that will take him to his new job as secretary to a local employer. Instead, another sleigh arrives driven by a young, personable man named Frank Rainer. Frank invites Faxon to join him on the way to the nearby home of his wealthy uncle, an industrialist named John Lavrington. Faxon is struck by Frank's "healthy face but dying hands," signs of a fatal tubercular condition (133).

Upon arriving at the house, George finds himself among a gathering of men called by Lavrington to witness documents attesting to Frank's coming to majority. Lavrington presides over the affair with a thin, cold smile that seems to contradict his apparent solicitude for the ailing nephew. He ignores suggestions from the others that Frank travel to Arizona for a cure and encourages him to remain in the house for the winter. Meanwhile, during the proceedings, Faxon is struck by the sight of a strange figure who appears behind Lavrington's chair. The barely substantial figure could almost be Lavrington's double, although the expression he directs toward Frank is menacing and deadly. There is a hatred in that face that disturbs Faxon: "The watcher behind the chair was no longer merely malevolent ... His hatred seemed to well up out of the very depth of balked effort and thwarted hopes, and the fact made him more pitiable, and yet more dire" (144). The moment comes to a climax when Faxon finds himself unwilling to gaze further at that dire figure, afraid that he will be overwhelmed by a "bottomless blackness that gaped for him" (146). But his resolve snaps—and after reluctantly catching a last glimpse of the horror, the panic-stricken Faxon quits the room and flees the "abominable air" of the house for the "purifying" night outside. What he sees and what it means are withheld from us. All we know is that he feels "he had looked too deep down into the abyss," and left questioning why he has been a participant in this evil:

> Why, in the name of any imaginable logic, human or devilish, should he, a stranger, be singled out for this experience? ... Unless, it was just because he was a stranger—a stranger everywhere—because he had no personal life, no warm screen of private egotisms to shield him from exposure ... A thousand times better regard himself as ill, disorganized, deluded, than as the predestined victim of such warnings! (148)

During his flight, Faxon is caught up by Frank, who has been dispatched by his uncle to bring him back to the house. It was a cruel directive, and, sure enough, the boy collapses in a spill of tubercular blood.

In the story's epilogue, Faxon leaves the country and aimlessly wanders the world, barely conscious that he has failed in some way to save young Frank. The youth's death has conveniently provided his uncle with the funds that enabled him to escape a disastrous stock market crash.

What begins as a richly atmospheric gothic horror story concludes with a fine, Jamesian meditation on the failure of conscience: Had Faxon not fled the scene, he might have "broken the spell of iniquity" and saved Frank from his uncle's fatal greed. The "powers of darkness" might not have prevailed. Instead, he had closed his ears to "the powers of pity" that had singled him out "to warn and save" (154–55). And his last futile gesture had been to hold Frank's dying and bloodied body in his arms.

The Terror of Solitude

Aside from their common theme of isolation and solitude, "The Moving Finger," "After Holbein," "A Bottle of Perrier," and "All Souls'" stubbornly resist easy categorization. The first three are seldom included in any mention of Wharton's ghost stories. Indeed, their ghosts, if any, seem entirely of the imagination. The last, "All Souls'," although frequently anthologized and acknowledged as one Wharton's finest ghost stories, threatens to elude our comprehension altogether.

"The Moving Finger" (*Collected Short Stories* 1.301–13) describes the strange fascination a portrait painting exerts upon two men in love with the same woman. Has their mutual possession of the painting, in turn, possessed them? Ralph Grancy is so besotted with his wife that he commissions his friend, Claydon, to paint her portrait. Claydon, curiously, grows so obsessed with the portrait that he seems to prefer it to the original. It is said that "he had been saved from falling in love with Mrs. Grancy only by falling in love with his picture of her" (303).

Then, one day, Mrs. Grancy suddenly, unexpectedly dies. Five years pass. Mr. Grancy keeps the portrait near him, worshiping in solitude her "bright, unappeasable ghost." Observing this, Claydon wryly comments that he has "never before known how completely the dead may survive" (306). Meanwhile, observers are aware that now the painting has been subtly been altered, *aged*, as if to accompany Mr. Grancy into middle age. This is Claydon's work. He had reluctantly acceded to Grancy's commission to *age* the painting. "Do you think," Grancy demanded of him, "she would have wanted to be left behind?" (307)

Years later, the situation grows stranger when, after Grancy's death, the painting is willed to Claydon. A visitor to Claydon marvels that the painting seems "to have recovered the radiance of youth" (312). Indeed, the painter has erased the signs of ageing. "[Mr. Grancy] wanted me to make an old woman of her," he explains, "but now she belongs to me" (313).

"After Holbein" (*Collected Short Stories* 2.532–50) is a personal favorite. It depicts the strangest dinner party in ghostly fiction.[9] Wharton is at her most wickedly amusing as she introduces us to dinner party hostess Mrs. Jaspar and dinner guest, Mr. Warley. The scent of the grave clings to both. They are specimens of a vanished society, trapped now behind display cases and between the pages of old scrapbooks. Although they walk among the world of the living, we expect them momentarily to fade suddenly into the thin air.

This evening Warley, a veteran of thirty years of New York dinner engagements, is preparing for his evening out. He's accustomed to only the "right houses" whose hostesses offer the best dinners and guests. Lately, however, he has been suffering brief memory lapses, has grown rather stiff in the joints, and has the sensation of "chattering with cold inside" (532). This night he leaves his faithful valet

---

9. Although Wharton did not include it in *Ghosts*, and although it is not usually included in relevant discussions, it is my contention that the guests who attend this extraordinary dinner party are just this side of the grave. The title, explains Lewis, is probably a reference to the "Dance of Death" woodcut by Hans Holbein the Younger, in which a lavishly dressed lady and a gentleman follow the skeletal figure of Death.

and decides to walk—where? Surely not to old Mrs. Jaspar's. He knows the poor old lady, once the high priestess of New York society, still imagines herself to be a leading hostess. Her invitations are prepared but never more sent out. He imagines her "coming down every evening to her great shrouded drawing room, with her tiara askew on her purple wig, to receive a stream of imaginary guests" (535).

Now out on the sidewalk in the bracing cold air Mr. Warley sets out for—again, where? As he ruminates, the scene shifts to Mrs. Jaspar's house, where she is preparing her makeup, her wig, and her jewels for the evening's dinner. She hears the carriages driving up and the bustle of arriving guests. But when she majestically sweeps downstairs on wobbly legs, she seems not to be aware that there are no carriages and no arriving guests. Nor does she notice that, aside from the servants, there is no one sitting at the table—excepting Mr. Warley (for he has found his way here, after all). The dinner itself is a curious thing: Newspapers stuffed into a bowl become to their eyes a bunch of beautiful orchids; the mashed potatoes become oysters; and a bottle of Apollinaris becomes a bottle of Perrier-Jouet, '95. The conversation is lively, sparked by the quips of Mrs. Amesworth (who died years before). "Very good talk," Warley muses to himself as he takes his leave (550). Was there yet another engagement? He can't remember.

He takes a step forward. But where the pavement had been, "now there was nothing" (550).

"A Bottle of Perrier" (*Collected Short Stories* 2.511–31) is a real gem, distinguished by a steadily mounting sense of horror against the dreamy backdrop of an Arab palace lost in a vast desert. Young Medford has come here to enjoy the hospitality of his friend, the archaeologist Henry Almodham. While he waits for Almodham's appearance—he is reported to be away inspecting some ruins—Medford succumbs to the lethargy of the place. He lapses into a state where time and agency are meaningless: "The silly face of his watch told its daily tale to emptiness" and "the spasmodic motions of man meant nothing" (514). Days pass with only the servant Gosling for company. The water from the well is growing foul and the case of Perrier water, badly desired by Medford, has been lost. Gosling evades questions about Almodham's continued absence. Medford grows suspicious. The palace is becoming a prison. He wonders if Almodham never left in the first place, but is lying, concealed, spying on him. His isolation grows intolerable, and "he felt himself shut out, unwanted—the place, now that he imagined someone might be living in it unknown to him, became lonely, inhospitable, dangerous" (528).

As day by day Gosling's behavior seems increasingly malevolent, Medford wonders if the servant has slain Almodham, leaving his ghost to roam nightly among the towers and battlements. "[Medford] could almost feel Almodham reaching out long ghostly arms from somewhere above him in the darkness" (529). He knows now his life might also be in imminent peril.

Matters come to a climax when Medford barely escapes Gosling's attempt to throw him down into the well. Indeed, this is the well into which Gosling had hurled Almodham days before, the source of the only water in the place. As Medford and Gosling confront each other in a stalemate, "the moon, swinging high above the battlements, sent a searching spear of light down into the guilty darkness of the well" (531).

Finally, we come to "All Souls.'" We've been waiting. And so has the house that is its setting. It is perhaps the *quietest* story in the genre and its house the emptiest. Maybe. All Soul's Day seems to have had a special significance for Edith Wharton. Her autobiography, *A Backward Glance*, bears on the dedication page the inscription: "To the friends who every year on All Souls' Night come and sit with me by the fire." We don't know in this instance if she means *departed* or *living* friends. Elsewhere, she clarifies the remark, noting that this is the day when she thinks about "all my dear, dead friends" (quoted in Dwight 18). Only Walter de la Mare's "All Hallows" rivals its deceptive calm and quiet dread.[10] The narrative voice, surely Wharton's own, rejects the "turreted castles patrolled by headless victims with clanking chains" as the only proper settings for ghosting. Rather, "the comfortable suburban house with a refrigerator and central heating"—"as soon as you're in, *there's something wrong*"— sends a chill down the spine (293).

It is the last day of October and early snows are gathering. Newly widowed Sara Clayburn, against the advice of friends, has decided to remain in Whitegates rather than relocate to the big city. "Here I belong and here I stay," she declares (293). The house is open, airy, high-ceilinged, with electricity, central heating, and all the modern appliances. One afternoon, on All Souls' Eve, the snows are beginning to fall as Sara returns to the house after a walk. She meets a strange woman who vaguely explains she is on her way to the house to "see one of the girls." Presuming this refers to one of Sara's servants, Sara dismisses the encounter and continues on her way. But a stumble and a bad ankle sprain confine her to bed. The doctor is called in and orders her to remain quiet and as immobile as possible until a further examination can be done.

That night, after the servants have left her, Sara lies alone enveloped by a stillness so oppressive it robs her of her sleep. Something is very *wrong*. Her imagination begins to work overtime. With the first glimmer of dawn, she has the odd sense that furniture items are "stealthily regrouping themselves, after goodness knows what secret displacements during the night" (298). No one answers the summons of her bell. All the appliances, the telephone, and power sources have been cut off. No fire has been set in the grate. The servants have disappeared. An icy chill sets in. The snowy winter

---

10. S. T. Joshi pronounces "All Hallows" de la Mare's most powerful weird tale (*Unutterable Horror* 418–19). The massive, empty cathedral known as "All Hallows" seems to be open to a *transformation* of some unspecified kind, as if the decaying structure is *restoring itself* for some strangely "sinister and intimidating" purpose. As the terrified verger declares, "There are other wills than the Almighty's" (317).

light is relentlessly stark and bleak. And the "inexorable silence" has a quality she has never felt before: "It is as though it were not merely an absence of sound, a thin barrier between the ear and the surging murmur of life just beyond, but an impenetrable substance made out of the worldwide cessation of all life and all movement" (303). It seems to accompany her painful steps through the rooms, "as though she were its prisoner and it might throw itself upon her if she attempted to escape" (305).

She stumbles and loses her cane. Somehow, wracked with pain, she gets back to her bed and lies there in a house utterly and finally empty. She is so alone, "that the nearness of any other human being, however dumb and secret, would have made a faint crack in the texture of that silence, flawed it as a sheet of glass is flawed by a pebble thrown against it" (308). In my opinion, these are among the most compelling and disturbing pages in all of Wharton.

She reawakens to a house that's back to normal and attended by a solicitous doctor and servants. Against her protests, they deny her claims that during the mysterious thirty-six hours the power was shut off, the telephone line cut, the maid's bell silent, and the fireplace cold and untended. Why, Sara wonders, are they all lying to her?

But the weeks and months pass, and she gradually regains her sense of normalcy and calm. When the next All Souls' Eve arrives, events begin to repeat themselves: Sara again encounters the strange woman approaching the house. Alarmed, she leaves Whitegates in a panic and relocates to New York City, never to return.

An epilogue suggests that one of Sara's servants has been indulging in satanic rituals and that witchcraft from a nearby coven is responsible for the strange events that assailed her. All Souls' Eve, after all, admits the narrator, "is the night when the dead can walk— and when, by the same token, other spirits, piteous or malevolent, are freed from the restrictions which secure the earth to the living on the other days of the year" (316).

This concession to Gothic witchery is all very well and good, but it won't do. We know better. What assails Sara Clayburn is something else. Something worse. Something final. What afflicts her is "the fear that she might lie there alone and untended till she died of cold, and of the terror of her solitude" (308). The veils of Sara's life of privilege, comfort, and companionship have been ruthlessly ripped apart, isolating her in an innate, inescapable existential state, alone with the silent ghost of her mortality.

Written at the very end of Wharton's life, herself a woman who, like Sara, had been blessed lifelong with privilege, opportunity, and all the comforts of wealth and society, "All Souls'" is, declares Linda Costanzo Cahir, "the epigrammatic capstone not only to Wharton's life but to much of her fiction. Many of Wharton's characters are gregarious souls who lead lone lives. Even while participating active-ly in their societies, they remain souls-apart, and, by the end, go through experiences that leave them, in the end, fully alone" (87). Alone, that is, with the "dark undefinable menace" that had dogged her since her youth.

Wharton's diary entry in 1924 states: "What I recall is of a lone life, and what I have gone through has made me alone" (quoted in Cahir 87).

Works Cited

Bleiler, E. F. "Introduction" to *The Collected Ghost Stories of Mrs. J. H. Riddell*. New York: Dover, 1977. v–xxvi.

Blum, Deborah. *Ghost Hunters: William James and the Search for Scientific Proof of Life After Death*. New York: Penguin, 2006.

Cahir, Linda Costanzo. *Solitude and Society in the Works of Herman Melville and Edith Wharton*. Westport, CT: Greenwood Press, 1999.

de la Mare, Walter. "All Hallows." *The Collected Tales of Walter de la Mare*. Ed. Edward Wagenknecht. New York: Alfred Knopf, 1950. 288–319.

———. *The Return*. In Edward Wagenknecht, ed. *Six Novels of the Supernatural*. New York: Viking Press, 1944.

Dwight, Eleanor, ed. *Edith Wharton: An Extraordinary Life*. New York: Harry N. Abrams, 1994,

Fedorko, Kathy A. "Edith Wharton's Haunted Fiction." In Lynette Carpenter and Wendy K. Kolmar, ed. *Haunting the House of Fiction: Feminist Perspectives on Ghost Stories by American Women*. Knoxville: University of Tennessee Press, 1991. 80–107.

Hamlin, Joanne. "The Private and Published Louisa May Alcott." *Helicon Nine* No. 4 (Spring 1981): 84–90.

Joshi, S. T. "Introduction" to *The Cold Embrace: Weird Stories by Women*. New York: Dover, 2016.

———. *Unutterable Horror: A History of Supernatural Fiction*. 2012. New York: Hippocampus Press, 2014. 2 vols.

Kerr, Howard. *Mediums and Spirit-Rappers and Roaring Radicals: Spiritualism in American Literature, 1850–1900*. Chicago: University of Chicago Press, 1972.

Lewis, R. W. B. *Edith Wharton: A Biography*. New York: Harper & Row, 1975.

Stemman, Roy. *Spirits and Spirit Worlds*. Garden City, NY: Doubleday, 1976.

Tibbetts, John C. *The Furies of Marjorie Bowen*. Jefferson, NC: McFarland, 2019.

Wharton, Edith. *A Backward Glance*. New York: Touchstone, 1998.

———. *The Collected Short Stories of Edith Wharton*. Ed. R. W. B. Lewis. New York: Charles Scribner's Sons, 1968. 2 vols.

———. *The Ghost Stories of Edith Wharton*. New York: Popular Library, 1976.

Wood, Ann D. "The Scribbling Women and Fanny Fern: Why Women Wrote." *American Quarterly* 23, No. 1 (Spring 1971): 3–24.

The Mysteries of the Worm

Darrell Schweitzer

You who would learn the mysteries of the Worm
must first enter into the kingdom of the Worm,
waiting in that narrow house
until all flesh is stripped away,
all putrid organs devoured,
and even bones are left
rotting in the damp and the dark.

Then, assuming no demons or angels await
to carry you off,
you sink down through the world
like a stone dropped through pond scum
to grovel before the Worm King on his throne.

Perhaps you will become wise.

To climb back out
of that abyss
is a rare thing indeed.
Few try.
Fewer still succeed.

Those are the ones we fear.

The Slug

Jon Bockes

"You sure it was this cave?"

"It's all one cave, man. They all connect into each other, so yeah. It's this one."

Jeff snorted, blowing dust out of his nose. He'd come here to see foreign locales, meet exotic women, and have a good time.

But now he was in this dirty cave because Dustin had to chase rumors of weird shit.

Who cared if there were stories of a giant slug or whatever living down in these Chinese caves? You could have a giant slug in a zoo and he still wouldn't care.

Dustin had insisted it was a big deal. "This isn't some ancient legend. People saw it recently."

"Oh, yeah, great. I always wanted to see a giant slug."

Dustin, apparently, had not realized he was being sarcastic.

If he hadn't gotten so drunk the night before last, he wouldn't have given Dustin half his money to go rent the equipment. If he hadn't woken up hung over—and alone, for fuck's sake—he might have been able to talk him out of the trip.

But once Dustin had rented the stuff and booked the tickets on the bus, he didn't want to let that money go to waste. 'No refund' policies were bullshit.

A day's travel by bus—away from the cities with the clubs and girls and everything interesting—and here they were.

He'd admit that the big karst pillars were pretty cool. Not worth all this, but they were cool. He took a few pictures.

"Send me those later," Dustin said. "I'm so glad you brought your good camera."

They'd started down into the caves. There was a tour group, but Dustin slipped the guide a few bills and he pretended not to notice as they wandered off. Jeff wondered if he'd get in trouble for that. This was China: wouldn't they do something terrible to him?

I mean, he hadn't seen anyone being tortured, the place was actually pleasant and the people nice. But they probably didn't do that stuff out in the open.

It had taken a few hours to get off the beaten path, but now they were in areas that no one had gone down before. The caves here were pristine: there weren't even footprints in the dust.

"Try not to step on the cave pearls," Dustin said.

"Pearls? Are these like valuable pearls, or—?"

"They're natural rock formations. Just try not to step on them!"

Of course, they weren't the valuable kind of pearls. He sighed.

"How long are we going to stay down here looking for this slug?"

"Our bus tickets back aren't until tomorrow afternoon. We could stay most of the night."

Jeff thought that was a bad idea. He didn't scare easily, but they were not expert spelunkers or anything close. These caves didn't seem dangerous at all; the tunnels were surprisingly smooth and large. Dustin put down markers as they went, so they could find their way back out.

But still. At night there might be animals about or something.

He mentioned that thought. "We're in a cave," Dustin replied. "Past the mouth there's no difference between night and day."

Jeff kept quiet after that. Dustin was in one of his "smarter-than-thou" moods, and he hated feeling dumb in comparison.

They walked on, and he would glance down occasionally, aiming to avoid any of the "cave pearls." If there really were such things. The floors seemed cleaner here, as if something had scrubbed up the dust. It seemed weird, but he didn't bring it up to Dustin. His friend would just lecture him on how it was some natural process or something.

He was surprised when he did start to see little white spheres on the ground, though.

"Hey, I think I found some of those pearl things you were talking about," he said.

Dustin turned back, shining his light first at Jeff's face, then toward the ground.

Dazzled, Jeff covered his eyes, and when he uncovered them he saw Dustin kneeling.

"Wow, this is a huge one," he said, peering at the stone.

Jeff could imagine that, for a pearl, it was pretty big. Maybe three fingers wide.

"You think they're valuable?" he asked.

"Don't be stupid. We can't sneak these out in our pockets; they'd catch us. And anyway, I don't think so. Only a geologist or something would want them." He frowned. "Maybe they're so big because—"

A white object dropped down and hit Dustin on the head. He flinched; it was a pearl as big as the others, which went bouncing away into the darkness after hitting his skull. Jeff followed it with a sharp flick of his flashlight.

"Ow! Damn it, Jeff, that—"

Dustin started to lift his head, but before his eyes even met Jeff's something enormous came down. Jeff felt the rush of air as it hit the ground, making a heavy thump that shook the cave.

It was almost black, and Jeff stumbled away from it. Was the cave collapsing? The thing was like a pillar, somewhat smooth, not like rock. It had an oily sheen and it had come down—

Right on top of Dustin. He looked down, seeing the red splatter. It hadn't just been air that hit his legs. The bottom of his pants were soaked in blood.

"Aahhhh—" he breathed, panic overwhelming every other sense. He ran.

Stumbling over rough patches and stalagmites, he went as fast as his legs could take him. He'd been the sporty one with the good legs, he was fast.

But when he glanced back, it was like a solid wall of the strange oily blackness. It was keeping up with him.

A scream escaped his lips and adrenaline made him faster. He looked forward again just in time to avoid hitting a wall, and darted down one side path. He didn't know which was the right one, he didn't even remember a Y-section.

The black thing hit the wall in front of him. It was again like a pillar, a thick limb that flattened against the stone like a gel. He turned, slipping on a wet patch, and tried to go the other way.

Boom. Another black pillar hit that wall, trapping him.

Pressing his back against the wall he'd almost crashed against, he faced the thing that followed him.

It wasn't a cave collapse, though he'd already realized that at some point.

It was a giant black mass that bubbled and oozed. It had extended huge arms that simply grew out of its shapeless body; those had been the pillars that blocked his way. Now it was coming closer.

His flashlight went over it, and he realized it was not uniformly black. An enormous eye, alien and bizarre, like no animal eye he'd ever seen, was looking at him. Its pupil shrank under the light, but it seemed otherwise unbothered.

It was the slug thing Dustin had wanted to find. It had to be.

He had found it, a lot closer than he probably wanted. Oh god, Dustin . . .

The pillar-like arms of the thing seemed to be melting, drooping down in great, thick droplets as it brought them closer to him, hemming him in even tighter.

The giant eye also came closer, but now its movements were slow. It was savoring this.

He was terrified beyond all reason; a warmth in his pants told him that he'd lost control of his bladder. There was no escape here, but he wasn't going to go down entirely like a punk.

The thing kept getting closer, and when it was only a few feet away he threw his flashlight as hard as he could at its eye.

He expected it to flinch, maybe even recoil. It didn't even blink.

The flashlight bounced off its eye. Parts of the plastic case shattered off and it fell to the floor, flickering but still working.

With nothing left but words, he used them. "Fuck you!" he yelled. "Go to hell, you fucking slug!"

Then he heard Dustin's voice.

"Don't be stupid."

It was him, his voice. Said in the exact same inflection as when his friend had rebuked him only a little while ago.

"This is a huge one. I don't think—you—can sneak out. Damn it, Jeff, it would catch—you."

Nearly every word, Dustin's voice. Exactly as he'd said them.

Except for the word "you." That was in his voice.

His. It had been listening and it understood. It was echoing the words back to him. Talking to him in the words it had overheard.

He felt dizzy.

"You understand me?" he asked.

"Understand you," it said. Its voice was his.

He noticed that a hole had opened near its eye, and it vibrated in time with the words. A slew of other holes opened around the eye, and a cacophony of voices came pouring out. He didn't know these voices, but they were all people. Some were in English, others Chinese. The latter he couldn't understand; his grasp of the language was poor, especially when the voices were panicked. And screaming.

But the ones in English: it was all too clear that they were the voices of previous tourists the thing had met.

"Oh god, what is that?"

"It's got Ted!"

"Please god, please god, please god."

"Run, run, get away!"

"Jesus, please deliver me—"

They all stopped, cut off at the same instant, and the slug crashed one of its huge limbs down to the ground for emphasis.

And he understood that it had been killing people who came down here. Learning from them.

Was it telling him this just to terrify him?

Its limbs were pressing in closer, and he realized that smaller tendrils were growing off of them, coming toward him. He flinched back, cracking his head on the stone wall. He hardly noticed.

"Don't move," a voice said from the creature. It was a man's. "Won't hurt, just a moment. Better not." Each fragment of sentence spoken in a different voice.

He screamed and flailed, and the small tendrils wrapped around his limbs, holding his arms with a strength that seemed far beyond their thin girth.

"Don't be stupid," Dustin's voice said again.

He didn't get a chance to reply. Something horribly cold, slimy, and oily pressed against his head from both sides.

He felt a tickling in his ears, then a sharp pain. He yelled, but heard nothing.

It had pierced his eardrums. He felt as if he were floating, and he wondered if this was what dying was like. He envied Dustin, that he had gotten to go so quickly. This seemed worse.

Worse . . .

Worse . . .

The word echoed in his mind strangely, feeling as if it were not his own thought. What in God's name . . .

Name . . .

Name . . .

What is your name?

"Jeff," he said, automatically. His mouth moved, but he didn't hear himself say it, even if the movement came naturally.

Jeff.

He heard his name, spoken by an alien voice, within his mind.

A connection was forming, a bridge, between the thing and

him. He was feeling its intrusion more and more, and flashes of memory—strange, distorted visuals from a hundred eyes. It felt cold inside his head, as if something with a body temperature lower than his were inhabiting him.

Memories, words, thoughts, images came to mind, triggered by something. He thought of his parents, of his girlfriend back home, of triumphs and failures, embarrassments and crowning moments.

His emotions flickered through various states; one second he felt insanely happy, the next sad, and the next terrified. Switches in his brain being flipped at random.

Was it intentional? Or just accidental that it was making him see these things?

Then he just felt calm. He felt . . . a oneness with the world around him. Any desire he had to fight drained away.

The presence in his mind was becoming something . . . not pleasant, but tolerable. He felt a connection to it as if it were a part of him.

Information began to flow both ways, and it suddenly made sense why it had crushed Dustin. It was simply a practical move: if the two had fled in separate directions, it could only catch one. While leaving some alive had brought more people down to it, that was both good and bad.

Not that it feared people. He couldn't understand why, though; when he considered it, there was simply a gulf of emptiness, a vastness that was larger than anything he could imagine.

It was intelligent, more intelligent than he was. It wasn't torturing him, it wanted to understand. It had encountered others and learned small bits from them.

But at some point, it had encountered a man who knew much about the human brain. A . . .

The word didn't exist in its vocabulary, but his mind was able to provide the word. Surgeon.

Yes, a surgeon, one who specialized in the brain.

When it picked his mind, it learned so much about the meaning of the structures in the organ. Its confusion and need to learn made sense, as now he knew that the thing normally had nothing like a brain.

It was not a slug; what a horribly inaccurate term to use. It was nothing like any other life form that existed on earth. Not alien, but a whole different type of life.

Even the origin of the pearls was made clear; its viscous body absorbed dust as it moved, which it compressed and expelled in that form.

It was to him that it was applying the surgeon's knowledge of the brain. He found himself smiling. This was an honor for him, in a sense. A massive step down for the being even to be interested in something like him.

Something tickled his mind about that, it bothered him, but it was hard to understand why. He was like an ant before a human.

But sometimes humans took an interest in ants, didn't they?

Dustin liked ants. That memory flickered through his mind, and he was startled to recognize a thought that was purely his own.

Dustin was the smart one, not him. He was just a dumb jock, but at least that meant he was strong. He focused, trying to reassert control over his own body and break free from the grip of the thing. But his limbs would not obey him, and all he found himself doing was straining until he saw stars.

"Get off me!" he yelled, but heard nothing through his ruptured ears. Oh fuck, had it gone into his brain through his ears?

A thought, purely alien, rumbled through him like a seismic wave. Unlike the whispers from earlier, this was overwhelming, and he found himself almost physically rattled.

Dustin was the smart one. I should have kept him alive, the thought said. You'll just have to do.

"What in God's name are you?" he asked. Or maybe he screamed it; he couldn't tell his own volume anymore.

A thought that formed itself into sounds slid into his mind, and he knew it was the name of the beast. The name itself was like a stab of fear, of wrongness, that seemed like a cruel and terrible stain on reality.

Worse than that, he felt a despair so crushing, so all-consuming, that it drained him of all hope, all will to struggle. It was a mere glimpse into the slug and he saw as well its greatest desire: an ending to all things.

His arms went slack, and he could not even attempt to resist anymore. His arms were yanked, pressure exerted upon his shoulders. He couldn't turn his head, but he looked as far to the sides as he could.

The thing was engulfing his arms in its body, consuming him. He felt it beginning to encapsulate his head. A black, tar-like substance dripped down his face, going over his eyes and then even his mouth. He couldn't breathe, but he did not care, and he was glad it was ending.

There was a wrenching feeling and a sharp pain. But it didn't last long.

With shuffling steps, a man emerged from the cave.

"Where have you been?" Li Qiang said, both annoyance and concern in his voice. His English was imperfect, but still understandable to most Americans. "You were supposed to come out much sooner!"

It was one of the dumb Americans who had slipped him money to be able to go off the beaten path. He never should have taken their money; it always led to problems when tourists did that.

The man didn't reply, but he looked a bit pale, the guide thought. "Are you okay?" he asked.

"Okay," the man replied, his voice a little odd.

"And where is your friend?"

"Friend okay," he replied.

Li frowned. He spoke English well enough to know that was wrong. He was about to ask for more, but then the man reached out, pressing a roll of bills into his hand. It was a lot of money.

The American said nothing but smiled at him. It looked strange, but not distressed.

A shiver went down Li's spine, and he didn't know why.

"You want me to be quiet?" he asked.

"Be quiet," the man replied.

The guide nodded. The American had a ticket back to the city, and he didn't want the man to miss it. As he led him to the bus, he almost spoke a few times. But there was just something about this American that creeped him out. It hadn't been like this yesterday. Had he just not noticed because his friend had done most of the talking?

The idea that he had killed his friend didn't escape Li. But he was not eager to report it. Small bribes would get minor punishment, so long as he admitted to it. If the man had killed his friend, however, he might be considered an accessory to murder.

He was grateful when the American got on the bus heading back to Guilin. He would go and look for the other American later, but he didn't want to do it while this one was here.

Li didn't feel safe around the man. Some instinct seemed to give him pause.

He'd never felt that unsafe before, at least not outside the caves. It was a new feeling, and he didn't like it.

The only time he did feel that way had been those few instances when he had gone deep into the caves himself. Sometimes, when he'd gone too far, alone, he'd felt as if something were watching him.

Now, as the bus pulled away, he saw the American move to sit at the very back. His head moved as if he were coughing, and once he stopped, he seemed to be holding something in his hand. He casually dropped it out the window.

Li wasn't sure why, but he approached the spot. The road here was asphalt, and the thing the man had dropped was white, easily visible as it rolled toward the side of the street where it sloped down into a ditch.

He met it at the edge and picked it up.

The American couldn't have coughed this out. It was a pearl, as wide as three of his fingers.

He had seen things just like this before, in the caves. In those deep places where he had felt the eyes upon him.

The bus was nearly gone out of sight now, and he had the sudden urge to run and make a phone call and get it to stop.

He was breathing faster, an unreasonable panic spreading through him.

He was too afraid, because he had a feeling he knew what had walked out of that cave—and it was not a tourist.

The bus stopped at other stations, more weary, city-bound tourists climbing aboard. Seats grew scarce.

A middle-aged woman moved down the bus, looking for a seat, and hoped that she wouldn't have to spend the rest of the trip standing. At the very back, she saw space next to a young man who looked as if he were also American. He was tall and muscled, and she smiled politely to him before sitting down.

"Those caves are something, aren't they?" she asked him cheerfully.

He seemed to mull over his reply for a time before answering simply. "They are something."

"I'm so glad I decided to come here. There's still such an untamed beauty about this place."

The man looked out the window as if noticing the trees and forests for the first time. "Yes." He said it oddly, as if trying out the sound for the first time.

"Are you okay?" she asked.

"Yes," he said again. He smiled, though she found it forced. "Tired."

She chuckled. "Oh, I know! The caves are so deep, it's like they go on forever."

"Not forever," he replied. "I wish they did."

"What, do you want to walk all the way home down there?" she asked, amused.

He stared at her for a long time. "They don't go home. But they also don't go where I want."

She was starting to regret picking this seat, and fell quiet. The bus rumbled along, but after a time she couldn't help but ask another question.

"We're close to the city," she said. "Just a flight home for me, my vacation is almost over. What about yours?"

The young man smiled again. It was a genuine smile, but one that disturbed her for reasons she couldn't put into words.

"Yes," he answered. "The end is close."

Et in Arcadia Jack

Adam Bolivar

I came upon a laughing youth,
    Who frolicked in the grass;
He made me feel my years in truth,
    And by him lay a lass,

Who played upon a haunted lyre
    An ancient mournful tune,
Which filled me with a strange desire
    To dance beneath the moon.

A troop of faeries soon emerged,
    Wild-haired, besot with glee;
My mind right then to madness verged;
    The youth, by Zeus, was me!

And in the grass I found a key,
 Which opened wide the thorn;
I entered it; it beckoned me
 Into a land forlorn.

Bright summertime turned gloomy black,
 Into a sullen dream;
I walked with poise for I was Jack,
 And by me flowed a stream.

The lass was here; she wore a hood
 Like blood all scarlet red;
The only thing in this drear wood
 That wasn't of the dead.

She sang her tune, that ancient tune;
 An owl screeched from a tree;
Her wings held stars, her eye the moon,
 And it was fixed on me.

But Hades had no hold on me,
 Nor could Death's scythe come near,
For I was Jack; I had the key
 To fly from sphere to sphere.

Finding Sherlock Holmes in Weird Fiction

Nancy Holder

NOTE: I have expanded upon some of the material from a previous essay, "Finding Sherlock Holmes in Science Fiction and Horror," which was published in *Sherlock Holmes Is Everywhere!* I used material from that essay in a presentation by the same title at the West Coast Sherlockian Symposium, 12 October 2019, in Portland, Oregon. Page numbers for the Sherlock Holmes stories are taken from the Doubleday edition of the canon. My edition is published by Barnes & Noble. A simple way to verify the possession of a Doubleday version is to ensure that the preface by Christopher Morley is included.

To begin at the beginning, or the birth of a fictional superstar:

Philip Gold, a member of the Antiquarian Booksellers of America and a leading expert on collecting "Sherlockiana," opined in "Clues on Collecting Sherlock Holmes," a brief article for the online book aggregator AbeBooks.com, that Sherlock Holmes is probably the most recognized figure in all literature. People from the world over who have never read a Sherlock Holmes story know who Sherlock Holmes is—and this was true even before the recent explosion of interest engendered by the Robert Downey, Jr. films and Holmes TV shows starring Jonny Lee Miller (*Elementary*) and Benedict Cumberbatch (*Sherlock*). Gold went on to estimate that as of 2006 (fourteen years ago!) more than 30,000 works relating to Sherlock Holmes had been published, and more are published each year.

As of 12 June 2020, members of 261 Sherlock Holmes societies and recognized Baker Street Irregular "scions" play "the Grand Game," a metafictional exercise in writing, reading, and discussing yet more articles about Holmes and his world as if he and Dr. John

H. Watson, and all their company, were/are real people (McSwiggin). This conceit runs deeper, asserting that Watson actually wrote the stories in the Holmes canon (with a few exceptions), and that Sir Arthur Conan Doyle merely served as his "literary agent"—since, being the more famous of the two authors, "Conan Doyle" was able to use his name to get Watson into print. As an "invested" Baker Street Irregular (my canonical name is "Beryl Garcia"), I am one of these True Believers and I play the Game. In this essay, I will include an argument that the Game provides a convenient portal for authors to build weird fiction around him.

Despite his characterization as a nonbeliever in the fantastic, Holmes has been imagined and re-imagined in all the subgenres that weirdness contains, with successful presentations in bona fide, more narrowly defined weird fiction as well. There is a demonstrable continuum of the weird running through the original Holmes works by Conan Doyle that propels this popular character into the speculative genres of science fiction, fantasy, and horror and into the realm of authentic weird.

First, a bit of background about the creation of Sherlock Holmes. In 1882, Scotsman Sir Arthur Conan Doyle (1859–1930) was a medical doctor with a skimpy practice in Portsmouth, England. Conan Doyle initially aspired to life as a busy physician enjoying a robust, part-time writing vocation on the side. After graduating from medical school, he struggled to make a living, succeeding at neither of his endeavors. Although he attempted to level up professionally by specializing in ophthalmology, he abandoned his studies in Vienna halfway through. After a severe bout of influenza, in 1891, he decided to abandon his medical practice and concentrate on his writing (Lellenberg et al. 293–94).

Conan Doyle was a born storyteller, regaling his fellows as a child at a Catholic boarding school with stirring tales of derring-do in return for pastries and admiration (Lellenberg et al. 29). His first published work was "The Mystery of the Sasassa Valley," published in 1879 while he was still in medical school. Sporadic sales of medical articles (he was the first physician to debunk the supposed cure for tuberculosis claimed by Robert Koch [see Goetz]) and fiction sales followed—with the emphasis on sporadic.

At twenty-seven he wrote (in less than three weeks) *A Study in Scarlet,* the first story starring Sherlock Holmes. After some rejections, it appeared in the 1887 issue of *Beeton's Christmas Annual.* This "shilling shocker" replete with evil Mormons did not garner much interest, nor did Holmes's second appearance, in another novel, the exotic *The Sign of Four* (a.k.a. *The Sign of the Four*), published in *Lippincott's Monthly Magazine* for February 1890.

Conan Doyle then decided to switch to the short story form for subsequent Holmes stories and, more importantly, fixed on the notion of Sherlock Holmes and Dr. Watson as recurring characters in an ongoing series of such stories, essentially creating a brand. The first Holmes short story, "A Scandal in Bohemia," was extremely well received when it was published in the *Strand Magazine* in July 1891.[1] It was the first of twenty-three stories that Conan Doyle wrote for the magazine before (seemingly) killing Holmes in a face-off with his nemesis, the criminal mastermind Professor Moriarty. (The order of stories in the Doubleday version reflects the fact that one story, "The Adventure of the Cardboard Box," was published later in the United States than in England.) Conan Doyle dispatched Holmes because Holmes was overshadowing everything else he wrote. He himself felt that the Holmes stories did not represent his best effort, and wished to concentrate on (and be recognized for) weightier work. Though he also created another series character, Professor Challenger, he wrote poetry, historical novels, two histories of the Boer War, and toward the end of his life devoted himself to writing and lecturing about his great passion, Spiritualism.

But throughout his life, Holmes was the "one fixed point" that readers clamored for, and after a ten-year break Conan Doyle resur-

---

1. "When 'A Scandal in Bohemia' was published in *The Strand Magazine,* circulation rose immediately" (Willis).

rected Holmes with the novel *The Hound of the Baskervilles* (serialized in the *Strand* in 1901–02). More Holmes short stories and another novel followed. In total, the Sherlock Holmes "canon" of novels and short fiction contains four novels and fifty-six short stories.

Holmes pastiches—including some written by Conan Doyle himself—emerged concurrently with Holmes's early appearances. J. M. Barrie, author of *Peter Pan* and a friend of Conan Doyle, wrote an anonymous "skit" titled "My Evening with Sherlock Holmes," which was published in the 28 November 1891 issue of the magazine *Speaker*. Arthur Bartlett Maurice and Frank Sidgwick discussed Holmes in the *Bookman* and the *Cambridge Review*, respectively, in the first decade of the 1900s (Lellenberg et al.). In 1913, *Sherlock Holmes Saving Mr. Venizelos* (English translation) was serialized in Greek in *Hellos*, a Greek magazine. It is also considered to be the first Greek detective novel (Wikipedia).

The image of Sherlock Holmes that the public carries—deerstalker cap, Inverness cape, curved Calabash pipe—is the result of Sidney Paget's illustrations for the *Strand* and, in America, Frederic Dorr Steele's Holmes portraiture in *Collier's Weekly* and other publications, as well as Holmes's portrayal by the actor William Gillette (1855–1937). Gillette depicted Holmes on stage and screen, appearing more than 1300 times onstage, in a silent film, and on the radio (*The Conan Doyle Encyclopedia*). While it is true that the literary Holmes sensibly would have worn a flapped cap on the occasions when he went to the country, when he was in gaslamp London he would have more correctly worn a top hat or bowler. He also smoked cigarettes and cigars, and may have taken snuff from a jeweled snuff box given to him by the King of Bohemia ("A Case of Identity" 191). He favored three types of pipes, none curved like a calabash (*Pipes and Cigars*). Ironically, in pastiche, the presence of deerstalker plus curved pipe is enough for readers to deduce that the character they are reading about is Sherlock Holmes. (This post-literary positioning is not, of course, unique to Sherlock Holmes: in current popular mythology, Dracula cannot walk in daylight, though in Bram Stoker's original novel, he can . . . and does.)

Another way to code for Holmes is to use the term "consulting detective." Conan Doyle was inspired by two precursors. Edgar Allan Poe's C. Auguste Dupin was an amateur who chose to solve mysteries for fun. He was unaffiliated with a police force, unlike Conan Doyle's second major inspiration, Émile Gaboriau's Monsieur Lecoq, who worked for the French Sûreté (Blathwayt). Holmes chose to make a profession of solving crimes and was, therefore, the world's first consulting detective.

Rather than relying on chance, coincidence, and/or lucky breaks, which can be found in detective fiction contemporary with Holmes (such as "Who Killed Zebedee?" by Wilkie Collins, published in 1881), Conan Doyle crafted Holmes such that scientific observation and logic served as his primary deduction tools (O'Brien). In "The Adventure of the Copper Beeches," Holmes declares: "Crime is common. Logic is rare. Therefore it is upon the logic rather than the crime that you should dwell" (317). Holmes deals in facts based on hard evidence: "It is a capital mistake to theorize before one has data. Insensibly one begins to twist facts to suit theories, instead of theories to suit facts" ("A Scandal in Bohemia" 163). Though Holmes is often portrayed as a machine-like logician, giving rise to discussions and presentations of him as someone on the autism spectrum, he despairs over his failures, is chivalrous toward women, and resorts to injectable drugs to ease boredom. However, another prevailing popular culture set of markers to indicate that the main character is Sherlock Holmes is that of a mystery-solver indifferent to social convention, clipped in manner, and uniformly disdainful of those who cannot keep up.

Unlike his creator, Holmes has no truck with the unexplained and zero interest in the occult. In "The Adventure of the Sussex Vampire," he declares: "This agency stands flat-footed upon the ground, and there it must remain. The world is big enough for us. No ghosts need apply" (1034). Yet Conan Doyle painted the

Holmes stories with wide brushes of the exotic: a puzzling family chant ("The Musgrave Ritual"); a poison that drove victims incurably insane ("The Adventure of the Devil's Foot"); the glamor of faraway India, and the murderous Andaman native Tonga with his lethal blowpipe (*The Sign of Four*); a voyeuristic visit to a Chinese-run opium den ("The Man with the Twisted Lip"); and the lurking, offstage menace of the violent American "secret" society, the Ku Klux Klan ("The Five Orange Pips").

Elements of science fiction and horror creep into the stories as well; so do cosmic awe and wonder. In *The Sign of Four,* Holmes says, "How small we feel with our petty ambitions and strivings in the presence of the great and elemental forces of Nature!" (121). And in "A Case of Identity":

> Life is infinitely stranger than anything which the mind of man could invent. We would not dare to conceive the things which are really mere commonplaces of existence. If we could fly out of that window hand in hand, hover over this great city, gently remove the roofs, and peep in at the queer things which are going on, the strange coincidences, the plannings, the cross-purposes, the wonderful chain of events, working through generations, and leading to the most outré results, it would make all fiction with its conventionalities and foreseen conclusions more stale and unprofitable. (190–91)

The Holmes story steeped most thoroughly in the traditional elements of horror is *The Hound of the Baskervilles.* This paean to Gothic sensibilities revolves around an ancient curse, a deadly monster on a desolate, boggy moor, and family secrets; it is drenched in an atmosphere of foreboding that matches Poe at his most eloquent.

Poe's literary fascination with premature burial was a possible reality that deeply troubled Victorians. To avoid this awful fate, they created "safety coffins" with spring-loaded lids, breathing tubes, and pulleys designed to ring aboveground alarm bells if the worst occurred (Tarazano). Conan Doyle exploited this creeping fear in "The Disappearance of Lady Frances Carfax," wherein the unconscious victim (Lady Carfax) is imprisoned inside an unusually large coffin in a secret compartment specially built beneath the actual corpse.

In "The Adventure of the Sussex Vampire," Holmes is asked to investigate a case that points to vampirism. Though he scoffs at the notion, his minute observations of the aberrant behavior of the dysfunctional members of the Fergusons, a blended family, provide clues as productive as the forensic evidence he collects—and the bizarre mystery is solved.

"The Adventure of the Creeping Man" offers a taste of science fiction—and a nod to Robert Louis Stevenson's *The Strange Case of Dr. Jekyll and Mr. Hyde.* (Though Stevenson and Conan Doyle never met, they admired each other's work [Wilcockson].) In this story, an elderly professor injects himself with langur serum to make himself more virile, to please his much younger bride-to-be. The freakish result is that the serum turns him into an atavistic sort of monkey-man who lurches down the halls and scales the walls of his home by means of ivy vines, terrifying his daughter, whose bedroom is on the second floor. Likewise, in "The Adventure of the Bruce-Partington Plans," stolen blueprints for a super-high-tech submarine go missing in 1895. Though the story was published in 1908, this was still a time when submarines were viewed much as contemporary readers might regard the technical marvels in James Bond or Mission: Impossible films. Conan Doyle's readers would have readily envisioned a War of the Worlds–style invasion of enemy submarines gliding beneath the waters of the Thames.

Writers of every generation since the birth of Holmes have written and/or edited material about him, including such luminaries in speculative fiction as Isaac Asimov (BSI), Poul Anderson (BSI), Anthony Burgess, Caleb Carr, Michael Chabon, David Stuart Davies (BSI), August Derleth (BSI), Philip José Farmer, Christopher Fowler, Neil Gaiman (BSI), Anthony Horowitz, Manly Wade Wellman (BSI), and many, many others, some of whom will be discussed later. (Disclaimer: I have written Holmes into pastiches, comic books, articles, and an online storytelling game.) There are so many pastiches that it is very nearly a rite of passage for authors to pen one (or many), as have Stephen King, Kim Newman, Naomi Novik, and Philip Pullman, and so many of my acquaintance that I hesitate to begin naming them all, for fear of overlooking someone.

Manly Wade Wellman and his son, Wade Wellman, wrote *Sherlock Holmes's War of the Worlds*. Holmes is a time traveler in *Exit Sherlock Holmes: The Great Detective's Final* Days by Robert Lee Hall. Recent science fiction and fantasy offerings alter Holmes such that he is a sorceress (*The Affair of the Mysterious Letter* by Alexis Hall) and a drug-addicted spacer teamed up with a sentient ship (*The Tea Master and the Detective* by Aliette de Bodard). Holmes is paired with doctors other than Watson in the anthology *Sherlock Holmes and Dr. Was Not* (edited by Christopher Sequeira; I have a story in this). And yet, despite changing Holmes's gender, setting, or companion, the marked state of the main character is transparently Sherlock Holmes.

The vast field of horror pastiches generally pits Holmes and Watson against concrete, if supernatural, adversaries: Loren D. Estelman's *Sherlock Holmes vs. Dracula* and Fred Saberhagen's *The Holmes-Dracula File* are straightforward examples. Holmes has also frequently gone up against Jack the Ripper, in books such as *A Study in Terror* by Ellery Queen (the pseudonym for the writing team of Frederic Dannay [BSI] and Manfred Bennington Lee);[2] *The West End Horror: A Posthumous Memoir of Dr. John H. Watson* by Nicholas Meyer (BSI); Michael Dibdin's *The Last Sherlock Holmes Story;* and dozens of other novels, novellas, and short stories. Enemies are unmasked; their vulnerabilities are pinpointed; they are (generally) vanquished. Though dressed in the clothes of horror, many of these pieces are in actuality classic Holmes caper-mysteries: the forces of evil may respond to mystical incantations or magical amulets, but

---

2. This is a novelization of the film by the same name; paperbackfilmprojector asserts that science fiction author Paul M. Fairman wrote "the Holmes section." See paperbackfilmprojector.blogspot.com/2012/05/study-in-terror-by-ellery-queen.html

respond they do. As Holmes says, "[W]hen you have excluded the impossible, whatever remains, however improbable, must be the truth" ("The Adventure of the Beryl Coronet" 315). As unworldly as Holmes's adversaries may appear to be, once he accepts that they are what they could not possibly be, he can quantify their natures and puzzle out the laws/rules/limitations of their existence, and apply his methods to defeat vampires, serial killers, revenants, zombies, mummies, werewolves, mad scientists, madmen, and maniacal cults. Thus they are creatures of materialism—concrete, limited, fathomable—and thus their stories do not "leave you [the reader] with many more questions than answers, " to quote Michael Moorcock's foreword to *The Weird: A Compendium of Strange and Dark Stories*, edited by Ann and Jeff VanderMeer (xii).

One might assume that pitting Sherlock Holmes against the crawling chaos of the Cthulhu Mythos of Lovecraft would yield tales that shambled into the sphere of truly weird fiction. Two candidates are both series of three novels: Lois Gresh's *Sherlock Holmes vs. Cthulhu* (*The Adventure of the Deadly Dimensions, The Adventure of the Neural Psychoses,* and *The Adventure of the Innsmouth Mutations*) and James Lovegrove's *Cthulhu Casebooks* series (*Sherlock Holmes and the Shadwell Shadows, Sherlock Holmes and the Miskatonic Monstrosities,* and *Sherlock Holmes and the Sussex Sea-Devils*). However, while both authors craft "creeper" horror stories from Lovecraftian tropes and details, neither can be said to transcend the convention of monster-to-be-fought to enter an intentional landscape inhabited (if that word can even be used) by the nihilistic deities that dwell out of space and time as created by Lovecraft.

There is a novel that approaches this benchmark, however, and that is *The List of Seven* by Mark Frost. There is a caveat: the main character is not Holmes, but Arthur Conan Doyle himself. Yet throughout the novel there are nods to the Holmes canon, and the overpowering presence of Conan Doyle-as-creator-of-Sherlock-Holmes is such that one Amazon reviewer described the book as "a love letter to Sherlock Holmes" and another assumed that the story is intended to serve as the catalyst for Conan Doyle's creation of Holmes. Indeed, it is difficult to engage fully with the text due to the temptation/distraction of embarking on a metafictional hunt for Holmesian Easter eggs.

This novel moves toward the territory of fiction that is strange, but not easily pigeonholed into the publishing boxes of genre—horror, science fiction, fantasy. It approaches the realm of interstitial fiction, requiring the reader to participate in the formation of its meaning by means of dwelling on an unknown and relentless off-page menace that hovers slightly out of reach. Nor does it answer the questions that commercial speculative fiction traditionally answers: *This is the villain. This is why he's doing what he is doing.*

The story opens with Conan Doyle attending a séance, at which a murder supposedly occurs, and he is attacked by hooded, faceless men, then saved by Alexander, a man he is unsure he can trust. He falls in with a second man, Jack Sparks, who informs him that Alexander is his brother, a bad seed from birth. Alexander tries to persuade Conan Doyle that Jack is insane.

As the novel progresses, Conan Doyle's loyalties ricochet back and forth à la *The Magus* by John Fowles. Once it becomes clearer that Jack is the brother to trust (and the prototype for Sherlock Holmes, down to and including his drug use), Conan Doyle becomes his Watson. The two join forces with other allies to stop Alexander's murder spree; as they move more deeply into the story, they discover that Alexander is part of the Dark Brotherhood, but they are uncertain what the ultimate agenda of the Dark Brotherhood is. In addition, the Dark Brotherhood serves a darker purpose, and weird phenomena occur that are beyond their ken: a house and one of Conan Doyle's books both melt in an interdimensional event. The story twists when Conan Doyle learns that he has been targeted for elimination because he sent out a novel that inadvertently mirrored some of the rituals and vocabulary of the Dark Brotherhood.

Madame Blavatsky, the founder of Theosophy, figures in the attempt to expose a nefarious conspiracy to help "the Dark Lord, the

Dweller on the Threshold" (who has other, unmentioned names) to break through from the other side, in part by being born into this world, as in Lovecraft's "The Dunwich Horror." Conan Doyle and company discover that pixies, faery folk, and other mythological creatures are real; as a prisoner Conan Doyle is served huge haunches of meat from enormous animals and uncannily oversized vegetables. As Vamberg, one of his captors, explains:

> "These elementals of the earth had once been united under the governance of a unifying spirit. . . . [A] powerful entity, worshiped by primitive people of the world in a variety of guises throughout history. A being tragically, savagely misunderstood by our religiously intolerant Western forbears—I won't mention any names—
>
> ". . . [W]ho have systematically engaged in brutal, senseless persecution of this entity and its legions of worshippers. The ascendancy of Western man, with his paltry, self-centered concerns and small-minded monotheistic obsessions, finally succeeded in driving this being out of the physical plane altogether, into a twilight, purgatorial existence." (460)

The novel ends with a momentary pause in the mayhem and the promise of worse to come in a sequel, almost losing its status as weird-ish by an epilogue that includes an appearance of baby Adolf Hitler—perhaps the Dark Lord's new vessel?

The Six Messiahs, the sequel to *The List of Seven*, reduces "the haze of distance," a term coined by sometime-weird author M. R. James, by imbuing six characters with visions of an impending apocalypse. Reminiscent of Stephen King's *The Stand*, the characters travel to an ersatz religious community of "The New City," in the American desert. It is ruled by Jack Spark's evil brother Alexander, and to defeat the great evil Alexander himself must be killed. Thus "the central wonder" is revealed, and though he has supernatural powers derived from the Dweller on the Threshold, in this story the unnamable is more "Dark Lord incarnate" than amorphous, creeping dread.

There are many forays into Holmes-based science fiction: the aforementioned *The Tea Master and the Detective* and *Exit Sherlock Holmes: The Great Detective's Final Days. Exit* poses intriguing questions until the mysteries fade once Holmes reveals that he and Moriarty are time travelers. Numerous anthologies of short science fiction include *Sherlock Holmes in Orbit, The Science Fictional Sherlock Holmes,* and others.

Two Sherlock Holmes pastiches by Neil Gaiman (BSI; canonical name: "The Devil's Foot") are worthy of note. One is planted firmly in the Cthulhu Mythos, and another is a tender fantasy about immortality. It was first published in the Lovecraftian anthology *Shadows over Baker Street.* As it is presented on Gaiman's website, the Hugo- and Locus award-winning "A Study in Emerald" describes an England called Albion, and the type font and graphics are decidedly steampunk. Winks at Spring Heel Jack, Vlad Tepes, and Dr. Jekyll feature in advertisements peppered throughout the text, created to look like a broadside. In "Emerald," the Great Old Ones warred against the human race, defeated it, and have ruled over humanity for seven hundred years. They are now perceived as benevolent, higher beings. "A Study in Emerald" assumes a substantial working knowledge of the Holmes canon, such that it becomes apparent [spoiler alert] that the narrator and his companion "the detective" are not Watson and Holmes, but Professor Moriarty and his lieutenant, Colonel Sebastian Moran. Holmes and Watson are the perpetrators in this story, members of the Resistance attempting to overthrow the Great Old Ones.

In "The Case of Death and Honey," also awarded a Locus award, Sherlock Holmes attends his dying brother Mycroft, who declares: "It is a crime, Sherlock . . . My death, in the specific. And Death in general. . . . A crime against the world, against nature, against order." To solve the crime of Death, Holmes travels to China, where he eventually brews tea with honey from a certain species of bee kept in hives on a specific hillside. He invites the owner of the bees to partake, and they both become immortal. He then sets sail for England: "I shall seek out Watson, if he still lives—and I fancy he does."

Although these two stories do not "ask more questions than they answer," they work with the Holmes tropes in interesting ways, pushing the envelope of what connotes a Holmes story.

Pushing further are the last of the two Holmes pastiches to be discussed, the metafictional novel *Holmes Entangled* by Gordon McAlpine, and the weirdest novel of all, *East Wind Coming* by Arthur Byron Cover.

In *Holmes Entangled*, Sherlock Holmes is the author of a found manuscript, who may or may not also be a multiverse version of the "private investigator" whom Jorge Luis Borges contacted in Buenos Ayres, Argentina, in 1943. (This framework allows McAlpine to depart from Conan Doyle's distinctive Dr. Watson voice, and the resulting narrative style makes for a straightforward, if anachronistic, read.) Borges informs the detective that he knew how to find him because he "dreamed of [him]."

He is being shadowed by a blond man with a gun, he tells the detective, and is so possessive of the manuscript that he insists upon sitting across from the detective while he reads it in its entirety. The framing device gives way as Holmes details a case in which Arthur Conan Doyle, "a writer of minor repute," approaches him for help after Conan Doyle attends a séance in which the then-current British Prime Minister Stanley Baldwin manifests himself in spectral form, though Baldwin is altered in significant ways: he was disabled in an accident when he was twenty-nine and never became prime minister. Furthermore, the spectral version suggests to Conan Doyle that he locate Holmes to investigate how there can be two of him ... and directs him to St. John's College at Cambridge, where Holmes is lecturing, in disguise as a German named Heinrich von Schimmel.

Like "the regular" Conan Doyle, this Conan Doyle is one of the world's leading authorities on Spiritualism, and he succeeds in enlisting Holmes's aid in unraveling the mystery of what he saw that night. Holmes agrees in part because Conan Doyle reminds him of Watson, who has, in this version, passed away. Holmes enlists the aid of Watson's widow, and eventually the two contrive to stash Conan Doyle in a safehouse to keep him from getting in their way—and also to ensure his safety, as it turns out that the British government is aware of the existence of multiple dimensions of existence—quantum mechanics—and wishes to keep such forbidden knowledge a secret.

Others aware of this explosive discovery include C. Auguste Dupin, who lends Holmes and Mrs. Watson a hand. In this version of the universe, Charles Baudelaire was Dupin's chronicler, not Edgar Allan Poe. But Poe was also an initiate, and was killed to quash his knowledge of the existence of multiverses (thus ending the mystery of his bizarre death in our dimension). Ernest Hemingway intrudes while Holmes and Mrs. Watson are reading about Poe's death to ask for Holmes's autograph.

The twists and turns in the novel are punctuated by questions of existence and meaning. Mrs. Watson says:

> "Well, if there existed countless versions of all of us, wouldn't we each be every manner of sinner, saint, and everything in between? In one universe or another, I mean. And, if that were so, then God's judgment on our souls would be impossible. Heaven and hell? All of it, threatened. And with that, the ultimate power of the Church." (123)

In this story, Holmes and Mrs. Watson contrive to persuade Conan Doyle to authenticate the Cottingley fairies in order to destroy his reputation, so that no one will believe his assertions that multiple dimensions exist. Mycroft is a "vile murderer." One might assume that the antagonists who pursue Holmes, Mrs. Watson, and Conan Doyle are specifically the Church and/or the government, but that is not clear.

However, the epilogue of the novel bookends the framing story of the opening, as Borges and "the detective" argue about whether Sherlock Holmes would truly have believed in such a phenomenon as parallel worlds. Borges cites passages from several of "our" versions of works in the canon to demonstrate that Holmes was no materialist, and that he has been misinterpreted: *"[H]ow often is imagination the mother of truth?"* (*The Valley of Fear* 802).

Further conversation reveals that Borges not only dreamed of the detective, but also that the P.I. was a character he had created in his dream, working on a case he had invented for him. The detective is taken aback . . . but nevertheless shoots Borges so that he can get rich off the sale of the manuscript himself.

Outside, a blond man aims his gun through the P.I.'s window . . .

And there the novel ends.

The strangeness of McAlpine's work is no match for that of *An East Wind Coming,* one of three novels in *The Universe of God-Like Men* by Arthur Byron Cover. (Disclaimer: Cover, like others in this essay, is a friend.) Written in 1979, *An East Wind Coming* is a dense, hallucinogenic Holmes novel written in a style reminiscent of Kurt Vonnegut (though Cover does not mention the author among his many influences in his afterword). Lush with popular culture and literary references and asides, the core of the novel is a Holmes-versus-Ripper story, but it is so coded and dense, written in such a bombastic style, that it enters the realm of weird with full authority. Among the influences Cover cites in his afterword (which is a handy decoder for the occasionally oblique descriptors for his pantheon of characters: "the consulting detective" and "the good doctor" are obvious; "the ace reporter" is Lois Lane; "the universal op" is Dashiell Hammet's "continental op"; "the shrew" refers to Elizabeth Taylor's portrayal of Katherina in *The Taming of the Shrew*) include the Firesign Theatre; Kafka; Gogol; Nicholas Meyer's *The Seven Per Cent Solution;* Basil Rathbone's portrayal of Holmes; the detective stories of Jacques Futrelle; Goethe; Sergio Leone; and Rima the Jungle Girl.

Reviewers compare this "dark, rich and unusual fantasy/science fiction novel" to Philip José Farmer's Wold-Newton universe (Amazon review as quoted on the back cover copy of the reissue of the novel by Strange Particle Press, 2016); "Imagine Michael Moorcock's *Dancers at the End of Time* reinvented by a chimera of Kim Newman, Philip José Farmer, and Belgian nihilist surrealist Jacques Sternberg and you'll get an idea of the strange atmosphere of this dense and mindwarping novel" (*Magazine of Fantasy and Science Fiction*, back cover copy of the reissue).

In the *God-Like Men* series, the population of Earth has been decimated and replaced with God-like Men (and women) who can transform themselves into anything they can think of becoming. But these beings, lacking meaning, take on the personas of literary, cinematic, popular culture, and comic book characters because they are easy to replicate and available. They lack purpose and meaning. When Jack the Ripper ("the demon") begins slaying them, "the consulting detective" stirs from his torpor of existential indifference to solve the crimes.

In the second paragraph from the end of the novel, the good doctor writes:

> It is [in] this compassionate spirit [of hope] that I submit these memoirs of tragedy and achievement to the public. It my intention that they play their part, however minor, in the collective journey of our race, in the great mysteries of the cosmos which, once unraveled, will eradicate the misery that has been preventing us from realizing our full potential for eons. (394)

While he does conclude on a more pessimistic note, the fact remains that this "decadent smorgasbord" conflates a Holmes story with a far-out, whacked out journey to fully weird fiction—the weirdest in this overview.

And what of Baker Street Irregulars and Game players such as I? We have embraced the reality of Sherlock Holmes and Dr. Watson as men "who have never lived, and so can never die." We can accept with ease that therefore, at least in this quadrant of the multiverse, they exist. To quote Maurice Lévy, from *Lovecraft: A Study in the Fantastic:* "It is well known that the truly fantastic exists only where the impossible can make an irruption, through time and space, into an objectively familiar locale" (36–37).

Works Cited

Barrie, J. M. "My Evening with Sherlock Holmes." (*The Arthur Conan Doyle Encyclopedia*, www.arthur-conan-doyle.com/index.php/My_Evening_with_Sherlock_Holmes)

Blathwayt, Raymond. "A Talk with Arthur Conan Doyle." *Bookman* 2, No. 8 (May 1892): 50–51. *The Arthur Conan Doyle Encyclopedia*. www.arthur-conan-doyle.com/index.php?title=A_Talk_with_Dr._Conan_Doyle

Bodard, Aliette de. *The Tea Master and the Detective*. Burton, MI: Subterranean Press, 2018.

Conan Doyle, Sir Arthur. *The Complete Sherlock Holmes*. 1905. New York: Barnes & Noble, 1992.

Cover, Arthur Byron. *An East Wind Coming: The Universe of God-Like Men Series*. New York: Berkley, 1979.

Dibdin, Michael. *The Last Sherlock Holmes Story*. New York: Pantheon, 1978.

Estelman, Loren D. *Sherlock Holmes vs Dracula*. Garden City, NY: Doubleday, 1973.

Frost, Mark. *The List of Seven*. New York: William Morrow, 1993.

———. *The Six Messiahs*. New York: William Morrow, 1995.

Gaiman, Neil. "A Study in Emerald." 2003. Website version: www.neilgaiman.com/mediafiles/exclusive/shortstories/emerald.pdf

———. "The Case of Death and Honey." In Laurie R. King and Leslie Klinger, ed. *A Study in Sherlock: Stories Inspired by the Holmes Canon*. New York: Bantam, 2011.

Goetz, Thomas. *The Remedy: Robert Koch, Sir Arthur Conan Doyle, and the Quest to Cure Tuberculosis*. New York: Gotham, 2014.

Gold, Philip. "Clues on Collecting Sherlock Holmes." www.abebooks.com/books/rarebooks/Avid-Collector/Sep06/sherlock-holmes.shtml

Gresh, Lois. *Sherlock Holmes vs. Cthulhu: The Adventure of the Deadly Dimensions*. New York: Titan, 2017.

———. *Sherlock Holmes vs. Cthulhu: The Adventure of the Neural Psychoses*. New York: Titan, 2018.

————. *Sherlock Holmes vs. Cthulhu: The Adventure of the Innsmouth Mutations*. New York: Titan, 2019.

Hall, Alexis. *The Affair of the Mysterious Letter*. New York: Ace, 2019.

Hall, Robert Lee. *Exit Sherlock Holmes: The Great Detective's Final Days*. New York: Scribner, 1977.

Lellenberg, Jon, et al., ed. *Arthur Conan Doyle: A Life in Letters*. New York: Penguin Press, 2007.

————. "The Ronald Knox Myth." *Sherlock Holmes Journal* 30, No. 2 (Summer 2011): 53–58. www.bsiarchivalhistory.org/BSI_Archival_History/Hard_Knox.html

Lévy, Maurice. *Lovecraft: A Study in the Fantastic*. Tr. S. T. Joshi. Detroit: Wayne State University Press, 1998.

Lovegrove, James. *The Cthulhu Casebooks, Book 1: Sherlock Holmes and the Shadwell Shadows*. New York: Titan, 2016.

————. *The Cthulhu Casebooks, Book 2: Sherlock Holmes and the Miskatonic Monstrosities*. New York: Titan, 2017.

————. *The Cthulhu Casebooks, Book 3: Sherlock Holmes and the Sussex Sea-Devils*. New York: Titan, 2018.

McAlpine, Gordon. *Homles Entangled*. Amherst, NY: Seventh Street Books, 2018.

McSwiggin, Mike. In conversation, Zoom meeting, Scintillation of Scions Cocktail Party, 12 June 2020.

Meyer, Nicholas. *The West End Horror: A Posthumous Memoir of John H. Watson, M.D.* New York: Dutton, 1976.

O'Brien, James. "Sherlock Holmes: Pioneer in Forensic Science." *Encyclopedia Britannica.* www.britannica.com/topic/Sherlock-Holmes-Pioneer-in-Forensic-Science-1976713

Peterson, Robert C., ed. *The Science Fictional Sherlock Holmes.* n.p.: The Council of Four, 1960.

Pipes and Cigars. "Russ's Views on Sherlock Holmes." www.pipesandcigars.com/faq/on-sherlock-holmes/1818123/.

Poggiali, Nathaniel. "*A Study in Terror* by Ellery Queen." *Paperback Film Projector* (16 November 2015). paperbackfilmprojector.blogspot.com/2012/05/study-in-terror-by-ellery-queen.html

Potts, Liza, "caretaker." *Sherlockian.net: The Portal About the Great Detective: Societies and Locations:* www.sherlockian.net/celebrating/locations/

Queen, Ellery. *A Study in Terror.* New York: Lancer, 1966.

Reaves, Michael, and John Pelan, ed. *Shadows over Baker Street.* New York: Del Rey, 2003.

Resnick, Mike, and Martin Harry Greenberg, ed. *Sherlock Holmes in Orbit.* New York: MJF, 1995.

Saberhagen, Fred. *The Holmes-Dracula File.* New York: Ace, 1978.

Sequeira, Christopher, ed. *Sherlock Holmes and Dr. Was Not.* Melbourne: IFWG Press, 2019.

The Arthur Conan Doyle Encyclopedia. "William Gillette." www.arthur-conan-doyle.com/index.php/William_Gillette

Tarazano, William D. "People Feared Being Buried Alive So Much They Invented These Special Safety Coffins." Collaborator Content, U.S. Patent and Trade Office and *Smithsonian Magazine* (26 October 2018). www.smithsonianmag.com/sponsored/people-feared-being-buried-alive-so-much-they-invented-these-special-safety-coffins-180970627/

Wellman, Manly Wade, and Wade Wellman. *Sherlock Holmes's War of the Worlds.* New York: Warner, 1975.

Wikipedia. "Sherlock Holmes Pastiches." en.wikipedia.org/wiki/Sherlock_Holmes_pastiches

Wilcockson, Ray, writing as "Altamont." "Robert Louis Stevenson's Letters to Doyle, *Markings* (21 June 2012). altamarkings.blogspot.com/2012/06/robert-louis-stevensons-letters-to.html

Willis, Chris. "The Story of the Strand." *Strand Magazine, History.* strandmag.com/the-magazine/history

Confessions

Stefan Grabinski

Translated by Mark Samuels

Introductory Note

The fiction of Polish author Stefan Grabinski (1887–1936) is eminently worthy of the attention of serious devotees of the literary weird tale. Since 1993, several volumes of his superlative stories have appeared in English translations, all by Miroslaw Lipinski (with one exception). These are the collections *The Dark Domain, The Motion Demon, In Sarah's House* (translated by Wiesek Powaga), *On the Hill of Roses,* and also the eerie novella *Passion.*

Grabinski's is an extraordinary literary realm riddled with bizarre metaphysics, *genius loci,* scarred eroticism, and the insane dead. To state that Grabinski deserves a place among the very greatest of weird fiction authors is, I hope, a claim that continues to gain ground.

In his essay "Confessions" ("Wzynania"), first published in the magazine *Polonia* # 141 (1926), Grabinski candidly reveals some of the motives lying behind the creation of his macabre stories, his personal struggles with ill-health and poverty, and his widespread critical neglect and even misinterpretation—disadvantages under which he was forced to labor until his death from tuberculosis at the age of forty-nine.—*Mark Samuels*

If one were to ask what I think the dominant feature of my own work is, I would say a feeling of great amazement, both wonder and fear at the same time—amazement at life and its mystery. "In the beginning there was astonishment"—this is how I would begin the first chapter of my autobiography. The wondrousness of life and its manifestations, the mysteriousness of events, the strangeness that we detect at almost every turn, I saw this even from my infancy, even before it was mingled with the adolescent sensation of anxiety. And then, subsequently, I detected it with the mature reflection of a man who is now forty years of age.

This, then, is my leitmotif, my basic "attitude" toward life and its affairs, the central rhythm through which vibrates the vital pulse of my consciousness. A secondary phenomenon is a passionate, stubborn, tenacious desire to explore wonderful, intoxicating depths, a desire to understand the elements, to bring mastery and order into the chaos of life-phenomena using the creative thought of my artistic worldview. There are those who deny me this right, hinting that my "philosophy" is an uncaring one and that it should remain as a purely private matter; what is more, they are trying to pigeonhole me with formulas of occult or psychiatric inquiry. They accuse me of being a cold, undercover doctrinarian in order to try and cut off my access to human sympathy. The only sure recourse for me against these "allegations" is the ascendancy of the "profane"; the opinions and remarks of my readers—those who do not go astray and analyse, but who, with the intuition of sympathy, share in my creative struggle . . .

Religion became the first way to marshal my imaginative life. In it I found a temporary shelter, a temporary haven, from the sea of storms that broke over my childhood. Raised under the watchful eye of a loving mother who was steeped in the spirit of a deep and sincere religious faith, I was myself a passionately devout child. But even then, my faith had marked mystical features; I felt the secret connections between the earth and the world beyond. I was already seeing life events, histories, and the fate of familial relations and outré acquaintances, all hidden deep under the surface of their ordinary meanings: I looked at everything as an enigma wrapped in a mystery. I saw symbols everywhere; my view both of the world and its people was already "parabolic." I felt the beauty of nature particularly strongly: even the simplest and most primitive landscape was a closed, newly individualized whole animated by a thought—it had its own strange, mysterious soul. Today I would equate this attitude of mine toward nature and so-called "dead things" with "panpsychism" . . .

As time passed, conventional faith was no longer enough for me; my awakened intellectual and sensual life cast me adrift: I felt the ground of dogmatism beneath me undermined. There was a period of rebellion and doubt. It was inflamed and intensified by painful transitions—chronic debilitations, more than five years of illness, hospitals, operations for a hand infection, and the lingering spectre of death. These were woeful experiences; the events between my fifteenth and twenty-first years cast a deathly pall over my later life—a shadow-cursed futurity. It was during this period that I learnt of the mysterious horror of existence and became convinced that Evil is just as powerful as Good. An outpouring of bitterness from those times produced my first tale, "Tawny Owl," written in 1906 and published in 1909 in a collection entitled *Exceptions: In the Shadow of Faith* (under the pseudonym Stefan Żalny).

There was a period of hard struggle in my life, difficult financial conditions, study at the university, lectures, medical treatments necessary to keep an impoverished man healthy; a gray void with almost no vivid memories for a decade. At that time, my first truly weird compositions were created, such as "The Menacing Farmhouse" (1908), "On the Hill of Roses" (1909), "Shadow" (24 March 1913), "A Villa by the Sea" (14 April 1912; later transformed into a play), "Strabismus" (1912), "On the Tangent," "Fumes" (15 July 1913), "Grey Room" (1915), and "In Sarah's House" (1915). Some of these tales, which appeared in Lwow magazines and dailies, were finally collected together as the book *On the Hill of Roses* (Krakow, 1918). The last two of these tales, together with several others I wrote later, made up the contents of further volumes entitled *Deranged Pilgrim* (Krakow, 1920) and *An Uncanny Tale* (Lwow, 1922). In 1919, the first edition of *The Motion Demon* was published in Krakow, and in 1922, *The Book of Fire* in Lodz.

From 1908 to 1918, I created in complete isolation, without even minimal moral support. In fact, I worked in a vacuum, in almost complete spiritual solitude, literally not finding anyone to encourage me to create and persevere except for my mother. I also sometimes had moments of severe self-doubt concerning the value of what I was writing, and said doubt was eagerly confirmed by the ironic smiles of the editors and publishers of literary journals in Lwow.

For nine long years, no one deigned to draw attention to the fact that I had created a new literary genre that has not appeared in Poland before. I am a pioneer of *phantasy* in the strictest sense of the word, of a *non-romantic fantasy*, with a singular and autonomous character. When one knows of literature only via a fifth of a tenth, and then solely in meager and scanty translations, when even I myself had not heard anything about the existence of Gustav Meyrink or Robert Louis Stevenson . . . it was through my own efforts I expressed the vision of life I had created; and it proved a Sisyphean endeavor. As a reward I received scant praise, some figurative pats on my shoulder and . . . a list of my "influences." As a general example, without wishing to prejudice the reader, I was advised of the influence of E. T. A. Hoffmann upon me, whose work I still hardly know and who is, for me, the quintessence of this genre of fantasy that I hate: boring, lengthy, and chaotic German romanticism is exactly my antithesis. Robert Louis Stevenson was cited only via Karol Irzykowski's article about me. In any case, it was not until a few years later (when I had mastered English) that I could actually read this author. Only three people in Poland drew attention to my work and were able to assess, in part, what I myself had brought to literature: from the older generation they were Wilhelm Feldmann and Józef Jedlicz, and, from the younger, Wilam Horzyca. In particular, I refer to the last article concerning *On the Hill of Roses* and *The Motion Demon* in the Warsaw magazine *Pro Arte* (March 1919 and in issue 6 of 1919), which was rendered in a beautiful prose style of precision and with a depth of thought that caught the tenor of my work perfectly and comprehensively.

However, this is not about the critics, it is about me—what I wanted at that period, how and what I was striving for in my work.

My amazement at the alterations in my life due to the agony that had blighted my youth was soon tinged with an apprehension of the fear and terror that is inherent in the unknown. The mystery of existence aroused both curiosity and dread. And these two aspects, wonder and fear, which, as I have said, constitute the essence of my works, were now augmented by the third element: the proactive imagination, with thought imposing order upon the chaos of mere phenomena and the creative will seeking to master the secrets of life and death. It cannot be denied that in taking this path of discovery there were echoes of my youthful religiosity, for I continued to regard the world as itself a symbol, one full of profound meanings; and in each separate manifestation of existence I sought for its spiritual core. I have an affinity with the works of Plato, Gustav Fechner, Henri Bergson, and William James, though I confess that ethical issues were not my primary concern; I first wished to validate my belief in the existence of an underworld and to confirm absolutely that the grave does not put an end to all things. The proof that this is so was provided by an examination of recondite and morbid states of the human soul, of certain latent psychic powers long thought dead, and of the *genius loci* of abandoned topographical regions. These are the subjects and concerns of my literary works. Allow me here to delineate some of them in particular because they have often been the victim of misinterpretations and error.

In "The Menacing Farmhouse" I sought to depict the brutalizing effects of a wild and desolate landscape on a sensitive individual trapped by destiny. His hideous crime, which forms the climax of the tale, is the result of a combination of two factors: that of sleeping in an abode within such an accursed region and also of the probable onset of a melancholic derangement. In the tale "On the Hill of Roses," the abnormally heightened sense of smell in the protagonist allows him to call up visions of the past, whose traces and palimpsests persist in an isolated villa.

Another variation on the theme of the *genius loci* and its effect on an individual is "Gray Room," in which the protagonist struggles against the recalcitrant soul of a former tenant. In "Shadow" a fratricidal murder is established in an amazing way as a consequence of replaying itself on a window curtain. "Strabismus" deals with the theory of the psychic duplication or possession by a deceased adversary (it is not merely a case of split personality, as one bungling critic claimed, even while erroneously applying the scientific label "schizophrenia," which is a different form of mental illness altogether—it will not do to confuse one malady with another).

In "A Villa by the Sea," which was latterly expanded and adapted into a stage play utilizing the symbol of Ryszard Norski's telepathic influence on the character Wrzecki, I delineated the enigmatic region of the human soul, which is free from the laws of physics and which, consequently, points to immortality as being its quintessence.

The story "On the Tangent" bears the mark of my most profound experiences and is an expression of my belief in the mystical ordering of the world; in it the character Wrzecki realizes that certain incidents that people think are accidental are actually part of a mysterious chain of events leading the individual to an ultimate fate determined by the will or by destiny.

The story "Fumes" (again from 1913), which I consider to be one of my best works, appeared at one time in Warsaw's *Pro Arte* journal. It caused a ruckus and almost resulted in a court trial. Someone dared to attach the hideous label of "pornography" to this tale of the metapsychical. The analysis showed only a lack of comprehension and insight. My prosecutor, a person unknown to me, was probably led astray by conflating the fantastical with realism, colored by the suggestion of homosexuality. Undoubtedly the story contains a gender problem, but is only so from a perspective of metaphysics. In my opinion, gender, as such, does not exist in the other world and the so-called feminine and masculine are confined to the sphere of this phenomenal world and subject to the stipulations of evolution and species differentiation. To demonstrate my theory I utilized our own native Polish belief in the so-called "Nocnice" or night-demon, a kind of medieval incubus, haunting a low tavern, and which takes the form of a male or female according to the gender of each "guest." Thus is explained the constant duplication and the alteration in sex between the host and the red-haired girl.

In "The Domain," the artist's imaginings are given substance and shape as persecuting specters, confined to a desolate villa that represents the soul of their creator. "The Problem of Czelawa," whose full meaning will be explained in my forthcoming dissertation on originality, raises, via symbolism, the issue of the relationship between our human empirical (earthly) self to our transcendental self and has nothing to do with the mental disorder of self-dissociation (which is the subject of Stevenson's *Dr. Jekyll and Mr. Hyde*) despite the insistence of some superficial critics. "Smoke Settlement" is a tale of the fantastic, rooted in the beliefs of totem-worshipping primitive peoples, and marked by the conviction that human spirituality does not perish but is an expression of the inextinguishable desire to surpass earthly concerns.

The tale "The Glimpse" (the last in the series *An Uncanny Tale*) is an attempt at a new approach to the problem of God and the Ineffable, and a symbolic representation of the creation of a yearning for "other shores"; the yearning awakened in the soul of one thought to be a maniac. I once wrote extensively and comprehensively concerning my opinions on the aetiology of some of the higher forms of insanity in the journal *Skamander* (February 1920). This article, entitled "From My Workshop," analyzed my tale "Machinist Grot" and also formed something of a commentary upon the whole collection entitled *The Motion Demon*. Only a separate study could do justice to the book. Such an undertaking here would significantly extend the framework of these "Confessions" and, therefore, I will not attempt to do so. I will instead limit myself to drawing the reader's attention to the fact that almost all the tales in that collection deal with different aspects of the same subject-matter or have their birth in one theme: railway motion and its profound, although seemingly lifeless, poetry. Only two people, both poets themselves, Józef Jedlicz and Wilam Horzyca, grasped the true tenor of this popular book, and for this I offer them my warmest thanks.

The final story cycle I have had published thus far is entitled *The Book of Fire,* and it is the weakest and least artistically successful. It constitutes a meditation upon the mysterious soul of this element of nature. The subject-matter, so to speak, gave me the topic for my first weird novel, *Salamander,* which emerged from the embers of the fiery prelude that was *The Book of Fire.* However, this would be only an external reading of the case. In point of fact, my novel has little to do with its smoldering elder sisters. *Salamander,* which has been correctly identified by one of the critics as the first Polish novel about sorcery, is again a work of symbolism and forms a new chapter in my literary output; it marks a transition toward ethical issues— the fight between Good and Evil.

This issue is explored in even greater depth when the symbolism of the struggle between white magic against black is transferred to the fields of philosophy and, partly, to politics, as in my newly published novel *Shadow of Baphomet.*

To conclude, I will add that the problem of Arhiman and Ohrmuzd still attracts me with irresistible charm and I intend to return to it in the near future, perhaps in a completely different mode of artistic expression.

Lwow, April 30, 1926.

Counter-Current

Michael Aronovitz

Even though Esther was six years old she knew what "NO TRES-PASSING" meant. She could read middle-school books like The Giver and Drums, Girls, and Dangerous Pie, thank you. Her big brother Isaac was nine. He played chess. He could do algebra. He was a show-off, and as usual, he wasn't going to go listening to his kid sister when he was playing "bad boy" with his friend Rickie-Jay on the other side of the rickety maroon picket fencing.

Esther walked along the ramshackle dividing line snaking its way down to the water; between the posts the boys looked jumpy and weird like an old-fashioned movie.

They were in the restricted area, where twenty feet or so beyond them there was an old wooden lifeguard tower missing the seat and a shanty behind that with its slanted overhang spilling dry green overgrowth that moved in the breeze. Esther halted, grabbed two of the fence slats, and put her face in between them. Down near the surf, both boys had their shirts off, sand caked on their legs and their ankles like slave-mud. They were trying to yank something straight out of the darkened beach floor. It looked like a big game board made of old wood or gray stone. They'd been unsuccessful trying to strain it up and out, and so they'd started hauling on it back and forth as if sharing an oar.

Something breathed on the air like static on clothes, and far out to the right the sky bristled. Lightning splintered across the horizon under black clouds that looked like Daddy's brow when he was thinking, and Esther grinned brilliantly into the glare, eyes glistening. It was a magic picture of a crooked crab tree dancing on the back of the water.

It flickered and thunder boomed out over the ocean. Esther felt it as much as she heard it, in her ankles and at the back of her throat, and she screeched with glee, bunny-hopping in place, hands folded in the praying shape under her chin.

Down left, the boys howled and clamped their hands to their ears. They were spiky stick figures posing for a moment, then dirty, hollering monkeys, hopping over the part of the fencing flattened down by the surf and running past Esther back up to the beach house.

Rain swept in across the dark water, which had become a marvelous witch's brew filled with invisible kings in their lacey robes diving into each other. They roared in some strange ancient tongue, and the downpour came on in a rush.

Esther closed her eyes, turned her face upward, and held out her arms. The rain felt like a million angels, a million kisses, a million whispers bursting with the secrets of the sea. Mommy was going to be mad. She had told Esther to "Go get the boys." That meant not getting soaked, not having her tuck-bun come out, her summer dress clinging. Mommy was a weirdo. She made Esther sad sometimes, because she was either mad or unmad, never happy like a smiley emoji. Mommy played solitaire on her laptop. Mommy watched CNN. Mommy worked on drawings with STRAIGHT LINES on her drafting board in the loft, and she sometimes took off her glasses, looked at Esther, and sighed. It was a nice sigh, because it meant Esther could crawl up into her lap for a hug, but Mommy never laughed, EVER.

Esther took a last, loving look at the shore. The low waves were tumbling in closer than before, and they backtracked leaving the sand flat and glistening. Over where her brother and his friend had been, the object half-stuck had been left at an angle. Esther blinked. She was sure the shape had been that of a game board with squared edges, but now the top had corners that curved. It looked like one of the tombstones in the old cemetery they'd gone to for gravestone rubbing last month at camp. She'd left her sneakers on the bus so she could walk barefoot, and she'd gotten a rash.

She moved down to the place where the fence potato-chipped down the sand. Daintily, she tiptoed between the splintery posts, careful not to step on the twisted wire ties, and super careful in the restricted area, avoiding the shining edges of the pointy shells.

A wave slithered up the sand, covering her feet and then receding, making things pull as if the world was balanced on the head of a pin.

The object in the sand moved a bit in the direction of the water's retreat.

What . . . ?

It was loose, and it was also no tombstone. It was an old boogie board. Esther took tiny steps forward and stopped at the edge of the crater her brother and his friend had worked into the sand. It was smoothed at the edges now, a murky puddle popping raindrops. The object leaned against the far edge, bobbing. She bent her knees, put her hands on them, and squinted. Scratched into the age-spotted Styrofoam, it said,

I liv in the oshin

mi name is jimmy

Esther put both hands over her mouth and held in a mischievous giggle. She wasn't supposed to talk to people she didn't know. She reached for the board, pursed her lips, and yanked it out of the hole. The surf came on, tumbling up to her ankles, and she gave a joyful cry, prancing back up the beach ten paces, splashing through the water as it drew back, making the world reel again like a carnival ride.

She dropped to her knees and laid the board flat. The bottom of it had wavy marks shadowed on it like the ceiling in the sun room last year when it had "water damage." Esther had frowned when Daddy had called it that, too. She liked the shape of it, pretty, like river-ripples.

She poked her tongue out the corner of her mouth, and scratched into the board,

Esther.

Picking up the board was hard because it sucked to the sand for a second, but she popped it free, wrapped her arms around it, and ran down to the water. Rain thundered around her. The board was almost as big as she was, and when she gave it a hurl she almost fell over.

It fell to the roil of dark waves and floated, close, then away.

"Esther!"

Mommy. Esther looked down at her feet. She was in trouble.

The shower had been love-a-licious, rain washing rain, ha. After dinner, Mother had braided Esther's hair silently right there at the table. Daddy moved to the living room and folded himself into his chair, slowly crossing one long skinny leg over the other, opening his magazine importantly.

"Choices," he said. He looked across back at Esther for a long meaningful moment and then let his glance fall down to the page.

"Yes, bad choices," Isaac added. He was lying at his father's feet on the floor in front of the television. He was on his stomach with his shins up behind him making an X-shape. He was playing Scrabble with himself.

"Enough," Mommy said softly, "we've discussed it."

Esther crawled out of her lap and padded in to her usual place behind the sofa across from the stairs so she wouldn't have to see Isaac. There, she sat with her ankles tucked under her and bent over her iPad plugged into the wall with the charger thing so she could play Peppa Pig: Paintbox and pretend she wasn't listening.

"But she's such a liar," Isaac said.

"She's imaginative," Mommy said.

"Not the issue," Daddy said. "She should have delivered the message to come into the beach house to her brother more expeditiously. And her mother shouldn't have given such a directive to a six-year-old."

"Third person isn't necessary, dear," Mommy said softly. "I'm sitting right here."

"Then it's settled then," Daddy said.

"Yeah," Isaac said, "but she's such a liar."

"Am not . . ." she muttered.

"Are so!" his voice said with a laugh in it. "Your ocean-boy, Jimmy? Yeah, that's funny. A kid died last year, pulled in by rip currents. He was a first grader named Jimmy Sweeney. You can Google it. I'll bet she did. Ma, can you check the browsing history on your laptop?"

"She wasn't looking in my laptop, honey."

"How do you know?"

"She's not allowed."

"Oh my God," he cried. "You let her get away with everything!"

He stomped past and moved off up the stairs. Esther smiled savagely. Then she stopped; that was mean. Thunder rumbled outside, and her mother was saying something about punishments versus creativity. Then something about rewards, and Esther immediately pushed up and bounded out from behind the sofa.

"Rewards?" she said, beaming. "Can I have Slime?"

This earned her looks from both parents, dining room, living room, both different flavors, yet both saying "no." Esther pushed out her bottom lip and stared at her toes. For some reason she thought she was going to cry.

"May I go upstairs?" she said, lifting her head cautiously. "I want to listen to the rain."

"Of course," Mommy said. "I'll be up in a bit to read to you."

Esther nodded and made for the stairs, going heel to toe like a tightrope walker. Mommy wouldn't "be up in a bit." She was drinking wine. Daddy was drinking out of the glass shaped like an upside-down triangle, and once Isaac retreated to his room he rarely came out, like an ogre lurking in a cave.

She was going upstairs to listen to the rain.

Then she was going to get Mommy's laptop, sneak it back to her room, and take it under the covers like a secret in a tent. She hadn't Googled Jimmy Sweeney as Isaac had said.

But she was going to now.

Esther had the covers pulled up to her chin in the darkness. She'd used Mommy's code, her birthday numbers, to look in the computer for the boy Jimmy Sweeney. There had been a picture. He had yellow hair that stuck out like straw, a ton of faint freckles, buckteeth, and a bright red birthmark on his neck. He died swimming by himself in the waters off the public part of the beach three blocks away, where you needed a tag to get in or a lanyard. The Google said he'd loved soccer. And horses.

Esther had unplugged her Goodnight Moon nightlight and left it on the carpet. The dark was like a big painter's canvas . . . a picture frame she could fill with the face of the lost Jimmy Sweeney. What did his voice sound like? Was he smelly like her brother? Why couldn't he spell "ocean"? Did he ever ride a horse, or did he just like drawing them or watching movies about them? Did he play soccer or was he just in love with Alex Morgan like everyone else?

She smiled wistfully. What was it like to live in the ocean? Did the seagrasses wave to you when you went by like a parade? Did the fish all show off for you their beautiful scales flashing rainbows? When you slept, did the currents swing you gently like "Rock-a-Bye-Baby"? The air conditioner was making noise as it usually did, but in the black backdrop it was different somehow, making rich watercolors ebb and flow across the darkness like waves.

Esther had almost surrendered to the rhythm of forgetfulness, when her eyes fluttered open. It was disturbing, the same way it felt when Isaac crept up behind her and clapped his hands hard.

She'd had a thought!

And oh, how she hated thoughts, especially when they surprised her!

Suddenly she'd remembered dance class for some reason, "Ballet 4–7" it was called, in the room above the music store that smelled like cobwebs and books. It hurt her feet and the teacher was mean. Mommy had said it would "take time," and Daddy had said the floor there was "forgiving," made of "semi-sprung" wood or something, but it hadn't felt like forgiveness when she fell on it.

She smiled again. In Jimmy Sweeney's "oshin," the floor was soft sand, and you only fell in slow motion. The water hugged you, protected you, made you graceful. Esther pictured herself doing pique turns and pirouettes "en pointe" among the coral reefs shaped like statues and honeycombs. So pretty and peaceful, and she fell into the silky current of dreams.

She woke up when she heard something. Outside her door something that bumped, or knocked, she wasn't sure which. Everything was strange, like being lost at the mall. The bed felt big in the dark, different from before, as if she were a peanut in a kangaroo pouch with no floor or walls.

"Isaac?" she said. The air conditioner hummed. Calming. The tide.

It wasn't just endless darkness, not if you looked to the sides instead of straight up as she'd done making picture frames in what seemed like years ago. The air conditioner had a tiny yellow light on, meaning Daddy had to clean the filter. Above it, you could see the barest outline through the shape of the blinds. On the other side of the room, up on the bureau, the clock said "2:19" in squared-off red numbers.

She went up on her elbows and saw that there was a thin bar of light under the door.

Then, there was a shadow in it.

Middle, a few inches right, it was Isaac, it had to be, going up on one foot, trying to scare her. It was his favorite ghost story, "The One-Legged Scissor Man," but Esther knew he'd gotten it wrong when he tried retelling it back home at Boy Scouts in the den when she'd been making pumpkin spice cupcakes with Mommy, standing on the kitchen chair pressing handprints in the flour on the cutting board. She knew it was really "The RED-Legged Scissor Man," an awful German poem that Ms. Brittany, the substitute, read them a month before by mistake at the Play 'N' Learn. It was a story about a monster-man who cut off your thumb if you sucked it, but Isaac made it into a one-legged groundskeeper with a set of extra-long hedge cutters who chopped off your leg because he got his caught under a ride mower. STUPID!

The shadow under the door moved. Slowly, to the left. It was smooth. There was no bunny-hop.

"Isaac!" she said. "How did you DO that?"

She turned to her stomach, pushed her feet over the edge of the mattress, and did the slow-slide off the side of the bed. Even though she was mad, she remembered at the tipping point to make her hands into claws. That way she could rake them into the contour sheet so the last six inches to the floor wouldn't be so surprising.

After landing, she straightened her nightgown. The mattress was blocking the view of the door, making it seem as if there was a hole in the darkness. She took a deep breath and walked to the front of the bed, letting her left-hand trace along the edge. At the corner, she saw that the shadow under the door had vanished. It was just a bar of faint light now.

Esther approached, expecting a dark shape to appear suddenly on the other side, her brother standing on one foot wearing a scary face and holding a pair of big garden hedge cutters. She got to the door, went up on her toes, and turned the knob. Pulled and backed off so the door could sweep open.

No Isaac.

The hallway was dim, shadows stretching across the walls. Down to the right Mommy and Daddy's door was closed, as was Isaac's, and the bathroom light was on as it always was from around the sharp corner of the laundry room. Esther didn't like it in there, and she always held her pee until morning. The washer and dryer were stacked on top of each other, and at night they looked like a person.

Esther turned to the left.

There was a soccer ball at the top of the stairs.

"Jimmy?" she said. Moving closer, she saw that the ball was scuffed, its pentagons and blacked-in triangles faded, the rest muddied and watermarked, but she could make out the black and gold lettering, "Brine—Phantom X," near the bottom.

She approached and tried to pick it up, but she kicked it before her hands could clap shut. Normally that would have sent her into a fit of laughter, but the bouncing ball wasn't funny. It hit the fourth step down, making an awful "boing" noise, and rebounded so high it almost hit the ceiling.

It came down with front-spin, kicking off the stair second from the bottom, doing a ricochet in the alcove off the cloak closet door and the bottom of the banister, next rolling out into the living room.

Esther gasped.

The front door was open. But that was WRONG, because Mommy said it wasn't allowed! The soccer ball quivered. It must have been the wind. The rain had stopped, but Esther could hear the whistling in the archway. A door clapped open down the hall, far right; it was Isaac. She froze, hands up by her neck. He was wearing his shark print jammies and he had the heel of his hand in his eye, rubbing it. He thumped down to the bathroom without noticing her, and Esther looked back down the stairs.

The ball was gone.

She stared, closed her mouth, rubbed her ear. Then she made her way down, gripping the posts one by one under the handrail. At the bottom she usually hopped off the landing into the living room like a broad jump for a prize, but this time she lowered herself with a little lady step, walking carefully on the slate gray decorator tiles where "shoes always came off!"

Through the doorway the clouds looked black, the moon behind them a pale sleeping eye, the sand like the moon, both marbled and pitted. She slipped outside and went to the edge of the porch. The sunning chairs were sunk in so you couldn't see their legs, and the badminton net had sagged in the middle. Down toward the waves the soccer ball sat on a small mound of sand, and Esther giggled into both hands. It looked like a planet on a dune saying, "Mommy, I'm lost . . ."

It started moving. Just a wiggle at first, next rolling off, skittering along the beach to the right. It wasn't magic, the wind had picked up, and as the ball changed directions, skipping along the sand the other way, then a foot back and five forward, Esther felt the breeze mimic the pattern on her face. The waves tumbled softly onto the shore; everything was dancing.

The ball rolled close to the waterline.

Esther leapt off the porch. The sand was cool and hard, good for running. Her steps were darts, but not quick enough. By the time she got to the place where the texture of the beach dampened, the soccer ball was bobbing in the current. Twice it almost came back to the shore, but twice it withdrew further, each time ignoring Esther's calls to please, please come back to play tag with the wind. Soon it was a speck. Then a memory in the darker part of the ocean, and Esther grabbed the hem of her nightgown in her fists, trying not to cry.

Before her then, about fifty feet out, the waves changed. It was the foam, the white bubbly part, churning and whirlpooling into a shape. It was an outline at first rising out of the froth, just points that became flickering ears above wide glass-ball eyes on either side of a muzzle with big flaring nostrils. Seawater dripped off of its broad barrel-ribs, and it rose on long and powerful legs, stamping its hoofs, a great white horse with a majestic long flowing mane.

It started to come forward, splashing the skin of the water, not in a trot, but a princely march the way they did in parades. Esther stood spellbound upon the cool sand just out of reach of the current, and by the time the magnificent beast came ashore she'd noticed that it bore a strange rider on its back.

It was a skeleton, limp arms dangling, and she hadn't seen it at first because it wasn't sitting upright, yet lying on its tummy where the saddle would be, draped along the spine. Its skull lolled and bumped softly on the horse's front shoulder. Its fingers were splintered. The bones were spotted and caked in places with what looked like those "calcium deposits" Daddy muttered about when he soaked the shower head in that lemony stuff. There were threads of seaweed hanging off the ribs. One of the eye sockets had black algae oozing out of it, and his big cracked teeth looked bucked-out and smiling.

"Jimmy?" she said. He smelled strongly of sea-life and saltwater.

The horse strutted past, close enough to touch. Esther didn't, but as it passed she reached after it, turning, seeing nothing behind her now but sunken beach chairs and a sagging badminton net. Her heart was racing, eyes shining, and she ran back to the house just bursting with stories.

Nobody believes me . . .

Determined, Esther had crawled out of bed, skipping her day-nap. Mommy and Daddy and Isaac were out front having beach time. Mommy had the tri-fold face reflector-thing and the lotion that made her look shiny. Daddy had brought out the umbrella and had on his socks with his sandals because even in the shade he said the tops of his feet burned. Isaac had brought out his summer reading packet, but as always, he was probably just playing Fruit Ninja on his iPhone.

Esther was sitting with her legs tucked under her in her special place behind the couch, drawing. She'd found a tablet of oversized construction paper at the bottom of her closet, and she was using a Sharpie to make a picture of Jimmy and his horse. She'd never been very good at art, but here, in her private nook, hunched over the bright yellow paper, she'd amazed herself with her creation.

The horse's ears were slightly too big, the muzzle too long, but the legs had come out PERFECT, especially the lower parts just above the hoofs below the knees that were angled back instead of straight as if spring-loaded. The nostrils were slightly uneven, but that made them look as if they were billowing! She'd almost messed up the mane, initially sketching the strands coming too high off the neck, but she worked the mistake into a flowing effect of what seemed a combination of water and flame.

The boy Jimmy was more—a stick figure. Since he'd been draped to the horse's back it had been hard not to double the lines, so she just drew a misshapen skeleton head, his bony feet, and his dangling spindle-fingers. Esther was pretty sure he wouldn't think it rude that you had to fill in the rest of him with your imagination. He was a ghost, after all . . .

She pushed up to sit a bit straighter, cocked her head, and added a couple of dots to be the foam, a few falling off the wide chest and some off his tail. She smiled. Now they'd know she wasn't making it up! It was the best thing she'd ever, ever drawn, even though she had pressed her palm onto the paper a few times, leaning, making it waffle a little and crease.

The door came open. Sounds of seagulls and surf and feet on the foyer tiles. The conversation was in the middle somewhere.

"She's eccentric," Mommy said.

"Autistic is more like it," Isaac said.

"Keep your voice down. Go check on her, please."

Isaac's feet pounded up the stairs, thumped above, thumped back, and thudded in return down the stairs.

"Asleep with the covers over her head like usual," he snorted. He moved off to the kitchen. The fridge door opened, and Esther's face burned. It was super-hot upstairs, so they always kept her door closed to conserve the air conditioning. He hadn't even opened it; she'd have heard. So should have her parents who clearly weren't listening.

"I'm concerned," Daddy said softly.

"No need," Mommy said. "Jerry Cohen is on the board. He can arrange for her to be identified immediately and they'll look after her, I'll make sure of it."

"She's not special ed."

"Maybe, maybe not, but she's peculiar. And if you run enough testing something's bound to come up. Everyone does it nowadays as a matter of course, and I'm going to make damned sure she gets every advantage."

"They pull her out of class and the other kids will know."

"There isn't that kind of stigma anymore; in fact, it's the opposite. Twenty-nine percent of the district gets services for children with disabilities. It's on the website."

"Disabilities."

"Of course, yes, but please, dear, you tend to be blunt. The studies say we should establish an atmosphere of sensitivity. Table-tact. Never use the words 'disabled' or 'damaged' or 'handicapped.' Our precious darling is 'special' and she doesn't need to hear anything else."

They moved off to the kitchen.

Esther's face was wet. She slowly let her hands fall upon her drawing. She crumpled it into a trash-ball and pushed it under the couch.

Isaac suddenly realized that he'd left his reading packet outside, probably flapping all over the beach like a wounded goose. He scraped back his chair, elbowing the table by accident and making the juice in the glasses move.

"Linoleum," said Dad. He was reading the Wall Street Journal.

"Manners," Mom added, thumbing through her phone. Her reading glasses were perched on the end of her nose. Neither had looked up. Isaac bolted through the living room, opened the door, and stepped out onto to the porch.

The sun was blazing. The gentle ocean shimmered, and Isaac could have sworn he saw a fire-white horse wading into it twenty feet out, making a path straight away toward the skyline.

He squinted hard and put his hand across his brow like a salute. There had been something on the horse's back, a figure draped along the spine as if sleeping. The details of the shape were hard to make out exactly, but there had been a pinkish tint to it, the same as Esther's favorite knit summer dress.

Both of Isaac's hands were up at his eyes now, one draped over the other, palms curved making a tunnel.

There was no horse.

But there was something pink floating on the water. It disappeared beneath the surface, and Isaac tore back into the house. He clumped up the stairs and raced down the hall. He had been asked to check on his sister. He hadn't, of course—I mean, why the heck would he? She slept like a log and acted like a turd, so why risk waking her up, yo . . .

He ripped open her door.

Whew. She was there as she always was, a lump with the covers pulled over her head, whew. At least he wasn't going to get into trouble.

His breath caught in his throat. The shape under the comforter was bigger than Esther by at least half a foot.

And the room smelled strongly of dead fish and saltwater.

Delirium Vivens

Nicole Cushing

I draw a Circle for the King of Ghouls
and summon him into my bedchamber.
He is the thief of corpses and my love.
When he arrives we sing a hymn to Hell,
and soon the rank waters of Jordan rise
up from the ground and make a red whirlpool
which plunges us into the tomb of Christ.

The King sucks marrow from the savior's bones
then grasps me by the chin and gives a kiss
in which I taste scourged eons, scabs of gods,
and grim blasphemous lust, too foul to fake.
His eyes commence to sparkle like a wind-
stirred, fading cinder through some cold, sick night—
a fevered, fecund gaze, throbbing with need.

After our tryst, mad bishops catch our scent
and chase us from the tomb with whips made from
the skins of infidels and suicides.
So off we swim, back up the Jordan's depths
into my secret room, where we devour
the shriveled husks of dead mice and await
the next chance to partake of Communion.

"The Weird Dominions of the Infinite": Edgar Allan Poe and the Scientific Gothic

Sorina Higgins

The Gothic genre frequently brings what Edgar Allan Poe calls "the weird dominions of the infinite" ("Revelation" [1844]) into threatening contact with human characters. Poe was arguably "the watershed figure of the gothic" (Perry and Sederholm 2); his tales obliterate the distinctions between matter/spirit, Gothic Other/reader, and fact/fiction by providing a pseudo-scientific basis for voices from beyond the grave. In two stories from the 1840s, Poe plays with genre conventions: "Mesmeric Revelation" (1844, rev. 1845)[1] masquerades as a philosophical-religious dialogue-catechism, while "The Facts of M. Valdemar's Case" (1845; later titled "The Facts in the Case of M. Valdemar") uses a scientific cover-story. Both were widely read as nonfiction, terrifying the reader with the possibility that even dying cannot save the soul from monsters. In this paper I offer a genetic analysis of these texts to reveal how "Valdemar" offers a Gothicized Doppelgänger of "Revelation," transforming the genre as a result. Through this analysis, I argue that the similarities of plot, character doublings, narrative shifts, and pseudo-scientific credibility of these stories create their own misreading of genre, exponentially increasing their Gothic terror.

The first of the two stories I will examine is entitled "Mesmeric Revelation" (hereafter cited as "Revelation"). It was published in the *Columbian Lady's and Gentleman's Magazine* in August 1844. This piece is not Gothic—at least not in its first version. The 1844 publication presents itself as a sober, scientific account in the form of a

---

1. All citations to "Mesmeric Revelation" are from the original 1844 publication in the *Columbian Lady's and Gentleman's Magazine* unless otherwise noted.

philosophical dialogue and/or religious catechism. A Mr. Vankirk, who has long been skeptical about the immortality of the soul, has recently discovered he is able to "perceive a train of convincing ratiocination" while mesmerized ("Revelation" 67).[2] This logical chain of thought calls into question his previous materialism. He sends for his mesmerist, who puts him into the sleepwaking state, and they engage in a dialogue about the nature of matter, spirit, soul, and God. The most remarkable claim that Vankirk makes while mesmerized is that there is no such thing as spirit: all is matter. What is traditionally called 'spirit' is really "unparticled matter" or "infinitely rarefied matter" (68, 69). Thus the tale postulates a monism whereby mind is God at rest, thought is God in motion, and death is "the ultimate life" (69). While there is nothing Gothic about this religious monism, it does lay the foundation for later spiritual surprises.

The story ends with a metaphysical twist. In the last paragraph, an "alarming expression" on Vankirk's face startles the narrator-mesmerist into waking him immediately. Then "he fell back upon his pillow and expired. . . . in less than a minute afterward his corpse had all the stern rigidity of stone" (79). Rigor mortis, "the stiffening of a body," does not occur instantaneously after death; rather, it "begins in six hours, takes another six to become fully established, remains for 12 hours and passes off during the succeeding 12 hours. It comes on quickly when extreme exertion has been indulged in immediately before death" (Marcovitch). The fact that Vankirk's body

---

2. Doris Falk provides this definition of mesmerism: "Mesmer and his followers had used the term 'animal magnetism' to indicate an autonomous physical force pervading both the animate and inanimate worlds, accounting for the mesmerists' therapeutic powers at the same time that it attracted iron to magnets, kept the stars in their places, and gave rise to the 'influence mutuelle entre les corps célestes, la terre, & les corps animés.' [F. A. Mesmer, 'Proposition 1,' *Precis historique desfaits relatifs au Magnetisme-Animal* (London, 1781), p. 83]. When mesmerist and patient were *en rapport* they both became conductors of the magnetic fluid or, as some practitioners held, of a newly discovered 'imponderable' comparable to—or perhaps identical with—electricity, light, or electromagnetism" (Falk 536).

enters full rigor mortis immediately after the narrator-mesmerist wakens him suggests that he has been dead for some time—at least six hours, unless mesmerism constitutes "extreme exertion." However, except for a description of the alarming facial expression (which is quickly replaced by a smile), the narrator's tone is calm, dispassionate, and objective; the fact that Vankirk is dead for much of the story is surprising, but not horrifying. In fact, his tranquil conversation and deathbed smile suggest that the afterlife is a beneficent condition in which the perceived differences between matter and spirit fall away, allowing unity of the self with God.

Later, Poe revised "Mesmeric Revelation" and added an additional shock. For publication in the Wiley & Putnam edition of his *Tales*, which was released on June 5, 1845, he added these three additional sentences: "His brow was of the coldness of ice. Thus, ordinarily, should it have appeared, only after long pressure from Azrael's hand. Had the sleep-waker, indeed, during the latter portion of his discourse, been addressing me from out the region of the shadows?" ("Revelation" [1845] 57). These additions make explicit what was merely hinted in the 1844 version: Vankirk (probably) voiced his revelation from beyond the grave. The tone is darkened by the addition of the words 'coldness,' 'ice,' 'Azrael's hand,' and 'the region of the shadows.' These changes are not sufficient to make the story Gothic, but they offer the merest hints of something frightening or inimical to human happiness—at least to the happiness of the living who observe the deathly change.

The other story I will consider is "The Facts of M. Valdemar's Case" (hereafter cited as "Valdemar"), which is the Gothic double of the earlier tale. "Valdemar" was published in December 1845 in both the *American Review* and the *Broadway Journal*. In this second tale, as summarized by a weekly periodical shortly after its publication:

> Valdemar was in the last stage of a consumption—was thrown into the mesmeric state—there was about him every appearance of death—in this condition he spoke, saying he had been asleep, but was now dead—thus he continued for seven months, stiff, cold,

insensible, save when the passes were made over him, when he would speak—he was at last aroused, and instantly his body fell into complete, almost liquid putrefaction. ("Democratic Editors")

The plots and characters of these two stories are nearly the same: a man (called 'V'), who is dying of tuberculosis, is mesmerized (by 'P') on the last day of his life. While in the mesmeric state, he speaks from beyond the grave. The mesmeric trance preserves his body superficially in its outward condition, but meanwhile the processes of death continue beneath the static surface.

The two stories were published back to back in the collected *Works* of 1850, highlighting their similarities; the major difference between them, however, is generic. "Revelation" is a pseudo-scientific philosophical dialogue and religious catechism, while "Valdemar" is Gothic horror.[3] The important contrast resides in the *nature* of the supernatural and of the soul's existence after death. In "Revelation," the "unparticled matter" it postulates is benevolent, unity with it is desirable, and the afterlife is a happy condition; in "Valdemar," death is accompanied by unspeakable revulsion. Vankirk smiles at death; Valdemar's lips writhe away from his teeth. Vankirk enters rigor mortis; Valdemar is reduced to "liquid putrefaction."

Gothic literature is characterized by its evocation of horror, terror, suspense, or disgust of a very particular kind: fear of a supernatural or mysterious force beyond ordinary, material existence. This spiritualized fear sets it apart from other genres, even when materialist explanations are provided. While definitions of the Gothic abound, many emphasize the psychology of the characters, plot mechanisms, or superficial elements of setting rather than this fundamental fear of the spiritual Other. A Gothic novel, claims *The Oxford Dictionary of Literary Terms*, is "a story of terror and suspense, usually set in a gloomy old castle or monastery" (Baldrick). I believe this definition is both too broad, failing to specify the particular kind of fear or suspense, and too narrow, restricting it to a

---

3. See Faivre 44 for a discussion of the genre of these two tales.

common setting. An examination of the American Gothic in particular reveals that any setting may suffice—a house, village, forest, or cave—as long as it is haunted by the dread of something beyond materiality. Even if the supernatural is explained away at the end of the story, the fear of it resonates throughout the tale.

All common Gothic characteristics are calculated to frighten the characters and the reader. Many Gothic works feature "portraits, doubles, veils, the confessional, hunger, bleeding corpses, treasure chests, live burial, madhouses, deformity, inquisition, dismemberment, miscegenation, restlessness, surveillance, footsteps, inarticulate howls, nightmares, insomnia, fire, shipwreck and mob violence" (Kilfeather 81). These are all terrifying—but fear is evoked in many other genres as well, such as tragedy, mystery, horror, thriller, science fiction, or the daily news. What sets the Gothic genre apart from its literary cousins is specifically the sense of something malevolent beyond sensory appearances. It might be a ghost in the attic, galvanic energy, a multi-generational curse, inexplicable powers of transportation, or hidden supernatural abilities. The *specific* horror that the Gothic offers, I argue, is the suggestion that there is something beyond sensual perception—what Poe in "Mesmeric Revelation" calls "the weird dominions of the infinite"—and that it is inimical to the human.

This malevolent supernatural force distinguishes the Gothic from other genres, particularly fantasy. In the latter, the supernatural may be beneficent or may be a neutral force to be manipulated for good or ill by powerful adepts. What is fascinating in Gothic stories is that while characters are hideously terrified of the malevolent beyond, they yet long for contact with it and are willing to take enormous risks to try to reach, communicate with, or unite themselves to it. They walk down dark hallways, open forbidden doors, plunge into whirlpools, clamber through caverns, and submit themselves to hypnotists to try to learn what is beyond, even when they suspect the result will be madness, death, or damnation. It appears that there is an element in human nature that longs for connection with something greater and more mysterious than material reality.

Each of these two tales by Poe, then, takes a Gothic turn. The *volta* in "Revelation" occurred in its publication history, as Poe revised it to make its otherworldly nature clearer. The shift in "Valdemar" occurs two-thirds of the way through (at 2,311 words out of 3,595, to be exact), when the bright spots on Valdemar's cheeks, indicative of life, *"went out"* like "the extinguishment of a candle by a puff of the breath" ("Valdemar" 563–64; emphasis in original). There are several implications for the Gothic genre in the ways Poe deploys metaphysics, narrative, and gender in these two stories, taken together.

First, "Revelation" postulates that there is no division between matter and spirit. There is no material hiding place from spiritual threats, because spirit "not only permeates all things but impels all things" ("Revelation" 68). Since "Valdemar" succeeds so rapidly on the heels of "Revelation," follows the same plot outline, and was published right after it in the 1850 *Works,* I read them as in dialogue with each other, importing the metaphysics of "Revelation" into Valdemar's monstrous body and bed. This brings the Gothic Other home in theologically and practically terrifying ways: if the Gothic threatens humans with a malevolent Other, but there *is* no other (for natural and supernatural are one), then whatever mysterious supernatural force the character (or reader) fears is of the same nature as the self. If God is mind and thought, then a terrifying thought is God.

Critics have missed this metaphysical terror, claiming that Poe's Gothic is merely psychological. "The most unnerving quality of Poe's Gothic," writes Frederick S. Frank, "is its psychosomatic circumscription of mental space, that is, the mind closing in upon itself" (334). While it is true that a mind closing in on itself is terrifying, it is not as frightening as believing that the horrors of the mind are universal, infinite, and eternal, encompassing not only the self and this life but God and the afterlife as well. Frank comes closer to the truth when he writes that Poe's Gothic fiction progresses "from physical horror and dread to metaphysical horror and awe" (337) and that "Poe adds a dimension of metaphysical anxiety and crisis" to the genre (338). This is clear in "Revelation" and "Valdemar" paired in the context of revision and publication. Both stories capitalize upon the nineteenth-century belief that the mesmeric electrical fluid was "an intermediary presence," one of several modernist "hybrid formations emerging in interstitial cultural spaces" (Darvay 162). Poe takes advantage of the liminal, border-crossing nature of mesmerism in "Revelation" to postulate the single nature of matter and spirit; "Valdemar" makes that identification horrifying. When it turns Gothic, monism makes the monsters come home.

Scholars have also neglected the publication history and generic implications of these two stories. "Valdemar" is not included in Frank's 2002 survey of Poe's Gothic writings (330), and there is nothing about manuscript revisions to either story in Fisher's *Poe at Work*. Overlooking the significance of the revisions to "Revelation" creates a misunderstanding of how the Gothic is deployed in "Valdemar," which in turn leads to overgeneralizations about Poe and the Gothic. Frank, for instance, claims that "By concentrating the action of the tale and isolating the characters, Poe converted the physical spaces used by previous Gothic writers into constrictive mental spaces" (333–34). This claim is too reductive: "Revelation" and "Valdemar" together suggest not a constrictive space, but a vast, even infinite, spiritual realm in which the perceived differences between matter and spirit dissolve, and the body, freed from organs, will vibrate in unison with an infinitely rarefied ether ("Revelation"). In "Revelation," this state is blissful; in "Valdemar," it is a site of unspeakable Gothic horror. Poe does domesticate the Gothic, with terrifying implications, but not by restricting characters or readers to mental confinement. Infinitude can be at least as horrifying as constriction.

Furthermore, some readers have missed just how far Poe is willing to go to break down the matter/spirit dualism. Anthony Enns contextualizes "Revelation" when he claims that "Vankirk's statements clearly show how mesmerism was challenging the divisions between body and mind, materiality and immateriality" (71). But while Enns is right that "Mesmerism effectively allows the subject to occupy a liminal position between these categories," he is wrong to suggest that Vankirk believes "the body is neither fully concrete nor fully ephemeral" (71). In "Revelation," Poe does not suggest that the body is some third substance between the material and the spiritual. The point of the dialogue is exactly the opposite: that matter and spirit are the same. There is only one substance, not two or three. Enns misunderstands the radical, comprehensive nature of Poe's monism and thus misses the ways in which "Valdemar" inverts "Revelation," Gothicizing it with deeply disturbing implications. My examination of Poe's generic moves in these two stories provides a deeper understanding of both of them and of just what a pairing of these tales does to the Gothic.

In addition to uniting the self with a malevolent spirituality, both stories engage in a shift of narrative perspective such that the reader becomes identified with the narrator-mesmerist, rather than the patient-visionary. This shift has generic consequences due to the ways in which it relates the two stories to one another, leading to a misreading of genre, then inverts "Valdemar" for its shocking Gothic turn. Gillespie claims that Poe's "stories require us to first assume the role of hypnotic subject or patient before we can consciously perceive their more profound subliminal suggestions" (153); I do not think that either story identifies the reader with Vankirk/Valdemar. Instead, the opening of each is directed at outside readers, who can comfortably picture themselves observing these stories from a distance. At the beginning, both narrators encourage readers to repudiate doubters and skeptics and instead receive the story with an open, receptive mind. "Revelation" begins by describing certain "unprofitable and disreputable" people who would be unlikely to believe this account (67); readers are encouraged to side with those intelligent, well-informed readers who would believe it. "Valdemar" begins with a desire to set the record straight about a story whose garbled version the narrator suspects readers have encountered already.

Each story suddenly shifts the ground, destabilizing the reader's sense of complacency and putting the audience in a position of uncertainty. This point-of-view modification positions the reader as an ignorant questioner—the narrator known as 'P'—who is asking an enlightened individual for information. "Revelation" achieves its shift when the narrator-mesmerist says, as if frustrated, "I wish you would explain yourself, Mr. Vankirk" (68). The reader is likely to desire the same. Vankirk responds by turning the conversation upside down, taking control. He accuses the narrator-mesmerist: "You do not question me properly." "What then shall I ask?" the narrator inquires. Vankirk responds pontifically: "You must begin at the beginning," then scolds the still uncomprehending narrator: "You know that the beginning is GOD" (68). "Suddenly," Gillespie observes, "the hypnotized has become the hypnotist" (147). From this point onwards, the reader occupies the same perspective as the narrator-mesmerist. Rather than calmly administering a catechism with set responses, the narrator is forced into asking asking questions to which he does not know the answers. Gillespie provides an insight into genre when he shares his own reader-response: "I think this [awareness of our susceptibility] is actually more frightening in 'Mesmeric Revelation' than in the most explicit examples of the horror genre" (152). The metaphysical shockers in these stories may have terrifying implications for the readers' identification with the supernatural Other and inability to separate themselves from it.

Similarly, "Valdemar" begins with the narrator-mesmerist in a privileged, knowing position, separated from the reader, but this relationship eventually shifts. The narrator-mesmerist confidently describes medical details that the reader has no way of knowing. He also begins a kind of catechism, questioning Valdemar about whether or not he is asleep. But at the moment Valdemar dies and turns into an object of horror, the narrator emphasizes the implausibility of events and neglects to reassert the "factuality" of his narrative: "I now feel that I have reached a point of this narrative at which every reader will be startled into positive disbelief. It is my business, however, simply to proceed" (564). This is a destabilizing moment that counterintuitively can cause the reader to identify with the narrator-mesmerist, because both are now together in a state of uncertainty about what will happen next. Rather than merely observing a confident experimenter testing his hypothesis, the reader joins the perplexed mesmerist in awaiting the unfolding of a mystery.

The moment of the perspectival shift in "Valdemar" is also the moment of its generic turn: this story becomes Gothic at the moment when the patient dies. The narrator-mesmerist asks him "Are you asleep?" three times. After the second iteration, the physicians express the opinion "that M. Valdemar should be suffered to remain undisturbed in his present apparently tranquil condition, until death should supervene" ("Valdemar" 563). However, 'P' decides to disregard this professional advice; instead, he repeats his question. This triple repetition, reminiscent of so many triads in fairy tales and folklore, seems to be an evil spell, for it kills Valdemar:

> The eyes rolled themselves slowly open, the pupils disappearing upwardly; the skin generally assumed a cadaverous hue, resembling not so much parchment as white paper; and the circular hectic spots which, hitherto, had been strongly defined in the centre of each cheek, *went out* at once. I use this expression, because the suddenness of their departure put me in mind of nothing so much as the extinguishment of a candle by a puff of the breath. (563–64)

This is the moment of death, and it is at this instant that the story shifts from a quasi-scientific account to a tale of Gothic horror. The narrator describes the change with almost gleeful disgust:

> The upper lip, at the same time, writhed itself away from the teeth, which it had previously covered completely; while the lower jaw fell with an audible jerk, leaving the mouth widely extended, and disclosing in full view the swollen and blackened tongue. I

presume that no member of the party then present had been unaccustomed to death-bed horrors; but so hideous beyond conception was the appearance of M. Valdemar at this moment, that there was a general shrinking back from the region of the bed. (564)

As if to signal the generic shift, Valdemar changes from an enlightened philosopher in a catechistical dialogue to both monster and victim in a tale of Gothic horror. He is simultaneously the terrifying force beyond the grave and the tormented "sufferer" (565) trapped in an agonized body on this side of death. The hostile Other is equated with the haunted human victim.

Soon after this horrifying visual change, Valdemar utters the shocking announcement *"I am dead"* (565). Two interesting events occur in quick succession; both have generic implications. First, as if to distance the story further from the scientific genre in which it began, the text is marred by an aporia. The medical student—who was taking notes—swoons. It takes "nearly an hour" (564) before he regains consciousness, during which time no one observes Valdemar. If, in Poe's monistic system, Valdemar is identified with the supernatural Other, then this human-material-spiritual being is unobserved during that crucial hour when he has passed beyond the grave. The text is silent at the most important moment in the entire tale. No one is there to watch his metamorphosis from the rudimental body to the ultimate body. Furthermore, in contrast to "Revelation," the supernatural is clearly inimical to Valdemar. His death is apparently accompanied by great suffering, and yet no one is available to help him during the hour of crisis. Given his isolation and victimization, Valdemar's helplessness is more startling than his horror. He might be expected to rise up from the bed in all his grotesquerie and wreak vengeance on the ignorant and unsympathetic medical personnel around him. Yet he remains motionless, trapped in his agony like many a Gothic damsel in distress.

In fact, the Gothic genre may explain why Valdemar remains motionless (except for his quivering tongue) on the bed, even though he has become a Gothic monster that might be expected to rise to attack. I mentioned above that the two interesting events that occur in quick succession when Valdemar dies. The first is the fainting of the medical student already discussed; the second is the erasure of the only woman in either of these stories.

When "Valdemar" takes its Gothic turn, women are ushered out of the story. The narrator observes early on that "A male and a female nurse were in attendance" upon Valdemar in his illness, "but I did not feel myself altogether at liberty to engage in [the mesmeric experiment] with no more reliable witnesses than these people, in case of sudden accident, might prove" (562). He waits until a (male) medical student arrives to take notes, then he proceeds. There are no other female characters in either of these stories other than this one, silent, unnamed woman—and she leaves the room after the horror of Valdemar's death. Neither of the nurses can be persuaded to return. Later, different nurses are hired, and their gender is not specified. Thus, at the moment that the story turns Gothic, the solitary female exits, never to return. The woman leaves when the Gothic Other invades. From that moment on, the story takes place in a male world, with a male narrator-mesmerist, a male patient-victim-oracle, a male medical student, and male doctors.

Furthermore, vivid masculine sexual imagery accompanies the climax of the story. As the narrator-mesmerist strives to awaken Valdemar, he is disturbed by "ejaculations of 'dead! dead!' absolutely *bursting* from the tongue and not from the lips of the sufferer" (565). Obviously, 'ejaculations' here means 'exclamations.' However, according to the *OED*, ejaculation meant both "the hasty utterance of words expressing emotion" and "the discharging of the male sperm" as long ago as the seventeenth century ("Ejaculation, N."); both definitions, then, were available to Poe. While the speech-utterance is the obvious denotation in this context, the sexual meaning is strongly implied by the word "bursting" and by the transference of the speech from the lips (often seen as analogous to the female genitals) to the tongue (possibly a phallic symbol).

A superficial (mis)reading of this story in the context of the early development of the American Gothic genre, then, appears to suggest that Poe has erased women from the Gothic genre, creating an entirely male world for the climax of his tale. However, a closer examination reveals that "Valdemar" is not concerned with the gendered nature of the Gothic; instead, pregnancy and birth imagery are used to create an evil Doppelgänger of one story for another, with frightening metaphysical consequences.

Two factors argue against such a simplistic misogynistic reading. First, the narrator-mesmerist's comment about the unreliability of these witnesses may have more to do with social class, level of education, or field-specific expertise than with gender; one of the displaced nurses is male, after all, and the medical student would be conversant with the terminology necessary to take notes in a medical experiment. Second, feminine imagery persists after the one female nurse has left the building. The timeline for the experiment, for instance, covers nine months: "about nine months ago," says the narrator on the first page, he thought of performing a mesmeric experiment on a dying person (561). Seven months after putting Valdemar into a mesmeric trance, the narrator and doctors "finally resolved to make the experiment of awakening, or attempting to awaken him" (565); no reason is given for this decision, but it occurs at the end of the nine-month-long gestation of Valdemar's illness, mesmerism, and death. Vankirk in "Revelation" claimed that death was "but the painful metamorphosis" from rudimentary life into ultimate life (69), corresponding to the caterpillar's transformation into a butterfly. Death, in other words, is new birth. That is why Valdemar does not leap from the bed, monster-like, to devour the other people in the room: he is a baby, newly born.

But Valdemar's birth, to borrow from T. S. Eliot, is hard and bitter agony, like death. It is the caterpillar's metamorphosis Gothicized, and (monism notwithstanding) its bodily nature is certainly not downplayed. As if to emphasize the terrifying union of the Other and us, Poe brings the horrors of the unknown spiritual world vividly, disgustingly home—emphasizing fluids, odors, and viscous substances. When Valdemar speaks from beyond the grave, his voice seems to affect the narrator's ears the way "gelatinous or glutinous matters impress the sense of touch" (564). At the end of the nine months, when the narrator attempts to awaken the deathly sleeper, bodily fluids issue forth. A motion in Valdemar's eyes is "accompanied by the profuse out-flowing of a yellowish ichor (from beneath the lids) of a pungent and highly offensive odor" (565). The sudden, surprising, even shocking ending that rivals the grotesqueries of nearly any other Gothic work:

> As I rapidly made the mesmeric passes . . . his whole frame at once—within the space of a single minute, or even less, shrunk—crumbled—absolutely rotted away beneath my hands. Upon the bed, before that whole company, there lay a nearly liquid mass of loathsome—of detestable putrescence. (565)

The malevolent beyond has manifested itself in Valdemar's body and bed.

Apparently even Valdemar's *teeth* and *bones* have rotted into jelly; nothing solid remains. This means, then, that Valdemar has become "unorganized": freed from his organs. In "Mesmeric Revelation," Vankirk argued that death, because it frees the self from particulate matter, is a new birth into "the ultimate, unorganized life, [where] the external world reaches the whole body" in a blissful, nearly omniscient unification with God (70). "Valdemar" follows the same plot as "Revelation," but its ending—with its gelatinous substances, yellow ichor, and liquid mass—is a Gothicization of childbirth, a Gothicization of the death-into-life postulated in "Revelation." What is important here is not the gender of the author or characters, but the way in which birth imagery is inverted. This horrific domestication of the Gothic serves as a Doppelgänger of happy death: it is birth's evil twin.

In "Valdemar," then, Poe provided a Gothicization, a dark inversion, of the optimistic philosophy of "Revelation." However, the generic nature of both stories is masked by their putatively factual surfaces. Both stories were received as fact by readers due to their deceptive generic gestures. "Revelation" employs the conventions of philosophical dialogue and religious catechism; Vankirk even states that he has high hopes of the enlightenment to be gained by the combination of mesmerism with "the proper conduct of a catechism" (68). "Revelation" begins with a claim of fact and contains many of the trappings of a scientific experiment: a definition of terms, parameters for the experiment, the expression of a hypothesis, the goals of the experiment, the taking of meticulous notes, a profile of the patient/test subject, and a narrative of the case. "Valdemar" also begins with a claim of fact and also includes goals of the experiment, a profile of the patient/test subject with highly specific medical details, the acquisition of medical consent (see Altschuler; Ashworth), an examination of the patient, the securing of witnesses, the taking of meticulous notes, and a narrative of the experiment.

Furthermore, both stories maneuver readers into a position where belief is desirable. The narrator of "Revelation" says that those who do not believe in mesmerism are "mere doubters by profession—an unprofitable and disreputable tribe" (67). Of course, this makes readers want to position themselves with those savvy people who are neither unprofitable nor disreputable and who believe proven science. The narrator-mesmerist "flatters the reader's intellectual vanity by purposefully using the *argumentum ad populum* fallacy" (Gillespie 143), persuading the reader that the best course of action is to join with other enlightened individuals in accepting this account as fact. "Valdemar," too, makes its misleading generic gesture in the title, claiming to be "The Facts in the Case." The narrator states that the truth has been obscured, misleading the public, so that "It is now rendered necessary that I give the *facts*" (561). Savvy readers, both narrators imply, will believe these tales.

Many readers did just that. The reception history of these two stories is remarkable, most notably for how many readers accepted these tales as factual, scientific, medical accounts. Many scholars have already recounted the reception history (Faivre 35–44; Kofman; Mabbott 1024–28, 1228–32), detailing the many republications in journals with headings suggesting their truth, angry or jubilant letters to editors and to Poe demanding more proof of their authenticity, and Poe's teasing replies in which he often hedged his answers in ambiguous terms. "These misreadings of *Mesmeric Revelation* and *Valdemar*," Antoine Faivre recounts, went on in Europe for at least fourteen years after their first publication (43). Even twenty-first-century literary critics still want to receive these tales as nonfiction to some extent: Gillespie wrote in 2016: "Vankirk's extrasensory perceptions, then, may well be those of Poe himself, and thus may not be completely fictional" (144). In other words, the scientific cover-story succeeded extremely well at misleading readers about the genre of these stories.

Generic misleading has consequences for the Gothic. Specifically, as I have shown, "Valdemar" presents itself as nonfiction, but then enacts an inversion of the optimistic philosophical religion of "Revelation" about the afterlife. If "Valdemar" is *true*, then so are the Gothic horrors it presents: death is not a new birth into a blissful afterlife, monsters from beyond the grave are ourselves, and humans are one with the malevolent forces that threaten them. Even dying does not save the soul from monsters.

These stories, then, are tales of misreading; they even enact misreading. As I noted above, the narrative shift means that the reader is moved from the position of observant outsider to that of unenlightened narrator-mesmerist. This is a dangerous position to occupy, because the narrator is both a failed mesmerist and a failed author: he himself misreads the genre—and *kills* his patient! The narrator of "Revelation" thinks he is the catechist, but he really is the catechumen. He thinks he is the doctor offering palliative medicine, but Vankirk dies during their dialogue. The narrator of "Valdemar" thinks he is in "Revelation": a philosophical-religious dialogue-catechism. But he is in a Gothic horror story, and he did not learn the lesson from the inept narrator of "Revelation": his insistent, repetitive questioning kills Valdemar and creates a monster.

Characters in Gothic fiction often misread genre, frequently thinking that they are in a romance or a love story. This is a common enough occurrence that Jane Austen could invert and parody such an error in *Northanger Abbey*, the humor of which is largely driven by Catherine Morland's constant—and constantly frustrated—expectation of Gothic conventions. But what is remarkable about Poe's stories is that *readers*, not just the characters, misread the genre. These stories set up their own misreading so that both inside the tales and in their reception, the "playful dimension" of the willing suspension of disbelief "passed many people by" writes Faivre (45): readers failed to reinstitute disbelief once they finished reading the stories.[4]

Two specific examples of misreading, one more egregious than the other, should suffice for this point. The first is the most notorious: the case of Robert Hannum Collyer, a famous mesmerist. On December 16, 1845, Collyer wrote a letter to Poe, which Poe subsequently published in the *Broadway Journal.* Collyer wanted Poe to provide additional facts to prove that the account was true and deny those who would basely fling at it the contumely of being "merely a *splendid creation* of [his] own brain." He offers his professional opinion on the mesmerism of Valdemar, but he drastically misinterprets the story. He writes: "I have not the least doubt of the *possibility* of such a phenomenon; for, I did actually restore to active animation a person who died from excessive drinking of ardent spirits." It is important to understand what Collyer is saying here. He claims that he himself has raised a man from the dead by means of mesmerism. He claims that he believes Poe's story about Valdemar is true, based on its similarity to his own experience. In other words, he thinks that "Valdemar" is about a mesmerist raising a man from the dead—but "Valdemar" is about a mesmerist *killing* a man! A more extreme misreading can scarcely be imagined. Since the story maneuvers the

---

4. Even Faivre's excellent, systematic examination of misreadings fails to note the metaphysical implications of nonfiction reception.

reader into the position of the narrator-mesmerist, it is hardly any wonder that a reader-mesmerist should want the tale to flatter mesmerists by praising their healing and even revivifying powers, but alas, it does not.

It is no wonder that Poe replied to Collyer in ambiguous, ironic, and mocking terms: Collyer blithely inhabited the role of the ideal *mis*reader. Poe published Collyer's letter in the *Broadway Journal* on December 27, 1845, commenting:

> We have no doubt that Mr. Collyer is perfectly correct in all that he says—and all that he desires us to say—but the truth is, there was a very small modicum of truth in the case of M. Valdemar—which, in consequence, may be called a hard case—very hard for M. Valdemar, for Mr. Collyer, and ourselves. If the story was not true, however, it should have been—and perhaps "The Zoist" [another journal in which Collyer proposed to print "Valdemar"] may discover that it is true after all. (391)

Here Poe plays with Collyer, both enabling and mocking his misreading—as "Valdemar" itself does to any number of readers.

One reader who was not fooled was Elizabeth Barrett (later Browning). She wrote to Poe in April 1846, saying that "there is a tale of yours ('The Case of M. Valdemar') . . . going the round of the newspapers, about mesmerism, throwing us all into 'most admired disorder,' and dreadful doubts as to whether 'it can be true,' as the children say of ghost stories." Barrett reads the genre better than many another reader: "ghost story" suggests that it is a Gothic story of the truly supernatural kind. She understands the metaphysical implications of a story that presents death as a horrific birth into a new existence of torment and terror. She also understands how easy it is to misread genre, gently making fun of those who take the tale as fact, naïvely, like children.

It may not be surprising that only such a sophisticated and spiritually minded writer as Elizabeth Barrett Browning caught on to some of Poe's tricks. He was the nineteenth century's American master of mysterious horror, an expert at evoking supernatural or paranormal mysteries, especially in stories that appear to rely upon psychological or mechanistic materialism. However, many scholars have asked whether Poe really wrote Gothic stories or whether he only ever used the Gothic ironically (e.g., Frank 331). Perhaps the question is irrelevant, at least for "Valdemar," which is a tale of reading and misreading. This story, especially read as a dark double of "Revelation," encodes and enacts its own misreading, mocking readers who ingenuously received it as nonfiction. But Poe did enjoy a good hoax, and the deeper irony of "Valdemar" is that if it *were* nonfiction, it would be much more horrific than if it were Gothic fiction. Humans like to be scared—witness the popularity of roller coasters or horror movies—but prefer the terror to be neatly packaged within the covers of fiction. These two stories do not allow such tidy containment. In "Revelation" and "Valdemar," Poe takes the two kinds of usual Gothic modes (one with real supernatural terrors and one with purely materialistic explanations) and interweaves them inextricably. Poe manages to ground them both in science, at the same time doubling the fear of a malevolent force beyond ordinary material existence. The result is more terrifying than mere spooks and bogeys, because it removes any hope of a happy afterlife, and it does so in an ostensibly nonfiction genre. This method allows Poe to capitalizes on fear of ghosts and fear of self, fear of haunting and fear of madness. In "Mesmeric Revelation" and "The Facts of M. Valdemar's Case," Poe manufactures and manipulates misreadings, to the reader's eternal terror.

Works Cited

Altschuler, Eric Lewin. "Informed Consent in an Edgar Allen [*sic*] Poe Tale." *Lancet* No. 9394 (November 2003): 1504.

Ashworth, Suzanne. "Experimental Matter, Unclaimed Death, and Posthumous Futures in Poe's 'Valdemar.'" *Poe Studies* 49, No. 1 (December 2016): 52–79.

Baldrick, Chris, editor. "Gothic Novel." In *Oxford Dictionary of Literary Terms*. 4th ed. Oxford: Oxford University Press, 2015,

www.oxfordreference.com.ezproxy.baylor.edu/view/10.1093/acref
/9780198715443.001.0001/acref-9780198715443-e-506.

Barrett (Browning), Elizabeth. "To E. A. Poe." April 1846,
www.eapoe.org/misc/letters/t4604000.htm.

Collyer, R. H. R. H. Collyer to E. A. Poe (16 December 1845),
www.eapoe.org/misc/letters/t4512160.htm.

————, and Edgar Allan Poe. "Editorial Miscellany." *Broadway
Journal* 2, No. 25 (December 1845): 390–91.

Darvay, Daniel. *Haunting Modernity and the Gothic Presence in British Modernist Literature.* New York: Palgrave Macmillan, 2016.

"Democratic Editors." *Cincinnati Weekly Herald and Philanthropist*
10, No. 19 (January 1846): 2.

"Ejaculation, N." *OED Online,* Oxford University Press. *Oxford
English Dictionary,* www.oed.com.ezproxy.baylor.edu/view/Entry/
60031.

Enns, Anthony. *Mesmerism and the Electric Age: From Poe to Edison.*
Rodopi, 2006. *Baylor OneSearch, Summon 2.0,* gateway.proquest.
com/openurl?ctx_ver=Z39.88-2003&xri:pqil:res_ver=0.2&res_id=xri:
ilcs-us&rft_id=xri:ilcs:rec:abell:R03846408.

Faivre, Antoine. "Borrowings and Misreading: Edgar Allan Poe's
'Mesmeric' Tales and the Strange Case of Their Reception." *Aries*
7, No. 1 (April 2007): 21–62. *EBSCOhost,* doi:10.1163/
157005906X154700.

Falk, Doris V. "Poe and the Power of Animal Magnetism." *PMLA*
84, No. 3 (1969): 536–46. *JSTOR,* doi:10.2307/1261142.

Fisher, Benjamin Franklin. *Poe at Work: Seven Textual Studies.* Bal-
timore: Edgar Allan Poe Society, 1978.

Frank, Frederick S. "Edgar Allan Poe." In Douglass H. Thomson et
al., ed. *Gothic Writers: A Critical and Bibliographical Guide.* Westport, CT: Greenwood Press, 2002. 330–43.

Gillespie, Zane. "'Mesmeric Revelation': Art as Hypnosis." *Edgar
Allan Poe Review* 17, No. 2 (November 2016): 142–60.

Kilfeather, Siobhán. "The Gothic Novel." In John Wilson Foster, ed.
The Cambridge Companion to the Irish Novel. Cambridge: Cam-

bridge University Press, 2006. 78–96, /core/books/cambridge-companion-to-the-irish-novel/gothic-novel/BD3BE43570ED97 0168DE7611E3434853.

Kofman, Ava. "The 'Extraordinary Case' of Poe's Valdemar." *Method: Science in the Making* 3 (July 2015): 63–70.

Mabbott, Thomas Ollive, ed. *Collected Works of Edgar Allan Poe: Tales and Sketches*. Cambridge, MA: Harvard University Press, 1978, www.eapoe.org/works/mabbott/tom3t013.htm#pg1026.

Marcovitch, Harvey, ed. "Death, Signs of." *Black's Medical Dictionary*. 42nd ed. London: A. & C. Black, 2010, ezproxy.baylor.edu/login?url=http://search.credoreference.com/content/entry/blackmed/death_signs_of/0?institutionId=720.

Perry, Dennis R., and Carl H. Sederholm. *Adapting Poe: Re-Imaginings in Popular Culture*. New York: Palgrave Macmillan, 2012.

Poe, Edgar Allan. "Mesmeric Revelation." *Columbian Lady's and Gentleman's Magazine* 2 (August 1844): 67–70.

———. "Mesmeric Revelation." In Poe's *Tales*. New York: Wiley & Putnam, 1845, hdl.handle.net/2027/nc01.ark:/13960/t2q53sx9p.

———. "The Facts of M. Valdemar's Case." *American Review* 2, No. 6 (December 1845): 561–65.

———. *The Works of the Late Edgar Allan Poe*. Ed. Nathaniel Parker Willis et al. New York: J. S. Redfield, 1850, hdl.handle.net /2027/uva.x000177929.

The Crazy Mountains

Dylan Henderson

The proprietor and I were sitting at a table in a corner of the dining room, watching as the streets outside filled with snow. The mountains to the northwest, which my wife and I had seen from the highway, were no longer visible, nor were the cottonwoods along the Yellowstone River or the grain elevators west of the Northern Pacific. Even the storefronts across the street from the Grand Hotel were beginning to fade. Before long, the white haze that had descended so suddenly over Big Timber would swallow them, too.

I should have excused myself and joined my wife and children upstairs, but I was too tired and drowsy to rise. Despite the cold weather outside, the dining room of the Grand Hotel was warm, cozy even, the only source of light being an enormous fire of aspen logs, which crackled pleasantly as it burned. It was nearly midnight, and aside from a single waiter, who was reading a magazine at the bar, the room was empty.

My companion, the owner and general manager of the hotel, was an elderly man, closer to seventy than sixty, who smelled faintly of horses. A half-empty glass of bourbon, its amber contents glowing in the firelight, sat by his elbow.

"If you're looking for a place in town," Campbell said slowly, "you ought to consider the Keller House on Hooper, a few blocks south of the Lutheran church. The widow who owns it has been trying to sell it for years. She wants to move to Spokane to be closer to her son. You might also check with the college. It owns a couple of houses across from the high school. Every summer, a bunch of students from Missoula live there while they're working in the hills—you know, digging for dinosaur bones—but during the winter the college is always looking for tenants. Course, there are a few ranches for sale south of the Boulder if you're interested in farming."

The old man took a sip of bourbon and leaned his head against the back of his chair. His weather-beaten face and small, hazel-colored eyes reminded me of pictures I had seen in the Metropolitan depicting cowboys, ranchers, and frontiersmen.

"Actually," I said, "I've inherited a bit of property. My grandfather left me his farm on the North Fork of Big Timber Creek."

A look of consternation passed over the old man's face.

"Are you sure it's on the North Fork?" he murmured. "That's a long way from town."

"It is. According to the lawyer, it's almost twenty miles northwest of Big Timber."

The old man took another sip of bourbon. He seemed troubled.

"What did you say your grandfather's name was?"

"Vandenberg."

"I remember him," Campbell muttered. "No one in town would have anything to do with him or his friends. When I was your age, there used to be twenty or thirty people living up there—running wild."

As much as I liked the old man, I was baffled by his reaction.

"The lawyer," I said hesitantly, "referred to it as an 'artists' colony.'"

Campbell scoffed. His leathery face had turned an ugly shade of red.

"I wouldn't call it that," he said savagely, "though your grandfather did consider himself an artist. His masterpiece, such as it is, used to hang in the Dutch Reformed Church in Gallatin. I saw it there myself. I don't know where it is now. Thirty years ago, after the war with Germany, the congregation demanded that Reverend Dekker take it down."

Outside, the wind had begun to howl. The sound rose, higher and higher, until it drowned out everything else. Even the grandfather clock in the hall, which had been ticking loudly, grew still.

"What," I said slowly, uncertain how to proceed, "did he paint?"

Campbell shook his head. In the dying light of the fire, he looked older and weaker than he had before.

"Cities," he said hoarsely. "I guess that's what you'd call them. Course, some folks say he painted other things too, things he couldn't show in town. You know, I have one of his pictures in the attic if you want to see it. My wife bought it years ago. I should've burned the thing after she died, but I kept everything of hers."

After a moment's hesitation I followed the owner of the hotel up the stairs to a small room, no more than five feet high, beneath the roof. Small though it was, the room was filled with furniture, picture frames, books, clothes, and Oriental curios. While I examined some of the stranger items in his wife's collection, including a set of ancient pewter spoons, Josiah Campbell rummaged through the stack of paintings his wife had accumulated. Unlike the others, most of which appeared to be conventional landscapes, the one he selected had been wrapped in butcher paper and marked with a vulgar symbol drawn in red ink. Breathing heavily, Campbell hoisted the heavy canvas onto a table and, taking a knife out of his pocket, cut the paper covering the picture.

I gasped when I saw what was beneath it.

In a way, Campbell had been right. It was a city of sorts. And yet, it was unlike any city on earth. Built of enormous, moss-covered stones, which no machinery known to man could have moved, the necropolis occupied a treeless plain bordered by a long line of jagged mountains. Most of the buildings, if that is what they were, must have collapsed centuries ago, for they were now nothing more than heaps of splintered rock. The largest structure still standing was a crooked, ebony-colored steeple, which pointed, like a broken finger, at the starry skies above. As I stared, hypnotized by the bizarre scene before me, the skies over the city seemed to stir, as if the heavens themselves, like some sort of fetid swamp, were filled with malignant life.

Two days later, after the snows had melted somewhat, my wife and I saw my grandfather's farm for the first time. Incredibly, neither my father nor my grandmother had ever mentioned it, nor had they told me anything about my grandfather, Jan Vandenberg. Before I arrived in Big Timber, I knew only that in the winter of 1923 my grandmother left her husband and, taking their ten-year-old son with her, returned to Albany where her parents lived. After she arrived in New York, she refused to speak of her husband or the circumstances that had compelled her to desert him. I learned of my grandfather's death, not from my father, who had not spoken to him for more than fifty years, but from his lawyer, who contacted me several days after the funeral.

Not surprisingly, my wife was disappointed with the property.

"It's a ruin," she said miserably, "a complete and utter ruin."

We were standing on the back porch, watching our two children play in the farmyard. In the distance, the Crazy Mountains towered, gray and somber, over the snow-covered plains.

"We knew," I said softly, "that the house would need some work. I mean, be reasonable. The man was over a hundred years old when he died. He couldn't possibly have cared for a property this size."

"Christ, John, look at the barn," my wife murmured. "It's about to fall down."

"We'll fix it," I said, putting my arm around her shoulders. "You'll see. This is our chance, Judith. It's our Saratoga Springs. Just imagine what you'll paint with this view for inspiration. Imagine what I'll write."

Judith ignored me. Her gray eyes, reddened by the cold, were staring at something in the distance, as if she saw or recognized something in the forested hills that bordered the farm.

To my knowledge, neither Maggie nor her husband had told Judith about the affair. And yet, somehow, she seemed to know all about it.

"We should never have left New York," she said bitterly, turning her back on the farm, the children, and me.

All that week I worked on the farm. By Saturday I had repainted the walls in the kitchen, dining room, and parlor; sanded the pinewood floors, which were badly warped; replaced several broken windows; pulled down the dilapidated toolshed; and patched the roof, which had leaked horribly in several places. Of course, a great deal of work remained, but I was pleased with my progress. Each day, before the rest of the family woke, I would wander through the old house, marveling at its tall ceilings, tiled bathrooms, working transoms, and stained-glass windows. Despite my grandfather's neglect, the house had retained its beauty, and I couldn't help but compare it to the cramped apartment the four of us had shared in Brooklyn.

And yet, despite my growing fondness for the house, I slept poorly inside its walls. Late at night, long after everyone else had fallen asleep, I would hear something moving around outside. More than once I heard it fumbling at the back door. Of course, I assured myself that I was imagining things. Considering that our closest neighbor lived more than three miles away, it was natural to feel somewhat paranoid. And yet, I know I didn't imagine the prints I found in the snow beneath our bedroom window or the gibbering I heard one evening in the woods west of the farm.

To make matters worse, a similar sense of dread had infected my wife. Her illustrations, which had always been sunny and cheerful, grew somber, the faces she depicted haggard. More and more, she would stop working and, forgetting her brushes, stare through the window at the mountains that rose so abruptly out of the surrounding plains. She seemed to be searching for something in those hills, something that, though close, remained invisible beneath the pines.

On Sunday, a week after we had moved into my grandfather's farm-house, one of our neighbors, a middle-aged rancher named Everett MacDonald, visited us after church.

Eager to display the progress I had made, I gave him a brief tour of the house, the fields, and the remaining outbuildings. Though somewhat taciturn, he inspected everything carefully, especially the tools and equipment my grandfather had left behind, and commented politely on the renovations.

"Does it ever snow like this in New York?" he asked as we

trudged through the north pasture.

"Sometimes," I said honestly, "but the snow in New York isn't this white. It's gray—like ash."

"You don't miss it, do you?" he asked.

I paused for a moment, letting the snow collect on my face and in my hair. I could feel the sting of the wind on my bare cheeks.

"After it snows," I said slowly, "the city grows quiet. For an hour or two everything stops. Everything becomes very still. Then the city begins to stir. People pour out of the buildings. Out of nowhere, cars appear. The crowds return. They churn the snow into muck. They ruin everything."

The rancher nodded.

"Well, there aren't any crowds out here. Truth be told, there are fewer people out here than there used to be. Most folks don't like living so close to the mountains."

"Why is that?" I asked, thinking of the crude, oddly bearded sculpture I had found in a closet upstairs.

The rancher seemed uneasy.

"I don't know. You hear things. Some folks complain about the grizzlies. Some say they can't sleep in the shadow of the mountains. I know the Crow always avoided them."

I glanced at the granite peaks to our right. They seemed larger—and closer—than ever. It was as if the mountains had sprouted additional ridges during the night.

"I do have strange dreams," I murmured, staring at the mountains, "dreams of another world."

MacDonald didn't reply.

"At the Grand Hotel," I said, changing the subject, "I saw one of my grandfather's paintings. I think about him a lot. He lived alone, way out here, for so long. . . . It's not surprising that his art became . . . well, somewhat disturbing."

The two of us were walking beneath the pine trees on the western edge of the farm. In the distance, about a quarter of a mile away, the roof of our farmhouse, its clapboards gray against the snow, rose above the dwarf elms that surrounded the house. When I squinted, I thought I could see a solitary figure wandering beneath the trees.

"I didn't know your grandfather very well," MacDonald said slowly. "No one east of the mountains did. Around here, decent folks avoid people like him."

"Why?" I asked, watching the lone figure stagger towards the open fields. "Why did everyone shun him?"

The rancher shook his head.

"A long time ago, when my little brother and I were hunting along the North Fork, I saw him—dancing in the woods. Even though I was just a boy, I could tell . . . I could tell that there was something wrong with him."

The thing I had seen near the house was less than a hundred yards away. It was shambling, head down, toward the woods. I called to it, and when it heard me, it stopped and, sniffing at the air, turned its shaggy head. Only then did I recognize my own flesh and blood.

By nightfall, my son had fully recovered. He seemed tired, exhausted even, but otherwise healthy. Both his temperature and his pulse were low—but not abnormally so for a five-year-old boy. Around seven I carried his blanket, pillow, and mattress downstairs and arranged them in front of the fire I had built in the grate. My son lay down next to his sister and, while I read to them, stared blankly into the flames. After a while, the two drifted off to sleep.

"You didn't see him out there," I said to my wife later that night. "He didn't seem . . . normal. It's as if he didn't know who he was. And then, my God, his face . . . His expression, Judith . . . It was unrecognizable."

My wife didn't answer. She was sitting on the edge of the bed, staring into the darkness outside. Through the window, I thought I could see the granite peaks west of the farm gleaming in the moonlight.

"I don't think you care about him," I said, suddenly angry. "You know, you don't play with them. You don't talk to them. You don't

Penumbra

listen to them. Why don't you just admit it? You've never cared about either one of them."

My wife looked at me for a moment. Then she lay down and, covering herself with the blanket, turned off the light.

My dreams that night were truly hideous. I dreamed I roamed an alien city, a vast, otherworldly necropolis built of Cyclopean stones beneath a row of serrated peaks. I could sense, in a way I cannot describe, other things in the darkness—shaggy, wolfish things that stalked the narrow streets of that nightmarish citadel or watched the city from their dens in the rubble. At times I could hear them feasting noisily or gibbering to themselves; I often smelled them; but I only saw them once. Beneath a pyramid of broken stones, I watched as a congregation of the things gathered around their sacrifice, the tentacles around their mouths wriggling hungrily. The high priest, if that is what it was, shuffled forward and took the victim's head in its paws. As it began to feed, the others danced and writhed in ecstasy.

And then, just before I awoke, I dreamed I was in the foothills west of the farm. I remember waiting, near the edge of the woods, for nightfall. When it came, I crawled beneath the barbed-wire fence and, lumbering through the snow, approached the lonely farmhouse. When I scratched at the door, my claws digging effortlessly into the walnut, it swung open, and the darkness outside poured into the house.

I wrote little that week. I told myself that I needed to spend more time with the children, but the truth is that I couldn't write. A sense of dread was growing within me, poisoning everything. At times I thought I was going mad. My children, who had always been happy and carefree, became listless and withdrawn. I often heard them moaning in the middle of the night, as if in the grip of a nightmare, but in the morning they never remembered anything. Once in a while, when they thought I wasn't observing them, they would suddenly shed their apathy, as if it were a mask or a disguise, and perform odd, ungainly rituals.

Sometime in January I stopped working on the house. By then I had grown to hate my grandfather's property and loathe the other-worldly peaks that pressed, closer and closer, against the farm.

Whenever the weather permitted, which was no more than once or twice a week, I would drive into Big Timber, leaving the children at home with Judith, and spend the day at the Grand Hotel or the Carnegie library on McLeod Street. One day, while perusing the library's archives, I came across a reference to my grandfather, who in 1923 had been charged with a litany of vague crimes, the most substantial of which was trespassing. Several of his associates, including Jacob DeWitt, Pieter Verhoeven, and Gerrit DeVries, were also indicted, but as far as I could tell, the charges had been dismissed. Further research, however, uncovered additional charges in 1927, 1932, and 1948. In the early 1920s, more than two dozen individuals, less than a quarter of whom were Dutch, were tried for blasphemy.

When I arrived home that evening, eager to tell my wife what I had discovered, I found her wandering around the backyard in her nightgown, as if she were looking for something, her pale skin as blue as the ice in the river.

Everything deteriorated after that. Our son, who had done so well in New York, seemed to regress. He talked less and less, and when he did, much of what he said was nonsense. Something about his behavior disturbed me, and despite the love I had always felt for my children, I found myself avoiding them as much as I could.

In February, the weather grew worse rather than better, and enormous drifts, sheltered from the wind, developed behind the house and the remaining outbuildings. Though I was desperate for company, I spent almost every day indoors, struggling to write. The four of us rarely saw anyone, most of the farms east of the mountains being deserted; but one evening, while I was gathering kindling for a fire, I thought I heard several of our neighbors in the woods west of the house. When I approached, they stopped whatever they had been doing and stared at me, their thin faces sagging hideously, as if I had encroached upon something sacred. That's when I noticed the snow at their feet, which their dancing had churned into mud. Long after I had turned from that strange scene and, badly shaken, fled into the woods, I could still smell the odor, which I can only describe as canine, that the clearing had secreted.

The next day I saw a realtor in Billings. He promised me that he would look for a buyer, but I knew, before I had left his office, that there was no hope of selling the property. The realtor had tried to be tactful, but I could tell by his sickly smile what he really thought.

Around the first of March, a friend of ours, who had published two of my novels and dozens of my wife's illustrations, visited the farm. He had spent the past two weeks skiing near Bozeman, and before he returned to New York he wanted to discuss something with me. The two of us stayed up late that night, discussing my previous books and arguing about contemporary authors. Around eleven, shortly after my wife retired, he asked me if I had seen any of her latest artwork.

"I haven't looked at her work in a long time," I said with a sigh, "and she hasn't read mine."

Elliot nodded, his blue eyes glowing sympathetically. The bitterness and rage I felt must have been alien to him.

"Maggie showed me the letter you wrote to her. Your friends are worried about you, John. If you're so unhappy here, why don't you leave this place? Why don't you come back to New York?"

Through the window, I could see the Crazy Mountains rising above the plains, their peaks gleaming malignantly in the moonlight.

"I can't," I said, staring out the window. "We can't afford to leave."

Elliot, leaning back in his chair, studied me for a moment. I could hear him tapping the bowl of his pipe against his armrest. The pungent smell of Algerian tobacco, which Elliot had discovered in France, filled the parlor.

"You can't stay," Elliot said finally. "Listen to me, John. There's something wrong with your wife. There's something wrong with Judith."

I thought I could see something outside, a black shape slouching across the field.

"Has its hour come round at last?" I murmured, trying to peer through the frost-covered panes.

"It's just a bear," Elliot said, reaching inside his satchel and pulling out a manila envelope. "Look at these, John. Look at them. That would've been the cover."

He handed me the pictures. My hands shook when I saw what they were.

"What are these?" I whispered.

Elliot didn't answer immediately.

"That . . . thing there," he muttered, trying to relight his pipe, "is the White Rabbit. Look closely at its mouth. I don't why it . . . looks like it does."

"This . . . is Alice's Wonderland? This . . . city?"

I pushed the all-too-familiar pictures away. I felt sick.

"Now tell me, John. What's wrong with her?"

I shook my head, unable to speak. When I looked up, I saw my son standing in the doorway, a blank, faraway look in his eyes. I motioned to him, and he crossed the room and, without saying a word, climbed into my lap. I pressed his head against my chest and began to stroke his short blond hair.

"There's something wrong with all of them," I whispered, my hands still shaking. "I think she's doing something to them, Elliot. She's drugging them or—I don't know—poisoning them or hypnotizing them or something. God knows why. Maybe . . . I don't know. Maybe she knows about what happened in New York."

My son's hair, I now realized, was slightly sticky. Elliot was watching the boy, a look of horror on his handsome face.

Just then my fingers touched something, something small and round behind my son's ear.

"There's something here," I murmured, my voice dropping. "Elliot, bring that lamp over here."

Elliot didn't move. His blue eyes bulged.

"Don't do that," he said, watching me pick at the waxy protrusion. "John, don't touch that."

I could feel the soft wax crumbling beneath my fingernails. When I held it to my nose, it smelled foul—like some kind of discharge.

My son showed no reaction when I took a pen out of my pocket and began to dig the last of the wax out of his skull. When I had finished, a perfectly round hole, about the size of a pencil eraser, was visible behind his right ear. Over the course of the next hour I found six more.

Nearly delirious, I dragged my daughter out of bed. While she sat on the floor of her room, crying, I began to pick through her hair. Beneath her blonde locks, her skull was pitted—like a cheese. Judith, her expression unreadable, watched from the doorway. She wouldn't let me touch her head, and I didn't dare touch my own.

Past that point, I can remember only bits and pieces. Elliot must have left soon after I discovered my son's injuries, but I have no memory of him departing. I suppose I followed him outside, for I remember staggering through the snow, which was almost as high as my waist, and feeling the cold wind on my face. Somewhere nearby, an elk moaned, as if it were in pain. The smell of pine trees filled the air, and I heard their limbs creaking in the wind. As long as I live, which I hope will not be much longer, I will never forget the way the snow-crested mountains glimmered beneath the stars that night or the way my wife's pale face reddened when I confronted her or the way the trigger of my grandfather's ancient rifle felt when I fingered it.

When the madness that had gripped me finally receded, I was stumbling through the foothills west of the farmhouse. My fingers, toes, and ears were numb from the cold, my feet and back sore. At some point a branch must have lashed me across the face, for I could still taste the blood in my mouth and on my upper lip.

And then, just before dawn, I saw it. It was loping westward, its shaggy head down, its thin, hairy body black in the starlight. The thing paused for a moment and, sniffing at the air, turned. I saw its eyes twinkle when it saw me. Then I heard, as if from a great distance, the crack of a rifle, and the acrid smell of gunpowder stung my nostrils. The creature dropped to its knees, the tentacles that grew around its mouth wriggling angrily, and vanished into a thicket of young hawthorn trees.

Later that day, while my wife and children sat silently on the sofa and watched me, I began to barricade the house. By nightfall I had nailed every window shut and reinforced both doors. After that, I sent the children to bed and, taking a ladderback chair and my grandfather's deer rifle with me, stationed myself behind the front door. My wife watched me for a moment and then, without a word, followed the children upstairs.

Time passed slowly that night. I dozed fitfully, sometimes dreaming of my grandfather and the awful things he and his friends had done in the wilderness, sometimes dreaming of a long-dead city, which crouched beneath a row of jagged, evil-looking peaks. Around midnight an unfamiliar sound pierced my dreams, and I awoke, my hands and face wet with sweat. After the last of the dreams had cleared, I heard, or thought I heard, something trudging through the snow outside.

My hands shaking, I rose and, standing atop the chair, peered through the transom. There was something outside. I could see it, a shape blacker than the shadow cast by the farmhouse. It was shuffling through the snow, its movements awkward and ungainly. Then I saw its bearded face, and I fired through the transom.

Instantly, a thick, sulfuric cloud filled the hall, the fumes stinging my eyes and throat. Outside, the thing shrieked. Then the door shuddered, its walnut panels quivering, as the creature hurtled itself against the portal. For a moment I thought I saw something through the transom, but before I could reload, the thing was gone. The house grew quiet, the night outside still.

Frantic, I tried to reload the gun, but the bolt had jammed. No matter how hard I tried, I couldn't pull it back. Outside, the thing had begun to make an odd cooing sound, which resembled, to the extent that it resembled anything on this earth, the call of a mourning dove. And then, to my horror, the children heard the sound. I could hear them pounding on the door to their room as they called to the creature outside.

When the ceiling started to quiver as the two began to dance, a sense of overpowering fear surged through me. My knees weakened, and for a moment I thought I might fall. Then I saw my wife standing on the stairs, the look in her eyes unrecognizable, and I screamed at her, my voice cracking, and staggered after the thing.

For almost an hour it circled the house. I stayed inside, following from room to room, trying to catch a glimpse of the thing through the windows, but it was all but invisible in the darkness. Sometimes it would pause to claw at a shuttered window or sniff beneath a locked door, but for the most part it kept moving. And then, suddenly, it stopped. According to the clock in the hallway, it was a little after one in the morning.

My knees shaking, I sank down into an armchair and, cursing softly under my breath, wiped the sweat from my forehead. Despite the cold, my skin was hot to the touch, and no matter how much I tried I couldn't stop trembling.

My wife, who was no more than a pale shadow moving through the dark house, sat down across from me. I thought for a moment that she might say something, but she didn't. She simply sat there, her face turned toward the mountains, those awful mountains I knew from my dreams.

I wanted to say something. I wanted to hone my words until they were sharp enough to cut her, to slice through her sickening apathy. And yet, in the end I didn't do anything.

"You did this," I murmured. "You."

It was all that I could say.

As I sat there, the room grew dim, the furniture blurry. A feeling of weariness had descended upon me, and I struggled to keep my eyes open. Before they closed completely, I saw my wife standing in the hallway, the children beside her. I heard the front door creak on its rusty hinges, and then, right before the nightmares began, I heard a soft, wet, slobbering sound, as if an enormous dog were licking its chops.

When I awoke, my family was gone.

The Fantastic Flame

Leigh Blackmore

I dreamed I saw a flaming pillar twined
With pulsing colours, reaching to the sky,
Resplendent, awesome, glowing. In my mind
It twisted up, a million miles high.

I stood and trembled like a bird whose wings
Were fluttering in death, whose beak still gapes.
And in the flame I witnessed vanished things—
Obscure gods and unfamiliar shapes.

Beneath the steadfast stars' exotic spray
The vast, bright pillar burned with spirit rare
And forms diverse—o suns; of time; decay
Of permanence. It bore a poisoned air.

It seemed I heard mysterious music—vague,
Ethereal, indefinite and remote.
I wondered, as the forms like fiery plague
Coiled lithe within and on my psyche smote.

To tread the stars the flaming pillar tried,
Transcending all, but could not last for long.
And so its flame died down; I almost cried
As, too, died down its deadly, beauteous song.

The Psychic Sleuth Who Survived

Lee Weinstein

Literary psychic detectives have come and gone over the past century, from Kate and Hesketh Prichard's Flaxman Low (1898–99) to such current characters as Jim Butcher's Harry Dresden and Mike Carey's Felix Castor.

Some, such as the series *True Ghost Stories* by Jessie Adelaide Middleton or *The Ghost Hunters* series (1906) by Allen Upward, have disappeared into obscurity, and a fair number, such as Blackwood's John Silence and Dion Fortune's Dr. Taverner, have been kept alive only through occasional reprintings of the original stories. For example, Seabury Quinn's Jules de Grandin stories from the original *Weird Tales* magazine, which were among the most popular stories to run in the magazine, were briefly resurrected when reprinted in mass-market paperback in the mid-1970s but soon faded from view. Aside from an expensive limited edition for collectors in 2006, there were no further popular editions or continuations of the character by subsequent authors.

Only one literary psychic detective, to my knowledge, has persisted in popular culture as a living character.

Thomas Carnacki, created by William Hope Hodgson, first appeared in the *Idler* magazine in 1910 in a story titled "The Gateway of the Monster." Five more stories appeared during Hodgson's lifetime and all six were collected in the volume *Carnacki the Ghost-Finder* (1913), published by Eveleigh Nash to good reviews. The London *Bookman* said the volume "comprises half-a-dozen of the 'creepiest experiences imaginable" and concludes, "Mr. Hope Hodgson plays deftly on the strings of fear" (142).

An additional three stories were published decades after Hodgson's death. All nine tales were collected by August Derleth and published under his Mycroft & Moran imprint and with the same title in 1947.

This expanded collection was favorably reviewed by the *Chicago Sun:* "The tales bear their thirty-odd years pretty lightly and the best of them ought to become the anthologist's delight" (72). The book also rated a brief mention in the *Saturday Review:* "Carnacki's exploits with real ha'nts better than his 'ghost breaking.' Stories vary in merit but general effect is amply shivery" (34).

Since then Carnacki has taken on a life of his own. Unlike Quinn's de Grandin, he has been in print from numerous publishers from the 1970s onward. He has appeared in two TV adaptations: "The Whistling Room" on *Chevron Theatre* (22 August 1952), repeated on *Pepsi Cola Playhouse,* 1954; and "The Horse of the Invisible" on PBS's *The Rivals of Sherlock Holmes* (18 October 1971), a rebroadcast from the BBC.

Carnacki rated a listing in *Queen's Quorum* as one of the most important detective characters since 1845. And just as the further adventures of Sherlock Holmes have been written by other hands, Carnacki has been adopted by newer authors. Among others, twelve further adventures of Carnacki have been written by A. F. Kidd and Rick Kennett (*No. 472 Cheyne Walk*), and ten Carnacki stories by William Meikle have been collected in *Carnacki: Heaven and Hell.* He appears as a character in John R. King's *The Shadow of Reichenbach Falls* (2008), in which he teams up with Dr. Watson, and in *The League of Extraordinary Gentlemen: Black Dossier* (2006) and later in *The League of Extraordinary Gentlemen: Century 1910* (2009) by Alan Moore and Kevin O'Neill. Leigh Blackmore, in his essay "Things Invisible" (181–82), notes that Kim Newman, Barbara Hambly, Guy Adams, Alberto Lopez Aroca, and others have used Carnacki in stories of their own, and Andrew Cartmel has even featured Carnacki as a companion to the second Dr. Who in a novella titled "Foreign Devils."

Recent additions to the growing list of Carnacki material are the anthologies *Carnacki: The New Adventures* (2013) and *Carnacki: The*

Lost Cases (2016), both edited by Sam Gafford, and an original audio drama, *The Haunting at Ravenglass* by Ian Gordon, produced by HorrorBabble (2019).

Blackmore (182) also notes an album of Carnacki-inspired electronic music, *Music for Thomas Carnacki,* and audio recordings of Hodgson's Carnacki stories by different readers from Librivox.

Journalist David Barnett, in a 2010 blog entry on Carnacki for the *Guardian,* notes that although he wasn't the first supernatural detective, he "has all the elements in such perfect proportions that he deserves to be crowned king of the occult 'tecs—especially in this, his centenary year."

Why has Carnacki had such staying power while other similar characters, such as John Silence or Jules de Grandin, have not? What is it about certain literary characters that enable them to outlive their creators? There are numerous examples in other genres such as Sherlock Holmes, Zorro, and James Bond.

Sometimes, as in the above examples, the critical factor in their continuing popularity involves crossing over into other media. *The Curse of Capistrano* (1919) by Johnston McCulley probably would have been a one-shot novel if it hadn't been discovered by Douglas Fairbanks and made into the popular film *The Mark of Zorro* a year later, prompting McCulley to continue writing Zorro stories and inspiring yet more adaptations.

Sherlock Holmes had been adapted into long-running plays in London and New York even while the original stories were still appearing in magazines. The popularity of James Bond was given a boost when President Kennedy revealed that he was a fan of the series, but it was the film adaptations of the character that found a permanent niche in popular culture and became the longest running series in film history.

This was obviously not the case with Carnacki. He was not adapted for the screen until 1952 and not again until 1971, both as individual segments of different anthology series. The 1952 adaptation of "The Whistling Room" was not very faithful to Hodgson's story. It was watered down into a conventional ghost story, in which the ghost was revealed to be a product of fakery—maybe. Alan Napier played Carnacki as a bit of a buffoon. It had none of the qualities that made the original story work so well. The 1971 BBC adaptation of "The Horse of the Invisible," with Donald Pleasance in the role, was considerably better but doesn't seem to have inspired further adaptations.

A second possible factor is brought up in the entry on Hodgson in *Twentieth-Century Literary Criticism*. After noting that "the Carnacki stories are considered the best of the 'occult detective' series that were popular at the time," the compiler goes on to say that "Perhaps the most innovative feature of the Carnacki stories is Hodgson's careful construction, which does not allow the reader to discover whether Carnacki has been investigating a real or faked supernatural event until the story's end" (229). But while this does add an intriguing element, it is not unique to the Carnacki stories.

A third possible factor is characterization. Sherlock Holmes has become a cult figure, to a large extent, because of his eccentric personality and almost superhuman abilities. Zorro's dual identity as a mild-mannered fop and a masked hero of the oppressed strikes a resonant chord that still echoes in such modern superheroes as Superman and Batman. Bond's depiction as suave playboy superhero in the films, gives him mass appeal.

In some respects it can be argued, and has been argued, that Carnacki is a not a very well-developed character. E. F. Bleiler, in his entry for Hodgson in his *Supernatural Fiction Writers* (426), says that in the Carnacki stories Hodgson played up his strengths (emotion and imagination) and downplayed his weaknesses (characterization and plot). H. P. Lovecraft in "Supernatural Horror in Literature" calls Carnacki a "more or less conventional stock figure of the 'infallible detective' type" (60). Kidd and Kennett in the introduction to *472 Cheyne Walk* call him a "generic stiff upper lip Edwardian Englishman." Albert Borowitz says in his entry for

Hodgson in *British Mystery Writers 1860–1919* that "he is not delineated strongly either in physical appearance or personality" (167).

There is some truth in these assessments. But although we know little about him, his appearance, or his background, Carnacki does come across as very human and very fallible. Like Holmes, he exhibits some rather eccentric behavior with his circle of friends, refusing to make any reference to his latest case until after dinner is finished and abruptly dismissing everyone from his home at the end with his genial "out you go." But unlike a Holmes, a Bond, or a Zorro, he is the antithesis of the superhero. His struggles as he attempts to convey his difficulties to his friends do not make him sound like a confident hero. As a typical example, in "The Searcher if the End House" he says of a ghostly child: "In an extraordinary way the child seemed not to be distinct from the surrounding gloom, but almost as it were a concentration of that extraordinary atmosphere; almost— can you understand?—as if that gloomy colour . . . came from the child. It seems impossible to make clear to you, but try to take hold of what I'm saying" (110).

But more importantly, unlike the "infallible detective type" to which Lovecraft compares him, Carnacki often displays anxiety and fear as he goes about investigating his cases. There is even a case in which he fails to end the haunting. And there are often questions at the end of each story that he is not able to answer because, as he admits, he himself doesn't completely understand what happened.

Compared to Flaxman Low, who comes across as an emotionless problem-solving machine, Carnacki comes very much alive as a character. Consider this passage from "Gateway of the Monster":

> A great black shadow covered it and rose into the air and came at me. I saw that it was the Hand, vast and nearly perfect in form. I gave one crazy yell and jumped over the pentacle and the ring of burning candles and ran despairingly for the door. I fumbled idiotically and ineffectually with the key, and all the time stared, with the fear that was like insanity, toward the Barriers. (54–55)

All this being said, it is unlikely that characterization per se is the key to Carnacki's longevity. It is there, but is not as strong or well-defined as in a character like Holmes.

A fourth factor is closer to the key. It is simply that most of the Carnacki stories are quite effective in inducing fright. No one could build up an atmosphere of fear and suspense quite like Hodgson. Bleiler was on the mark when he cited emotion as one of Hodgson's strengths. We feel with Carnacki when he breaks out in a sweat as he spends the night in a haunted room or experiments with his electrical devices.

But more than anything, it is most likely the somewhat Lovecraftian imaginative backdrop Hodgson created for his character that is mostly responsible for his lasting success. As Bleiler said, imagination is one of Hodgson's strengths.

Lovecraft's fiction has survived and built up a following largely because of the underlying philosophy that gives his work resonance. His stories are interconnected and based on the idea that mankind is an inconsequential speck of dust in the overall scheme of things, at the mercy of intelligent entities from beyond time and space. Hodgson has built up an analogous background. Brian Stableford, in an encyclopedia entry for Hodgson (274), characterizes Hodgson's uniting idea as "a marginal region separating our world from others." Our world is depicted as being under attack by what Hodgson calls "the Outer Monstrosities" and "ab-human creatures."

As I have stated in an earlier article, many of Hodgson's stories have hints and allusions to this underlying mythos, but it is laid out and developed to the greatest extent in the Carnacki stories. It differs from Lovecraft's in that Hodgson's universe is not an uncaring one. The forces of evil are counterbalanced by forces of good. Thus, in "The Whistling Room," Carnacki is saved at one point by an unknown entity whispering the last line of the Saaamaaa ritual at a critical moment. This good/evil dichotomy is also spelled out in *The House on the Borderland* and surfaces in *The Night Land* as well.

Stableford characterizes the first six stories as "inventive and engaging, but calculatedly trivial." However, he goes on to praise "The Hog" (first published in 1947) as a "visionary fantasy in which the meta-empirical realm is revealed to be dark and hostile, populated by degraded and malevolent entities . . . the recurrent note resonating within all Hodgson's most effective work" (275). It should be pointed out that the "calculatedly trivial" tales, such as "The Whistling Room" and "Gateway of the Monster," did lay down many of the elements elaborated upon in "The Hog" and have been anthologized on their own merits.

As Blackmore puts it, "it's [Carnacki's] exploits, and the carefully constructed milieu in which they take place, that continue to intrigue." Borowitz hypothesizes: "The detective's literary fame is probably due to his unique investigative technique, which combines a pseudoscholarship in occult doctrine, a variety of devices for protection against 'The Outer Monstrosities,' and the use of Hodgson's beloved photography and other practical means of recording intrusion into reputedly haunted houses" (167).

Carnacki indeed applies a scientific approach to his cases. As Samuel Bruce notes, "Carnacki was more than just an imitation Sherlock Holmes or John Silence—he was, in fact, one of the earliest examples of the 'scientific detective,' that is, he employs new gadgets (often of his own invention) made possible by scientific technology" (128). He begins by minutely examining every inch of the area thought to be haunted, to rule out human agencies. He then brings in the tools of his trade, flashlight, camera, gun, and state-of-the-art electrical gadgets such as his electric pentacle.

He consults the Sigsand Manuscript, Hodgson's equivalent to the *Necronomicon*, which dates from the fourteenth century, as well as the presumably recent book, *Experiments with a Medium* by a Professor Garder, thus applying modern technology to medieval beliefs and implying that medieval ideas of magic are actually phenomena with a scientific basis. The Electric Pentacle is similar and serves the same protective purpose as the "Earth-current"-powered barrier surrounding and protecting the Last Redoubt in *The Night Land*. In addition to the Outer Monstrosities, Carnacki refers to "aeiirii" and "saiitii" phenomena, and other—for the want of a better word—pseudo-Lovecraftian or perhaps proto-Lovecraftian phenomena. In "The Whistling Room" and "The Hog," Carnacki explains that saiitii phenomena involve an entity converting matter to its own purposes, and aeiirii phenomena involve materialization.

It is this consistent underlay, often cross-referenced between stories, that gives the whole a footing in reality. All this underlying mythos is mentioned in other stories but is explained in greatest detail in "The Hog," which in some ways resembles *The House on the Borderland,* just as "The Haunted 'Jarvee'" bears much resemblance to *The Ghost Pirates.*

To this one may add Carnacki's frequent references to other cases, some of which refer to previous stories, as the references to the "Gateway Case" in "The Hog," which refer to "The Gateway of the Monster," and many of which refer to unwritten stories, such as the "Noving Fur Case" or the frequently cited "Black Veil Case." The overall effect is of a consistent underlying universe. As French critic Lauric Guillaud notes in his survey of paranormal detectives, Carnacki's "metaphysical experiments . . . are no more than a pretext . . . used by the author to create a personal and original cosmology" (311).

In addition to Carnacki's human vulnerability and his dealings with the Hodgsonian mythos, there is one other factor that helps to explain Carnacki's burst of popularity in the past decade. The stories were written and set at the beginning of the twentieth century, circa 1910. Carnacki makes frequent use of the technology of the era. It should be noted that he is using the most modern high-tech equipment available when he constructs devices using vacuum tubes. The vacuum tube was invented in 1904, and the triode in 1907. In addition to the electric pentacle in his earlier stories, he makes use of an electrical apparatus to produce "counter-vibrations" in "The Haunted 'Jarvee,'" and in "The Hog" he has devised a machine that can record and play back the nightmares of man he is trying to save. He also uses an improved version of the electric pentacle using concentric rings of multicolored tubes. This period technology fits in quite nicely with the current popularity of the Steampunk genre, and that is undoubtedly what has won him a membership in the League of Extraordinary Gentlemen.

Hodgson's most imaginative work may have been *The Night Land* and *The House on the Borderland,* but the Carnacki stories may prove to be his most enduring creation.

Works Cited

Barnett, David. *Booksblog:* "Thomas Carnacki, King of the Supernatural Detectives." *Guardian* (London) (10 June 2010), www.theguardian.com/books/booksblog/2010/jun/30/thomas-carnacki-supernatural-detective.

Bleiler, E. F. "William Hope Hodgson." In E. F. Bleiler, ed. *Supernatural Fiction Writers.* New York: Charles Scribner's Sons, 1985. 421–28.

Blackmore, Leigh. "Things Invisible: Human and Ab-Human in Two of Hodgson's Carnacki Stories." *Sargasso* 1, No. 1 (2013): 176–97.

Borowitz, Albert. "William Hope Hodgson." In Bernard Benstock and Thomas F. Staley, ed. *British Mystery Writers 1860–1919.* Detroit: Gale Research Co., 1988. 166–68.

Bruce, Samuel. "William Hope Hodgson." In Darren Harris-Fain, ed. *British Fantasy and Science-Fiction Writers Before World War I.* Detroit: Gale Research, 1997 121–31.

Gafford, Sam, ed. *Carnacki: The New Adventures.* Warren, RI: Ulthar Press, 2013.

———, ed. *Carnacki: The Lost Cases.* Warren, RI: Ulthar Press, 2016.

Gordon, Ian. "The Haunting at Ravenglass." HorrorBabble 2019. Audio.

Guillaud, Lauric. "Paranormal Detectives." *Para*Doxa* 6, No. 3 (1995): 301–18.

Hodgson, William Hope. *Carnacki the Ghost-Finder.* Sauk City, WI: Mycroft & Moran, 1947.

Kidd, A. F., and Rick Kennett. *No. 472 Cheyne Walk.* 1992. Ashcroft, BC: Ash-Tree Press, 2002.

King, John R. *The Shadow of Reichenbach Falls.* New York: Tor/Forge, 2008.

Lovecraft, H. P. *The Annotated Supernatural Horror in Literature.* Ed. S. T. Joshi. New York: Hippocampus Press, 2000.

Meikle, William. *Carnacki: Heaven and Hell.* Portland, OR: Ghost House/Dark Regions Press, 2011.

Moore, Alan, and Kevin O'Neill. *The League of Extraordinary Gentlemen: Black Dossier.* New York: DC Comics, 2008.

———. *The League of Extraordinary Gentlemen: Century 1910.* New York: Top Shelf Productions, 2009.

Queen, Ellery. *Queen's Quorum: A History of the Detective Crime Short Story as Revealed in the 106 Most Important Books Published in This Field Since 1845.* Rev. ed. New York: Biblio & Tannen, 1969.

Stableford, Brian. "Hodgson, William Hope." In David Pringle, ed. *Horror, Ghost & Gothic Writers.* Detroit: St. James Press, 1998. 273–75.

[Unsigned.] Review of *Carnacki the Ghost Finder. Bookman* (London) No. 261 (June 1913): 142.

[Unsigned.] Review of *Carnacki the Ghost Finder. Chicago Sun Book Week* (6 February 1948): 72.

[Unsigned.] "The Saturday Review's Guide to Detective Fiction." *Saturday Review of Literature* 31, No. 7 (14 February 1948): 34.

Weinstein, Lee. "The First Literary Copernicus." *Nyctalops* 3, No. 1 (January 1980): 17–19.

The Hell of Mirrors

Manuel Arenas

Mary could not believe the cheek of that gauche little doomsayer. What kind of fortune was that? How could she say such horrible things, and why? Was she psychotic, possessed by a malignant spirit, or just meanspirited? Either way, it certainly would not do her prognosticating practice any good, and once Mary told her father, Helldorado copper mining mogul Anselm Worthington, about her insolence, Madame Catina would be back to dispensing philters and telling fortunes from a yellow-curtained tent with the bawds and boozers. Anyway, after giving the harridan a piece of her mind she got her money's worth to make up for the impertinence. On her way out of the sibyl's shop, as the spindly woman was putting away her tarot cards, muttering heatedly under her breath (some tawdry gypsy malison, no doubt), Mary swiped the first thing that came to hand—a vermeil hand mirror; it was tacky and hideous. Mary now held it in her hand, running her soft fingers, unblemished by any common labor, along the gaudy detail of the border frame; the entirety of it was fashioned into the gaping maw of a leering grotesque. As she paused to behold her own tawny-haired reflection in the glass, her sullen, doughy-faced doppelgänger peered back at her from within its gullet like a harried soul in a hellmouth. Mary blenched at the sight and quickly pulled the mirror away with a gasp.

Then, with a roll of her hazel eyes and a shilly-shally chuckle, she dismissed the thought, chided herself for her foolishness, and tried to recall what her former governess, Miss Amanda, used to tell her when she was a slip of a girl, about that divinatory ritual in which a young lady might see the countenance of her future husband by using a lit candle and a hand-held mirror. If memory served, to perform this minor feat of captromancy, one would take the aforementioned implements, then walk backward up a staircase peering into the mirror in the light of the candle as one did so, and eventually the image of a suitor would appear by their side. Mary was game, but she would have to wait until the rest of the household had retired before she could give it a try.

Holding a lit red candle in her right hand and the mirror in her left, she began her rearward ascent from the foyer, carefully minding her step while maintaining her gaze on the glass in front of her. The candle flame glinted off the gilded frame as in the reflected darkness of the unlit stairwell a figure commenced to take shape beside her. However, it was not the handsome swain she had hoped for, but rather a ghastly fetch, ashen-faced and bloody with a sanguinary trail spurting from an ugly head wound. Mary screamed, startled by the gruesome sight, and, losing her balance, took a tumble down the staircase, thwacking the floor with a horrible crunching sound that did nothing to ruffle the indifferent slumbers of her surviving family members.

With a quick flash of pain Mary was insensate. After an indeterminable period of time she awoke to extreme darkness. She could not see nor feel anything, but she was somehow aware, and in the pitch blackness she heard a familiar voice call her name—once, twice, then again. She knew but could not place the speaker, yet she followed its voice just the same. Presently a light appeared before her. Moving toward it, she saw a slight figure approach, its face obscured in the illumination. The figure reached out a radiant hand to Mary and she responded in kind, only to be seized in an iron grip that pulled her from the darkness into a dimly lit room.

Oddly, she found herself alone in a narrow hall that stretched as far as her eyes could see. The walls were covered in black wallpaper with red stripes that glistened in the lambent light of the myriad sconces that lined the room. Mary approached the nearest wall cautiously to examine the stripes she perceived ended just before the rim of the wainscoting in drips. She touched one hesitantly and with bated breath brought her ruddily splotched fingers to her face to inspect the smudge; it bore a metallic odor. Eyes widening, she gasped, "Misery me—it's blood!" As if on cue, an even bigger drop plopped onto her cracked cranium, prompting Mary to look up to discover its source: a grisly candle cast in her image that, as it melted, oozed an incarnadine residue that through some nefarious prodigy was comprised of the vital fluid.

Mary screamed, prompting the infinitude of mirrors, all bearing the leering maw of the vermeil hand mirror, to respond with an eruption of disquieting laughter: the derisive cackle of Madame Catina. Subsequently, their gilded mouths commenced to call out at intervals: "Bloody Mary! Bloody Mary! Bloody Mary!" At the sound of which Mary, unaccountably, was compelled to answer their respective invocations, racing from one mirror to the next to descry the faces of strangers who alternately screamed and jeered at her ghastly, ghostly countenance. And so she continues to flit from summons to summons, in perpetuity, screaming and clawing at the glass, striving to break free from her Gehenna of the looking glass, her Hell of Mirrors.

The Resurgence of a Fallen Angel: Echoes of *The Ghost Pirates* in "The Mainz Psalter"

Hubert Van Calenbergh

Ignored by critics in his home country, Belgium, Jean Ray[1] (1887–1964) chose to express himself in the language of Voltaire. In the early 1920s he turned to France for literary contacts. Thanks to authors like Jean Germain and most notably Maurice Renard, the French counterpart of H. G. Wells, the fledgling writer eventually established a strong foothold in Parisian artistic circles. As early as 1922 he obtained the much-coveted membership of the Société de Gens de Lettres, thus establishing his reputation as a French-language littérateur in both Belgium and France. Renard invited Ray to literary soirées in his Parisian home and introduced him to a number of colleagues. So when Ray's first book, *Les Contes du Whisky* (1925), appeared, by all accounts it set the stage for a glorious and fruitful career.

In spite of an open hostility on the part of (Belgian) Catholic reviewers who condemned the book as morally inappropriate, *Les Contes du Whisky* exploded like a bomb, especially in France. In *Le Figaro* Ray was dubbed the Belgian Poe, a nickname that stuck and would be bandied freely by cognoscenti in the years to come. Demand for the book surpassed all expectations: there were as many as twelve reprints in the year 1925 alone. *Les Contes du Whisky* actually

---

1. Jean Ray's real name was Raymond De Kremer. After an unexpectedly early release from prison in 1929 (possibly thanks to his uncle Edward Anseele), De Kremer was expelled from the French Société de Gens de Lettres and dropped by his publisher La Renaissance du Livre. Realizing that the name Jean Ray had become an embarrassment, De Kremer decided to use the name John Flanders as a new byline. However, the *nom de plume* Jean Ray would gradually resurface in the years to follow.

became the object of a cult following among French students; Maurice Renard's son Remi later testified that not a few of them could recite some of the stories in their entirety. In July a second book with more of the same fare, provisionally entitled *Rum Row,* was announced as "being in the works." Ray did indeed write five new stories that were subsequently aired in the periodical *L'Ami du Livre.* But the eagerly expected follow-up to *Les Contes du Whisky* did not materialize.

Photographs taken in the pivotal year 1925 show Jean Ray as a well-to-do gentleman. He possessed his own car, with a personal driver no less (highly unusual in Flanders); he would spend idle days in luxury hotels on the Belgian coast, mingling with the affluent, lazing on the beach with his wife and young daughter, or indulging in hunting parties in the hinterland. All this was done so ostentatiously that some acquaintances began to wonder about the provenance of Ray's sudden extraordinary wealth. And with good reason.

The final months of the year unexpectedly passed in a strange and ominous silence, as did the first two months of 1926. There was no more mention of a second book and no new stories appeared. Odd rumors began to circulate about a weapons traffic to Morocco and a smuggling operation to the United States (where Prohibition was in full swing). It was whispered that Ray owned a boat as well as two airplanes, that he was involved in the Siberian fur trade, that he operated a number of Dutch cinema complexes, etc. These tales form the nucleus of what scholars would later call *rayality,* or reality as Jean Ray perceived it.[2] At any rate, at the time many felt there was something in the wind, but it was too late to stem the tide.

---

2. Ray managed to create an entire body of lore around his person and would present its diverse components as solid fact even in televised interviews. This "legend" persisted until well after his death. Nowadays it is generally believed that he created it to account for the missing years in prison. Intensely aggrieved by his downfall, Ray ultimately came to believe his own legend. To humor him, a well-meaning critic launched the catch phrase "Avec Jean Ray, on ne sait jamais" ("With Jean Ray, one never knows").

On March 6 Jean Ray was officially arrested on the charges of malversation and large-scale financial fraud. Apparently he and an exchange agent named August Van den Bogaerde had been wheedling a number of upper-class citizens out of large sums of money since at least 1920. It would take another ten months before the case was heard in court. In the meantime Ray had to move out of his newly acquired home and seek shelter in one of the many wooden barracks that had been erected to accommodate victims of the Great War. Ray's new living conditions were appalling; his wife Virginie had to work as a seamstress in order to make ends meet, and his daughter Lulu was so ostracized by the children in her school that she had to be removed to another town. Ray was ultimately sentenced to seventy-eight months in prison.[3]

From the outset he behaved like a model prisoner and was granted certain liberties, such as being exempt from prison labor. He was allowed to correspond and receive books, and generally spent his days reading and writing in the prison library. Ray was overjoyed when he received his contributor's copy of *Les Maîtres de la peur,* an anthology that included his story "Irish Whisky." This volume was instrumental in establishing Ray as an important genre author alongside Poe, Ewers, Wells, Renard, and others. Feeling a strong kinship with Oscar Wilde, Ray wrote his own *De Profundis,* namely the poignant "Walls, Bars, Bolts (the Harsh Prison Life)."[4] Other writers who made an impression include Paul Verlaine, Jack London, Joseph Conrad (notably *Typhoon*), and William Hope Hodgson.

In prison Ray read a translation of Hodgson's *The Ghost Pirates* in *Revue Belge* and was so profoundly impressed that he set out to write a sea tale of his own. This became "Le Psautier de Mayence." The story is sufficiently original, even if Ray himself did not deny a

---

3. A detailed account of the trial can be found in Ray's *La Flandre Libérale* 304–27.

4. For the sake of convenience a translation of the title is offered. The piece first appeared in *Ons Land* as "Muren, tralies, grendels (het grauwe leven in onze gevangenissen)" (1931).

certain kinship with Hodgson's novel. Let us then take a closer look at both efforts and see if we can retrieve any clear-cut similarities. The comparison should be valuable, since "Le Psautier de Mayence" has been hailed as one of Ray's finest stories. Unfortunately, Ray knew no English, so we can only conjecture what he would have made of Hodgson's other novels, most notably *The House on the Borderland*, which was not translated in French until 1971.

Reading *The Ghost Pirates* one is immediately struck by Hodgson's solid workaday knowledge of all aspects of late nineteenth-century seamanship. The jargon deployed is so specific that a nautical dictionary would come handy indeed. This should come as no surprise, since from the age of fourteen the author spent eight full years at sea. In his sea tales Hodgson enthusiastically describes the dark atmosphere of a nascent mutiny, the dangers involved in the boarding of a derelict vessel, or the hazardousness of chores on deck and in the main rigging by stormy weather. He took a series of impressive photographs of his packet braving a cyclone ("Through the Vortex of a Cyclone"). One picture, showing a vessel strangely becalmed at sea, exudes the brooding menace reminiscent of the memorable discovery depicted in "The Derelict" (1912).

Hodgson had a love-hate relationship with the sea. He did not like the hard discipline; life on board was marked by bad food, inhuman treatment, and inadequate pay. But his father had died suddenly and the family needed a new breadwinner. Like all sailors, Hodgson eventually did develop a sense of awe for the beauty and sheer ruthlessness of the element to which he had entrusted his life. More than once he scornfully disparaged the sorry life of the landlubber who has no inkling of the strict discipline aboard a big sailing ship, or the deadly mishaps that can befall an apprentice. Not surprisingly the sea is a major constant in the twenty-four Hodgson poems left to us; titles such as "The Voice of the Ocean," "Grey Seas Are Dreaming of My Death," and "The Place of Storms" say it all.

Jean Ray's erudition, on the other hand, appears to be wholly second-hand, i.e., based on findings in reference books and nautical vademecums. Nonetheless "Le Psautier de Mayence" is suffused with enough realistic technical detail to warrant the reader's willing suspension of disbelief. It is possible that Ray, who was never a sailor, picked up certain details in the Harbour of Ghent. He is reported to have had long talks with fishermen during his stays in Zeebrugge on the Belgian coast. His much-vaunted smuggling experiences aboard the Fulmar are, however—just like the Fulmar itself—pure figments of his rich imagination. Nonetheless, in spite of his complete lack of nautical experience, Ray saw fit to imitate Hodgson in professing a deep-seated hatred of the sea.

Hodgson and Ray make use of an identical frame story: in both cases we are presented with a report written by a crew who have picked up the sole survivor of a sunken ship. The documents are signed by the captain and his officers, which is meant to authenticate the unbelievable happenings they narrate. Jessop, who survives the supernatural events on the doomed *Mortzestus*, is reasonably certain that not a single crew member on the rescuing vessel *Sangier* shall believe him. But at least he survives, while Jean Ray's protagonist Ballister ultimately succumbs to the wounds inflicted on him by his nemesis, the schoolmaster. That the frame of narration was borrowed from Hodgson is probable, but not sustained by any secondary literature or letters that I have seen. Both Hodgson and Ray use the device elsewhere; the short stories "A Tropical Horror" (1905) and "The Derelict" (1912) come to mind, as well as the novel *The House on the Borderland* (1908). In Ray's structurally complex novel *Malpertuis* (1943) frame narration is present on multiple levels. To be sure, the device is frequently used by a great many other authors. However, its specific context in the stories under consideration is so identical that a measure of doubt is plainly justified.

The motif of the phantom ship that the forces of nature do not seem fit to destroy, and which roams the seas for decades or possibly centuries, is a favorite with Hodgson. The terrifying seaweed-covered hulk that nearly collides with the *Mainz Psalter* was possibly inserted as a tribute; as in many a Hodgson tale, the wreck rises unexpectedly and spectacularly from the depths of the ocean: "A weed-encrusted derelict [!] that looked as if it had just risen from the bottom of the Atlantic nearly hurled itself into our bowsprit; the foul hulk was blown to smithereens against a foaming wall of rock that suddenly emerged away on the starboard quarter" (*MO* 94).

It is not clear what the mysterious schoolmaster plans to do with the *Mainz Psalter* or its crew, or what the ultimate goal of the "scientific" expedition he has mounted can be. According to crew member Lewellyn, there can be no doubt but that there is indeed such a goal. Lewellyn asserts that the vessel has entered another dimension, a suggestion strongly reminiscent of the theory put forward by the illiterate Jessop in *The Ghost Pirates:*

> "I should say it's reasonable to think that all the things of the material world are barred, as it were, from the immaterial; but that in some cases the barrier may be broken down. That's what may have happened to this ship. And if it has, she may be naked to the attacks of beings belonging to some *other state of existence.*" (*GP* 93; my emphasis)

It is seen that Lewellyn comes to exactly the same conclusion:

> "We are probably on a plane belonging to some *other state of existence.* You are well-versed in mathematics, that shall be of some help to you. Our familiar three-dimensional world is probably forever lost to us. I would say our present environment is part of the nth dimension [. . .]" (*MO* 100–101; my emphasis)

Lewellyn bandies impressive-sounding terms like "hyperspace" and "hypergeometry," haphazardly mingling astrology with modern science in the pseudo-authoritative way we encounter again and again in Jean Ray,[5] but it soon dawns on Ballister that his compan-

---

5. For an interesting analysis of Jean Ray's formal grasp of mathematics, see Van Herp.

ion, who is numbed by fear, is merely trying to convince himself they can escape the creeping terror that engulfs them. Jessop and apprentice Tammy (*GP*) agree to keep silent about the extraordinary happenings on the Mortzestus in order to avoid panic, mutiny or being put in irons as madmen. The duo Ballister/Lewellyn (*MO*) likewise decide to be discreet about their observations to keep the crew from becoming mentally unhinged.

Jessop's very first encounter with the supernatural—in the half-light an indistinct figure is seen clambering out of the sea; later it just as inexplicably returns to the waters (a particularly strong image!)—clearly made a strong impression on Ray: "a dark, wet shape jumped onto the deck. [. . .] To our amazement it looked like a clergyman, dressed in a dripping black vest. In the comparatively small head two tiny eyes burned like coal" (*MO* 113).

Hodgson's short story "The Haunted Pampero" similarly introduces a vaguely human figure who bluntly boards a ship in mid-sea. There is no evidence that Ray was familiar with the tale and it is doubtful that he knew enough English to have read it; at any rate, the passage is strikingly similar to that in *The Ghost Pirates*, a book that, as we have seen, he is certain to have read.

Mysterious vessels appear just under the surface and majestically sail by under the *Mortzestus'* keel. Is Jessop right in assuming that the *men-shadows* who have so far appeared on his ship belong to these phantom packets? What is the purpose of their assault? Williams does battle with them in the upper main to galant rigging and tumbles down onto the deck, while a fellow crew member disappears altogether. In "The Mainz Psalter" it is Turnip who falls to his death, while Walker vanishes without leaving a trace. In the depths under the schooner a red glow becomes visible. Ballister glimpses red-litten buildings with mighty towers connected by streets. Suddenly three gigantic tentacles lash through the air and a monstrous Kraken appears, but just as soon these visions disappear again. Any similarity with Hodgson's novel, then, is limited to a glimpse of something just under the surface that is but temporarily seen. The unexpected emergence of the monstrous cephalopod is a classic encountered in quite a few sea stories and hence a trifle gratuitous; it is as if Ray furiously resorts to spit and string to make the reader forget that the initial idea of supernatural submarine activity came from Hodgson.

In the end a powerless Jessop watches the *Mortzestus* being hijacked by a ghostly, determined and taciturn mob which wastes no time preparing the ship for an adventure of an altogether different kind: "Down upon the decks, there were the noises of a multitude working in a weird, inhuman silence. Then came the sqeal and rattle of blocks and braces aloft. They were squaring the yards. [. . .] and then I saw the sails fill suddenly" (*GP* 240).

Ballister and Lewellyn retreat to the captain's quarters where they will be safe. But they too unexpectedly have to deal with a new crew which takes charge without much ado:

> Indeed, it sounded as if the bridge had been invaded by a busy crowd. Before long there came a noisy creak from the wheel, and up in the rigging we heard the bustle of a laborious manoeuvre in progress. [. . .]
> "They're hoisting the sails!"
> The *Psalter* took a deep plunge and then swiftly heeled over to starboard. (*MO* 107–8)

The *Mainz Psalter's* annihilation is spelled right out. No ghostly crew is deemed necessary to navigate the ship straight into the depths; the schooner's destruction is assured by the last-minute interference of a furious schoolmaster who wants to talk Ballister out of destroying his precious occult books. Ballister is saved from drowning, but cannot avoid an ultimate and fatal confrontation with his mysterious employer.

Conversely, the fate of the *Mortzestus* is handled with excruciating realism. The men desperately do battle with an enemy they cannot understand; panic mounts and evolves into complete chaos as the ship begins to topple forward, diving headlong into its watery grave:

The jibboom was plunged right into the water, and, as I stared, the bows disappeared into the sea. [. . .] I watched the ocean lap over the edge of the fo'cas'le head, and rush down onto the main-deck, roaring into the empty fo'cas'le. And still all around me came the crying of the lost sailor-men. [. . .] there came a drear chorus of bubbling screams, a roar of waters, and I was going swiftly into the darkness. (*GP* 241)

Narration in "The Mainz Psalter" is adequately sustained by original imagery; combined with standard literary devices, it gives the story a cachet all its own. The hooligan who flees the watering hole upon catching a glimpse of the schoolmaster, the bizarre *tyroli-enne*-like clamor heard in moments of crisis, the unfamiliar night sky, the abnormal hues seen in the waves, the ship's rats who jump ship en masse—all are memorable occurrences who add to a mounting sense of dread.

On the other hand, the omission of a final explanation, however far-fetched, is a bit hard to swallow. Surely that perennial deus ex machina of a sanctimonious church-father who sees fit to warn off intrepid adventurers is a somewhat facile cliché, manifestly part and parcel of the time wherein the story was written. In Jean Ray's hyper-Catholic Belgium, it has to be remembered, the Church of Rome was emphatically present in every echelon of society, most notably in education and the arts. For his part, Hodgson may have had an Anglican clergyman for a father, but he never found it necessary to refer the reader to a supreme power. Such supernatural elements as we encounter in his work are invariably to be interpreted as little-understood natural phenomena.

In 1931 the Abbey of Averbode welcomed a destitute Ray into their roster of writers. Penning story after story for their exceedingly popular *Vlaamsche Filmkens* series under the byline of John Flanders provided him with a steady income when he had become persona non grata just about everywhere else. He became good friends with the Abbey's press officer Father Daniël De Kesel, who fully realized that the recruitment of this formidable storyteller was an acquisition of the first magnitude. In a way the prelate evolved into a guardian angel. Doubtless this bond instigated a new equanimity in Ray, and hence perhaps an acceptance of a more pronounced form of belief. But 1931 also proved to be an important year in another sense: it would see the appearance of Jean Ray's long-awaited second book *La Croisière des ombres*.

I can find no evidence of any form of outspoken religiousness either in *Les Contes du whisky* or in the many journalistic pieces written prior to Ray's incarceration. Toward the end of his life, however, the man's faith appears to have been sincere and unwavering. In Ray's posthumous *Mémorial,* in essence a collection of pensées scribbled in Ray's final years (not meant for publication), we find many meditations on the necessity of prayer, the unconditionality of belief, and so on. Even if Ray's faith contained elements of an unorthodox nature (e.g., his idiosyncratic view on the redemption of Judas Iscariot[6]), this remarkable about-face remains inexplicable.

In view of Ray's crushing despair and the concomitant spiritual annihilation he suffered in jail, he must have found the unmitigated bleakness of *The Ghost Pirates* a tall order indeed. The clerical intervention toward the end of "The Mainz Psalter," as unexpected as it is final, was likely added to counterbalance the supernaturalism in the story, not to mention the overt occult touches. On the whole, his reiteration of Hodgson's tale with the added 'bonus' of a divine intervention suggests that Ray's perusal of *The Ghost Pirates* was instrumental in crystallizing certain dormant views, ultimately effectuating nothing less than a spiritual rebirth.

Works Cited

de Lorde, André, and Albert Dubeux, ed. *Les Maîtres de la peur.* Paris: La Librairie Delagrave, 1927.

---

6. According to Ray Judas was as much, if not more, a saint as any of the other apostles.

Hodgson, William Hope. *Beyond the Dawning: The Poems of William Hope Hodgson.* Ed. Sam Gafford. Bristol, RI: Hobgoblin Press, 1995.

———. *The Ghost Pirates.* 1909. London: Holden & Hardingham, 1920. [Abbreviated in the text as *GP.*]

———. "The Haunted Pampero." *Short Stories* 89, No. 2 (February 1918): 95–103. In Hodgson's *Demons of the Sea.* West Warwick, RI: Necronomicon Press, 1992. 22–29.

———. *Les Spectres-Pirates.* Tr. Emile Chardome. *Revue Belge* (12 December 1927–1 February 1928).

———. "Through the Vortex of a Cyclone." *Cornhill Magazine* 3rd Series, No. 137 (November 1907): 643–63. In Hodgson's *Demons of the Sea.* West Warwick, RI: Necronomicon Press 1992. 54–63.

Ray, Jean. *Les Contes du Whisky*, La Renaissance du Livre, Paris 1925.

———. *La Flandre Liberale.* Ed. Arnaud Huftier and André Verbrugghen. Kuurne, Netherlands: Amicale Jean Ray, 2003.

———. "The Mainz Psalter." In Ray's *My Own Private Spectres.* Seattle: Midnight House, 1999. 89–115. [Abbreviated in the text as *MO.*]

———. *Mémorial.* Kuurne, Belgium: Sailor's Memories, 1998.

Van Herp, Jacques. "Des composantes mathématiques du fantastique chez Jean Ray." In Dominique Warfa, ed. *Jean Ray . . . en miroir.* Verviers, Belgium: P.O.C. Éditions, 1985. 85–95.

Door Skin

Belicia Rhea

The thing that lives in the forest waits deep within the trees. You go left, past the abandoned warehouse, past the shallow lake with the mutant fish, past the burned-down factory still in too close range of the city. After you head another sixteen miles northeast, when your feet wade in ticks and leaves and crunch unruly branches, fighting through terrain where no one goes, you're close.

Some bring offerings, though no one knows exactly what the thing likes. Those who've seen never make it back to tell. But it is known that the thing likes something, because they can hear it laughing and dancing and shrieking in the night when the moon is full in Capricorn.

What should I bring the thing? you wonder.

The important question you should be asking yourself is, what do I have to give? It can't be something material. Anyone can tell you that, from the line of the maimed that lay dead in a circle around the thing's pit still clutching their jewels, gold, flowers, and herbs. None of these will suffice.

If you want to know for yourself, keep walking ahead.

As you get closer, you'll feel it.

Saliva will start pooling in your mouth. Your jaw will hang with acid and bile spurting out of you, dog-sicker than you've ever been. The thing forces the insides out, takes them by surprise. Sometimes stomach contents aren't enough. Sometimes it wants the stomach.

When the thing is displeased, you'll know. It'll put you in back of the carcass line, holes gaping so wide from your torso you can count the rocks housed in a red ring through the other side.

By now if you can still stand, make sure to follow the trail of bodies along the spiraling circle. Look for a barren clearing in the center of the woods, where the plants start leaning away, nothing growing save for a lone tree, with an enormous trunk larger than a building, its dwelling.

This monstrous redwood may look dead, but it has lived for centuries. There is a layer like a sheet nailed on the front, ghostly pale across the bark. When you peel back the door skin, you might get stuck on the layers. Keep searching for the lip or nipple or groove that is the door handle. You might feel you are flipping through a heavy book, with the folds filthy and foul. There will be a ridge in the heart of the trunk, and that is the only way inside.

When you find the groove and pull open the door, it'll be wet in there. Rubbing your eyes, you'll realize it's also pitch-dark.

You might try to shine in a flashlight, then stand there in frustration, slapping the butt of it in your other palm, confused because it's a brand-new Maglite, uncertain if it's just the batteries.

But when you turn to shine it on the ground outside, it'll glow.

As you force yourself to enter, placing a foot into the black, you'll take a breath and hold it, wondering if it's safe to breathe. The pungent air will bite.

You'll think of the stories, the tales of schoolchildren who say it's the last hole to the center of the earth, who've dropped pennies inside and laughed, then one kid gets dragged down inside, and the other hears a penny finally clank the bottom fifteen years later in their sleep. But this is not the center of the earth. It's just a belly. The thing lives past this door.

When you are brave, when you crawl deeper, you might hear your name, someone calling, distant laughing, but it will echo until it recoils, crashing and overlapping to absurdity. Drips will ooze from your ears. Drums inside your head. You'll start to feel creatures crawling on you.

The thing has pets. Their little nails might leave scratches, tiny slimy fingers might catch your ankles and hold you down. When you double over, then fall, that sinking panic never goes and you aren't sure when you're going to hit ground.

Suddenly there will be new movement, what you assume to be wind, but in a moment you will find that it is hot and fetid, that it is breath, an exhalation. As you feel the teeth sink into your flesh, you'll know you've found it— that you're who's been found.

When you feel it peeling you, and watch your outsides layer over the alabaster door, you'll become a soft goop of a thing. Left only with your eyelashes to keep you warm.

You can stay with the others, slipping around, only if you've brought the correct offering.

The thing likes skin. Soft, dark, porcelain, tan, covered with ink portraits and lettering, moles and scabs, scars and bullet holes cut through all shades. The thing likes supple, full, or saggy, but most of all: infantile. Skin that smells like newborn. Skin that's still just made. If you come clutching a body of brand-new skin, the thing gives a reward.

The thing will make you a pet.

Waiting for others to come, you'll stay with the pets slipping around, watching the new arrivals get skinned. The tearing away from muscles like fabric ripping in half will sicken you at first, the door going heavier and heavier. But one day, millennia and eons of time later, you will notice a quiet. Then you will wake one century as the next thing—first in line for an offering, and you will shriek in delight at its smell. I know this, because the thing that lives in the forest is me.

Monstrous Tourism: Petromodernity in China Miéville's "Covehithe"

Rhonda Knight

In his 2012 keynote address at the International Conference for the Fantastic in the Arts, China Miéville put forth a playful taxonomy of monsters, starting with Freud's uncanny and moving through many other prefixed forms of the word *canny*. His proposed term *subcanny* refers to haunting monsters from the deep that are all the more terrifying in the imagination: monsters of potentiality, lurking below, emerging who knows where. His further neologism *postcanny* applies to "[m]onstrous, insurgent garbage." "Rubbish monsters were thrown out, not repressed," he says, but that does not make them any more comprehensible or knowable ("On Monsters" 386, 387). Yet, even as Miéville playfully riffs on the multitudes of possible not-*cannies* to label and sort potential monsters, he dismantles those very categories. Miéville concludes that while parsing and classifying monsters are entertaining thought experiments, these actions should not be ends to themselves, but tools that help "get at how and why, and to what end, [. . .] monsters do what they do" ("On Monsters" 391). He advises that classification can help with thinking.

This relates to the monsters in his short story "Covehithe" that are revenant, zombie-like oil rigs, named after the real structures that have been the victims of varied disasters, such as fires, explosions, and capsizing. These monsters act in instinctual and purposeful ways, emerging from the sea and destroying everything in their paths. Only after some tragic encounters do the people understand the rigs come to land to deposit eggs that later hatch into baby oil rigs that then return to the sea. Therefore, thinking about these monsters through the classifications of subcanny (monsters lurking in the deep) and postcanny (the return of the abandoned) demonstrates a new expression of cosmic horror.

H. P. Lovecraft characterizes cosmic horror through the roles of the unknown and the environment in creating the strongest expressions of terror. Miéville's oil rigs do the same as monsters of the Anthropocene that are "conjured by the cultural imagination to give shape to the many sources of anxiety brought on by the urgency of surfacing environmental issues such as plastic pollution, oil spill, deforestation, extreme weather, and forest fires" (Ulstein 50). As such, Miéville's story conjures up these monsters in order to satirize the Anthropocene's fraught relationship with petrochemicals. The story showcases the lifestyles of petro-tourists who track the revenant rigs. They appear as petro-hobbyists, petro-experientialists, and petro-activists, whose activities are enabled by the very oil culture that created the rigs and whose lifestyles contribute to the creation of more rigs, more environmental damage, and possibly more rig disasters.

As the rig monsters and petro-tourism contribute to a vicious circle of cause and effect, they participate in what Jeffrey Jerome Cohen calls a category crisis. In his 1996 essay "Monster Culture (Seven Theses)," Cohen explains that monsters resist binary thinking (40). Monsters are both "disturbing hybrids whose externally incoherent bodies resist attempts to include them in any systematic structuration" and "ontological liminalit[ies that appear] at times of crisis as a kind of third term that problematizes the clash of extremes" (40). For Cohen, this means that the monster, going back to its Latin roots—*monstrare* (to show), *monere* (to warn), and *monstrum* (a portent/a monster)—not only *is* the crisis but *demonstrates* its own etiology. As such, the oil rigs *are* threats to ecosystems and habitats, while they also *represent* oil culture's previous and continuing threats to ecosystems and habitats.

When Miéville introduces his revenant rigs, he contextualizes them through the Atomic Age monster Godzilla, who also emerged from a category crisis, Japan's attempts to deal with nuclear disaster.[1] *Godzilla* (1954) explains that the creature is a Jurassic dinosaur that managed to survive on the ocean floor until radiation from an atomic bomb caused it to mutate into a monster. This creature, an embodiment of Cohen's "third term," a hybrid of the world's animal past and atomic future, attacks Japan in precisely the same ways that American bombs and nuclear devices devastated the country. Tomoyuki Tanaka, the creator of Godzilla, said in an interview: "Mankind had created the Bomb, and now nature was going to take revenge on mankind" (quoted in Ryfle 19). In "Covehithe," Miéville references the beginning of *Godzilla* in which the boat *Eiko-maru* is destroyed by Godzilla.[2] The first oil rig that emerges Godzilla-like from the sea is the Rowan Gorilla I (capsized 1988). Before the rig makes landfall, "a fishing boat southeast of Halifax, radioed an SOS, under attack" (304). The Rowan Gorilla I came ashore and "walked through buildings, swatted trucks then tanks out of its way with ripped cables and pipes that failed in inefficient deadly motion, like ill-trained snakes, like too-heavy feeding tentacles. . . . It dripped seawater, chemicals of industrial ruin and long-hoarded oil" (304–5). This method of destruction recalls Godzilla's march through cities, destroying architecture, objects, and infrastructure. Even though Miéville clearly characterizes the Rowan Gorilla I as much more of a "sea monster"

---

1. In 2019 the Anthropocene Working Group, a panel of thirty-four geologists, biologists, geographers, anthropologists, historians of science, and experts in related fields, voted to mark the beginning of the Anthropocene "in the mid-twentieth century, when a rapidly rising human population accelerated the pace of industrial production, the use of agricultural chemicals and other human activities. At the same time, the first atomic-bomb blasts littered the globe with radioactive debris that became embedded in sediments and glacial ice, becoming part of the geologic record" (Subramanian). Thus, Godzilla could be the first monster of the Anthropocene.

2. The movie's scene itself is a reference to the 1954 incident of the *Lucky Dragon*, a fishing boat that was hit by a radiation blast from American nuclear testing. The crew members suffered immediate physical effects, and many died of cancers in the months following (Ryfle 20–21).

(subcanny) than Godzilla,[3] they both exhibit Anthropocene monsters' characteristics of scale, imagined as bigger, "faster-paced, and more out-of-control" than civilization and its infrastructure can handle (Ulstein 49).

Yet unlike Godzilla, who mutated from a living being, these resurgent oil rigs, "insurgent discarded" artifacts, return as animated corpses of machinery (Miéville, "On Monsters" 387). Rowan Gorilla I was the first to encroach on the land, but then there are more incursions. UNPERU (the United Nations Platform Event Repulsion Unit), a team of "scientists, engineers, theologians and exorcists, soldiers, veterans," attempted "to figure out what economies of sacrifice were being invoked, for what this was punishment" (305). They soon learn that the newly sentient rigs are participating in a cycle of life. As Miéville contends, the New Weird need not explain the impossible it creates but portray the impossible within "its own terms and systematicity" (Gordon 366). Thus, if "dead" objects act as sentient, "alive" organisms, then their participation in a life cycle is logical. Yet their existence itself, as "petrospectral presences," represents "an integral part of modernity's industrial unconscious" ("Covehithe" 306; Ingwersen).

"Covehithe" first appeared in the *Guardian* (22 April 2011) as part of a feature called "Can Fiction Change Our View of Oil?" which marked the first anniversary of the explosion of the Deepwater Horizon in the Gulf of Mexico. In explaining the reasons behind the *Guardian*'s feature, editor Richard Lea notes that oil is "all around us, seeps into everything we do, but we don't see it, we can't see it, because it's simply everywhere. It powers us into work, takes us on holiday, lights up our homes and cools our food. It washes us and dresses us and stirs our tea." Lea is describing a condition that Stephanie LeMenager has termed petromodernity: modern Western

---

3. Even by choosing the Gorilla class oil rig as the first known attacker, Miéville subtly references Godzilla, whose Americanized name visually evokes the word *gorilla* and whose Japanese name *Gojira* combines the word for gorilla (*gorira*) with the word for whale (*kujira*) (Ryfle 23).

life, which is "based in cheap energy systems long made possible by oil" (60). Along with almost all other facets of modern life, petromodernity sustains the modern idea of "leisure," a phenomenon that "displac[es] work from the center of modern social arrangements," according to Dean MacCannell (5). In the petromodern world, members of the privileged classes can more easily choose how they construct their leisure time. Leisure can be a cessation of activity or a motivated, intentional active practice, such as participating in a hobby or traveling. MacCannell demonstrates the irony that in this modern context leisure activities are often approached with the intensity of work or center on understanding the techniques embedded in the production of commodities. For example, some travel to marvel at the spectacle of the Hoover Dam, while others take guided tours of breweries or automobile factories (6–7). Miéville brings into sharp relief petromodern habits of leisure, in which petro-tourists demonstrate work-like attention to observing these artifacts of industry.

By setting the story in an existing English coastal village that itself exhibits qualities of the weird, Miéville demonstrates the ways that natural forces and the environment can easily erase petroleum's mark on the world. In "Covehithe," Dughan and his unnamed daughter travel to this Suffolk village, hoping to see a rig emerge from the North Sea. The real Covehithe has two distinguishing features: a ruined church, St. Andrew's, and a road that runs off the edge of a cliff, eroded away by the sea. Miéville describes the sight: "The road stopped abruptly, rag-edged, fell into nothing" (301). Dughan's daughter describes the location as "misbehavicious," a made-up word that connotes its liminality, eeriness and sterility:[4] "In the leafless trees of this region were cold, random and silent flares of light. Touch the soil, as Dughan did, . . . and it felt greasy, heavy, as if someone had poured cream onto loam" (301). As he and his daughter wait at this "decomposing road-end" for a glimpse of a monstrous rig, he tells her, "The sea's taking it all back." She asks,

---

4. See Ritson (134) on the location's hybridity and Miéville's neologisms that marry the organic with the technical.

"Is it still going?" "Being eaten?" (301, 302). The real-world answer is yes. Covehithe is losing meters of coastline directly inland each year. As Dughan's daughter phrases it, the monster Nature is eating what humans call the world. Andrew Hageman characterizes this scene through attention to the petromodern infrastructure that is easy for readers, petromodern subjects ourselves, to overlook: "Facilitating [Dughan's] journey is a swathe of petroleum that has been extracted, refined, poured, and smoothed over the land as tarmac. This tarmac infrastructure, which likely originated with an oil rig, is itself disintegrating due to a lack of infrastructural maintenance, particularly in the face of the coastal erosion" (5). All reports agree that the land currently named Covehithe, with its eroded road, few remaining dwellings, and massive ruined church, will be consumed by the sea in the next thirty to fifty years.

Along the Covehithe coastline the natural world is cannibalizing itself and all evidence of human habitation, while at the same time sunken and destroyed oil rigs, unnatural machinery, mysteriously heal underwater. Rejecting their former mechanical existence, they display animal characteristics. Thus, Covehithe, this threatened, isolated area, becomes the landing spot for a monster that challenges the dichotomy of animal and machine, where it will deposit eggs by using the mechanisms that were previously used to extract oil. Yet culture intervenes as the landscape is peopled with petro-tourists, hoping to spot a rig, and security guards, protecting the people from the rig *and* the rig from the people.

In his role as a petro-tourist, Dughan most closely mirrors a trainspotter, an observational hobbyist who focuses on petroleum-based transportation. Dughan lives his life inundated by media and information, such as computer forums and bulletin board sites that provide information about possible sightings or landings of the oil rigs. He constructs plausible locations from "hints and whispers," such as "[t]wo names he knew, erst-while colleagues, both announcing they'd be near Ipswich next week" (301). This lifestyle is enabled by oil culture: cheap and easy electricity and the hydrocarbons from which computers are built. An ex-soldier, Dughan once worked with UNPERU trying to prevent the oil rigs from coming ashore (305). Miéville hints that Dughan suffers from PTSD, which could be the reason no longer works for UNPERU. Dughan was trapped between the Rowan Gorilla I and the sea. He saw a third of his comrades killed in the violence of that encounter, crushed, caught in explosions, and trapped by pieces of the machinery. He has had "years of dreams and memories of trodden men" and now his daughter watches him carefully for "signs of angst, . . . flashback, . . . fear" (304). Dughan's loss of occupation robbed him of his former identity, which he has reclaimed by shaping his lifestyle around tracking the oil rigs. MacCannell explains that a lifestyle comprises "specific combinations of work and leisure" (6). For Dughan, his former work has taken over his leisure. His identity and his lifestyle as a rig spotter have become inextricably bound.

As Miéville echoes petro-hobbyists like trainspotters in Dughan, he also points out the tendency of fetishizing both the physical substance of oil and the abilities it gives the petromodern citizen by processing it into varied commodities. Sometimes these commodities are present, as the material objects of the petroleum industry, such as trains to be identified, classified, and catalogued. Dughan similarly fetishizes the materiality of oil rigs by collecting observations, knowledge, and experiences. He displays an encyclopedic knowledge of oil rig disasters, including names, locations, types, dates. When the oil rig comes ashore at Covehithe with twisted metal, "[o]ff-true and angular . . . lurch[ing] . . . landward in huge jerks," Dughan translates the rig markings for his daughter: "Under its stains and excrescences were more regular markings, stenciled warnings. Paint remnants: an encircled 'H'" (302, 303). Dughan immediately tells his daughter that it is Petrobras P-36 that sank at Roncador field in 2001 (303). Miévile uses Dughan's knowledge base to commemorate other real tragedies by showing Dughan remembering other "revisitors," such as *Interocean II*, Sedco 135F, and *Ocean*

Prince, in the moments that it takes for P-36 to come ashore (307).[5]

Notwithstanding Dughan's obsession with the materiality of the oil rigs as an observational hobbyist, in other parts of the narrative Miéville further demonstrates petromodernity's fetishization of oil through its invisibility, as energy, seemingly ubiquitous and limit-less. Michael Ziser explains how oil, compared to coal, whose ex-traction is marked by labor and human energy, implies excess: "Oil . . . is a liquid that in the most classic scenario flows to the surface almost of its own accord, gushing out in all directions. . . . Once struck, oil returns so much more energy than is required to produce it that it becomes an effectively costless substitute for human and animal labor (321).[6] Ziser quotes Karl Marx's estimation from *Capital* that so-called natural resources act as the "free gift of Nature to capital" (321). Marx advocates harnessing the power of Nature as a labor force. For example, he speaks of the monopolization "of the earth and its appurtenances," such as waterfalls (Marx 481). The way Marx ad-vocates using the energy of waterfalls and what humanity has since enacted in search of fossil fuels signals a deep-seated belief that "the environment," rather than being a balanced ecosystem, serves as a storage facility for energy we might access, now or later (Ingwersen). This perspective was created through generations of discursive prac-tices, which appeared long before Marx, but gave him an epistemol-ogy that promulgates a dichotomy between the natural (the environment, the wilderness) and the cultural (society, civilization).

Bruno Latour argues that this epistemology occurred during the Scientific Revolution and Enlightenment (67–72). Roger Luckhurst neatly summarizes Latour's point. Modernity classifies "the world according to a binary that sorts humans from nonhumans, subjects

---

5. Miéville follows common italicization principles for vessels in the names of these oil rigs. Anchored rigs are not italicized and mobile ones are.

6. Several scholars have discussed this concept of oil as "laborless." See Wen-zel (451), who points to Fernando Coronil's "'petro-magic', petroleum's false promise of wealth without work," and Ryszard Kapuscinski's similar state-ments about "the false promise of oil."

from objects. A politics emerges from this dispensation that is inflexible and often violent: nature is to be dominated" (9). Oil, then, existing in this dichotomy as an objectified nonhuman, must be dominated. Furthermore, because oil is deemed "natural" and because its product diversity and abundance have far outstripped any use value Marx could have ever imagined for it, Ziser explains that oil "would seem to justify almost any degree of fetishization" (321). As such, oil has become the preeminent, post-Marxian commodity fetish, which "obscures the complex socioecological processes through which crude oil becomes commodified" (Huber 226).[7] The petro-tourists' mobility in "Covehithe" demonstrates the role of oil fetishism in the commodification of experience.

In his narrative, Miéville also compares Dughan's hobbyist identity to other types of tourists who engage in wildlife tourism. Through his fetishistic activities of watching, cataloguing, and collecting oil rig sightings in locations worldwide, Dughan need not only be compared to trainspotters but also birdwatchers, whose hobby depends on careful watching and recording, as well as the deciphering of markings. Furthermore, Miéville distinguishes Dughan from more casual tourists who also participate in a leisure economy that mirrors wildlife tourism. Karen Higginbottom explains the wide range of activities that are classified as wildlife tourism. Traveling to an animal's natural habitat to see it, to hunt it, or to capture it are examples of wildlife tourism, but so is traveling to a zoo or attraction where animals are kept in captivity (2–3). Wildlife tourism has its roots in nineteenth-century European colonialism, as the wealthy became fascinated with the wildlife living in colonized countries. The rich traveled to see (and often to kill) exotic creatures, such as rhinos and lions (Ungvarsky). Current wildlife tourists display cultural capital relative to these former wealthy, upper-class travelers. Nowadays, wildlife tourists are older, often retired, possess a post-secondary education, and are, according to Susanna Curtin, "relatively affluent usually within

---

7. See Jameson (185–86), who helps contextualize the nature/culture dichotomy that Marx participates in through a discussion of historical reflexivity.

the higher income brackets" (18). In "Covethihe" they are mirrored by petro-experientialists who consume oil/energy in order to travel to sites to see oil rig creatures enact their cycle of reproduction, the laying of eggs and their subsequent hatching.

Miéville combines wildlife and event tourism to interpret his petro-experientialists as entertainment seekers who readily place themselves in danger from the unpredictable oil rigs. In their onto-logical analysis of nature-based tourism, May Kristin Vespestad and Frank Lindberg explain that in one form of nature-based tourism the tourists' excursions are commodified by "experience presenters," who carefully stage-manage activities, information, and packaging. This type of upsell directly targets consumers seeking an authentic experience (571, 576). In "Covehithe," Miéville patterns the oil rig tourism on sea turtle tourism by creating two events around which the tourists can structure their encounters. In the "laying event" the oil rig comes out of the sea to lay its eggs. When Dughan and his daughter are leaving the site in the wee hours, the commercial tour-ism for this event has already begun. Behind the cordons are a tour guide and a group of tourists who had been in nearby hotels. The tour guide says, "'We'll come back in the morning, when it's finished laying' . . . 'You can bring your cameras then—no danger then if you forgot to turn your flash off'" (311).

This tour guide's words parallel the words that *Christian Science Monitor* contributor Kennerly Clay heard from her tour guide on Tortuguero Beach, Costa Rica—"No camera. No flashlight. No cig-arette"—as she watched a green sea turtle come upon shore to lay her eggs. On the very same night, Clay and her husband see hatch-lings from another nest trying to find their way to the sea. While lucky sea turtle tourists can see the beginning and the ending of this gestational process in the same trip, the rarity of the oil rigs and lack of a natural habitat prevent this, so the maximum entertainment comes later with the "hatching event" in which the hatchlings uncover themselves and "totter . . . for the sea" (309). The security guard tells Dughan's daughter that in "a few months . . . it'll all kick off . . .

there's like a kid's club they have here" (309). Also, he says, "you can see the eggs on a live feed. They'll be digging down to them and they'll put cameras and thermometers" (310). This live feed reflects the current craze of zoos and animal parks broadcasting the births of charismatic species, such as pandas and giraffes (Céline et al.). In 2017, April the Giraffe had "more than 232 million YouTube live views" ("April"). Even though Miéville wrote this story before April was a sensation, the practice of commodifying animal births was already well established with pandas and other rare species.

Because of the rarity of the oil rig laying and hatching events, the tourists who travel to see them would form a very exclusive subset of "wildlife" tourist. As there are no predictable breeding areas or breeding seasons, the tourists would have to gain information, much the way that Dughan did, and they must be ready to travel quickly to an identified location for the laying and possibly return for the hatching. In short, this subset of tourists must have a fair amount of leisure time and money. The hatching event, because its location is fixed and can be better predicted because of the cameras, would attract a broader subset of the population. Research in wildlife tourism can predict the demographics and dispositions of experiential tourists who might travel to observe laying and hatching events. Curtin labels them "serious" tourists and reports that they "possess an environmental ethic," "are biocentric," "aim to benefit wildlife and the environment," and "expect an educative and interpretive element" (18). The irony, of course, lies in these self-identifying supporters of the environment's use of petroleum-based energy to sustain their hobbies and travels. Kennerly Clay, again, provides an analogy for such petro-tourists when she describes the travel she and her husband undertook to see the green sea turtles' laying event: "My husband and I have traveled from the central highlands of Costa Rica— three buses, a taxi, and a five-hour boat ride—to the western Caribbean coast, just miles from Nicaragua." Like Clay, many of the Covehithe tourists would have traveled long distances, expanding their carbon footprint, in order to be entertained and have an experience, but unlike Clay, their own actions, such as a camera flash, place them—rather than the organism—in danger.

Even as Miéville offers a critique of wildlife tourism in "Covehithe," this imaginary portrayal of petro-tourism is not so far-fetched. Oil tourism has already developed around various oil disasters. Following Kai Erikson's formulation of environmental disasters, Patricia Widener characterizes both the building of an oil pipeline and an oil spill as types of environmental disasters and shows how these disasters can engender tourism that can cause further ecological damage. The first step in her formula explains that the disaster must occur "in a place established as a promising tourism destination or constructed as an untarnished environment" (272). Tourists then discover the location in order to either experience it before disappears or to protest the disaster event retrospectively, in hopes of preventing the next one (272). Both groups, no matter their intent, can stress the local ecosystem and even cause "alterations, which are more subtle, yet as damaging, as an oil disaster" (266). Miéville hints at this final type of tourism when the security guard tries to size up Dughan's purpose. He thinks that Dughan at least is not one of the "oleophobe fanatics" there to attack the oil rig, nor does he belong to the "Oil Firsters," a violent group set to kill all people who are "investigat[ing] or exploit[ing]" the rigs (308). Through the security guard's caution, Miéville briefly introduces the third type of petro-tourist, the petro-activist. Each type of petro-tourist constructs its lifestyle through the fetishization of oil and the oil rigs. Yet, as each follows the lumbering footprints of the oil rig as it comes to shore, each also expands its carbon footprint to see them, catalogue them, photograph them, protect them, or to try to destroy them.

Drawing on the work of Bruno Latour, Moritz Ingwersen explains that it is not hard to find a "convergence between ecocriticism and Weird fiction" because the weird offers opportunities to consider the world fighting back against human incursion or a world that has divested itself entirely of humans. Miéville himself has described the weird as "an expression of upheaval and crisis" ("Weird Fiction"

513). Miéville's oil rigs, though aptly described as modern, mechanical entities, show his debt to H. P. Lovecraft, as Ingwersen has noted, in his moments of decadent descriptions and purposeful purple prose:

> In the glow of the thing's own flame, they saw the edificial flanks [of P-36], the concrete and rust of them, the iron of the pylon barnacled, shaggy with benthic growth now lank gelatinous bunting. . . . Pipes dangled from its roof-high underside, clots of it fell back into the sea. It wore steel containers, ruins of housing like a bad neighbourhood, old hoists, lift shafts emptying of black water. (302–3)

Here is the literal embodiment of Miéville's not-*cannies* in Lovecraftian syntax: the subcanny eldritch rising from the sea, bringing up bits of the sea's mystery coupled with the postcanny organism of waste, broken, ruined, and rusted. Petrobras P-36 and its ilk are not the Old Ones; they could be the New Ones, as they should frighten humanity much more than Cthulhu ever could, because humanity should see its own complicity in these monsters' origins.

Works Cited

"April the Giraffe is Expecting Again, and Tens of Thousands Are Watching." *Washington Post* (3 March 2019), www.washingtonpost.com/lifestyle/kidspost/april-the-giraffe-is-expecting-again-and-thousands-are-watching/2019/03/13/63bd142e-4116-11e9-9361-301ffb5bd5e6_story.html.

Céline Albert; Luque, Gloria M.; and Courchamp, Franck. "The Twenty Most Charismatic Species." *PLoS ONE* 13, No. 7 (2018), doi.org/10.1371/journal.pone.0199149.

Clay, Kennerly. "A Night on the Beach . . . with Some Busy turtles." *Christian Science Monitor* (6 October 2004), www.csmonitor.com/2004/1006/p11s02-trgn.html.

Cohen, Jeffrey Jerome. "Monster Culture (Seven Theses)." In Jeffrey Andrew Weinstock, ed. *The Monster Theory Reader*. Minneapolis: University of Minnesota, Press, 2020. 37–56.

Curtin, Susanna. "The Self-Presentation and Self-Development of Serious Wildlife Tourists." *International Journal of Tourism Re-*

search 12 (2010): 17–33.

Godzilla. Toho Co., 1954. Directed by Ishiro Honda. Amazon Prime Criterion Channel, 2019.

Gordon, Joan. "Reveling in Genre: An Interview with China Miéville." *Science Fiction Studies* 30, No. 3 (November 2003): 355–73.

Hageman, Andrew. "Bringing Infrastructural Criticism to Speculative Fiction: China Miéville's 'Covehithe." *C21 Literature: Journal of 21st-Century Writings* 7, No. 1 (2019): 1–10.

Higginbottom, Karen. "Wildlife Tourism: An Introduction." In Karen Higginbottom, ed. *Wildlife Tourism: Impacts, Management and Planning*. Altona, Australia: Common Ground, 2004. 1–14.

Huber, Matthew T. "Refined Politics Petroleum Products, Neoliberalism, and the Ecology of Entrepreneurial Life." In Ross Barrett and Daniel Worden, ed. *Oil Culture*. Minneapolis: University of Minnesota Press, 2014. 226–43.

Ingwersen, Moritz. "'Geological Insurrections': The Weird Return of Rust and Dust in China Miéville's 'Covehithe' and 'The Dusty Hat.'" *Academia*, 21 May 2020, www.academia.edu/34439685/ _Geological_Insurrections_The_Weird_Return_of_Rust_and_Dus t_in_China_Mi%C3%A9villes_Covehithe_and_The_Dusty_Hat_.

Jameson, Fredric. "Magical Narratives: On the Dialectical Use of Genre Criticism." In David Sandner, ed. *Fantastic Literature: A Critical Reader*. New York: Praeger, 2004. 180–221.

Latour, Bruno. *We Have Never Been Modern*. Tr. Catherine Porter. Cambridge, MA: Harvard University Press, 1993.

Lea, Richard. "Can Fiction Change Our View of Oil?" *The Guardian Online*. 15 April 2011. Accessed 21 May 2020. www.theguardian. com/books/2011/apr/15/oil-stories.

LeMenager, Stephanie. "The Aesthetics of Petroleum, after Oil!" *American Literary History* 24, No. 1 [*Sustainability in America*] (2012): 59–86.

Lovecraft. H. P. "Supernatural Horror in Literature." In *Collected Essays—Volume 2: Literary Criticism*, ed. S. T. Joshi. New York:

Hippocampus Press, 2004, pp. 82–135

Luckhurst, Roger. "Bruno Latour's Scientification: Networks, Assemblages, and Tangled Objects." *Science Fiction Studies* 33, No. 1 (March 2006): 4–17.

MacCannell, Dean. *The Tourist: A New Theory of the Leisure Class.* 1976. U of California P, 1999.

Miéville, China. "Covehithe." In Miéville's *Three Moments of an Explosion.* New York: Del Ray, 2015. 299–311.

———. "On Monsters: Or, Nine or More (Monstrous) Not Cannies." *Journal of the Fantastic in the Arts* 23, No. 3 (2012): 377–92.

———. "Weird Fiction." In Mark Bould, Andrew M. Butler, Adam Roberts, and Sherryl Vint, ed. *The Routledge Companion to Science Fiction.* London: Routledge, 2009. 510–15.

Ritson, Katie. *The Shifting Sands of the North Sea Lowlands: Literary and Historical Imaginaries.* London: Routledge, 2019.

Ryfle, Steve. *Japan's Favorite Mon-star: The Unauthorized Biography of "The Big G."* Toronto: ECW Press, 1998.

Subramanian, Meera. "Anthropocene Now: Influential Panel Votes to Recognize Earth's New Epoch." *Nature* (21 May 2019). Accessed 21 May 2020. www.nature.com/articles/d41586-019-01641-5.

Ulstein, Gry. "'Age of Lovecraft'?—Anthropocene Monsters in (New) Weird Narrative." *Nordlit* 42 [*Manufacturing Monsters*] (2019): 47–65.

Ungvarsky, Janine. "Wildlife Tourism." In *Salem Press Encyclopedia,* 2019. EBSCOhost, search.ebscohost.com/login.aspx?direct=true&db=ers&AN=137502300&site=eds-live&scope=site.

Vespestad, May Kristin, and Frank Lindberg. "Understanding Nature-Based Tourist Experiences: An Ontological Analysis." *Current Issues in Tourism* 14, No. 6 (2011): 563–80.

Wenzel, Jennifer. "Petro-Magic-Realism: Toward a Political Ecology of Nigerian Literature." *Postcolonial Studies* 9, No. 4 (2006): 449–64.

Widener, Patricia. "Oil Tourism: Disasters and Destinations in Ecuador and the Philippines." *Sociological Inquiry* 79, No. 3 (2009): 266–88.

Ziser, Michael. "Oil Spills." *PMLA* 126, No. 2 (2011): 321–23.

The Caves of Death

Gertrude Atherton

[Gertrude Atherton (1857–1948) was a prolific California novelist and author of such novels as *The Californians* (1898), *The Conqueror* (1902), and *Black Oxen* (1923). Her two short story collections, *The Bell in the Fog and Other Stories* (1905) and *The Foghorn* (1934), contain a number of weird tales. The following story appeared in the *San Francisco News Letter and California Advertiser* (25 December 1886).—Ed.]

I cannot tell whether I had been asleep hours or moments, but I awoke suddenly as if shaken from my unconsciousness by some unseen hand. And immediately I was aware that a change had come over the night. The moon still shone clearly down into the little amphitheatre of hills wherein I lay, the redwoods still loomed unswayingly on the mountain beyond, the stars still glittered undisturbed in the heavens above, but yet there was a change. And the change, I realized, sprang from other than earthly conditions. The air was full of unheard sighs, the night of unseen shapes. How I knew this I cannot tell, for I saw nothing, and no voice spoke; reason and analysis had no part in my knowledge, but a heretofore unknown consciousness seemed suddenly awake and abnormally acute. In a moment I knew that something had happened on the hill behind me, and I turned with a sense of expectancy which was almost foreknowledge, and looked up. Something had appeared over the brow of the hill and was slowly descending. What was it? A chariot, a carriage, a vehicle, ancient or modern? I could not tell. Its outlines and substance were too dim, too shadowy, too unsubstantial, too elusive, but perhaps it bore more resemblance to a hearse than to any other human object. But whatever it may have been, it was followed by another, then another, and another, in a funereal procession of a kind never seen on earth. The long, ghostly train wound slowly down the hill, and traversing the space at its foot, disappeared in a cave which yawned opposite. Would it never end? Hundreds and hundreds of these hearses, half seen, imponderable as a mountain, mist, vanished through the mouth of the cave, but hundreds still wound over the brow of the hill until I knew that the number had swelled to thousands, and that time had passed. I knew, also, what it meant. That newly awakened, or newly born Consciousness supplied the place of externally derived knowledge. It was the funeral train of the souls of the dead, coming from the graves of their bodies, under earth and sea, where they had gone for one hour to weep, and on their way to their yearly rendezvous in the Christmas House of Death.

How long it was before the last of those pale chariots floated down the hill, I cannot tell, but after a time I found myself following the procession into the cave below. And as the light and the familiar objects of the outer world were left behind, my consciousness of this midnight phenomenon became still more acute, and sight and hearing developed themselves into more than mortal sensitiveness. In the long line of hearses winding before me through the depths of the hills, I caught, again and again, a glimpse of what was now a point of luminous white light, now expanded into the semblance of a human form, then contracting into shapelessness, or vanishing into nothingness. The air was torn with cries and groans, and more than once a shriek, frail and shadowy as the thing that gave it vent, came to my ears. But this was not all. I had learned in the great world above that no sound, once born and given to the waves of the air, can die until time and space shall be alike annihilated. In that wonderful expanse above, where the atmosphere vibrated with the sounds of men, or the million audible manifestations of Nature, and where human Consciousness was happily limited, that endless continuity of sound was dumb to human ears. But in this long, dark, silent passage in the heart of a mountain no sounds penetrated either of nature or of man, and the ocular sensitiveness of which I found myself in possession, gave me a new and terrible power. The wails and groans, the, pale, wan shrieks, the occasional awful bursts of laughter, hollow as a dead man's skull, the feeble, colorless cry of the infant, the distant, dream-like sobs of pulsating wraiths, which once had lived in woman's form, the curses and cries of those who had sinned and died unrepentant, the smiling whispers of those few at perfect rest, echoed on and on and on in the vaulted roof above until sense was strained to the utmost limit of human endurance. Fainter and fainter they grew until it seemed as if sound, human or ghostly, could survive no longer. But the end never came. Softer, softer, remoter, hollower, more unearthly, more difficult of perception grew those terrible echoes of ghostly woe, and sharper grew the strain to follow. Nor would they blend. The ear followed the bitter cry of the murderer, the groping wail of the solitary babe, the sob of the woman for the lover she had left, down to their infinitesimal vibrations and in all their individual separateness. If it had lasted much longer, my soul would have joined that pale army before me in one terrific human shriek, which would have echoed through all Eternity, overriding those thunder bubbles of air which called it forth.

But presently I saw that my journey was over, and that things were about to occur which would consign sound to temporary oblivion. The last hearse had disappeared, I could not tell where, and I stood at the entrance of a vast succession of caves, wide and white, and illumined with a soft, dull radiance, which came from no visible lamp. Far down in their dim perspective that soft, cold light still shone, and I knew that endless caverns stretched beyond, and that mountain upon mountain must lie upon their heads. The floors, the walls, the mighty vaulted roof were of purest white, and softly polished, but of what they were composed no man could tell. That which lay about and looked down from above was finer than cobweb and denser than marble; it looked as if a sigh would blow it away, and as if the instruments of man would glance back, impotent, at its contact. It was so beautiful, so typical of stern and awful purity, so unearthly in its fairness that I took for a moment no note of anything beyond. The souls of sinners and saints, I knew, were summoned alike to these caves of loveliness and calm, that the latter might find more infinite peace and the former know greater anguish in the emblem afforded them of a bliss to be theirs, only after a punishment and probation extending over millions of years. Only from midnight until dawn of Christmas day were the gates to this wonderful realm thrown open, and in it all sounds, whether of joy or of pain, were inaudible save one. Far away, down in that dim perspective, I could see a white-robed choir, and the strains they gave forth, sad as the wail of a harp, and unearthly as the forms of the choristers, floated through all that vast expanse and filled the air with a sweetness and an infinite harmony which the imagination of no mortal who has not heard it can conceive.

After a time I lowered my eyes and looked about me. The great hall formed by the ever multiplying caves was crowded with luminous, shadowy, transparent forms, visible at last under this all-searching light, in dim but distinct outline. I passed into a cave at my right and saw the faint negatives of faces I had known in my youth. In a moment I paused before a familiar form. It was that of a man who had posed for a cynic in the existence above, and for a blasé man of the world in the small community he had never left, and in which he had found the Alpha and Omega of his experience of life. French novels had convinced him that in common with the world he had no morality, and French dinners had sent him to rejoice the spirit world prematurely. And in the spirit world he was not comfortable. He had been wont to argue to admiring friends that there was no God, no future, no soul; therefore, when he found himself in the future and at the disposal of a God who insisted upon recognition, he felt somewhat vague and upset. But he had another and yet more trying grievance. Having disbelieved in the existence of a soul it was discomfiting to find himself a soul, pure and simple, merely that and nothing more. He did not know from what point of view to regard himself; that he must admire himself went without saying; but it was hard to be obliged to learn the lesson all over again. He was very much worried and he longed for the old existence artificial, where no one had ever accused him of being an entity.

My attention was quickly diverted from him to a group just beyond. On the floor crouched a man young in years, but with the egotism of age speaking in every line. On a bench on a platform above him sat a thin, wiry, sardonic little man, his face "stamped deep with grins that had no merriment," his intelligent brow contracted in a savage frown, his coarse mouth set in a pitiless line. In his heart was a knife, and, as I gazed, he drew it slowly out and bent over the man at his feet. The motion was as deliberate as that of a snake curving itself to strike, and the other watched him with the fascinated gaze of the bird under the charm of the serpent. Then, with a swift motion, the arm of the man on the bench darted down and plunged the knife into the heart of the other, who rolled upon the floor, uttering voiceless cries of agony. Then I saw that the knife was not even as palpable in the form as the hand which had sent it home, but the wound it inflicted was sharp as the sting of Conscience. The man who had dealt the blow then raised himself upright on his bench and beckoned to a figure behind me. The figure approached and conferred with him, and I saw that he had been a man of much physical perfection, and I knew that the intelligence, which was all that was left of his earthly attributes, had once been of great service to the little man on the bench. At his back was a large and interesting army of retainers, one and all of whom bore the outlines of woman's form. Of all shapes and sizes, of all color and style, of all conditions, mental, moral and social, they formed a beautiful illustration of the variety which may exist in one man's mind. They all wore a mocking smile, and its meaning was obvious. Upon earth he had had the privilege of beaming upon one at a time, but here he had the whole collection, with all their various and conflicting characteristics perpetually evident to eye and ear. He turned, after a moment, and I saw his face. He did not look happy.

I wandered into the next cave, but found few faces there that I knew. Before I left it, however, I paused a moment before a group which no observer could pass without noticing. Leaning with what in flesh would have been a heavy attitude against the wall of the cave was a man. He had the brutish face of the criminal cast, haggard and lined with cowardice and shameful punishment, and in his hand was a knife from which ghastly colorless drops dripped, dripped, with eternal persistence. Before him stood a girl, young, beautiful, with a hideous, gaping wound in her throat. She was saying nothing to the man who had murdered her, even in silent spirit-thought; she uttered no reproaches or words of forgiveness. She merely *looked*— looked at him with great, wide, transparent, horror-stricken eyes; eyes fixed forever in the look he had seen flash into them as he dealt the blow which cut short her brief life on earth, and which were destined to follow him throughout all eternity.

I entered the next cave and paused before a strange picture. In the middle of the room, the light shining full on his villainous, unintelligent face and ignoble head, stood a man who, during the trial which scandalized Europe and America, had been the most talked of and best hated man in the Great Republic. But the man he had murdered knelt at his feet and kissed his hands. "I have power here," he murmured in that voiceless interchange of thought, which was all that was allowed in these halls of silence. "Command me as you will in return for the immortality you conferred upon me." "Yes," said the other grimly, "if it had not been for me, you would have had favors of another sort to-day. You had already made as many mistakes as man ever contrives to crowd into so short a space of time, and you were just about to mount your steed and go down hill at a gallop when I stepped in and saved you. Now you wear a martyr's crown, and half the children in the nation are named after you. Moreover, you have been remembered for more than four years; you can never repay me for that." "Never!" murmured the other. "You can command me to any extent you please," and he settled the martyr's crown more firmly on his brow. Another man came by at the moment and joined the group. He had been a man of splendid make, and he bore himself with the air of a personage who yet had not sprung from the alleys and gutters. He looked enviously at the kneeling man. "You are fortunate," he said. "I died in bed, and had only a paragraph and one headline, while you monopolized the entire sheet and all the pictorials. I did my duty for the allotted time, incurred but little reproach, and killed myself by the exertion, yet I am forgotten, and you are a saint. Such is human destiny." And he passed on.

I glanced from the group which had claimed my attention for several moments, towards a figure calculated to attract the notice of the passer-by. Not that he was particularly striking in appearance, for he had a heavy, rather fishy face, but his occupation was a somewhat curious one, and not to be defined at first glance. His fingers were wandering with great precision in the air, now as if pulling, now adjusting, now changing and substituting objects invisible to even my quickened sense. It seemed, however, as if a delicate vibrating sound should have followed those manipulations. Finally he confined himself to one movement only, and pulled and pulled and pulled with a methodical persistency which commanded my admiration, but with no change of expression on his stolid face, varying as the results must have been. The kneeling man rose and approached him. "The ruling passion strong in death," he conveyed. "Yes," replied the other with a frown and a sigh. "It is a great pity I couldn't have stayed longer. I wouldn't have needed a bullet." "No," replied the other, "you would have banged yourself with red tape." I smiled at this interchange of ghostly amenities, and went my way. Presently I met a woman whose face had been familiar to me in the brilliant societies of the world. She still bore vague, shadowy marks of beauty, and still held herself with the professional air. Her face assumed an aggrieved expression as she saw me. "I am not happy," she murmured. "No one admires me here." "That is unfortunate," I said. "Will nothing else satisfy you?" She opened wide the pale eyes which once had been so beautiful in their dark brilliancy. "What else is there?" she demanded. "You might recite," I suggested lamely. Her lip curled scornfully. "They do not appreciate my collection here," she replied. "I gave up trying to please them long ago. And they care nothing for my beauty, and toilettes I have none. My fame is gone! My fame is gone!" "Your notoriety," I amended mildly. "What is the difference!" she demanded. "All the newspapers babbled of me. And there is not a newspaper in spirit-land—woe is me!" "Would that I could dwell permanently in spirit-land," I sighed, and bade her farewell.

Suddenly I became aware that hours had passed, although no bell had tolled their flight; and I knew that the dawn of earth approached, for one and all of the ghostly multitude about me had turned their faces toward the choir, and were pressing down the long perspective of the caves. Just behind that choir, I knew, was an inner chamber, a holy of holies, which all who were forgiven were allowed to enter before departure, and experience one moment of a happiness which even that wonderful new Consciousness which had been granted me would not allow me to dimly picture. I followed the throng, however, and, looking through them, I saw the small band of the elect walking ahead and apart. When they reached the outer portals of the Chamber of Perfect Blessedness, the choir paused a moment, raising their eyes and their hands; then, when the fortunate few had passed within and the doors swung behind them, they burst into such a wonderful peal of song that I thought the wretched beings without must be compensated for what was denied them. But it was otherwise. They cast themselves face downward upon the ground and burst into a voiceless wail of anguish which I felt but could not hear, which thrilled all my being with its terrible dumbness, but which must find no outlet to disturb the immortal sweetness of sound alone tolerated in these caves of beauty and death.

Almost immediately the great doors behind the choir opened again and the few who had passed through them reappeared. And, although they had known but one moment of perfect bliss, their faces were transfigured with the radiance of what would preclude the possibility of further suffering in all spirit time to come. In re-ernbodiment they would again experience the trials of humanity, but in a modified degree, and until then they were exempt. They passed the prostrate millions, retraversed the long line of caves, and disappeared through the entrance into the darkness beyond. Then the others rose and with bowed heads followed, the music going with them in strains of sadness and compassion, and passed in turn into the gloom of the way by which they had come. Then voice came to them once more, and the beauty and melody and harmony of the past hours vanished for the moment from my memory. Shrieks and groans, wails and cries, curses and sobs once more rent the air. The turmoil of their coming faded into insignificance beside that of their going; the air seemed literally creaking and groaning beneath the burden cast upon it and of which it would never be freed. Again my ear strained itself to follow those dying waves of sound, until I longed for the peace of the outer world with a longing equaling in intensity that of the sinners before me for the one moment of happiness which awaited them in the twilight of coming centuries. But it was not in my power to pass that funeral train, and it was only after what, in my torment, seemed interminable hours that I stood at length under the stars without and watched the last filmy chariot of the dead pass up the hill and disappear over its brow. I followed, but when I reached the hill's summit no trace of that ghostly cortege could be seen. Nothing met my gaze but nature slumbering peacefully under her coverlid of dew. Then I glanced toward the east and saw a line of rosy light. The dawn had come. It was Christmas morning.

John Collier: A Weird Fantasist in Jester's Motley

Darrell Schweitzer

Of John Collier, the author of "Thus I Refute Beelzy," S. T. Joshi writes: "If he had chosen to devote a great proportion of his output to the explicitly weird, he would occupy a still greater place in the field than he does" (*Unutterable Horror* 576).

As for Collier's place in "the field" these days, he seems to be virtually forgotten, although for many decades his stories were standards in ghost-story and suspense anthologies, and, as listed by Wikipedia, a startling number of his stories have been adapted for television. Longtime viewers may particularly remember "Back for Christmas" on *Alfred Hitchcock Presents*. There was even a television movie of "Evening Primrose" in 1966. For the longest time he was a part of the standard vocabulary of critics and blurb-writers, so that any writer of polished, sardonic, fantastic stories (Avram Davidson, for example) was inevitably compared to Collier, and usually to the writer to whom Collier was most often compared, Saki.

But what about Collier's place in the weird fiction field? That, I think, is a matter of definition. I certainly do not agree with Joshi that the "one genuine tale of the supernatural" in Collier's work is "Thus I Refute Beelzy." About half of Collier's output contains some element of the fantastic, from his early short novel, *No Traveller Returns* (1931) to his final work, *Milton's Paradise Lost: A Screenplay for the Cinema of the Mind* (1973). One can also make a case for his first novel, *His Monkey Wife, or Married to a Chimp* (1930), although the fantastic element here is more clearly a conceit: a parody of a Victorian novel in which a blandly respectable Englishman, who once taught school to native children in Africa, is courted by and eventually marries a chimpanzee who sat in his schoolroom, absorbed his lessons, and fell in love with him. Otherwise, in shorter forms Collier wrote brilliantly ironic stories of domestic crime and murder. If anyone ever produced a story to match Lord Dunsany's famous "The Two Bottles of Relish," it is Collier. But Collier was primarily a fantasist, as Anthony Burgess points out in the introduction to *The John Collier Reader*, not of the immersive sort like Tolkien or most science fiction writers, i.e., not someone who creates a whole new world in his stories, but someone who describes intrusions of the fantastic into a sharply observed, real world.

This is actually not far from Lovecraft's idea of the weird as a form of *realism*, as cunningly devised as a hoax, with the real-world background meticulously observed so that intrusion of the unreal may be contrasted with that background, but made plausible by it. The difference with John Collier is primarily one of tone. He is a weirdist in a comic mask, or even in full jester's motley. While Lovecraft might insert sly in-jokes into his stories or even indulge in self-parody (as in "The Hound"), he never loses focus on the emotion of horror. Collier frequently goes all the way into satire or even farce, and is willing to distort realism considerably in the process.

"Thus I Refute Beezly" is a virtually perfect short story. I have used it in writing classes to show how a story may proceed like a one-act play on the page, with continuous action, no flashbacks, no lecture-lumps, but sufficient context to fill in character and background as needed. Any writer should be able to admire its prose and look with envy on Collier's description of a neglected back lot: "Here a little summer house was passing close by beauty on its way to complete decay."

The characters are indeed sketched in quickly. We meet the ineffectual Mrs. Carter and her friend Betty at tea, then get a glimpse of Small Simon, a boy who plays mysterious games at the end of that neglected back lot and won't associate with other children anymore. Enter Mr. Carter, also known as Big Simon, a dentist, a powerful, intimidating presence, who clearly likes to present himself as enlightened, modern, and reasonable, although his obsessive nature is revealed by the way he is constantly washing his hands with imaginary soap and water. Big Simon has modern ideas about rearing his son. If Small Simon chooses to play alone in the yard, rather than associate with others, that is his choice and he has made it. However, Small Simon must be taught what is real and what is imaginary. His playmate, Mr. Beelzy, is imaginary. It is all right to have an imaginary playmate as long as one recognizes it as imaginary. The boy disagrees. The father becomes angry. Amid his constant imaginary hand-washings, Big Simon makes several references to physical punishment. It would seem that all this enlightened, modern "psychology" is a veneer, and Big Simon is a harsh, even abusive parent. Small Simon is sent to his room, to be dealt with. Big Simon finishes his tea and goes upstairs. There follows a scream, and one of the most famous last lines in all weird fiction: "It was on the second-floor landing that they found the shoe, with a man's foot still in it, like that last morsel of a mouse which sometimes falls unnoticed from the side of the jaws of the cat" (*Fancies and Goodnights* 201).

It would seem that Small Simon has been doing something the modern scientific thinking of his father cannot accept: he has been conjuring demons in the back garden. Mr. Beelzy is of course Beelzebub.

If there is any tiny flaw or speck in the perfect amber of this story, it is Betty's offhand reference to something called *These Three*. ("Only different, of course. *She* was an unblushing little liar.") I tell my students not to do that, because generations of readers might puzzle over what *These Three* is, presumably a play or a novel long since forgotten. Internet research narrows it down fairly convincingly to a 1936 film, written by Lillian Hellman and directed by William Wyler, staring Miriam Hopkins, Merle Oberon, and Joel McCrea. The plot turns on three people's lives being wrecked by a malicious lie. Betty's comment seems to mean that Small Simon's lies are not malicious, and that maybe Big Simon is making too big a deal of them, as indeed he is.

This story differs only in degree from Collier's other fantasies. The ironic and satirical elements are sufficiently subdued so that the element of shock or fright comes through at the end. Not exactly

Weird Tales material, since that magazine tended to take its horror straight. It might have been at home in John W. Campbell's more sophisticated *Unknown,* and even was once published in a pulp magazine, in *Famous Fantastic Mysteries* in 1952, complete with a Virgil Finlay illustration; but Collier was not a pulp writer at all. The story was first published in the *Atlantic Monthly* in 1940, at a time when the fantastic was virtually taboo in "quality" magazines. There, presumably, the extreme perfection of its form and the element of satire "redeemed" it from the horrific shock at the end, not to mention the element of the supernatural. Otherwise the only fantasy one might find in the *Atlantic, Harper's,* or other such magazines in this period would have the occasional Jorkens story by Lord Dunsany, which, more often than not, treated the fantastic as a joke.

Collier had come a long way to be the author of "Thus I Refute Beelzy," publishing in the *Atlantic.* He was born in London in 1901. His father, one of seventeen children, could not afford a formal education and worked as a clerk. Young John got no formal education beyond prep school, but was otherwise educated at home and by his uncle, Vincent Collier, a novelist. This education seems to have been quite thorough, because Collier's early work is often downright erudite. John's father must have had money, despite his humble position, or else Uncle Vincent helped out, because when the young man was asked to choose a profession and he replied that he wanted to be a poet, he was indulged. For the next ten years he was allowed to live on a small stipend, plus whatever he could earn from miscellaneous writing. He served as poetry editor for *Time and Tide* magazine and was for a time a correspondent for a Japanese newspaper. Meanwhile he moved in elite literary circles and published some not very good poetry.

His Monkey Wife appeared in 1930. It was a modest success and has been frequently reprinted over the years. It is technically a fantasy, since the chimps in the story (not just Emily, the bride-to-be) are far more intelligent than real chimpanzees are, and even speak among themselves in their own language, in complete sentences, as when Emily encounters an old acquaintance from the jungle, now in a British zoo. The novel is best classified as an absurdist social comedy, something to be subversively placed on the same shelf with such writers as Max Beerbohm, P. G. Wodehouse, or E. F. Benson (in his Mapp and Lucia mode). The difference is that one of the persons in the story's love triangle (the teacher is supposed to marry someone else, who doesn't love him) is a chimp. It is also quite risqué. By the end, once they are married and it's legal, Collier makes it clear that the man is having sex with his new bride.

Some readers may have trouble with *His Monkey Wife* because of its style, which is very wry, filled with allusions, circumlocutions, and flowery phrases, like the Victorian or Edwardian novels it is intended to parody. What makes it readable is its dialogue. Collier was always a strong writer of dialogue, and when he became a screenwriter in the mid-1930s, his skill with dialogue was to transform his work utterly. (Hence that offhand reference to *These Three* in "Beelzy." Collier was working in Hollywood when that picture came out.)

In 1931 he published a thin collection of poetry and prose called *Gemini.* One suspects it may have been written earlier. This is the work of the struggling poet of the 1920s. It must have been because of Collier's networking through literary circles that such a book was published at all—a fine edition on handmade paper, with a vellum spine, signed, numbered, and limited to 185 copies. This is clearly for the collector's market, a speculative item for customers hoping that the then virtually unknown Collier would be famous one day. In that sense it proved a moderately good investment. The imprint is Ulysses Press, and given that Collier goes on at some length in the introduction about his admiration for James Joyce, and how Joyce's *Ulysses* seemed to him a wonderful example of poetic effects achieved in prose, one suspects that this book was aimed at a small coterie of ultra-modernist readers, early James Joyce fandom. In addition to the verse, the volume contains a prose piece called "Of Consolation through Murder." The title suggests one of Collier's later crime stories, and someone does blow his brains out at the end, but the whys and wherefores are difficult to determine. All this really shows is that the Joycean idiom was not suited to Collier.

Most of the verse is likewise dense and difficult, though the first poem, "An Address to the Worms," shows some of the macabre wit that would later come out in Collier's prose, as the poet offers himself as a god to grave worms:

> You've a good god in me: I'm one
> Who more than symbols shall provide;
> True body and blood, and bones beside:
> Which last shall span your cathedral,
> Dark, silent, and populous, where fall
> No foot-scrape sounds, nor rustle of rag,
> Sermon, cough, or clink of bag,
> A liquid, quiet! and, like your faith,
> Rich and alive, conquering death.
>
> *(Gemini* 9–10)

The exclamation point in the penultimate line may or may not be a typo. In today's world of OCR scanning we would assume so, and that the line should read "A liquid, quiet land," but in a book of handset type (produced by "members of the Handprinters Association"), one cannot be sure. The book has never been reprinted. It is worth noting, given the sentiments expressed in this poem, that Collier was an atheist.

The year 1931 also brought forth another such limited edition, *No Traveller Returns,* from the White Owl Press, with fine binding, handmade paper, and limited to 210 signed copies. This too has never been reprinted, and one can understand why a later Collier might have wanted it suppressed, but it is far more substantial and interesting than *Gemini.* The problem here is the prose, seen at Collier's sesquipedalian worst. The content is a satire against science, of which Collier takes a dim view. What might be described as a time-portal appears across the street from Professor Wilkinson's lodgings:

> That dry old stick, the Professor, noticed nothing at all until
> some months had passed. He was then much disconcerted by the

complete upsetting of certain mathematical formulae, from which he had of course experienced that extra-ordinary aesthetic pleasure, which only mathematicians are privileged to feel, unless perhaps Shakespeare and Giotto may have glimpsed some twinkling mirage of it. This super-artistic rapture has become so prized by many contemporary scientists that they are now eagerly implanting all heaven in a wild atom, in order that, having already told us they experience the purest of artistic truths, they may now claim to be seers of religious ones, as were their ancestors, the witch doctors before them. But as in every great eclectic renaissance a few obstinate temperamental primitives will survive, the good Wilkinson found it as impossible to join with his flexible colleagues as would St. Peter with the present pope of Rome. He was that sort of whole-hogger who feels that the abstract beauty of science must be founded on objective truth, and as, like the rest of his profession, he found more beauty in the celestial harmony of those two twos which make four, than in all the poems and creeds which have ever been created, so he saw no more advantage than of justice in the strenuous efforts of the modernists to lay claim to alien and barren fields. Accordingly, when he found his aesthetic joys to have been invalidated by a slight mistake in the formulae which invoked them, he determined to return to the ecstasies of simple arithmetic, much as a painter, who finds himself unable to imitate a cow, will decide to adopt the asceticism of peasant art, as opposed to others in the same case, who will proceed to a broad treatment of light and shade. (*No Traveller Returns* 15–16)

A close analysis of such a passage may find it to be entirely correct grammatically, and filled with barbed or clever asides, but the train of thought often tends to get lost by the end of the paragraph. Despite this, rather inevitably, the professor steps into the time-portal and finds himself in the future, whereupon he is immediately seized, stripped naked, and locked in a cage. He learns that this "utopia" of science is not particularly utopian. Women and all forms of wildlife have ceased to exist. Men are cloned, but everyone is reduced to eating a kind of nutritious mush, and so, wanting some fresh protein, the time-portal was built to lure in primitive humans from the past, who are to be eaten. The professor briefly escapes this fate and is put into a sideshow exhibition, where he is supposed to explain the philosophy of science, but for laughs. He is a failure, having taken himself much too seriously, and after a brief attempt at escape is recaptured and headed for the dinner table. Prominent contemporary figures including G. K. Chesterton, Hilaire Belloc, and Max Beerbohm are on the menu. The futurians swear by Einstein.

For the time being, Collier was still primarily a novelist. His next work, as many commentators have noted, is like nothing else in his canon. *Tom's A-Cold* (1933), published in the United States as *Full Circle,* is a science fiction novel. Those who describe it as "utopian" may be suspected of not having read it, because it depicts a future barbarism, set about the 1990, after civilization has collapsed due to plagues and wars. Englishmen are reverting to savagery, even though only two generations have passed and the grandfathers of young men can still remember the old world and are still trying to teach from such books as have survived. Small tribal groups live in fortified villages. Our hero, a big, rather thoughtless lunk, and his more intellectual sidekick (named Crab) spend almost the first half of the book scouting out and planning a raid against a neighboring settlement in order to steal women, who in this society are commodities, like livestock. Our hero insists on raiding one specific village because he lusts after a woman he has seen there.

This is a post-civilization story, akin to Stephen Vincent Benét's "By the Waters of Babylon" or George R. Stewart's *Earth Abides.* There had of course been many such before 1933, such as John Richard Jeffries's *After London* (1885) and John Ames Mitchell's *The Last American* (1889), not to mention many in the pulps, such as *Darkness and Dawn* by George Allan England (1914; fix-up of three serials from the Munsey magazines, 1912–13), and even *Beyond Thirty* (1916; later reprinted as *The Lost Continent*) by Edgar Rice Burroughs. The problem is that it is simply *not as good* as some of the more celebrated examples of the genre. Some critics have indeed praised it highly. John Clute writes in *The Encyclopedia of Science Fic-*

tion that "throughout the novel, very movingly, Collier renders the reborn, circumambient natural world with a hallucinatory visual intensity found nowhere else in his work." I must confess to having failed to discover this intensity in the book. It's actually rather dull, because of the slowness of pacing and the wooden nature of the characters. The prose itself is considerably simpler than that of some of Collier's earliest works, but it notably lacks his wit. It is understandable that he would have come to regard this book as a misstep. Later he would acknowledge it in "books by" listings in his books, but he would not allow it to be reprinted. (*No Traveller Returns* is not so acknowledged.)

Collier's last novel was *Defy the Foul Fiend* (1934), which, despite its title (taken, like *Tom's A-Cold*, from a passage in *King Lear*), has no fantastic content at all. It is semi-autobiographical, about a naïve and idealistic young man, educated at home and with few social skills (in the novel the bastard son of a dissolute nobleman), who at the age of twenty is thrust out, Candide-like, into society. The result may not be a literary masterpiece, but it is pleasant and readable. Collier did allow it to be reprinted later on. There was a Penguin edition in 1948. Two chapters are excerpted in *The John Collier Reader*.

It must have been at this time that Collier decided, as he had with poetry, that the novel was not the right medium for him. He had begun to write short stories as early as 1931 ("Green Thoughts"—about which more in a moment), but now he began to produce more of them. Equally important, he moved to Hollywood in 1935 and began a long and successful career as a screenwriter, which no doubt provided him the financial security to write short fiction, and also had a profound impact on the fiction he wrote. As Burgess notes in that introduction to *The John Collier Reader*, the later Collier, the one we think of when his name is mentioned, the author of "Thus I Refute Beelzy," has a screenwriter's virtues to a considerable degree: extreme compression and deft characterization through dialogue. He also shows an excellent sense of pacing. A screenplay is not allowed to drag the way *Tom's A-Cold* did. Nor is a short story.

As a screenwriter, Collier did not specialize in fantasy. Some of the more celebrated films he wrote include *The African Queen, I Am a Camera*, and *The Warlord.*

Collier the short-story writer began to emerge with "Green Thoughts" in 1931. This story is weird fiction, or science fiction of a sort, about an orchid enthusiast and his strange plant, which absorbs its victims and then sprouts blossoms in their image, which still retain part of the original consciousness. An uncle, his cousin, and a cat are thus absorbed. Part of the story is even told from the point of view of the uncle *after* he has become part of the plant, as he worries about his good-for-nothing nephew who wants his fortune. Unlike the many Collier stories in which nasty persons get their comeuppance at the end, this one concludes with the nephew victorious, approaching with a pair of shears. The story seems to meander in tone, from horror to comedy and back, and lacks the tight unity of later Collier short fiction. But if Collier wasn't paid off by the producers of *The Little Shop of Horrors,* he should have sued. He is not mentioned in the credits of the Corman film, and the best various sources can say is that it "may have been inspired" by the Collier story, which is admittedly in its turn something of a parody of H. G. Wells's "The Flowering of a Strange Orchid."

By the late 1930s, Collier was a prolific short story writer, for high-quality, mainstream publications like the *New Yorker, Harper's,* the *Atlantic,* and, late in his career, *Playboy.* His appearances in genre magazines, such as that printing of "Beelzy" in *Famous Fantastic Mysteries* or occasional stories in the *Magazine of Fantasy and Science Fiction,* or one in *Fantastic,* were reprints. He began to issue story collections as early as 1934, with *The Devil and All,* then recycled most of those stories and added more to produce *Presenting Moonshine* (1941), then *A Touch of Nutmeg* (1943), with the more or less definitive compilation being *Fancies and Goodnights* (1951), which won the International Fantasy Award. *The John Collier Reader* (1972) is a retrospective, though it adds a few stories not in *Fancies and Goodnights. Pictures in the Fire* (1958) also includes a few stories not found elsewhere. About forty are uncollected.

If we are to group Collier's short fiction loosely, it can be said to fall into three categories: stories about conventional supernatural beings (angels, devils, imps, and djinns), miscellaneous fantasies, and stories of domestic murder.

To survey some prominent example of the first category, other than the celebrated "Thus I Refute Beelzy": In "The Devil, George and Rosie" a misogynist is hired by Satan to run a new annex of Hell for women, but falls in love with a woman who is there by mistake. In "Fallen Star," an angel, captured by a demon, is sent to Earth as an amnesiac girl. She marries a psychoanalyst. The demon comes to claim her after seven years, but is himself psychoanalyzed, "cured," and becomes successful on Wall Street. In "Hell Hath Fury," an angel and a demon both incarnate on Earth as young women. They become rivals over a young man. The angel gets him. The demon, more true to her nature, gets a sleazy lout from a dance hall. In "The Possession of Angela Bradshaw," a young woman, engaged to be married to a dull fellow, seems possessed by a demon she rather likes. The demon is exorcised. It proves to be a poet, much more interesting than the fiancé, so she marries him. "Pictures in the Fire" combines demonology with Collier's Hollywood experience. A writer's agent contracts him to a movie producer, who is a demon. The demon becomes obsessed with an impossible, spoiled starlet who never actually acts (and probably can't). The writer escapes when the demon marries the starlet and is so distracted that he lets the writer's option expire. The demon vanishes through the floor with the starlet, into Hell.

Among the assorted fantasies, we find "Bottle Party," about a man who draws a djinn out of a bottle, then is trapped in it himself. "Variation on a Theme" is something of a throwback to *His Monkey Wife*. A gorilla in a zoo asks a passer-by for a fine suit of clothes. The man is not much taken aback by a talking gorilla, apparently. He is an author. The gorilla claims to be an author too. The man helps the gorilla escape and makes him his protégé. The gorilla is not only a crude lowbrow, but actually a fraud. He has no book. But out of vanity, he is spurred on to write one. Meanwhile the man writes a feeble satire. The gorilla's book is macho, virile stuff, sort of like a Mickey Spillane novel. Out of spite, the gorilla switches manuscripts. Both are published under the other's name. The man thus becomes a bestseller. The gorilla gets his comeuppance because the satire, however feeble, is also blasphemous, so he goes to jail. (Is Collier caricaturing himself here?)

The surprisingly gruesome "Rope Enough" involves a white man who learns the Indian rope trick. In this version the magician's assistant goes up the rope and refuses to come down until his master climbs up after him. Then the assistant's dismembered limbs, head, and torso drop down into a basket. The master descends, with a bloody sword in hand. Has he committed murder? He makes mystic passes over the basket and the assistant pops out, unharmed. But when the white man does this trick, he goes up the rope and refuses to come down because he finds himself in an exotic Oriental paradise surrounded by beautiful women. His jealous wife climbs up, confronts him, chops him into pieces, and does *not* revive him. The paradise has now adjusted itself to *her* tastes. She pulls up the rope after her. This is interesting in the context of Collier's domestic murder stories, because more often than not it is the irritating wife who ends up dead.

In "Incident on a Lake," such an irritating wife is determined to make her husband's life miserable. He inherits a large sum and wants to go traveling. She does everything possible to ruin the experience. When they go up the Amazon in search of a prehistoric monster, the wife conceals the monster's tracks, whereupon it eats her. The husband's experience is indeed ruined, because he is convinced there was no monster.

"In the Cards" likewise combines the fantastic with unloving spouses and death. A shabby fortune-teller's cards predict that a loutish man will come into money, then die shortly thereafter. She marries him for the money, hoping to be a rich widow. Then *she* inherits a million dollars, he murders her for it, and he is executed for the crime.

"Old Acquaintance" seems to be a mixture of infidelity and

ghosts. Monsieur Dupree of Paris has led a dull life for the past twenty years. He suspects his wife really loved their old friend Robert. She dies. Before telling anyone, he goes out for a cigarette, then a drink. He seems to meet his wife, with Robert. They go on a spree. Very drunk, he returns home. His wife's body is gone. Did she really die? Did she run off with Robert? Was he hallucinating? He follows the two around town. He meets someone who tells him that Robert has been dead for a month. Has he been following ghosts?

Much more explicitly ghostly is "Are You Too Late or Was I Too Early?" A man keeps trying to meet a phantom woman in his apartment. It turns out that *he* is the ghost of the previous tenant, and thus the two cannot meet.

Probably the best and the most famous of Collier's miscellaneous fantasies is "Evening Primrose," in which a poet drops out of society, resolving to live in a department store disguised as a manikin. He discovers that a whole such society of people exists. They come out at night, carefully evading the night watchman. The new society he finds himself in proves just as snobbish and nasty as the one he left. When he falls in love with a maid, he runs afoul of the sinister "Dark Men," who live in funeral parlors and can turn people into dummies permanently. All this is told in the form of a diary found on a counter top. The implication is that the poet, teaming up with the night watchman to rescue the girl, has not been successful, and the three of them will soon be seen in windows as manikins.

This is a wonderfully atmospheric story, which makes no literal sense. How would people spend all their daylight hours perfectly still, as a dummy, and not be detected? What happens when they have to go to the bathroom? If they are active at night, when do they sleep? But it doesn't matter. Deserted department stores are spooky places and the idea that an entire hidden society comes out at night is compelling. This is one of those stories, like Robert Aickman's celebrated "The Hospice," which does not explain itself, but has the emotional texture of a dream, which gradually turns into a nightmare.

Collier has other stories about dummies. "Special Delivery" is about a young man who works in a department store, who falls in love with a manikin and ultimately dies for her. In "Spring Fever," a sculptor produces an incredibly lifelike (male) dummy. He tries to go on stage as a ventriloquist, but his act is a flop. Meanwhile the dummy comes to life and runs off with his girlfriend. He considers making another girlfriend for himself, but thinks better of it and makes a poodle.

Now let us consider some of the stories about murder. None of these are fantastic, but, like the others, most of them are about love, quarreling spouses, and greed.

Probably the most famous of these is "Back for Christmas." A British professor murders his bothersome wife. After many difficulties he buries her in the basement without getting caught, then goes on a lecture tour in America. He was planning to tell people that they had divorced in America, but he had promised that he will be "back for Christmas." While in America, he receives an invoice from a contractor, who is about to dig up the basement to install a wine cellar, which the wife had ordered as a Christmas surprise.

In a similar league is "De Mortuis," in which a doctor has just finished cementing up the basement. His fishing buddies show up, so convinced he has murdered his wife and buried her under the cement that they justify it and explain how they will help him gain the perfect alibi. Actually he hasn't, but the opportunity is so good that when she returns, he lures her into the basement.

In "The Chaser," a young man, desperate for love, buys a love potion from a strange old man. The conversation explains how this potion will make the intended lady utterly, eternally, smotheringly devoted to her lover. The love potion costs one dollar. A "spot remover," i.e., an undetectable poison, costs $5000. Why the difference? Good business. Customers for the first potion inevitably come for the second.

Jealousy figures as large as murder in these stories. In "Think No Evil," a man becomes so obsessively jealous of his wife and the man he thinks she is cheating with that, in his quest for evidence of this non-existent affair, he forces the two "lovers" together until, indeed, they actually fall in love.

"Little Memento" is also about jealousy, but it is brought on by a busybody who by subtle suggestion and observation induces murders. He keeps a museum collection of sinister souvenirs from each murder.

Sometimes the method of murder is the point. "A Matter of Taste" gives the phrase "death by chocolate" literal meaning. The murderer gave the victim fifteen pounds of irresistible chocolates, and she ate herself to death. The investigators realize this and helplessly devour the rest of the evidence. Like several others of Colliers murder stories, this is almost a parody of a mystery story, reminiscent of Dunsany's *Little Tales of Smethers*.

What is the point of all these? There is no need to summarize every story Collier ever wrote. The patterns are clear enough. Virtually all Collier's stories, whether fantastic or not, are about love or the failure of love. They are about what James Thurber once illustrated as "The War Between Men and Women." In this sense, they are very much of their time, the same era that produced *The Honeymooners* and so many other comedies about battling spouses. It is not a surprise that so many of Collier's stories were adapted for television in the 1950s. Considering the number of stories in which husbands kill wives or vice versa, and for all it is perilous to try to discern the writer's personal views from his fiction—particularly a writer who is so remote from much of his fiction as Collier usually seems to be—the inevitable questions still come to mind. Was this guy ever married? Did he know anything about women? Was he genuinely a misogynist?

The answer to the first question is easiest. He was married three times. In 1936 he married a silent film actress, Shirley Palmer. This was of only brief duration. Between 1946 and 1954 he was married to Beth Kay (another actress). Between 1954 and his death in 1980, he was married to Harriet Hess Collier, by whom he had one son, John G. S. Collier. Considering that he lived through much of the twentieth century and both world wars, he saw much evil and doubtless developed a grimly cynical view of humanity. His Hollywood years probably did not do much for his idealism either. If he was ever like the naïve young man at the beginning of *Defy the Foul*

Fiend, he did not stay that way. So did he have a poor opinion of women or, more like Ambrose Bierce, a poor opinion of everybody?

In Collier's world, greed almost always overcomes love. One of the very few seemingly loving couples is that in "Over Insurance." They are so obsessively in love with each other that they virtually think the same thoughts. They then put 90% of their money into life insurance, so that if one dies, the survivor will be provided for. This makes them cash-poor, which makes daily life miserable. They both do indeed have identical thoughts. They poison each other.

A Collier love story may be completely absurd, as in "The Frog Prince," in which Paul proposes to marry the mentally backward Ethel, who plays with dolls at twenty-eight, and is enormously fat and ugly, but is also exceedingly rich. Paul confides this to his girl-friend, Olga, who disguises herself as a man and marries Ethel first. Then, after hormone treatments, Ethel loses weight and turns out to be a witty, handsome, clear-headed man. Olga resumes her female role as his wife. They live happily ever after. Paul gets nothing.

The most purely male-chauvinistic of all Collier stories may be one of his fairy-tale variants, "Sleeping Beauty." Still ravishingly beautiful after five years in a coma, a young woman is exhibited in a sideshow. Customers pay to see if they can awaken her with a kiss. A man becomes obsessed, spends his entire fortune to "buy" the lady, then revives her by medical means. Awakened, she proves to be vulgar, obnoxious, and ungrateful. Eventually he deprives her of her medicine, puts her back in a coma, and recovers his fortune by exhibiting her as the original sideshow operators did.

But the obnoxious male character can also lose. The husband in "Three Bears Cottage" is so niggardly that he quarrels with his wife over who got the better egg at breakfast. He feels that merely because he is a man, he deserves the best of everything. After breakfast he goes mushroom hunting. He finds one very delicious mushroom and one death's-head mushroom, which can kill instantly. He has his wife add them into toasted cheese sandwiches, telling her that he wants the death's-head, which is by far the tastier. He is playing reverse psychology here, assuming that she will greedily switch sandwiches with him and eat the "better" one, because that is what he, in her position, would surely do. But she doesn't and he dies.

A similar murderous husband perishes in "And Who, in Eden . . ." Exasperated by his wife's passion for pets, he decides to get her one more, a poisonous snake. He goes out into a (Florida) swamp and buys a snake from a local teenager. But things misfire and he gets bitten. Then it is revealed that the teenager cheated him and sold him a harmless snake. He died of a heart attack. The final twist is that the wife, who is appalled that her husband would try to kill her, is relieved to conclude he must have been joking.

There are a few stories on completely different subjects, such as "Witch's Money," which is a mordant fable about economics (greed, murder, but no romance), but overall we can see that Collier's great subject was men loving women (or substitutes, like the manikin in "Special Delivery"), men vs. women, or men and women murdering one another. Romance, even if begun well, almost always turns out badly, although there are exceptions. A lot of Collier characters enter romantic relationships with the most deceitful motives, and usually suffer for it.

This is the work of a writer considerably closer to Ambrose Bierce than to, say, John Norman. If women are playthings in his stories, so are men, or else they are villains and fools.

Many of his stories are fantastic or weird, but ultimately they are the exact opposite of the Lovecraftian ideal of the weird, in that they are primarily about human relationships, not about phenomena. The human beings are not spear-carriers; they are central. The fantastic elements themselves (all those angels and demons) are the kind of taken-for-granted comic supernaturalism that was so popular when Collier was writing, as seen in the novels of Thorne Smith or in plays or movies like *Here Comes Mr. Jordan* or *The Adding Machine*.

The strength of these stories is in their sardonic wit and their succinct perfection of form. Compare that very windy passage from *No Traveller Returns* to the following from "Halfway to Hell":

Louis Thurlow, having decided to take his own life, felt that at least he might take his own time also. He consulted his bankbook; there was a little over a hundred pounds left. "Very well," said he. "I'll get out of this flat, which stinks, and spend a really delightful week at Mutton's. I'll taste all the little pleasures just once more, to say goodbye to them." (*Fancies and Goodnights* 85)

Or this from "Pictures in the Fire":

Dreaming of money as I lay half asleep on the Malibu sand, a desolate cry reached me from out of the middle air. It was nothing but a gull, visible only as a burning, floating flake of white in the hot, colorless sky, but wings and whiteness and a certain deep pessimism in the croak it uttered made me think it might be my guardian angel.

Next moment, from the dank interior of the beachy house, the black telephone raised its beguiling voice, and I obeyed. It was, of course, my agent.

"Charles, I've made a date for you. For dinner tonight. Have you ever heard of a man called Mahound?" (*Fancies and Goodnights* 60–61)

Notice how quickly the scene is set, the characters introduced, and the main character has been propelled toward some action. Collier was not the sort of writer who would take fifty pages to get the hero out of bed.

The shortcoming of many of these stories is that they blend together in the reader's mind. They are like chocolates, and not the lethal chocolates of "A Matter of Taste" either, but fine ones, to be savored. Do not read them all at once. Reviewing them for this article, I found I had to take extensive notes, so I could remember which one was the gorilla story and which one was about the snake, and what "The Possession of Angela Bradshaw" was about. Collier was very good at what he did, but his miniatures are a specialized kind of art. You would not read Shakespeare's sonnets all at once either.

At this point it is worthwhile to consider Collier's last major work, *Milton's Paradise Lost: A Screenplay for the Cinema of the Mind.* It was not well received when it first appeared in 1973, critics almost universally saying that the author had overstepped himself for one reason or another. John Updike seems to have led the charge in the pages of the *New Yorker,* which greatly discouraged Collier, so that he wrote little in the last few years of life. At the very end he returned to the novel and was working on something called *Finding Ernie,* which has not been published.

But was the *Paradise Lost* screenplay a failure? Presumably it is described as being for "the cinema of the mind" because Collier assumed that it could not be filmed. Of course with today's technology, such as computer-generated animation, just about anything can be filmed. If the Star Wars and Lord of the Rings movies are possible, there is nothing in Collier's *Paradise Lost* screenplay that couldn't be filmed.

But that is a secondary point. The work as written is designed to be read. It is very visual and does indeed work like a movie inside the reader's head. What seems to have upset the critics was Collier's presumption, or his failure to be Milton. He was, after all, a twentieth-century atheist rather than a seventeenth-century Christian. He inevitably substituted some of his own ideas for Milton's. He also left significant parts of the original epic out, arguing, for one thing, that it is impossible to present God convincingly. Hence the scenes in Heaven are gone. What remains are the scenes in Hell and on Earth. The angels fall into the fiery lake. They gradually extricate themselves. Their burnt and mutilated forms are more or less restored. Satan rallies his troops and vows vengeance and defiance. At the gate of Hell, he talks his way past the two guardians, Sin and Death, convincing them that if he is successful in his intended mission, he will bring them vast numbers of damned souls. He flies to Earth, finds the Garden, and goes to work on Eve. By the end he has triumphed. There is no promise of any Redeemer to come. Satan seems to have won this round.

What is most interesting, in the larger context of Collier's work, is the depiction of Adam and Eve. This is the climax of all Collier's writings about the conflicts and contrasts between men and women. The original biblical myth of course blames the woman for the fall of mankind and the sufferings of the world. But does Collier? His Eve is no weak appendage of Adam. Adam is the one who seems a bit dull, a placid, contented, unimaginative fellow who is perfectly happy just to obey the rules and remain as he is. Eve is more intelligent, and restless. She does show some greedy traits. She wants to *own* animals rather than merely name them (68). But she also has a sense of legitimate grievance because God, at least through his Messengers, seems to be terribly sexist. When the ancient Raphael comes to warn Adam of the danger of Satan's approach, he pays no notice to Eve whatever. He has come to speak with Adam, as the man of the house (or bower, in this case). God does not recognize the female. Things are not quite harmonious in Eden. God seems to have wrought imperfectly. This gives Satan something to work on.

Milton tries to deal with the obvious paradoxes of the original myth in his own way. Collier's view is more modern, more cynical. If God knew what was going to happen, why did he allow it to happen? Collier actually suggests that there are some things, hatched by evil forces, which are beyond the sight of God. God sends Raphael to warn Adam, even though he knows (more or less) what is going to happen, for the sleaziest of reasons. This way, if/when Adam falls, he cannot say he wasn't warned. God seems to be covering up his own mistakes. So much for infinite grace and mercy!

Collier also makes some interesting changes on Genesis and on Milton. In the original *Paradise Lost,* when Satan announces his victory, all the devils are transformed into serpents. In Collier's version, they are transformed into the various heathen gods that will mislead mankind in the future. He also has an interesting idea about why God allowed the Fall of Man to happen. The perfection of God is static. Any action, any change in condition or circumstance implies a movement away from perfection. God is therefore trapped by his own perfect nature. Satan, on the other hand, has vast agency. Much of the time he seems more heroic than evil. Of course this much is true in Milton too. It has long been observed that in *Paradise Lost* Satan has all the best lines.

But I think the message of Collier's version of *Paradise Lost* is a summation of everything he had been writing about all along. We are imperfect creatures. Conflicts arise because of this. Our motives are not always the best. Eve eats of the fruit of the Tree out of discontent or ambition. Adam does so for a less admirable reason, because he thinks that God won't really punish him and he can get away with it. But he can't. Very few people in John Collier's fiction get away with much of anything.

Works Cited

Collier, John. *Defy the Foul Fiend*. New York: Alfred A. Knopf, 1934.

———. *Fancies and Goodnights*. Garden City, NY: Doubleday, 1951.

———. *Full Circle*. New York: D. Appleton & Co., 1933.

———. *Gemini*. London: Ulysses Press, 1931.

———. *The John Collier Reader*. New York: Alfred A. Knopf, 1972. With an introduction by Anthony Burgess. (Contains *His Monkey Wife*.)

———. *Milton's Paradise Lost: A Screenplay for the Cinema of the Mind*. New York: Alfred A. Knopf, 1973.

———. *No Traveller Returns*. London: White Owl Press, 1931.

———. *Pictures in the Fire*. London: Rupert Hart-Davis, 1958.

Indick, Ben P. "Sardonic Fantasistes: John Collier." In Darrell Schweitzer, ed. *Discovering Modern Horror Fiction II*. Mercer Island, WA: Starmont House, 1988. 121–27.

Joshi, S. T. *Unutterable Horror: A History of Supernatural Fiction*. 2012. New York: Hippocampus Press, 2014. 2 vols.

Kessel, John J. "John Collier." In E. F. Bleiler, ed. *Supernatural Fiction Writers*. New York: Charles Scribner's Sons, 1985.

Updike, John. "Milton Adapts Genesis, Collier Adapts Milton." *New Yorker* (20 August 1973): 84–86.

Warren, Alan. "John Collier, Fantastic Miniaturist." In Darrell Schweitzer, ed. *Discovering Classic Fantasy Fiction*. Mercer Island, WA: Starmont House, 1996. 68–75.

Notes on Contributors

Manuel Arenas is a writer of verse and prose in the Gothic horror tradition. His work has appeared in various journals and anthologies, and he is a regular contributor to *Spectral Realms*. He currently resides in Phoenix, where he pens his dark ditties sheltered behind heavy curtains, as he shuns the oppressive orb that glares down on him from the cloudless, dust-filled sky.

Michael Aronovitz has published two collections, *Seven Deadly Pleasures* and *The Voices in Our Heads*, as well as three novels: *Alice Walks, The Witch of the Wood*, and *Phantom Effect*. In 2011 his story "How Bria Died" was reprinted in *The Year's Best Dark Fantasy & Horror* (Prime Books), and in 2014 his story "The Girl Between the Slats" appeared in S. T. Joshi's anthology *Searchers After Horror*. He has published more than thirty short stories.

Leigh Blackmore, a lifelong enthusiast of the weird, lives with his family in Wollongong, New South Wales, Australia. He has edited *Terror Australis: Best Australian Horror* (1993) and *Midnight Echo 5* (2011) and has written the verse collection *Spores from Sharnoth & Other Madnesses* (2008). A nominee for SFPA's Rhysling Award (Best Long Poem), Leigh is a four-time Ditmar Award nominee for fiction and criticism. He is currently compiling a new collection of fantastic verse and completing a thriller novel, *The Eighth Trigram*.

Jon Bockes is a longtime reader of strange fiction. He has been involved in local arts leagues, online collections, and fanzines. Bockes has been a writer since his early teens and has been previously published in magazines, online, and in nonfiction works. He is a historian who also loves entomology, with varied interests in reading, including speculative fiction, historical fiction, cosmic horror, and nonfiction. He writes regularly on these topics on his blog, *Archives of the End of the World.*

Adam Bolivar is a Romantic poet specializing in the composition of folkloric balladry in traditional rhyme and meter. He also carves marionettes out of wood, tailors clothes for them, and compels them to perform in fiendish plays of his own authorship. Born and bred in Boston, Adam Bolivar currently resides in the gloomy dreamland of Portland, Oregon, with his beloved wife and golden-haired son.

Jason V Brock is a writer, editor, filmmaker, composer, scholar, and artist. His fiction and nonfiction have appeared in many venues, such as *Weird Fiction Review, Fangoria,* and others, and include a monograph about horror and science fiction in culture called *Disorders of Magnitude: A Survey of Dark Fantasy.* He has been nominated for several honors, including twice for the Bram Stoker Award. His documentary about Forrest J Ackerman, *The AckerMonster Chronicles!,* won the Rondo Hatton Classic Horror Award for Best Documentary in 2014. He resides with his wife and their reptiles in Vancouver, Washington.

Matt Cardin is a writer and editor of fiction and nonfiction exploring the intersections of religion, horror, creativity, apocalypse, and the weird and anomalous. He is also a college vice president and a long-time pianist. He books include *To Rouse Leviathan, Dark Awakenings,* and, as editor, *Born to Fear: Interviews with Thomas Ligotti* and *Horror Literature through History.* He co-edits the literary journal *Vastarien.*

Nicole Cushing is the Bram Stoker Award–winning author of *Mr. Suicide* and a two-time nominee for the Shirley Jackson Award. *Rue Morgue* recently included Nicole in its list of *13 Wicked Women to Watch,* praising her as an "an intense and uncompromising literary voice." Her second novel, *A Sick Gray Laugh,* was recently released by Word Horde. A stand-alone novella, *The Half-Freaks* (published by Grimscribe Press), also appeared in 2019. Nicole lives in Indiana.

Wade German is the author of the poetry collections *Dreams from a Black Nebula* (Hippocampus Press, 2014), *The Ladies of the Everlasting Lichen and Other Relics* (Mount Abraxas Press, 2019), and *Incantations* (Raphus Press, 2020), a selection of his verse in Portuguese translation that was also released as a digital audio album. A new volume of poetry will appear from Hippocampus Press in 2021.

James Goho is a writer and researcher who lives in Winnipeg, Canada. His most recent short story, "Calls from Home," appeared in the literary magazine *Fiction* #64. His next book, *Caitlín R. Kiernan: A Critical Study of Her Dark Fiction*, was published by McFarland in 2020.

Born outside a small town in rural Oklahoma, **Dylan Henderson** has lived almost his whole life within the confines of the Ozark Plateau. An avid reader, he spent much of his childhood studying literature, but at the age of sixteen he dropped out of high school and enrolled at the local community college. He now lives in Fayetteville, Arkansas, where he is pursuing a master's degree in English literature at the University of Arkansas.

Sorina Higgins is a Ph.D. candidate, Presidential Scholar, and winner of the spring 2020 Outstanding Research Award at Baylor University. She also serves as a faculty member at Signum University, online, where she was Chair of the Department of Language and Literature for the past five years. Her latest publication is an academic essay collection on *The Inklings and King Arthur* (Apocryphile Press, 2017), winner of the 2018 Mythopoeic Society Inklings Scholarship Award. Her interests include British and Irish Modernism, the Inklings, theatre, and magic; her dissertation-in-progress is tentatively titled *From Dramaturgy to Thaumaturgy: Staging Occult Modernism*.

Nancy Holder is a *New York Times* bestselling author and editor of books, comic books, articles, and essays. She has received five Bram Stoker Awards for her supernatural work and a Grand Master Award from the International Association of Media Tie-In Writers. She has written original material and novelizations for IPs such as *Buffy the Vampire Slayer*, *Crimson Peak*, and *Wonder Woman*. She writes the *Mary Shelley Presents* comic book series for Kymera Press.

Rhonda Knight earned her Ph.D. at the SUNY-Binghamton, where she specialized in medieval literature. A Professor of English at Coker University, she holds the James Wayne Lemke Endowed Chair in College Service and Leadership. She has published articles on a wide variety of subjects from *Sir Gawain and the Green Knight* to *Doctor Who*. She is currently co-editing a collection, "Fans and Franchises: Essays on the Changing Landscape of Fandom," centered on innovative storytelling in media franchises.

Curtis M. Lawson is an author of unapologetically weird fiction. His work ranges from technicolor pulp adventures to bleak cosmic horror and includes *Black Heart Boys' Choir, The Devoured,* and *Those Who Go Forth into the Empty Place of Gods*. Curtis hosts the Wyrd Transmissions Podcast. He lives in Salem, Massachusetts, with his wife and their son.

Michael D. Miller is an adjunct professor at Aquinas College, Grand Rapids Community College, and Kendall College of Art & Design, a National Endowment for the Humanities medievalist summer scholar, and the author of the *Realms of Fantasy* role-playing game for Mythopoeia Games Publications. His poetry has appeared *Spectral Realms* and *Alien Buddha Press,* his scholarly articles in *Lovecraft Annual,* his reviews in *Dead Reckonings* and *Dim Shores,* and his essays in *Crackpot Press* and *Marchxness.*

Michael Parker was born and raised in Green Bay, Wisconsin. He holds master's degrees in philosophy and Spanish. He is a voracious and omnivorous reader with a special interest in weird fiction. He currently resides outside Green Bay with his best buddy: a black standard poodle named Charlie.

Belicia Rhea is an emerging writer from the desert of Tucson, Arizona. She often uses storytelling to illuminate the darker sides of the human experience, to acknowledge epidemics of violence toward women and vulnerable groups, and to examine themes of fear and the unusual. This is her first publication.

Mark Samuels lives in Kings Langley, England. He is the author of six short story collections and of three novels, the latest of which is *Witch-Cult Abbey* (Zagava Books, 2020). Zagava is now in the process of reprinting all his earlier work in deluxe limited editions throughout this year and the next. In 2020 Hippocampus Press published a selection of his best horror stories under the title *The Age of Decayed Futurity*.

Darrell Schweitzer is a former editor of *Weird Tales* and a poet, short story writer, novelist, critic, and anthologist. PS Publishing recently issued a two-volume retrospective of his work, *The Mysteries of the Faceless King* and *The Last Heretic*. Fedogan & Bremer issued a collection of his Lovecraftian stories, *Awaiting Strange Gods* (2015). His major verse collections are *Groping toward the Light* and *Ghosts of Past and Future*. He is overdue for another one.

John Shirley has written numerous novels, including *Demons, Crawlers, Wetbones, Cellars, Bleak History, City Come A-Walkin', Bioshock: Rapture*, and *The Other End*. His story collections include *Black Butterflies*, which won the Bram Stoker Award. His new novel *Stormland* is coming out in 2021 from Blackstone Books. *Weirdbook* magazine recently published a special John Shirley issue containing the new novella "Swords of Atlantis," short stories, and poems. He is co-screenwriter of *The Crow*.

John C. Tibbetts is Professor Emeritus at the University of Kansas in Film and Media studies. His books include *The Furies of Marjorie Bowen* (McFarland, 2019), *The Gothic Worlds of Peter Straub* (McFarland, 2016), *Those Who Made It: Conversations with the Legends of Hollywood* (Palgrave Macmillan, 2015), *Peter Weir: Interviews* (University of Mississippi Press, 2014), and *The Gothic Imagination* (Palgrave Macmillan, 2012). Most of these contain John's paintings and illustrations. John has researched, written, produced, and narrated two radio series, *The World of Robert Schumann* (broadcast worldwide on the WFMT Radio Network) and *Piano Portraits* (broadcast on Kansas Public Radio). He was awarded in 2008 the Kansas Governor's Arts in Education Award, presented by Governor Kathleen Sebelius.

Hubert Van Calenbergh has been interested in weird fiction since the age of ten, when he read his first Lovecraft story. He has translated Jean Ray and Hanns Heinz Ewers, and is currently working on a volume of short stories. His native language is Dutch, but he also likes to express himself in French and English. He resides in Ostend, Belgium. Other interests include guitar playing and soundscaping.

Lee Weinstein is a retired Philadelphia librarian with a lifelong interest in science fiction, fantasy, and horror. He edited a collection of Edward Lucas White's horror stories, and his essays have appeared in *Studies in Weird Fiction, Supernatural Fiction Writers,* the *New York Review of Science Fiction,* and elsewhere. He was a contributor to *Horror Fiction through History* and is an ongoing contributor to the online third edition of the *Encyclopedia of Science Fiction.*